PITCH BLACK

Elise Noble

Published by Undercover Publishing Limited

ISBN: 978-1-910954-05-8

Edited by Amanda Ann Larson

Cover art by Abigail Sins

www.undercover-publishing.com

www.elise-noble.com

No pressure, no diamond.

CHAPTER 1

AS I SPED along the highway, the rain fell harder than the last man I shot with my faithful Walther P88.

Ahead, a fork of lightning lit up the sky, closely followed by the angry growl of thunder. I accelerated around a truck driving slowly, or as normal people would say, sensibly, and kept the pedal flat to the floor. The drive to Dulles International Airport usually took two hours, but at this rate, I'd do it in just over one. Either that or end up wrapping my car around something solid.

At that moment, I didn't particularly care which.

A bend came up, and the back end of the car broke loose, swinging from side to side in a wild fishtail. I grappled with the steering wheel, knuckles white, and managed to keep the vehicle pointing in the right direction. My Dodge Viper didn't like the weather any more than I did. Metallic black, with an 8.4-litre V10 engine, it looked mean and sounded meaner.

Not exactly your typical girl's car.

But, as my husband had pointed out when he handed me the keys on my birthday, "You're not a normal girl, Diamond." The nickname he gave me on the night we met had stuck through the years.

Fuck, I missed him.

Soon the road evened out, and the car settled back

into a more-or-less straight line. The highway was almost empty. Only long-distance truck drivers and a few desperate souls crawling along in the slow lane were crazy enough to be out in this storm. Fortunately, all the cops were most likely tucked up in their squad rooms too, munching on donuts and mainlining coffee, far too busy with the important things in life to worry about little old me, merrily barrelling along I-95 at twice the speed limit.

I flicked through the radio stations until I found one playing rock. Bon Jovi belted out "Livin' on a Prayer," which seemed quite appropriate given how fast I was driving.

By the time I hit the outskirts of Centreville, the rain had slackened to a steady drizzle. The road was mirrored with puddles, the rippling reflections of the streetlights twinkling up at me. Just in case a stray cop was hanging around, I slowed down to somewhere near legal as I drove through town.

I'd kept a careful eye behind me on the way, and I was confident nobody had tailed me, especially with the speed I was driving. Even so, I made four consecutive right-hand turns to be on the safe side, doubling back on myself and driving through a residential area. Only once I was satisfied I was alone did I make my way back to the main road and continue on to the airport.

The long-term parking lot stretched out before me, and I carried on to the back. I didn't want my vehicle to stand out, although I appreciated that was wishful thinking with the Viper. Still, it wouldn't have to remain unspotted for long. I only needed a day or so's head start to disappear, and I figured it would be a couple of hours before anyone even started looking for me.

I opened the minuscule trunk and climbed out to collect the leather travel bag that lived in there, then threw it on the passenger seat while I slid back into the driver's side. Once I'd closed the door, I unzipped the outside pocket and pulled out the wallet I'd stashed there several months before.

The car's interior light bathed me in a soft glow as I dumped the contents into my lap and took a quick inventory. Everything that should have been there was present and correct—a United Kingdom passport and driver's licence; a matching credit card and a few thousand in cash, split between dollars and sterling; plus the other assorted detritus one normally accumulated. The body of the travel bag held spare clothes, toiletries, a Smith & Wesson .38 Special, and a butterfly knife. Everything I might need for an impromptu weekend away.

I didn't have all that stuff by luck. The man who trained me spent years stressing the need to be prepared at all times, and I'd taken it to heart. I could have been a fucking Girl Scout, if it wasn't for the fact that while most little girls were learning the basics of how to cook an egg using a piece of cotton and a safety pin, I was busy learning how to survive in the real world.

He'd also taught me to act like a cold-hearted little robot, and I called on every one of those lessons now.

Don't think, don't think, don't think. Just *do*.

Lock those *damned* emotions away.

The passport photo made me look as if I'd just been rolled out of the morgue, and for good reason. Tramping through the jungle in Belize on a survival training exercise never did much for my appearance, and I'd spent a week living off twigs and berries and nasty-tasting wriggly things while trying not to get eaten myself. I'd gone the final forty-eight hours without sleep as the trainers decided to play a fun new game that involved them hunting us like animals. Anyone they caught got treated to a nice trip to a facility that made Guantanamo Bay look like a five-star hotel.

No, I didn't get caught.

I figured I'd sleep on the plane on the way back, but the pilot went down with food poisoning. That meant I'd ended up flying the bloody thing instead while the pilot alternated between throwing up and pouring coffee into me. I crawled into work for a meeting straight after we landed, and following that, when I was just about to pass out on the sofa in the corner of my office, my assistant walked in with a make-up artist and photographer for another round of passport photos.

All that seemed a lifetime away. Right now, I was barely capable of brushing my teeth, let alone taking on a team of the best special forces the US had to offer.

From the bottom of the bag, I fished out a wig and a fresh pair of coloured contact lenses that matched the ones in the picture. I'd already had a wig on all day, and my head was hot and itchy. I'd have liked nothing more than to fling the damn thing under a moving car and then climb into the shower to wallow in misery, but I couldn't allow myself that luxury. Instead, I swapped out the honey blonde bob for something longer in a dull, mousey brown. The fringe tickled my eyebrows. That was going to get old, fast.

I went on autopilot, changing my identity as I'd

done many times in the past. The only difference was the quake in my hand as I popped the mud-coloured contact lenses out of their blister packs. Even though I had 20:20 vision, I wore a pair of contacts most of the time because, in my line of work, my piercing violet eyes were far too noticeable. Despite all the practice, it took me four tries to get them in, and I bit my lip hard, trying not to scream in frustration. As the metallic tang of blood filled my mouth, I relished the pain. Anything to distract me from my thoughts was welcome.

A pair of wire-rimmed glasses completed the effect. When I looked in the mirror, I bore an uncanny resemblance to the morgue shot, which was both a good and bad thing. Good because it meant I was unlikely to get hauled off going through passport control. Bad because it served to remind me of just how horrific the last nine days had been. Things had started out terrible, then this afternoon, they'd progressed into a nightmare of such epic proportions I wasn't sure I'd ever wake up.

Or if I even wanted to.

Still, I didn't have time to sit around basking in self-pity. I needed to get moving.

I fished my three phones out of my handbag and threw them into the glove compartment. Anything relating to my true identity—credit cards, driving licence, my real passport—joined them, as did the gun and knife. Some say it's liberating to go without a cell phone, but I didn't feel that. No, I just felt...lost. Sure, I may have had a habit of going through phones faster than a frat party goes through beer, but I normally managed to keep at least one of them with me.

After a moment's deliberation, I gave in and

retrieved one mobile, removed the battery, and returned it to my handbag. I couldn't use it—turning it on would allow the people I worked with to locate me instantly—but I felt better having it with me. Call it a comfort blanket. A connection, however tenuous, back to my life. I allowed myself that one concession.

Five minutes had passed by the time I removed my tailored black jacket and stilettos. The jacket in particular, a military style that accentuated my waist and drew attention to my chest, was too noticeable. I hadn't wanted to wear the outfit, but my assistant picked it out and I was too tired to argue.

I replaced them with a pair of grey ballet pumps and a shapeless cardigan. My white shirt and black trousers were plain enough to keep. An olive green wool scarf provided the final touch, leaving me looking like a librarian who got dressed in a thrift shop. In the dark.

Finally, I tugged my wedding ring off and swapped it onto my other hand. I couldn't show the world I was married, but I wasn't going to be parted from that last connection to my husband, even if every glance at it made my eyes prickle with tears.

"I will not cry," I whispered to myself as I climbed out of the car. "I will not fucking cry."

I swung my travel bag over one shoulder and my handbag over the other then headed for the terminal. The rain had slackened but it was still falling, a persistent drizzle that made me wish for an umbrella. I sighed and carried on. The walk would only take a few minutes, and I wasn't going to dissolve. It was just one more shitty nail in the coffin of the second worst day of my life.

The airport was busier than I expected, and a quick glance at the departures board showed every flight was either delayed or cancelled due to the storm.

"Fuck it," I muttered under my breath, as I paid homage to my British roots and headed for the nearest queue.

Grumpy passengers milled around the check-in desks, berating the airline staff as if it was their fault the planes were running late. To my right, a red-faced man chewed out one poor girl who looked on the verge of tears.

"I'm holding you personally responsible if I miss my meeting," he yelled, spit flying as he got in her face.

"I'm sorry, sir." What else could she say?

The old me would have called in a favour to ensure the arsehole got rewarded with a cavity search as he went through security. New me stared blankly into space as I waited my turn.

When I finally reached the ticket counter, I still hadn't decided on a destination, but as my passport was British, it seemed sensible to aim for mainland Europe and avoid the need for a visa. Preferably an English, French, German, Spanish, or Italian speaking country as I was fluent in all those languages, but I'd get by anywhere. It wasn't as if I wanted to talk to anybody when I got there.

"Where do you want to go?" a harried-looking employee asked. He glanced at his watch, no doubt counting down the seconds to the end of his shift.

"What tickets are available for Europe? On planes

that are actually going to leave soon?"

He tapped away at his computer keys. "We've got... London Heathrow...and...Egypt...and.... No, that's it."

"Egypt isn't in Europe."

"It's not?"

His blank face told me I'd be wasting my time with a geography lesson.

"Are you sure that's all you have?"

England was at the bottom of my list as the border controls were stricter, meaning I'd need to be more creative if I wanted to travel outside the country. This passport would be compromised soon, and the way things were, it wouldn't be as easy as it usually was for me to get another.

"Yes, I'm sure," he said, glowering at me like I was a mosquito he wanted to swat. "Do you want the ticket or not?" He tapped his fingers on the desk and looked pointedly back down the queue, which grew longer with each passing second.

I didn't have a lot of choice. I needed to get out of the US sharpish or I wouldn't be able to make a clean break, and there weren't any other viable options.

"Yes, I'll take it," I told him, digging out the cash to pay. It would have to do.

I cleared security without any hitches. I hadn't been expecting any because the guy who sorted out my passports was the best. Over the years, he'd procured sources for blank documents from any number of different countries so whatever he produced for me was indistinguishable from the real thing.

As I collected my bag from the scanner, I was pleased to note that karma had raised her ugly head and the obnoxious guy from the check-in line was having his carry-on luggage emptied out by a security guard.

At least it wasn't just me that little bitch hated at the moment.

The departures screen told me I had a while before I needed to head for the gate, so I stopped at a newsagent and bought a couple of magazines to try and occupy myself on the trip. Usually when I flew commercial, I spent most of the time working, but with my employment status somewhat hazy and my head filled with rocks, that wasn't a viable option. Plus the pounding in my temples at any sudden movements told me thinking wasn't a good idea right now.

I wandered aimlessly around the shops, fitting in nicely with the tourists. The amount of crap you could buy at airports never ceased to amaze me. The only reason I went to them was to leave again as fast as possible, but some people seemed to treat the terminals as shopping destinations in their own right. I marvelled as one family staggered past carrying, among other things, two designer handbags, a games console, a surround sound speaker system, and a pair of cowboy boots. Good luck trying to stuff that lot into the overhead lockers.

With nothing better to do, I bought a hot chocolate with whipped cream in a vain attempt to make myself feel better then slumped into an empty chair outside the cafe to watch the display monitor.

Twenty minutes passed... Thirty... Why did time go more slowly when a girl's heart was breaking from the inside out? After an interminably long time, my flight status changed from "Wait" to "Boarding." I trudged to the gate and joined the rest of the throng as we were herded onto the plane like cattle, turning right into economy class as directed by an overly perky air hostess. Once my bag was safely stowed above my head, I buckled myself into my seat and closed my eyes.

Please let this trip go quickly.

Nobody listened, and we hung around on the tarmac for another half hour before the plane took off. I relaxed an infinitesimal amount as the wheels left the ground. The first part of my plan had gone as smoothly as I could have hoped, but now I was left to deal with the worst bit. Loneliness. I only had my thoughts for company now. As soon as the pilot turned out the seatbelt light, I took the only sensible option—pressed the "call" button and ordered a large gin and tonic.

"Ice and lemon?"

"Yes, and actually, make it two."

I needed something to help me forget.

Memories and frustrations and pain took over in my mind, and I wished I could flip an off-switch to give myself inner peace. But I couldn't, so alcohol would have to substitute.

With little to distract me, my thoughts turned back to earlier in the day. Darkness descended as I recalled the events that led me to be sitting there, eating tiny cardboard crackers out of a plastic wrapper with my arse slowly going numb, instead of being back at home with those I considered my family.

Chapter 2

I'D SAY I woke at dawn that morning, the day of the funeral, but the truth is I never really slept. As soon as the sun cleared the horizon, I headed into the office to work on the case that had occupied my every waking moment, as well as my dreams, for the past week.

The murder of my husband.

I felt like my heart had been ripped out, set on fire, and then put in a blender. My head told me I should be out looking for his killers, that they needed to pay for what they'd done, but inside I was paralysed.

My friend Daniela had moved into my house and each morning, she'd herd me out to the car and drive me to the office. We had a routine now.

"How are you feeling?" she'd ask.

"A little better," I'd lie.

"We're getting closer. We'll find them; I promise."

Dan was heading up the investigation and had a team of our best people working for her, but so far, every lead had petered out. I offered little help as I sat behind my desk, staring at the wall.

"Hey, watch it!"

I looked across as one of our technicians bumped into a chair, waking Evan, who'd been slumped sideways in it.

"Sorry."

Evan shook his head. "No, it's me who should apologise. I shouldn't have snapped."

Tension crackled through the air. Not a minute passed without somebody yawning, and tempers were frayed. The equipment in the company gym took a battering as the guys tried not to vent their frustrations on each other. The punch bags bore the brunt of it, and we'd replaced two of them already.

Nick stomped in at ten, wearing a scowl. "Every cop I've spoken to in Mexico is either corrupt or incompetent."

"You didn't learn anything, then?"

"Apart from how to swear more creatively in Spanish? No."

He'd been trying to trace the true identity of the sorry excuse for a human being currently on ice with the coroner. The team had narrowed his origins down to somewhere south of the border, but the fact that a good portion of his face was missing left us struggling to pinpoint things any further.

Nick sat back on the couch in the corner and sighed. I wasn't the only person my husband's death was affecting. Nick had been one of his best friends.

"Do you want me to make you a drink?" I asked. Playing barista was all I was good for at the moment.

He managed a small smile. "Coffee would be good."

At least it gave me something to do, although when the machine flashed the "change water filter" light at me, I wanted to kick it. My tolerance of menial tasks had dropped considerably.

At 11 a.m. my office assistant, Sloane, gently nudged my arm. "It's almost time."

"Did Bradley bring something for me to wear?"

"It's hanging on the back of your bathroom door."

Her voice cracked as she spoke, and I knew she'd been crying. She'd tried to hide it, but her puffy eyes had telltale smudges of mascara around them. I wanted to give her a hug, to tell her to cry if it would make her feel better, but I couldn't. I was afraid that if she started sobbing, then I would too, and I didn't cry anymore. Ever.

No matter how much of a wreck I was inside, to anyone looking at me, I was the ice queen. I never got upset, never got emotional. Not in front of anyone but my husband, anyway. He was the only person who saw the real me. And now he'd gone, that girl was locked up inside, and I'd thrown away the key.

Sloane had arranged cars to take everyone to the church, but I decided to drive myself instead. I couldn't take another pity-filled glance or offer of help, no matter how well-meaning everyone was. I collapsed into my Viper and sat for a few minutes, forcing myself to breathe deeply until I was calm. The others had left before me, which was just as well, because when I arrived at the church, it turned out the media circus had come to town.

We'd suspected a handful of reporters might turn up, but it must have been a slow news day because there were dozens of them milling around in the parking lot. All the local press had arrived, plus a bunch of freelance paparazzi and even a TV crew. When I pulled in, a virtual stampede started towards my car.

My husband and I had done everything we could to keep a low profile, but when someone got killed in an undeniably attention-grabbing way, it had an unfortunate tendency to entice the media scum out from the rocks they usually resided beneath. There was even a crowd of the public, peering through the drizzle from under hoods and umbrellas, ghoulishly waiting to catch a glimpse of the "Black Widow," as the press had dubbed me. Give them ten out of ten for originality, huh?

I hoped they were getting good and wet.

Barely resisting the urge to drive the Viper straight through the lot of them, I pulled to a halt next to our other cars. My friends were waiting when I got out, and they formed a barrier to shield me from the circling sharks. One held an umbrella overhead, and we moved towards the church as one mass with the guys at the front shouldering any particularly persistent reporters out of the way.

Their shouts echoed in my ears.

"Look this way," one yelled before Dan pushed him aside.

"Come on, just give us a picture," another called.

As if.

I kept my head bowed, wishing the service was over before it had even started. A couple of my team stayed behind by the doors to keep reporters out of the church. A few of them tried to talk their way in by claiming to be friends or relatives, demonstrating they had as little respect for the dead as for the living.

I sat down on the front pew next to Nate, my husband's best friend and business partner. Another of my girlfriends, Mack, took the other side. She dabbed at her eyes with a tissue, not as concerned with hiding her emotions as I was. Bradley leaned forward from the row behind and squeezed my shoulder in a show of support. He'd foregone his usual riot of colour and put on a black suit, but his watch was pink, and he had a diamond in his ear. He just couldn't help himself.

I nearly lost it when the pallbearers carried the casket in. Six of my husband's oldest friends shouldered the burden, the grief on their faces mirroring my own. The casket was a plain oak affair, with brass handles and a simple arrangement of orchids on the top. He wouldn't have wanted something fancy, and it was closed of course. In fact, the whole thing was more for show than anything else, as firstly, there wasn't a whole lot left of him, and secondly, what was left had pretty much been cremated already.

The pastor stood up and droned on for a lifetime. Well, about twenty-five minutes, but it seemed much longer. His whole speech came across as insincere—hardly surprising as he'd never met my husband. The part where he said our kids would miss their father terribly was particularly touching, considering we didn't have any.

Still, I couldn't totally blame him. I'd refused to give him any personal details, so he tried his best, and I had to be grateful for that. I blocked out the rest of his words and concentrated on staying calm.

Just breathing.

In and out.

In and out.

When he'd muttered his final prayer, we all trooped outside for the burial. It was still raining, which at least gave me a good reason for hiding under an umbrella once more. The last thing I wanted was to wake up the next day to find my face plastered across the front page. I wouldn't put it beyond the reporters to photoshop a big grin on my face to show me "gleefully celebrating" the death of my husband, just to stir things up a bit.

As I watched the casket being lowered into the ground, my heart sank down with it. Never again could I love anyone the way I loved that man. When he died, my soul died too. I'd been reduced to a shell, mechanically doing the bare minimum to work and stay breathing but not caring whether I ultimately lived or died.

I was alive but no longer living.

The pastor sprinkled a handful of dirt on top of the casket then Dan nudged my arm and gestured towards the black rose I clutched in a death grip. A thorn dug into my thumb, and I relished the pain, relished the trickle of crimson blood because it broke through the numbness. But at Dan's urging, I forced my fingers to loosen and threw the single flower into the grave.

That was it. Over.

My soulmate was gone.

CHAPTER 3

AS THOSE PRESENT started to leave, I stayed frozen to the spot. My flesh crawled at the lingering glances from people not sure whether they should come over and speak to me or just go. I was in no mood to talk to anyone, so I was grateful when my closest friends once more formed a wall to protect me from the crowd. Thankfully, their actions deterred most people from coming over.

I say most, because there's always one.

In this case, the "one" was my husband's Aunt Miriam. Not my favourite person on a good day, and if I'd made a list of the people I least wanted to cross paths with today, her name would have been right at the top of it, written in bold and underlined. She powered in my direction like a super-tanker, mourners scattering out of her way as she dragged her long-suffering husband along behind her, set on a collision course with yours truly.

Nick's grip tightened around my elbow, and he silently asked me with his eyes if I wanted him to get rid of her.

"I'll deal with it," I whispered. Despite the circumstances, this wasn't his battle to fight.

She ground to a halt in front of me, her ample figure carelessly squashed into a Chanel suit, teetering on a pair of Louboutin heels that I was surprised hadn't buckled under the strain. I doubted her unsteadiness was entirely due to the unsuitability of her footwear, however. Miriam was fond of a few glasses of wine with her lunch. Or sometimes instead of her lunch. And for glasses, read bottles.

I schooled my expression into a blank mask as I prepared to face a woman who made the Ugly Sisters look like Cinderella, and who had as much tact as a herd of buffalo. As usual, Miriam got in before me. She always had to have the first word and the last. And most of the ones in between.

"I thought I should let you know how sorry I was to hear about Charles's death," she said, her voice dripping with more insincerity than the pastor's.

She was the only person who called my husband Charles. He'd despised the name, but she still insisted on using it even when he continually asked her not to.

"It was good of you to take the time to come, Miriam. I'm sure he would have appreciated it."

Not exactly true, because my husband cared for Miriam about as much as I did. He'd have appreciated it more if she'd moved to the next state. Or better still, the next continent.

"I always said he'd come to a nasty end if he kept associating with those unsavoury characters. If he'd become an accountant like my William, I'm sure all of this could have been avoided. A man needs a well-respected job to get on in life. You don't see any of William's friends at the country club getting murdered," Miriam said.

Even in a situation like this, she couldn't resist giving me a lecture. Miriam classed any man who rode a motorbike, or had a tattoo, or didn't have a nine-to-five office job as an "unsavoury character."

Most of our closest acquaintances fitted into one of those categories, whereas Miriam's son, William, was about as exciting as a jellyfish and with slightly less backbone. William's wife wasn't too enamoured with him either. Only last week, I'd seen her stumbling out of the Quality Inn on the outskirts of town accompanied by the pizza delivery guy from Giuseppe's. She'd worn the satisfied smile of a freshly fucked woman as she busily untucked her skirt from her knickers. The Quality Inn was one of those classy establishments where the honeymoon suite came with a mirror on the ceiling, a vibrating bed, and free all-you-can-watch porn.

Still, this was a funeral, and I didn't want to cause a scene, so I kept that little story to myself.

"He made his own decisions in life, Miriam."

"Don't we all know it? Some of them were worse than others."

She looked pointedly at me when she said that, leaving me in no doubt which decision of his she was referring to. Miriam thought I was a trophy wife and a gold-digger. I knew this because she told my husband exactly that about a week after our wedding.

No "congratulations." No "I hope you have a lovely future together." I think her exact words were, "You've done what? Is she a hooker? I hope you've got a good lawyer." Like I said, Miriam held me in high regard.

As I forced myself to resist the call of the Beretta Bobcat I knew Nick had strapped to his ankle, she continued, "And as for that security company he started..." She shook her head and her double chin wobbled. "Charles could have been a man of leisure, travelled the world. But what did he decide to do? Install burglar alarms and advise little old ladies on what locks to put on their front doors. A waste if you ask me."

I didn't ask her. And as a matter of fact, he'd made a pretty decent living, as did I, and his life had been a damn sight more exciting than William's.

"You're entitled to your own opinion."

She had that smug little smile of a person convinced they were always right down to a tee. Oh, how I longed to remove it.

"By the way, when is the will being read?" she asked.

Ahhh. The real reason for her sudden interest became clear. She wanted money, yet she had the nerve to call me a gold-digger. Now probably wasn't the best time to break it to her that there wouldn't be a formal reading of the will, because I was the only person included in it, and I already knew what it said.

"Nothing's been arranged yet," I said truthfully.

I wasn't about to give her the bad news at the funeral and have her raising hell. The reporters camped outside would have had a field day with that. If we were somewhere else, I'd have told her that her numbers hadn't come up just to see the look on her face. If I was really lucky, she'd get so pissed she'd give herself a stroke.

"Well, be sure to let me know when it's organised. It's never good to delay these things, you know."

I didn't have to answer because Miriam turned on her heel and left, trailed by her poor hubby. He was a good deal younger than her and had started out as the pool boy before he made the biggest mistake of his life. Another man blinded by money. There wasn't a lot else to love about her, and unsurprisingly, he seemed to have spent the last decade regretting their union. The poor guy's only hope left in life was that she'd cark it first so he could finally get some peace. She'd never divorce him because he'd get half of her cash—not that there was much left seeing as she'd drunk most of it.

Somewhere in the years since their marriage, the dumb schmuck had lost his hair and gone soft around the middle. Now, he looked more like the Pillsbury Doughboy and less like the arm candy that Miriam originally chose. From the way she always snapped at him, the feeling of disharmony was mutual. They spent most of their time sitting around the country club, bickering. It truly was a match made in heaven.

I watched Miriam's super-sized backside disappear towards the parking lot, where she ploughed through the waiting mob of reporters like they were skittles. Strike one for Miriam.

"Ready to go?" Nick asked.

I looked up at him. Over the past few days, he'd developed worry lines around his eyes, and the dark circles underneath showed the toll recent events had taken. And it wasn't just him. I saw the same effect on all the team. After what happened at the Green Mountain Hotel, life would never be the same for any of us.

I took a deep breath and did a mental check. My hair looked okay, my eyes were dry, and I was calm enough that I wouldn't lose it at a photographer. In truth, I wasn't ready to leave my husband for the final time, but I knew I couldn't stay.

"Better get it over with," I replied.

My guys immediately formed up again, and we headed back towards the cars. Between the umbrella above and the bodies around me, there wasn't much for the press to see. I kept my head down, careful not to make eye contact with any of them, but that didn't stop them yelling more questions as we pushed past. They were worse this time.

"Is it true you're being investigated over your husband's death?"

Like I was going to answer that.

"Was your husband an enforcer for the Russian mob?"

Seriously?

"Did your husband die over an arms deal gone wrong?"

That guy must have been on a break from the Hollywood slot.

"Were you having an affair with another man?"

None of your fucking business.

"Was your marriage in trouble?"

Fuck.

"Did you hire someone to kill your husband?"

Off.

Curses hovered on the tip of my tongue, but I refused to let them fly. Some of the reporters had digital recorders, and they'd have just loved to get my tirade on tape. They were fishing, hoping someone would take a bite so they could splash their trash across the front page. They obviously hadn't managed to dig up anything good on my husband's life or death, or on me either, and I refused to get riled or let them see me upset. But that someone could think those things hurt more than I cared to admit.

We made it over to my car, and I bleeped the locks. Nick pulled open the driver's door and looked down at me.

"Still sure you want to go by yourself? I can drive if you like," he said.

"Let you drive my car? Nice try, but you've got to be kidding me."

"Thought that would be a long shot. I can just ride with you if you want company?"

"I need a few minutes on my own. I'll meet you back at the house later."

In reality, I felt as if I was going to break down, and I didn't want Nick or anyone else around to witness it. I'd never been good at expressing my feelings. I guess most people learned that sort of thing from their parents, but I'd never had that education. The overriding emotion my mother showed me as a child was indifference, interspersed with the occasional angry outburst.

The last time I cried was etched vividly in my mind. At eight years old, I'd just had a run-in with my mother's latest boyfriend, a skinny man everyone just called Dog. I always found that odd because he smelled perpetually of fish and looked like a rat. That evening, he'd just taken his belt to me for the heinous crime of eating the last tin of baked beans.

"Those were mine, you little bitch. You don't take what's mine."

"I-I-I didn't know."

I'd felt sick with hunger, and there wasn't any other food in the house, but he lifted up my top and thrashed me, anyway. One, two, three, four, five lashes. My back burned, and I started to cry.

That only made him angrier.

"Shut up. Shut up! You're always snivelling. If I hear you do that again, I'll take more than my belt to you."

With every word that passed his lips, I shrank back further into the corner. I knew he meant what he said.

So, I never cried after that.

Emotions like hope and happiness were foreign concepts to me. At school, I'd always been the outcast. A memory of seven-year-old me flitted through my mind, rushing out the door at the end of another day in hell. Or rather, St. Joseph's First School. I'd almost made it to freedom when a foot across the threshold sent me sprawling. A dainty foot encased in a pink patent pump with little bows. I followed the leg upwards and found Katie Mitchell sneering at me. As her little gang of cronies looked on, she'd raised her heel and ground it down on my Mickey Mouse pencil sharpener. I'd coveted that thing in the newsagent's for weeks before I finally plucked up the courage to steal it.

Katie's pretty shoes were no match for my ugly second-hand lace-ups, and when I kicked her in the shin, the teacher came running at her wail. I got sent to the headmaster's office. Again.

Even now, I could still feel the condescending looks of those kids, and their cruel taunts would forever play in my head. I never got invited for play dates or to birthday parties, and even if I had been, I could never have reciprocated. My mother resented being lumbered with one child without having to care for somebody else's for the day as well. Not that she did much caring.

I'd been fending for myself for as long as I could remember while also looking after my mother as best I could. She'd never kept a job for long, and money was always tight. A good weekend for me meant finding enough food to have a meal on both days and managing to stay out of range of whichever waste of space boyfriend she'd installed in her bed that month.

The one emotion I became overly familiar with as a child was fear. Fear is a choice. An important lesson and one I learned too young. First, I worked out how to hide it, and then how to conquer it. Succumbing to fear never helped my situation, but acting scared encouraged people to take advantage of me. Standing up to the school bullies meant they left me alone, even if it did get me labelled as a problem child.

At home, the most sensible option was to avoid my mother's boyfriends. The best of them ignored me back. Others took their anger out on me, shouting for every perceived wrong before they raised their fists, but they weren't the worst. No, those were the men who had a special spot reserved in hell, the ones who started out nice, too nice, but then touched me in ways that even at that age I knew were wrong. I'd spent a lot of time hiding under my bed, and when I outgrew that, the wardrobe became my refuge. By the time I got too big for the wardrobe, I was old enough to keep out of the house altogether.

As an eight-year-old girl, I'd perfected the art of the blank face and still body. A faultless mask. It served me well as a child, and it continued to do so as an adult. Nick, one of the few people who knew anything about my upbringing, took a good look at me and understood I'd shut down.

He wrapped me up in a hug and leaned over, dropping a soft kiss on the top of my head.

"Okay, baby, I'll see you soon."

Please, just leave me alone. If I hid myself away like the scared child I once was, nobody could touch me. Not the hordes who thought they were helping and not the cops, either.

We'd given them a chance to do their thing in the fortnight since my husband died, but they hadn't made a whole lot of progress. In fact, they hadn't come up with a single line of enquiry other than to question me, and I knew I didn't kill him, so I was already one step ahead of them there.

I also had access to my husband's files, which the cops didn't, and with his line of work, there might be a link in those to whoever murdered him. My investigators were better than the police anyway, of that I was sure. If the killer was going to be found, it would be by us, not them.

Nick closed the car door, and I started the engine. As I pulled forward, my foot on the throttle giving a warning growl, an explosion of flashbulbs lit up the grey sky. Thanks to my illegally tinted windows, the reporters weren't going to get much, but I still wanted to jam their cameras into their mouths and force them to chew on the jagged remains. Death by telephoto lens.

Teeth clenched, I showered the rabble with gravel as I pulled out of the parking lot then floored it towards the highway that would take me home.

CHAPTER 4

MY HOME, ONCE my sanctuary but not anymore, lay a half-hour drive from the church. Two weeks ago, I would have enjoyed the journey, but today I barely saw the road. My thoughts kept coming back to how I was going to get through the rest of my life without the man who'd been a constant in it for the last fourteen years. We may not have spent all our time together, but barely a day passed without us speaking. My husband had been the one person who truly understood me.

He saw my frustrations and failures when they got me down, but made me get back up and try again until I succeeded. He had confidence in me when I had none in myself. He was the one I let off steam to when I got home at night, and he took my grumpiness with good humour, most of the time at least.

He wasn't only my husband, he was my best friend. I might have taken his name, but I'd given him my heart.

For all that, our marriage wasn't what people thought. Our relationship had evolved over the years, but it never became a traditional husband and wife arrangement, that was for sure. Yes, I wore his ring, but there'd never been any sex, and we'd had our fair share of disagreements. At the end, the trust between us was absolute, but it took us a while to get there.

For three months after we met, I hated him, then that hostility turned into a grudging respect and over the next year, friendship. Fast forward two years, and I'd found out just how awkward it was to get permanent residency in America. Going back to England wasn't an option, not when the company I'd helped my beloved tormentor to build was taking off. Then one drunken night in Vegas when I was moaning about all the paperwork and interviews to get a green card, a friend had jokingly suggested we get married and bypass most of it.

We both had enough alcohol in us that it seemed like a reasonable idea, and two hours later we left the Little White Wedding Chapel as Mr. and Mrs. Our prenup was written on a cocktail napkin—he kept his guns; I kept my knives—and we'd tipsily agreed that if either of us got serious about somebody else, we'd get a divorce. Somehow, that never happened, and nearly twelve years later we'd still been hitched.

Except now he'd gone, and I missed him more than I'd ever imagined I could when we tied the knot all those years ago.

I'd driven a couple of miles down the road when my phone vibrated in my jacket pocket. It was standard procedure for me to have three phones, and the same for the other key people I worked alongside. Each of these phones was designated as green, amber, or red.

The world and his dog had the number of my green phone, which spent most of its life diverted to Sloane. She was pretty busy.

Employees, friends, and a few clients had my amber number. Mostly I answered that one, but not today. I had no interest in speaking to anybody, let alone someone unimportant. In fact, I wasn't sure I could summon up the energy to deal with that type of call for the foreseeable future.

But the red phone was different. It was for emergencies only and was never, ever, turned off or diverted. Not a lot of people had the number, and most who did had been at the funeral with me.

And it was the red phone ringing.

Sweat seeped out of my palms as I pushed the button on the steering wheel to answer the call. What could possibly have happened in the five minutes since I'd left?

"Speak to me."

An unfamiliar voice rasped from the speakers, distorted electronically but definitely male. The line crackled, making him sound even more sinister as he barked orders at me.

"Stop investigating your husband's death. No more questions, and don't cooperate with the police. If you stay on your path, everyone close to you will die as he did."

"Who the hell is this?" I asked, though I didn't expect to get an answer. Not when the caller had gone to so much trouble to disguise his voice in the first place.

"That doesn't concern you. The only thing you need to worry about is keeping out of my business. Of course, if you insist on continuing, I'll be forced to demonstrate more of my toys."

Even disguised, his voice had a jovial lilt at odds with his words. He was playing a game with me. A deadly game, but I didn't understand the rules.

"What do you want?"

"Nothing. I want you to do absolutely nothing. Do you understand?"

What should I say? *What should I say?* If I could have reached across the airwaves and torn his windpipe out, I would have, but instead, bile rose in my own throat as I forced out an answer.

"I understand."

What other option did I have?

The line went dead as the bastard hung up, leaving me with only the demons in my head for company.

Fuck, I was a mess. I had been since my husband died. He'd kept me grounded and thinking straight, but with him gone, the monsters locked up deep inside me went for a jailbreak.

I saw a side road coming up and took it, barely slowing as my heart pounded against my ribcage. The back end of the car kicked out on loose gravel as I slewed round the corner before snapping back into line. I changed down a gear to get some acceleration, and the engine screamed in chorus with the demons.

A mile along the lane, I pulled over, leaving a trail of rubber behind me. The old ranch house I'd parked in front of looked fittingly desolate for the situation, with the front door hanging off its hinges and the porch sagging under years of neglect.

My legs shook as I climbed out of the car and started pacing, desperately trying to gather my thoughts together. They rebelled against order, a jigsaw puzzle where none of the pieces fitted.

I'd very much suspected my husband's death was arranged by someone who bore a grudge against him, or maybe me, and now that had been confirmed. The men who pulled the trigger were dead, but they were only hired help. The fucker who ordered the hit was still out there, toasting his success and racking up his phone bill.

I should have been furious, I knew that, but the anger wouldn't come. The place where it should have been was frozen like the rest of me. Where was the pain? The agony? I'd rather have felt anything but nothing.

Now I had a decision to make. Did I carry on with a search that had proved fruitless so far or back off? My friends' lives were at stake, and I couldn't face another funeral. Not when it might be Nick or Dan or someone else I was close to lying in that casket.

Dammit, why couldn't I concentrate? Logic got sucked into a black hole of oblivion as I scuffed my stilettos in the gravel.

If I told the team, they'd want to carry on regardless, of that I was certain. I could hear Nick's voice in my head right now.

"We're trained professionals. We'll be okay."

Dan would say the same, and so would everyone else. But what if they weren't okay?

We may have hit a nerve with our questions so far, but whose nerve was far from clear. We'd put out so many feelers, who knew which one caused the killer to react? Narrowing it down would take time, more questions, and possibly more deaths. The bastard had already proven he didn't mess around.

Short of locking everyone I cared about into a nuclear bunker for the foreseeable future while I tripped around chasing leads on my own, I had no way of keeping them safe. I didn't even have a nuclear bunker, so that option was out, anyway.

In the end, I gave up and let my broken heart make the decision. I couldn't risk anybody else getting hurt. I'd already lost my soulmate, and the thought of the others getting picked off one by one was something I couldn't entertain.

I had to shut this down, but how?

My head throbbed, and I rubbed at my temples, trying to relieve the pressure. The events of the last fortnight were sucking me down like quicksand. I hadn't felt so out of control of my own mind and body since I was a teenager. Back then, my husband taught me to take all the anger and fear and channel it into whatever was necessary to fix the problem, but this time I couldn't see a solution.

Deep breaths.

Take deep breaths.

I forced myself to count to five on each inhale and exhale, but the weight on my chest only got heavier.

My husband's voice echoed in my head, deep and gravelly, always so calm. He'd know what to do. He always did.

"It's like a fire, Diamond. First you get it under control, then you put it out."

He'd told me that more than once.

But I couldn't extinguish it, not yet. To do that, I'd have to take out the source, and I didn't have it in me right now. But I could stop fanning the flames.

How? By stopping the investigation, at least until I got my head straight and came up with a game plan that gave us a reasonable shot at winning.

I thought of what waited for me at home—the cops, the pity, and worst of all, the constant reminders of my husband. Memories lay everywhere in that place. I'd never get the space I needed to think things through there.

Soaked through from the rain, which was no longer a drizzle but a steady downpour, I got back into the car. Out of habit, I had my iPad in my handbag, and it only took a few minutes to log onto the server at work and use my administrator privileges to clear out the files relating to the investigation. That would put the brakes on things. They could stay in my personal cloud storage until my sanity returned.

As guilt ate away at me, I replaced them with a single document:

I have to leave. All this—I can't deal with it right now. And I need you to put a hold on the investigation. I can't tell you the reasons why, but I'm safe and I'll be back to explain. I just need some time. Please. Take care of each other, okay?

Looking back, it was a shitty thing to do, but at that particular moment, I couldn't see a better option. Making stupid decisions is easy when your brain's fucked.

Logic—flawed logic—told me that although my friends would be upset, and even more so when they couldn't find me, being upset was better than being dead. I was doing the best thing for them; at least that was how I saw it at the time.

With my heart a cold lump of lead, I turned off my red phone, started the engine, and set the navigation system for the airport.

It's always darkest right before it goes pitch black.

CHAPTER 5

THE FLIGHT TO England was one of the more unpleasant ones I'd taken. Okay, I'll admit I'd been spoiled over the past few years, first with business class and then my own jet, but that was only so I could deal with my never-ending stream of calls and emails. On the other hand, I'd also taken military transport in some of the shittiest countries in the world, and half of those planes didn't even have seats, let alone trolley service.

So when I say it was bad, that meant the flight sucked.

When I booked my ticket, the only seat left was in the middle of a row of three, near the back. I spent the eight-hour flight wedged between a snoring salesman with a body odour problem and a stomach the size of the national debt, and a teenager who only stopped playing computer games long enough to throw up into a paper bag.

"Don't worry," he told me, after he'd puked for the third time. "It happens every time I fly."

Well, if it always happens, I've got a suggestion—don't eat a super-sized McDonald's in the departure lounge right before you get on the bloody plane. I'd seen him doing exactly that.

Between that pair, the toddler behind me who

reckoned he was the new David Beckham, and the bachelor party in front that managed to drink the plane dry of vodka before we got halfway over the Atlantic, I'd had enough. I was seriously regretting not stuffing my gun into a diplomatic pouch and bringing it along.

By the time we landed, the entire cast of *Riverdance* was holding a rehearsal in my head. As I only had hand luggage, I avoided the crush at the baggage carousel and half crawled, half sleepwalked over to the railway station to catch the Heathrow Express into West London. Morning or not, all I wanted to do was sleep, so I checked into some dive of a hotel on a backstreet in Bayswater.

I slept for most of the day, but not well. Six times, the headboard in the next room banging against the adjoining wall woke me, accompanied by the wild cries of a woman faking an orgasm. Yes, all through the morning and early afternoon. It takes a special kind of desperate to pop out for a quick fuck along with your coffee and McMuffin, but I guess there's a market for everything.

Finding a hotel that didn't rent its rooms out by the hour jumped to the top of my to-do list.

By evening, I'd found a room smaller than my closet at home, having forked out an obscene amount of money for the privilege. At least I'd had lunch and stocked up on painkillers for my headache, as well as shopping for the essentials.

I spent the evening dying my hair, and also my eyebrows, careful not to use so much dye I ended up looking like Bert from Sesame Street. Once I was nice and mousey, I chopped the front bit into a fringe and checked myself out in the mirror. I looked bloody awful. Perfect.

Before I drifted off to sleep, I considered my options. Staying in London long term wasn't one of them—I knew too many people, plus there was CCTV everywhere. It would only be a matter of time before I ran into someone who recognised me.

I'd spent my life cultivating a long list of contacts. There was a standing joke among my friends that I could be out walking in the middle of the Amazon rainforest and a local tribesman would appear from behind a tree saying, "Hey, how are you? Long time no see!" Usually my number of acquaintances was useful, but now I found it a hindrance.

So, if not London, where should I go?

Europe brought the risk of another border crossing, and there would be too many people looking for me—my own team and fuck knew who else? That left the rest of the UK.

After I'd slept on it, I decided heading to the countryside would be my best plan. I'd find somewhere to hole up for a few weeks until my mind consented to shake hands with logic again.

Old me had a plan for everything. And a spare plan. And an alternate plan for the spare plan. And a backup plan for that. New me couldn't decide between cereal and toast for breakfast. Someone had sucked my brain out through my nose and replaced it with termites.

Without a driver's licence in my new name, the best plan I could come up with was "get on a train." Sure, I could have stolen a car, but in my current frame of mind, I'd probably screw it up, and I was too tired for a police chase today.

Guilt nibbled away at me as I shoved my belongings

into my bag. How were the people I'd left behind feeling? Angry? Exasperated? Disappointed in me?

Probably all of the above.

I was a coward for running, so I deserved their contempt. I didn't know how else to cope, though. At work, I was used to confrontation, but in my personal life, I shied away from uncomfortable situations.

I only hoped my friends would forgive me when I went back home.

In the meantime, there I was. Ashlyn Emily Hale. Thirty-two years old on my passport, twenty-nine in reality. I had no home, no job, no qualifications, no friends, and not much money. I'd been in worse positions, but for the last decade and a half, I'd had my husband to support me through them. Now I was on my own, and it brought back stark reminders of a childhood I'd spent my life trying to block out.

An hour later, I sat on a train chugging out of Paddington station. At first, I couldn't decide whether to head north or west, so I'd flipped a grubby penny, and west it was. My husband had been the one who carefully evaluated every decision, weighing up the pros and cons. Without him, I was reduced to heads or tails.

As it was a Saturday, I'd hoped the trains would be less crowded, but the one I ended up on was almost as bad as the plane. It was a stopping service, and drunken revellers returning from what appeared to have been an all-night office Christmas party filled the carriage. It was only the end of November, for crying out loud, but they'd started the festive season early. I guess they didn't want to waste any precious drinking time.

By the time we reached Slough station, I'd been serenaded by a group of elves, had a drink spilled on me by a reindeer, and gotten my arse groped by Father Christmas. Normally, I could remain calm through anything, but my legendarily rock-solid nerves were becoming well and truly frayed around the edges.

Then, just after two Christmas trees, an angel, and the three wise men had started a conga line along the middle aisle, the driver announced that the train had broken down and we all had to get off. I didn't know whether to be pleased or cross.

On the plus side, I'd get away from the Christmas calamity, but the downside was I'd have to move, and it all felt like too much effort at the moment.

Life had been pretty good for the last decade. Maybe I'd used up my quota of happiness and that little bitch, karma, was going to send things downhill from now on.

How much lower could I go?

Because right now, I was at the bottom of the Mariana Trench. Did she expect me to grab a spade and dig down to the fires of hell underneath?

With no other choice, I lifted my bag down from the luggage rack and made my way onto the platform, where a rail employee in a hi-vis jacket was herding passengers onto a hastily procured bus. I spotted two snowmen and a red-faced Christmas pudding heading towards it, weaving from side to side.

A sigh escaped my lips. I needed to find an alternative.

"Excuse me, is there a bus stop around here?" I asked hi-vis guy. "I'm not sure I want to take that one."

He eyed up the Christmas pudding, who'd got stuck in the bus door and was being tugged free by a shepherd and the Virgin Mary, and gave me a look of sympathy.

"Sure, love, there's a bus station just across the street."

I traipsed over to the building he indicated, a space-age monstrosity that appeared to have been modelled on a giant slug, and hopped on the first bus leaving. Looked like I'd be heading north after all.

The bus wound its way through towns and villages for a couple of hours, and I lost track of where I was. I rested my head on the window, staring without seeing, my mind blank. The glass misted up, and I was on the verge of nodding off again when the driver tapped me on the shoulder.

"You'll have to get off now, I'm afraid. This is the last stop, and I have to take the bus back to the depot for shift change."

Where the hell was I?

In a daze, I followed him to the door and climbed down. The bus chugged away, and as it receded into the distance, I found I'd been deposited in a small village. Time warp sprang to mind, and not the Rocky Horror version.

My stomach gurgled, reminding me it was almost lunchtime. I wasn't hungry, but as I'd given up on making the breakfast decision, I knew I should have something. I'd lost half a stone over the last couple of weeks through being too miserable to eat, and while I might end up looking like a supermodel, I'd make myself ill if I kept that diet up.

The tiny high street was terribly quaint. If not for the brand new Range Rover parked outside the post office and a teenage girl texting on her smartphone as she walked, oblivious to everything around her, I could easily believe I'd travelled back half a century.

I walked past a small supermarket with old-fashioned produce displays stacked in the windows and paused outside a bakery. The delicious aromas drifting out of the door tempted me, but I couldn't see anywhere to sit down in there. The temperature hovered in the low single figures, too cold to find a bench and eat outside.

So I carried on, barely glancing at the hardware store, the hairdresser, or the florist, until I arrived in the car park of a pub. A faded wooden sign creaked above my head, swaying in the breeze.

The Coach and Horses. That looked like my best option.

I had to stoop as I crossed the threshold. The inside was dim and dingy, all dark wood and low ceilings studded with blackened wood beams. A nook to my left housed a roaring fire, so I snagged a menu and curled myself into one of the leather wingback chairs set in front of it.

After I'd been there a few minutes, a kind-looking woman in her fifties came over, wiping her hands on her apron.

"What do you want, love?"

The grown-up in me knew what I should pick—salad or soup, or maybe a grilled chicken breast with steamed vegetables. But the child I'd regressed to wanted comfort food.

"I'll have the macaroni and cheese, with a side order of chips and some onion rings," I said, feeling a little guilty but beyond caring about it.

The food came out quickly, piping hot and steaming. If Toby, my nutritionist, saw me now, he'd drag me out by my feet before I could raise the fork to my mouth. I could just imagine him. A sharp intake of breath, followed by, "Don't you dare! That's got so much oil on it, America's gonna invade the plate."

It was bloody delicious.

After eating that amount of stodge, I felt tired, so I spent the rest of the afternoon hiding out by the fire, reading the newspapers that were scattered on the coffee table next to me. By 4 p.m. I started feeling guilty. Guilty that I'd just spent four hours doing nothing. I normally spent every waking minute on the job. I never had time to just *be*.

My mind churned. I should be working towards catching my husband's killer. There wasn't much I could do without tipping the man off, but I had the files to review. Even if I wasn't doing that, I should at the very least be finding myself a job and somewhere to live. The cash I had with me wouldn't last long, and I didn't know when I'd be ready to go back and face the remnants of my life.

I knew that was what I *should* be doing, but I couldn't bring myself to actually do it. I picked up the paper and began to read again instead. The lives of Hollywood Z-listers had never been so fascinating.

Ten minutes later, the barmaid interrupted me.

"Can I get you anything else?"

"No, thanks. I was planning to leave soon." Just as soon as I could drag myself away from the nice warm fire and an article about the dangers of false eyelashes.

"Visiting someone, are you?"

"Er, no."

"It's just I haven't seen you around here before. I thought you must be stopping in to see someone."

I'd only been in the countryside from time to time on assignment, and I'd forgotten how nosey its inhabitants could be. In London, everyone studiously ignored everybody else, and if you did accidentally make eye contact, people automatically assumed you'd escaped from the nearest secure hospital and gave you a wide berth.

"I'm only passing through."

"Lower Foxford's a funny place to pass through. It's not really on the way to anywhere," she said, eyeing me a bit suspiciously.

"Perhaps passing through is the wrong term. I didn't exactly plan where I was going, and this was where I ended up."

"Argument with the boyfriend was it?"

Well, thanks, that'll do. "Yeah, it was."

She laid a hand on my shoulder. "Oh, you poor love. Are you planning to go home, or do you need somewhere to stay for the night?"

"I could do with a place to sleep if you know of any hotels around here?"

She chuckled. "This village is far too small for a hotel. The nearest one's in town, but that's a fifteen-minute drive or half an hour on the bus. We've got a bed and breakfast, though."

I'd been so zoned out on the journey that I didn't even know which town she was talking about. "A bed and breakfast will do fine."

"In that case, I'll get you the number. It's ever so nice, really homely. And Carol, who runs it, will cook you dinner if you like."

I hadn't gotten around to buying a phone yet. I needed to pick up a cheap, pay-as-you-go mobile, but it had slipped my mind before I left London. It wasn't like I had anyone I was planning to call, but it might be handy for situations like this.

"Could you give me directions instead? I forgot to pick up my phone when I left."

"Of course, it's not far."

CHAPTER 6

ARMED WITH A map the barmaid had hastily scribbled on the back of her order pad, I found Carol's bed and breakfast within fifteen minutes. *Melrose* was a chocolate-box cottage on a quiet lane, white with wooden beams and a thatched roof, straight out of the pages of one of those fancy magazines dentists kept in the waiting room to remind you how inadequate your life was. Even in winter, the garden looked beautiful, all manicured lawn and neatly edged flower borders. A stone cupid peeped out from between the bare branches, his arrow aimed straight at my fucking heart.

The curtains twitched, and I'd just lifted my hand up to knock when the door swung open and a tiny lady greeted me with a wide smile and curious eyes.

"Hello, dear. Elsa from The Coach and Horses said you'd be stopping by. I've opened up a room for you, and the electric blanket's already on."

Why wasn't I surprised she knew I was coming?

"Ashlyn Hale. Or just Ash, if you like. I wasn't sure you'd have a room available at such short notice."

"Oh, I'm rarely fully booked. Most people who come to Lower Foxford are visiting family or friends, so they already have somewhere to stay. I just run this place as a hobby. I get lonely on my own." With her cheerful demeanour, she'd keep smiling through Armageddon.

"I won't be great company, I'm afraid."

"Don't you worry about that, dearie. Elsa said you'd had a tiff with your boyfriend. You just need a good night's sleep and everything'll look rosier in the morning."

Yeah, right. Unless reincarnation was a thing, we were shit out of luck on that one.

"Let's hope so, eh?"

She must have sensed my hesitation. "It was a big argument, then?"

"Er..."

"You don't have to give me the details now. We can have a nice chat about it over dinner. I'm making toad-in-the-hole to start and chocolate brownies with ice cream for after. The ice cream's from my own special recipe."

"I ate a really big lunch—I'm not sure I've got room for dinner as well." Or the interrogation that would inevitably come with it.

"You need to eat." Carol reached out and patted my stomach. "Look at you—you're already fading away, and that's not good for a girl. I'll show you up to your room. You'll have time to take a bath, and I'll knock on your door when dinner's ready."

Before I could get a word in edgeways, I found myself being marched up the stairs. What was the point in trying to argue? Instinct told me Carol could outmanoeuvre even the most hardened negotiator. Next time my company had a hostage situation, they should call her in. She'd probably win the bastards over with cookies.

The room may have been basic and a little too pink, but it represented a definite step up from my digs in London. I tested the weight of the chest of drawers. Yes, I could drag that across the door at night. Anything to keep myself inside. By the time Carol came back, I'd checked my exit routes and fitted in a quick shower with freesia-scented shampoo.

Carol held off on the questioning through the main course, and I suppose I should have been thankful for that. At least her brief reprieve gave me time to come up with a cover story.

Usually, thinking up a plausible tale on the fly came naturally, but today I struggled. My heart wasn't in it, and Carol's incessant chattering about the inhabitants of Lower Foxford as I'd picked at my toad-in-the-hole had left my concentration in tatters.

"Marjorie Smith crashed her car into a tree last week after she left The Coach and Horses. I'm not saying she'd been drinking, but it's quite a coincidence, don't you think?"

"Mmm, sounds like it."

"And Vera saw Mrs. Melton's daughter in the chemist buying a pregnancy test kit this morning. She's only been dating the butcher's son for a month, and they're not even married." Carol shook her head. "Youngsters these days. Always rushing into things."

My initial suspicions had been right—Carol wasn't just a branch of the local gossip tree, she was the trunk. Everyone in the village, and undoubtedly half the people from the surrounding area, would soon know anything I told her.

As I pondered my escape, Carol bustled off to the kitchen and came back with the brownies. Once she'd deposited a family-sized portion in front of me, she couldn't contain herself any longer.

"So, what happened with this boyfriend of yours then?"

I took a deep breath, looked her in the eye and did what came naturally. I lied.

"My fiancé. Ex-fiancé." I arranged my face into a suitably devastated expression and added a sniff for effect. "Three days ago, I got a migraine while I was out shopping, so I went home to rest, but as soon as I walked into the house, I heard noises coming from upstairs."

These brownies were pretty damn good. Maybe I hadn't lost my appetite after all, merely misplaced it. I forked in another mouthful while Carol salivated for the good bits.

"I almost called 911 because the house was meant to be empty, but then I figured I'd probably just left the TV on. It was supposed to have one of those energy-saving timers, but that never worked properly, and... Anyhow, I crept upstairs and realised the noises were coming from our bedroom. Kind of...grunting." I screwed my eyes shut in mock disgust. "When I pushed the door open, Jamie was in there doing the deed with another woman."

Carol's mouth dropped open in horror. Or perhaps glee, since this was gossip gold.

"What did you do?"

I gazed past her. Lying was always easier if you didn't look the person in the eye.

"First, I froze, but then I turned to run to my best friend's house. Beth lived three doors up, and we'd been so close since we met at a yoga class three years ago and she recommended these really comfortable pants that—" I pursed my lips. "It was her! When Jamie moved, it was her underneath him. In *my* bed!"

"Did you kick his ass?" Carol asked.

I turned my laugh into a cough. This imaginary situation was anything but funny, but seriously? How many sweet little old ladies said that? She'd been watching too many US dramas.

"If I could turn the clock back, I'd have booted him up the backside, but I wasn't thinking straight. I mean, they were *naked*. No, I ran right out of there."

Carol reached over and squeezed my hand. "That's quite understandable, dear."

"Well, I threw my engagement ring at him and left, but now I wish I'd kept it. I could have pawned the diamond."

"You know for next time."

Next time? Boy, she had a high opinion of me, didn't she?

"I guess."

"But how did you end up in Lower Foxford?"

"I got worried he might come after me, so I ran to the bus stop and jumped on the first bus to arrive. Turned out it was going to the airport. So I got on a plane. Then a train, then a bus, and then I ended up here." I gave a helpless shrug. "I'm a bit lost."

I kept that last part close to the truth. Pretending was easier if you threw in a few facts, I knew that from years of experience. And when I first met my husband, he'd imparted a few words of wisdom: if you can only be good at one thing, be good at lying. Because if you're good at lying, you're good at everything. Words to live by. I'd taken his advice to heart, and like everything else I did, I practised. Practice made perfect.

"You said you flew?" Carol asked. "Where did you live?"

"In America."

"Oh my, that's a long way to come. No wonder you look tired."

That was my cue to yawn. "I haven't gotten much sleep over the past few days."

"So, what are you planning to do now? Are you going to go back home and sort things out?"

I shook my head. "I never want to see that pig again. There's not much to go back to, anyway."

"What about your job?"

"The house was Jamie's, and I didn't work. He said I didn't need to, that he earned enough for both of us. I thought we'd be together forever. How could I have been so stupid?"

"One of those control freaks, was he?"

"Something like that. I'm glad I scraped my house key along his Mercedes on my way down the driveway."

Carol clapped her hands with glee. "Did you do anything else?"

"No, that was it, but the scratch went from the bumper to the boot."

Ashlyn was pretty tame. If these events had been real, darling Jamie would have been fighting for his release from prison in a country that paid lip service to human rights.

Carol tilted her head to one side, but her tight grey curls didn't move. "You say you came from America, but why do you have an English accent?"

"Because I grew up in London. I moved to the States to be with Jamie when I was twenty-one."

"Twenty-one? Golly, you were together a long time then."

"A third of my life: wasted." I gave a convincing groan. "It took him eight years to propose. That alone should have told me something, right? I think he only gave me a ring because I talked about getting a job. He obviously figured that if I was his wife, I'd be back under his thumb, and I fell for it. I'm an idiot."

"They say love is blind. You're not the only woman to have the wool pulled over her eyes by a man thinking with his little head instead of his big one."

Oh, Carol. What would a normal girl do right now? Giggle. So I giggled.

"I know, but it doesn't make it hurt any less."

"Well, we'll just have to take your mind off things. Keep you busy. That's what worked best for me after I lost my Len. We were married for forty years."

Forty years, and she still talked fondly of him. I felt a pang of jealousy. If my husband had lived, would we have lasted four decades? I liked to think so.

"I'm so sorry, Carol. Losing Len must have been far worse than what happened to me."

In fact, it was closer to the truth than I cared to admit.

"It happened almost ten years ago now, dear. Time's the greatest healer, but my friends were a huge help too. At first, I didn't know how to go on without him, but now I can look back and smile at the good times. Nobody will ever replace Len, but I know he wouldn't have wanted me to sit around moping, so I've filled my life with other things."

Her look turned wistful, and I knew she was thinking of her late husband. I couldn't help thinking of mine too. Was there life after death? I'd never believed in it, but now I wondered. Was he up there, willing me to get my act together? I hoped Carol was right and time would heal my cracks, because I didn't see what else would help. I gave a sniff, a genuine one this time, and Carol snapped her eyes back to mine.

"Enough about me," she said. "We need to get you back on your feet. Tomorrow I have a fundraising lunch for church and then bingo at the village hall in the evening. You can come to those. It'll do you good."

Was she serious? Seniors' bingo and a church fundraiser? Apart from the funeral, my last visit to a place of worship had involved a sting operation on a pastor who liked the younger members of his congregation a little too much.

And by lunch, did Carol mean making it or eating it? I could manage the eating part, but cooking had never been my strong suit.

"It's ever so nice of you to offer, but I wouldn't want to put you to any trouble."

"Nonsense, it's no trouble at all. It'll be terrific fun."

Well, if she said so. In my current state, I didn't have the energy to argue with the force that was Carol. Tagging along seemed like the easier option.

"Another custard cream, dear?"

A white-haired lady held out a plate with one hand while pushing her glasses back up her nose with the other.

"I've already had six, thanks."

I felt hideously out of place at the church lunch, firstly because I was the only person not wearing chintz, and secondly because I was the youngest by at least three decades. The way everyone stared at me, I could have been a zoo exhibit.

Maybe I should've invested in a plaque to save answering endless questions.

Name: Ashlyn Hale
Species: Barely human
Habitat: Found on every continent, usually in a hostile environment.
Traits: Excellent hunter, adopts camouflage when threatened. Thought processes can be unexpected.

After four cups of tea, two trips to the toilet, and the aforementioned biscuits, I was grateful to escape to the kitchen. *Please, someone give me a damn knife.*

"Can you make the shortcrust pastry?" a lady with a purple rinse asked.

I stared blankly at her. Didn't pastry come frozen in packets?

"You don't know how to do pastry?"

"Sorry."

"Well, can you help chop the vegetables?"

Oh yes, I could do that. Playing with knives was a particular skill of mine. I forced myself to slow down, but I still sliced three cucumbers perfectly in under two minutes, avoiding the temptation to close my eyes while I did so. Didn't want to scare the old dudes.

Lunch took the entire afternoon, and afterwards, most of the people present went straight from the church hall to the village hall for bingo. I'd expected a subdued affair, but I'd underestimated this crowd.

The alcohol flowed, and one old gent produced a couple of bottles of home-brew. I had no idea what was in it, but from the way it burned my throat it had to be 160 proof. I practically had to carry Carol when we left.

"Don't forget your raffle prizes," one of her friends said.

I'd tried to leave them behind on purpose, but now I pasted on a smile.

"How very remiss of me."

I tucked my toiletry basket and Carol's fruit cake under the other arm, and Carol wrinkled her nose.

"Mildred Armitage made that. Her cakes are always far too dry."

I caught Mildred watching us from over her beak-like nose. "Sorry, but we'd better take it back with us. You can use it as a doorstop."

I thought after that evening I'd earn a reprieve from more socialising, but no such luck.

"The tea dance is today at three," Carol told me over breakfast the next morning.

I stifled a groan. Where did Carol get the energy? I hadn't slept well, and the last thing I wanted was to go out again.

"I'll have to pass."

"You have something else on?"

"I fancy some time on my own."

"Don't be silly, dear. Sitting alone won't help matters." She snapped her fingers. "Vera mentioned yesterday that her son's looking for a nice young lady.

I'll invite him over to keep you company."

Spend the evening with a random bloke? No thanks. I went to the tea dance.

Between eating cakes and the endless cuppas, I gained a few new friends by taking some of the old boys for a spin—well, more of a shuffle—around the dance floor. I'd been a bit concerned about their artificial hips and the like, but Carol insisted it would be okay.

"Are their hearts up to this?" I asked.

"If they're not, at least they'll die happy."

My husband had taught me to ballroom dance soon after we met, insisting it was a useful skill for undercover work at posh functions. I'd grown to love it, and even though he pretended it was a chore, I knew he'd secretly enjoyed it too. And boy, could he move. He'd had a particularly dirty tango in him, but we'd reserved that for the privacy of our own home.

Those memories overshadowed the evening, because now we'd never dance again.

The day after the dance found Carol and me at the parish council meeting, which wasn't so much a meeting as a bunch of self-important idiots bickering.

"I'm not on the council myself, dear," Carol said. "But the Women's Institute has an outing there each month. The arguments can be quite entertaining. It's a bit like *Jeremy Kyle* but with better refreshments."

She was right. It was all I could do to stop myself from smacking their heads together after an argument about whose turn it was to organise the litter patrol for the Best Kept Village competition.

I hated to admit it, but Carol's distraction technique had some merit. With all the bullshit she organised to fill my days, I didn't have time to dwell on more painful subjects. Still, I couldn't help wishing for something more interesting to do. The old guys were kind, but I felt out of place being the youngest by thirty years, and I could easily live without discussions over the best brand of incontinence pad. Perhaps if they drank less tea, they wouldn't need to worry about that. Yes, I was English, but I was sick of bloody tea. My palate craved a decent espresso, but asking for one would have been sacrilegious around here.

And while I could cope with my waking hours, the nights gave me more problems. Rather than sleeping, I'd lie awake for hours, thoughts tumbling through a mind filled with darkness. How had my life turned into such a mess so quickly? And more importantly, what was I going to do about it?

CHAPTER 7

I SAT UP in bed, sweat dripping off me. The mattress was damp, the outline of my body dark against the maroon sheets. Had I cried out in my sleep? I'd certainly screamed in real life when it happened.

Once again, I'd relived my husband's death, the moment seared into my mind like the climax of a horror movie. I'd have done anything to rewind the film.

Calm, Ash. Calm. I tried to slow my breathing as I listened for signs of movement in the house, but the only noise was a car on the road outside. Good, I hadn't woken Carol.

I rolled out of bed, my steps silent as I crossed to the window and looked out on the moonlit world. Sleep wouldn't come again that night, I knew from experience. It would just be me and my wayward thoughts until morning, and as always, my husband was on my mind.

Always a planner, he'd organised what would happen if one of us died young, but now I realised that had just been paperwork. I'd been left with his share in a security business, his house, his cars, even a fucking jet, but I'd also gained a gaping chasm in my chest, because a part of me died with him.

There were so many things I wished I'd said. Above

all, I should have told him I loved him, really loved him, in the way I'd pretended not to for fear he wouldn't feel the same way. I'd have sold my soul to the devil to be held in my husband's arms one last time. He'd been the person who kept me sane, and now I'd lost my damn mind.

Lucifer wasn't dealing, though. My husband was gone, and I was still here.

Which meant I needed to plan. I couldn't risk going home yet, but with cash dwindling, getting a job was a priority. A job that wouldn't lead to my name popping up in any databases, and one that didn't require a reference.

That left two options: low-paid, manual work or something illegal. The latter would certainly pay better, but I didn't want to walk down that road at the moment. Not because I had a problem with breaking the law—the world ranged from black to white, and I'd always walked on the dark side—but because I didn't trust myself not to get caught, not with my head screwed up the way it was.

By morning, I'd set myself a time limit to start looking for work. One week. One week to get my head in order. One week of living in a bubble before I had to rejoin the real world. One week, and the clock was ticking.

Little did I know that luck would be on my side for once. Only two days had passed when Carol informed me of another outing.

"The horticultural society committee's meeting

tomorrow morning, and Vera's making her chocolate fudge cake. You don't want to miss that."

"Could you bring me a slice back?"

She gave me a dirty look over her glasses.

"Okay, okay. I'll come."

What could I say? I was a sucker for dessert.

The village hall held the ubiquitous long table, a variety of old people, a tea urn, a table of plants with handwritten price tags, and—hallelujah—the promised chocolate cake.

Without Toby on my back, I was eating too much junk food, and I didn't have the energy to work it off. At this rate, I'd be straining at the seams of my newly purchased yoga pants and reciting the number of the local takeaway in my sleep. It was a slippery slope to the life of a couch potato, and I stood perilously close to the edge.

I took a seat next to Carol and tuned out as the conversation turned to gardening. My horticultural knowledge covered three areas—what I could eat to survive, which plants had healing properties, and those I could use to poison people. The characteristics of a prize-winning dahlia passed me by.

A huff from Carol brought me back to the present.

"Fenton Palmer doesn't know his aster from his elder."

The man at the head of the table sighed. "But he's agreed to sponsor the show, so we have to let him be on the judging panel. We've booked the hall, and now we just need to agree on the classes."

Oh dear. Eight voices got louder and louder as the committee began arguing. They must have been getting tips from the parish councillors, because nobody wanted to listen to anybody else, and they couldn't agree on anything.

While fascinating to watch, my nerves were wearing thin. If this discussion kept up, I'd miss lunch, and Carol had promised sticky toffee pudding for dessert. Fingers tapping, I waited for the next gap in the conversation, which took such a long time to appear I began to think the manned probe to Mars would arrive back sooner, and that hadn't even taken off yet, for crying out loud.

"Why don't you have a vote?" I asked. They looked at me like I'd grown another head, so I elaborated. "How about we put all the ideas on a list, and each one that gets six or more votes goes on the schedule?"

There were murmurs of assent from around the table.

"About bloody time someone came up with a sensible idea," a man wearing a tweed cap muttered. He looked as if he'd be more at home on a tractor.

We soon had the number of classes down to thirty-five, which everyone agreed was reasonable, and I looked at my watch. Eleven thirty. I just had time for another slice of cake before we went back to Carol's. And yes, it was damn good cake.

I was trying to balance my teacup and plate in one hand while I pulled out a chair with the other when the tweed-cap man sidled up to me.

"George," he said, sticking his hand out.

I gave up and put everything down on the table. "Ashlyn." I held out my hand. "Nice to meet you."

"I was wondering if you're going to be a permanent member of the committee? We could do with some younger people, especially ones who've got their heads screwed on straight and don't try to include a class for the potato that looks most like Elvis."

A genuine suggestion, and one that had garnered three votes.

"Afraid not. I'm staying with Carol at the moment, but I'm not sure how long for. I need to look for a job, and I doubt I'll find anything suitable near here."

"What kind of a job?"

"I'm not exactly sure. Maybe waitressing or bar work. Or cleaning. Something casual."

"Do you know anything about horses?"

Horses? As a matter of fact, I did. I had one back home in Virginia—just one more thing I was missing.

When I acquired him, I hadn't been planning to buy a horse. I'd been planning to buy a cold drink and a plane ticket to the Arctic, seeing as I was driving back to the airport from a meeting in southern Spain in heat so oppressive I thought my brain was going to melt out through my ears.

Traffic had slowed to a crawl as I drove past a livestock market, and when I slowly edged to the front of the queue, I saw what was causing the hold-up. A black horse going crazy in the middle of the road. Nostrils flaring, it stood up on its back legs, and the guy on the ground was struggling to hold onto the rope. The horse leapt sideways as two more swarthy men whacked it with plastic piping then it lashed out with its hooves. That drew forth a string of swear words and another beating.

Now, I may not have been shy with my fists, but I couldn't stand cruelty to animals. Nothing gave a man the right to take his frustrations out on an innocent creature like that.

The heat forgotten, I leapt out of my car and strode towards the little scene. As I got closer, I realised the horse was covered in scabs and scars, and that made my blood boil. No wonder the poor thing was sweating and showing the whites of its eyes.

The temptation to put all three men on the ground, or better still, six feet under it, was immense, but while there was no doubt in my mind I could have done it, that wouldn't have helped the horse. Getting myself arrested was never going to be constructive.

No, I used my wallet instead. After five minutes of "negotiation" and a liberal application of Euros, I was left at the side of the road holding a snapping horse on a rope as the men trundled off in their decrepit lorry.

A dozen phone calls later, I'd managed to find a sympathetic vet, and with the help of some tranquillisers and a lot of swearing, we got my new purchase onto a horse transporter. He lived at a rehabilitation yard in Spain for a few months, and when he'd healed up well enough, I took him home. The staff at the rehab place held a party when he left. I knew this because I saw the photos on Facebook. There was a good reason I'd christened my darling pony Satan.

In the first three months of ownership, I went through six grooms, and I'd begun to lose hope when I found an old cowboy called Dustin who understood him. Although my horse still had his moments, he mostly behaved himself. Right now, he lived in luxury at my place in Virginia with Dustin's mare to keep him company, and we'd shortened his name to Stan.

But that wasn't a story I could tell George.

"I know a little about horses. I took riding lessons when I was a kid and helped out at the local stables."

"Well, if you're interested, I'm looking for a groom to work at my stable yard. The last girl ran off with a bloke she met at the travelling fair without giving any notice, so I'm a person short."

"How much does it pay?"

"Only minimum wage, I'm afraid. Cash every Friday."

Sounded perfect. At least horses wouldn't ask questions about my state of mind or try to drag me along to the needlepoint club. I was sick of pasting on a fake smile from dawn to dusk.

"Can I come and take a look around?" I asked.

"I'm in all day tomorrow."

I set off on foot after breakfast the next morning, sheltering from the rain under a golf umbrella Carol lent me. George had given me directions, and as I reached the outskirts of the village, the houses got progressively bigger and more expensive.

The walk took twenty minutes, and the bottoms of my jeans were soaked through by the time I got there. Well-kept paddocks stretched into the distance on either side of the driveway, and the horses in them raised their heads to peer at me curiously as I trekked past.

"Where can I find George?" I asked a girl sweeping the stable yard.

She pointed at a house to the left then leaned on her broom as she watched me walk towards it.

The bell echoed, followed by the din of dogs barking inside. The sound made me miss my Doberman, Lucy, who I'd left back at home with Dustin. He always dog-sat when I was away, and he tended to spoil her. At least she'd be getting plenty of walks.

When the door swung open, an excited pack surrounded me, ranging from a tiny Yorkshire terrier up to a German shepherd with a huge tongue lolling out the side of its mouth. George appeared behind them, wearing the country uniform of cords, wellingtons, and a waxed jacket. All he needed was a shotgun and a brace of pheasants, and he could have stepped straight from the pages of *Country Life* magazine.

"I hope you're all right with dogs," he said.

Bit late if I wasn't.

"Yes, they're fine," I said, stifling a laugh as the Yorkie humped a chair leg.

"Come on, we can talk while I show you the yard."

George herded the dogs back inside and pulled the door shut, then motioned at me to follow him.

Hazelwood Farm was a livery yard, a hotel for horses if you like, and judging by the looks of the place, it had a five-star rating. I'd rather have slept in one of the stables than the dive I'd ended up in on my first night in London, at any rate.

George led me around, showing me where things were and asking me to demonstrate different tasks, none of which were taxing. How hard could it be to fill a bucket of water or clean out a stable? The yard was beautifully kept, split into three large barns, each with eight horses.

"Each girl looks after one barn. It's an early start to

feed and muck out, then the horses get put to bed at five. You'd take it in turns with the other girls to do a late check," he said.

"What days would I work?"

"Monday to Friday, with a half-day over the weekend. I've got a couple of part-time teenagers who come in to do the rest on Saturday and Sunday."

"Is there any riding?"

"No, we have someone else who does that. You get a nice long lunch break. Would you be happy with that?"

"Sounds reasonable."

"The job's yours if you want it, then."

"It sounds like just what I'm looking for."

"Good, good. The accommodation's a bit basic, but I can pick up your belongings if you don't have a car. How soon can you start?" he asked.

Accommodation? Now, that was an unexpected bonus. It looked as if another of my problems had been solved. I gave him a smile, my first genuine one since I'd arrived in the country.

"I can start tomorrow if you like?"

CHAPTER 8

AT THE END of my first week at Hazelwood Farm, southern England was in the midst of a cold snap. When my alarm went off just before 6 a.m., the moon shone from a clear sky, and Jack Frost had left his lacy fingerprints on the inside of the windows.

At least I had the afternoon off today. Maybe I could clean my lovely new home? On second thoughts, if I removed the dirt, the whole place might fall apart. Plan B: walk to the bakery and buy a donut. Okay, two donuts.

When George had mentioned accommodation, I'd been surprised but pleased at the prospect of saving money on rent, not to mention my thirty-second commute to work each day. And although Carol had been sad to see me go, she was heading off on a seniors' cruise next week, so I doubted she'd miss me too much.

Then I saw where I'd be living, and I almost went back to *Melrose*. The mobile home squashed between the hay barn and a boxy red-brick cottage had certainly seen better days, say, twenty or thirty years ago.

Judging by the window frame held together with duct tape, maintenance of the staff accommodation didn't come high on George's list of priorities, most likely falling somewhere between attending London Fashion Week and growing a potato that looked like

Elvis. The hot water only worked when it felt like it, and trying to heat the place with the single bar electric fire was akin to melting a glacier using a Zippo lighter.

While I'd stayed in some shitty places in my life, for the last fourteen years, I'd had the luxury of going home to a mansion at the end of each trip. My stay here at Hazelwood Farm had no expiry date, and I was sick of fucking cockroaches.

I crawled out of bed, and my breath fogged in the chill as I walked the few short steps to the tiny bathroom. *Please, say the damned pipes hadn't frozen again.* Yesterday, I'd had to borrow a hairdryer to thaw them out. A bonus would be if the shower was warm, but I couldn't expect miracles.

I turned the tap on over the grimy, soup bowl-sized basin and did a silent fist pump when the water slowly dripped out, the flow gradually increasing as the ice build-up cleared. Once I'd done my bit in the bathroom, I returned to the freezing bedroom to get dressed, although I'd rather have gone into hibernation at that point. Layering was definitely the way to go in this weather.

Carol had held a whip-round of various acquaintances, who'd donated a selection of clothes ranging from unfashionable to downright scary. I was now the proud owner of a waxed jacket, and the knitting club had gone overboard with the scarves.

Suitably attired, I stood in front of the cracked mirror to put in my contact lenses. My roots were still good at the moment, but I'd need to buy hair dye in the near future, even if the thought of shopping filled me with dread.

So far, I'd gone through each day like a robot. *Do*

this, do that, don't think, don't feel. The numbness still hadn't begun to shift. Would I ever feel like myself again?

"Miss you," I whispered, turning my head to gaze at the blackness outside. When I returned to the mirror, I barely recognised the desolate stare of the broken woman looking back at me.

Before my husband's death, I'd been full of energy, perhaps too much on occasion. We'd always worked as a team, complementing each other. I'd had the tendency to jump straight into things, adapting to circumstances on the fly because I wanted to get the job done and done quickly. My husband had been the thinker, the planner, preferring to run everything through in his head and work out the best course of action before he took a single step. We'd learned from each other, and together, we'd achieved what others thought was impossible.

Not anymore.

My mind was black inside, the darkness a cancer eating me from the inside out. And living in that shadow, all I could do was get on with things as best I could.

The cold wind hit me as I stepped out the door. I had eight horses to muck out, and the longer I procrastinated, the more they would shit.

I checked the temperature on the phone I'd bought from some dude in The Coach and Horses, kind of cheap, but I was almost sure it was kosher. Bollocks—it wasn't due to rise above freezing all day.

With it being a Saturday, the part-timers from the village had arrived to do the horses in the other barns. The girls I worked with during the week, Susie and Hayley, were having in a lie-in in the cottage next to my trailer. They'd invited me over for dinner a couple of times, and the place wasn't in much better condition than mine, although it stayed slightly warmer.

When I got to my barn, the first thing I did was defrost the taps with a kettle full of water, careful not to spill it because the walkway would turn into an ice rink if I did. I might do all right on a pair of skates, but the horses wouldn't.

One by one, I tied them outside and mucked out their stables. The effort warmed me up, and by the time I'd finished, I'd shed my jacket and was wishing I hadn't put on thermal leggings under my jeans.

Then came my favourite part of the job: grooming the horses. So peaceful, just me and them, and I liked to brush their coats until they shone. I didn't have the radio on like the other girls, preferring the silence, interrupted only by the munching of the neddies eating their hay and the occasional quiet whicker.

But those moments were the calm before the storm, and sure enough, the thunder started half an hour later when two of the owners, Jessica and Marianne, strode into the barn. One of them turned the music on at full volume as she walked past, and the pair of them clattered around as they hauled stuff out of their lockers.

Their voices had no mute button, and before I was halfway through brushing the horses, I was all too aware that Marianne had just been dumped by her boyfriend. Not only that, the boyfriend was an arsehole who didn't understand her, she could do better than him anyway, and he'd been sleeping with a girl who'd had breast implants and a nose job.

Jessica, on the other hand, had been out clubbing last night, and her cell phone, keys, wallet, and dignity were just the beginning of what she'd lost in the process. She claimed to be hungover, but I had my doubts about that. If she was at death's door as she claimed to be, she wouldn't be screeching so loudly.

Throughout their conversation, they ignored me. After all, I was just the hired help, there to pick up their shit and keep out the way. I was used to that. In fact, I'd used the ploy many times over the years. People barely noticed the invisible army of worker ants—the maids, the handymen, the meter readers, the cleaners. Did you know that the best way to break into a building was to put on a hi-vis jacket and carry a toolbox?

Shh, don't tell anybody.

Shit shovelled, I stowed my wheelbarrow and hung up my fork. The next job was preparing the horses' food in the hay barn and the feed room, and a good thing too. My ears had suffered enough, and I was out of aspirin.

CHAPTER 9

I HEADED FOR the hay barn first. Filling the twenty-four haynets that got hung up in the stables for the horses to eat would take half an hour. They got one in the morning, one at lunchtime, and another in the evening. It wasn't my favourite job because of the dust, but at least it was quiet.

I was stuffing haynet number twenty when Susie and Hayley walked past, Susie pushing a wheelbarrow and Hayley carrying a mucking-out fork.

"What are you doing out here? Don't both of you have the day off?" I asked, knowing full well that they did.

"Uh, we thought we'd give you a hand," Susie said, carefully avoiding eye contact.

"I've been out here almost four hours. Nearly everything's done. Now, tell me the real reason you've dragged your asses out into the cold to shovel shit."

"Portia Halston-Cain's just arrived," Hayley said, as if that explained everything.

Portia owned three of the horses in my barn, but she rarely visited on weekdays, so I hadn't met her yet. Gameela, Samara, and Majesty, her Arabians, were all stunningly beautiful, but according to Susie, she only ever rode two of them.

"Why doesn't she ride Majesty?" I'd asked.

"That horse is far too clever for her. He's worked out she's not a good rider, so he just dances around until she falls off," Susie said, trying, and failing, to keep a straight face.

"Why the hell doesn't she sell him to somebody who *can* ride?"

"Because then she'd have to admit she can't. Plus he's pretty, and she imported him from Qatar for some stupid amount of money that she never misses an opportunity to brag about."

Majesty reminded me of Stan, which meant even though he was an arsehole, I still liked him. Plus he had the measure of his owner, which made me even fonder. Still, none of that explained why Susie and Hayley were traipsing out to see her.

"From what I've heard, Portia being around is a good reason *not* to be out here."

"Her brother's come with her," Susie said, a faraway look in her eyes.

"So?"

"Just wait until you see him."

Wait until I saw him? Yeah, I could wait. I finished filling the haynets then returned to the barn to fetch the feed buckets, and when I walked in, it seemed as though everybody at the farm had gathered there.

Susie and Hayley were walking up and down, looking for non-existent poop, while Jessica and Marianne brushed horses that had already been groomed. Half a dozen girls whose horses lived in the other barns pretended to talk to them, and a couple more hovered around Arabella, another of the owners. Arabella was sitting outside her horse's stable, stuffing her face with crisps.

All heads pointed in the direction of Samara's box, and I could hear a high-pitched whine coming from inside. A whine I could only assume came from Portia.

"She's got dirt on her rug. She needs a new one."

A male voice replied, smooth, low and seemingly exasperated. "If you get her a new one, she'll get that dirty too. She's a horse. She doesn't understand she needs to stay clean. Can't we just get it washed?"

"No! That's not the same. She doesn't want a used rug. Besides, this colour doesn't suit her."

"But you chose the colour," the man said.

"Well, it was difficult to judge the exact shade in the shop. But now she's wearing it, I can see it doesn't suit her."

"She probably doesn't realise that."

Ooh, wrong thing to say. I felt sorry for the guy as Portia's voice rose in both pitch and volume.

"Well *she* might not know, but everyone else does, and they'll think I'm a stupid colour-blind person who can't even pick a rug that matches her horse. Sammy *can't* wear it anymore. And Majesty and Gameela need new rugs too, because if Sammy has one and they don't, they'll think I love her more than them."

Impeccable logic there. I bet horses talked about things like that all the time while the humans were asleep.

The poor bloke sighed and admitted defeat. "Okay, get them new rugs. Just make sure they're the right colour this time, because you're not buying more next week."

Now she'd got her own way, Portia's voice turned sickly sweet. "Ooh, you're the best brother ever."

The guy emerged from the stable, and there was a collective intake of breath from everyone except me. He breathed deeply himself, leaning against the wall outside Samara's stable with his eyes closed. His clenched jaw and balled fists suggested he was a man on the edge.

I took the opportunity to get a good look at him. Just over six feet tall, he had tousled, dark blond hair a month past needing a cut and a day's worth of stubble. Were his jeans well-worn or designer? Hard to tell these days.

Three months ago, Bradley, who looked after my wardrobe as well as my diary, had presented me with a pair full of holes and informed me they cost over a thousand dollars. I'd counted up—sixty dollars per hole. He hadn't been impressed when I told him to go with the cheap ones next time and I'd do the holes myself.

Next time. A sigh escaped. When would that be?

I shut down that wayward thought and looked back at Portia's brother. Surely he must be freezing in only a T-shirt and a beaten-up leather jacket? Still, his lack of clothing let me see his goods, and I ran through my mental checklist. The verdict? Not bad. I'd had better. I worked with better. In the department I ran, every day was Diet Coke Break day. But yeah, in Lower Foxford, I could see why Mr. Halston-Cain warranted a fucking fan club.

I checked the thermometer on the wall. Judging by the flushed faces around me, the temperature seemed to have risen by a couple of degrees, but the mercury remained steady.

Good grief.

While the rest of the girls gawked, I collected up the buckets and headed off to the feed room. I'd long since learned to see past people's looks and judge them on what sort of person they were, so although I freely admitted the guy could have his own calendar, I didn't feel the need to swoon.

Before I reached my destination, my stomach let out an almighty grumble, reminding me I'd skipped breakfast in favour of five extra minutes under the duvet.

I decided to nip inside and make myself something to eat before I carried on. After all, there were enough people on duty in my barn that I felt like a spare part. The horses never got that much attention on weekdays, and some of them were looking downright confused by it.

Back in my trailer, I stuck two slices of bread in the toaster, and when they popped out, I covered them in butter and raspberry jam. Toby's voice prattled on about the amount of saturated fat in the butter and the sugar content of the jam, but I ignored him. At least the bread was wholemeal, and I poured out a glass of orange juice to go with it. Having one of my five-a-day would offset the butter, right?

Hunger temporarily banished, I walked back towards the feed room. What were the chances of getting Portia's brother to stop by every day so people would do all my work for me? That way, I could get an extra hour in bed.

The feed room was a converted stable, dingy because it didn't have any windows. I flicked on the light then cursed myself for jumping when I found said brother sitting on a feed bin in the far corner.

"What on earth are you doing here?"

"Uh, checking my emails." He held up his phone to prove it.

"Which requires darkness?"

"No, but..."

I thought back to the posse hanging around in the barn. "You're hiding?"

"Yeah." He gave a sheepish shrug. "Normally, no one comes in here."

"I can't really blame you."

I'd hide too if I was like the Pied bloody Piper for socialites and stable girls.

"So it's okay if I stay?"

"If you want. I'll admit I was hoping you'd stick in the barn a bit longer so your groupies would clear the cobwebs and scrub out the water drinkers, but I can see why you wouldn't want to."

He chuckled. "Thanks. I promise I won't get in your way."

The grin he flashed revealed a perfect set of white teeth. Either he had great genes, or his dentist was on speed dial. They looked even lighter offset against his tan. How did he get that in winter? Holiday or tanning salon?

"What makes you think you'll be any safer in here with me?" I asked.

"You didn't shriek or faint." He gave a wry laugh, but sadly there was some truth in it.

"I'm not the shrieking kind. Or fainting."

I got on with making up the feeds, scooping the right amount of conditioning cubes and chaff into each bowl according to the chart on the wall. Then I added the supplements. The horses got so many, the shelves looked like a branch of GNC. It seemed to be a competition among the owners as to who could pump the most extras into their beloved steed. Some of them got more vitamins than food.

"Do you need a hand with those?" Portia's brother asked as I picked up a pile of bowls to carry to the barn.

"Nah, you'll get mobbed. Just stay here."

He was being a gentleman, but he clearly hadn't thought his offer through.

"Good point. You won't tell them where I am?"

"Your secret's safe with me."

An hour later, after Portia had ridden Samara and the group of admirers had dispersed, her brother re-materialised in the barn. As I watched the pair walk back to his car, I felt sorry for him. Sitting in a cold feed room couldn't have been his favourite way to spend Saturday morning. Why didn't he stay at home? Or at the gym or on the sunbed? I suspected they were both places he frequented.

"Do you want to have dinner with us?" Susie asked before she disappeared inside.

"Sounds good." Anything was better than my own cooking.

It wasn't that I'd spent my life trying out recipes that always went wrong. It was more that I'd never needed to cook. When I was a kid, we rarely had proper food in the house, and as I got older, someone else made me food or I ate things that didn't need cooking. My microwaving skills were legendary, and I knew how to build a campfire, but I didn't know where to start with ingredients.

Maybe I should buy a recipe book? It would give me something constructive to do with my evenings rather than watching crappy TV re-runs. And worse, the files on the cloud drive kept taunting me. Part of me wanted to buy a laptop and start looking at them, but at the same time, they scared me. I didn't want to anger my husband's killer, and I didn't want to make my nightmares any worse than they already were.

The nightmares were a monster that fed off the black parts of my soul. Each one started with an event from my past then twisted it into a horror that consumed me. I was a helpless participant, unable to stop the visions in my head until I woke.

And that wasn't the worst of it. I remembered every vivid detail of the nightmares, but it was the night terrors and the sleepwalking that terrified me.

Nothing was as bad as finding out I'd done something in the middle of the night I had no memory of. Nothing. Especially when that something involved hurting somebody I cared about. I'd seen some of the most horrible things imaginable, but what scared me most was my own mind.

Over the years, I'd learned the medical details and tried every treatment possible. The only thing that had helped was talking through the worst of it with my husband, a therapeutic debrief if you like, but I no longer had that option.

No, my only choice was to stick with Carol's strategy of using time to heal and hope for a miracle.

Chapter 10

ON SUNDAY, I ate a bowl of Coco Pops for breakfast then found my jeans no longer did up. It had only been a matter of time. When Hayley headed into town an hour later, I hitched a lift and bought some workout gear. My mind might have gone soft, but I could at least stop my body from following suit by exercising and eating properly again.

Remember that old saying, Ashlyn? You are what you eat. Since I'd discovered the bakery in the village, I was in danger of turning into a donut. Sweet as they were, I didn't want to end up looking like one.

The afternoon brought a grey sky and steady drizzle. According to the weather forecast, it was there to stay, so I made myself woman up and go outside, anyway. Nearly a month had passed since I'd been to the gym, and boy did I feel it. Mucking out was no substitute for a twelve-mile run. I battled up slippery hills and along frozen tracks, returning two hours later splattered with mud and nursing a stitch. Back in my trailer, I did what I could in the way of push-ups, squats, lunges, and crunches until I collapsed on the grubby floor, unable to move.

Shit. I was a mess.

Still, the exhaustion contributed to me getting a reasonable night's sleep, so I couldn't complain. I woke up on Monday morning ready to face the week ahead, a week that passed un-memorably in a blur of nothingness, mindless days of shovelling crap and carting hay around. After work each evening, I ran a lap of the village under the glow of the street lights, followed by circuits of bodyweight exercises. My strength was slowly coming back, but did I ever ache.

The only break from my new and thrilling norm was a trip to a pub in the next village with Susie and Hayley on Thursday evening. The opportunity to avoid cooking seemed too good to pass up, although with hindsight, I should have stayed home with a packet of instant noodles.

Because I'd only eaten half my jacket potato when a man slid into the seat beside me uninvited. Two of his buddies dragged chairs up to the end of the table, and the uglier of the pair waved at the barmaid and held up three fingers.

"All right, ladies?"

The first interloper pressed his leg against mine as he twirled his Range Rover keys around his finger and gave me a leering grin. His boots had clearly never seen mud in their lives, and he was wearing a cravat. A fucking cravat. I rolled my eyes at Susie and Hayley—I just couldn't help it.

I'd only seen one person wear a cravat in real life before, a few years ago when my husband and I were invited to a charity clay pigeon shoot on Lord Something-or-other's country estate. Our esteemed host turned up full cliché, in gaiters, a cravat, and a tweed jacket with matching flat cap. He'd also brought at least two hip flasks, and I'd had to gently confiscate his gun before he did any damage. My husband had a quiet word, and the man's son hauled him into the back of a Land Rover and drove him home.

I had a feeling it wouldn't be so easy to get rid of the newcomers.

"His name's Henry Forster," Susie whispered as the sleaze next to me stared at the barmaid's tits. "His dad's a property developer. He's got stacks of money, and he shags anything that moves."

Oh, he did, did he? Well, he wouldn't be shagging me.

"Can I get you a drink?" he asked, ignoring Susie and Hayley as he addressed my chest.

"No."

He seemed taken aback for a second, but he didn't get the hint. "How about dinner?"

"No."

"Ah, a woman who plays hard to get. I like a challenge." He shuffled closer, and I jabbed an elbow in his side, but he only grinned. "Feisty. Why don't we skip the small talk and head back to my place? I've got a Ferrari in the garage we can take for a spin."

More like a crash, with the amount of beer he'd drunk. I could smell it on his breath as it washed over me. "No."

"Come on; it's a 360 Modena."

Oh, well in that case...

"No."

I had an Aston Martin in my garage. Big fucking deal.

Henry's fingers crept up my arm, and I resisted the urge to break them. I needed to keep a low profile, and getting arrested for assault wouldn't help matters.

"Excuse me, I need to use the bathroom." I shuffled

out from the bench seat and hurried to the ladies',
followed by a wobbly Hayley.

"I think Henry likes you," she said when she arrived
a few seconds later.

"I got that."

"What are you doing?" she asked, looking beyond
me to the window I'd just opened.

"Planning my escape."

"Out of the window?"

"Doors are so last year."

"Aw... Me and Susie are going out to a club with the
other guys. Susie knows them from school. You sure
you don't want to come? It'll be fun."

"I'm sure. I'd rather have an early night."

Or lie on a bed of burning coals or shave my legs
with a cutlass.

"You need the number for a cab?"

"I'll walk. It's only a couple of miles, and the moon's
bright tonight."

She stepped forward and gave me a hug. Weird.
Few people ever hugged me, mainly because they were
worried I'd shoot them.

"I'll see you tomorrow, yeah?" she said.

I forced a smile. "Yeah. Have a good time."

Tomorrow evening, I'd stay in.

Saturday came all too soon, and I was scheduled to
work again despite being exhausted. I'd barely slept for
three nights, and I knew I'd been sleepwalking at least
once because I woke up on the bathroom floor,
freezing. The lack of rest left me cranky and slow, and

mucking out took twice as long as usual. I found myself hoping Portia would bring her brother along again so I could get a hand with the sweeping.

My wish came true half an hour later when his silver Porsche 911 pulled into the car park. He unfolded himself from the seat and followed Portia into the barn, head down and shoulders hunched. I checked my watch and started a countdown. Sure enough, in less than ten minutes, Susie and Hayley emerged wearing full make-up and freshly laundered jeans. I smirked and held out brooms to them as they passed.

"Might as well make yourselves useful."

Susie looked blank. "What? Oh..."

Hayley had the good grace to act sheepish as she accepted her broom. "Thanks."

"You're welcome. Enjoy."

Sweeping sorted, I carried on to the feed room, pleased to avoid the bitch-fest undoubtedly taking place in the barn. I was halfway through preparing the feeds when Portia's brother slunk in.

"You don't mind if I just...?"

"Be my guest." I waved over at the bin where he'd perched last week.

"Thanks. It's worse than usual this morning. They seem to have turned up with reinforcements. One of them's actually wearing a dress, and I'm pretty sure her eyelashes aren't real." He rolled his eyes, but there was weariness in them rather than humour.

"Why do you come, then?" I asked, continuing to scoop snake oil into bowls. "Couldn't you just drop your sister off and go home?"

"I wish. I promised mother I'd spend time with her, and if you met my mother, you'd know it was easier for me to stay."

I hadn't seen my own mother since I was ten years old, so I didn't really understand the whole family obligation thing, but hey, whatever.

"Well, if you're set on staying, do you want a cup of tea or coffee? It's bloody freezing, and I was just about to make myself one."

"I'd love a coffee. Shall I come with you?"

"Your choice. I can bring it out here if you like."

I headed back to my trailer, and he followed. Thankfully, we didn't have to pass the barn on the way. I could only imagine the uproar if any of the girls saw him disappear into my tumbledown palace.

I made the coffee, managing to find two mugs that had only minor chips out of them. Portia's brother took his black like me, which was just as well seeing as I didn't have any milk. As he sipped, he looked round with obvious disdain, taking in the delights of the shabby sofa in my tiny lounge and the kitchen with its wonky table complemented by two mismatched chairs.

"You live here?" he asked.

"No, I have a mansion to go home to."

"Sorry. I didn't mean to sound condescending."

"Don't worry about it." My feelings about the place were the same as his. "Yes, I live here. If you want to sit down, I'd suggest the left-hand side of the sofa or the chair with the orange seat. The brown one's wobbly and the other end of the sofa has a broken spring." In fact, the only thing the sofa was good for was blocking the door so I couldn't get out and wreak havoc at night.

He lowered himself gingerly onto the unbroken end, leaving the chair for me. "You haven't been here long, have you?"

"About two weeks now. Just getting used to the joys of the British winter."

"You're not from around here, then?" His eyes widened "Wait, you're not that girl who torched her boyfriend's house, are you? No, no, you can't be. She's from America. Forget I said that."

"Gossip sure travels fast around here. Yes, I came from America, so it's probably me they're talking about, but I sure as hell didn't torch anyone's house. Did you hear that from Carol?"

"No, my mother heard the story from someone at her bridge club."

"Wonderful. You probably know a warped version of my life history, and I don't even know your name."

He stuck his hand out, a little reluctantly it seemed. "Luke Halston-Cain."

"Ashlyn Hale." I shook his hand, hoping mine wasn't too grubby. "Ash'll do, though."

"If it's any consolation, I don't think it's your entire life history. Just that you split up with your fiancé, who cheated on you with a team of high school cheerleaders plus your maid of honour the week before your wedding. You got revenge by running his car into one of the cheerleaders and driving it into a lake. Then you set fire to his house before you did a runner to England. Don't think I missed anything."

He eyed up the door, and I knew what he was thinking—can I escape from this madwoman?

"Bloody hell. Almost none of that happened, I swear. If it had, I'd be in jail, not working here, although this place probably isn't much better than a prison cell."

Certainly, most of the prisons I'd seen had fewer

cockroaches.

"Too bad," Luke said, finally breaking into a grin. "I always wondered if a cheerleader would bounce."

"Half the village must think I'm a raving lunatic. No wonder the guy in the grocery store kept giving me funny looks."

"Don't worry. The gossip-mongers do this to everybody. When I split up with my last girlfriend, my mother heard at the country club that I'd dumped her by text message after finding out she was pregnant with my child. Oh, and I'd started dating a lingerie model with an eating disorder. Mother had a meltdown. I nearly lost my hearing when she yelled at me about how rude it was to communicate by text message, and it took me three days to convince her she wasn't going to be a grandmother."

"So, just to clarify, no dumping by text message?" I asked, returning his smile.

"If you must know, I got sick of being treated like a walking wallet, and I told my ex that over dinner at my house. I take it you're not a closet arsonist, then?"

"The only part that's true is that I caught my fiancé cheating and I left. I keyed his car, but that was all. He bloody deserved it."

"Sounds like a fair trade to me. Now we've established you're not a psychopath and I'm not a heartless bastard, we can have a normal conversation."

"Okay." What did he count as a normal conversation? I stuck to a safe topic. "Weather's not looking good today."

"This is England—when does it ever?" Luke leaned back on the sofa and took a sip of coffee. "So, I'm curious. If you're not on the run from the law, why did you choose to work here?"

I could hardly tell him the truth, could I? "I don't know many people in England anymore, and this job gives me somewhere to live while I work out what to do next."

"What about your parents? Couldn't you stay with them?"

"I haven't spoken to them since I emigrated. They weren't keen on Jamie, and they didn't agree with my decision to drop out of university." I shrugged. "I guess I don't want to hear 'I told you so.'"

"They might have mellowed over the years."

Maybe, if they actually existed. I didn't want to discuss my fantasy life any longer. "So, what about your family? How come you ended up human while Tia's a contender for brat of the year?"

Okay, so that was a little rude, but if he took offence, he could leave. At least then I wouldn't have to deal with more questions.

"There's not much left of my family. Just me, my mother, and Tia."

"I'm sorry." Both for his lack of family and because he was related to Tia.

"Don't be. Our dad died over a decade ago. It's common knowledge."

Even so, he didn't like talking about it. I could tell by the way his nails dug into the arm of the sofa.

"Still, that must have been hard."

He gave a hollow laugh. "I survived. Now it's Tia who's the problem. I know she's a brat, but I don't know what to do about it. I spend most of my time at work, so I only see her once or twice a week, and she's worse on every visit."

"You don't live with her, then?"

"I moved out when I hit eighteen. Tia lives with Mother on the other side of the village."

"What does your mother say about her behaviour?"

"She doesn't." He shrugged. "Like mother, like daughter."

Oh.

Luke put his cup down, and we sat in silence for a few seconds before he broke it. The silence, not the cup.

"So, what are your plans for the future? Are you going to stick around here?"

A good question, and one I wasn't about to answer. I looked at my watch instead. "Sorry, I've got work to finish. You can stay here if you like."

"Do you make a habit of letting virtual strangers hang out in your house?"

"Look around. Do you see anything worth stealing?"

My cash was hidden in a tampon box in the bathroom, and I couldn't see him poking around in there. Beyond that, I didn't care.

"I guess not. Thanks, it's more comfortable than the feed room."

But only marginally. He didn't need to put that into words—I could tell by his grimace as he went into the kitchen to dispose of our cups.

"Just try not to let anyone see you leaving, or I'll never hear the end of it," I said.

"Gotcha."

The barn had emptied out since Luke was nowhere to

be seen. Jessica, Marianne, Portia, and Arabella were all riding. Portia's other two horses were standing in their stables looking bored, and the rest were in the fields. I spent a peaceful hour cleaning saddles and bridles before clattering hooves signalled the return of the horses.

The instant she saw me, Portia flung Gameela's reins in my direction. "Untack her, would you?"

I was tempted to say no, but I thought of the grief it would cause George and nodded instead.

The little witch turned to Arabella. "I'm going to jump Samara. Where the hell is Luke? He needs to carry things." She pulled out her phone, tapped at the screen, and demanded Luke report for duty immediately at the outdoor arena.

Poor guy.

I made Gameela comfortable then helped to tack up Samara. Luke slunk back into view, followed by half a dozen groupies who'd materialised out of nowhere.

As he walked past, he cut his eyes in my direction and muttered, "Give me strength."

Sorry, but I barely had enough of my own right now. I offered a half-smile instead.

A little while later, I'd finished tidying up the piles of grooming kit and tack dumped everywhere, and that meant I was done for the morning. But there was still no sign of Portia. Before going back home, curiosity made me take a detour to the arena to see how she was getting on with her show jumping. I didn't even know Samara could jump. Arab horses weren't exactly renowned for it.

Oh dear. When I rounded the corner, it soon became apparent from the mess of poles on the ground that Samara *couldn't* jump. Portia was sitting in the sand, crying, while Luke tried to hold onto the horse and calm his sister down at the same time. I jogged across and took Samara, leaving Luke to deal with Portia, who deserved an Oscar for her performance.

"Stupid horse," she screeched. "She tripped over; that's why I fell off. She didn't even try to jump the fence properly."

Samara fidgeted beside me, shifting her weight off her left foreleg and flicking her ears back in a sign of discomfort. I struggled to give a shit about Portia, but her horse was a different story. Fearing the worst, I trotted the mare up, and sure enough, she was lame.

Whatever happened, the poor horse had come off worse than her owner. I led Samara over to where the drama queen was being fawned over by the rest of her coven, biting my tongue so hard it hurt.

"Portia, Samara's injured."

"And? What am I supposed to do about it?"

"How about looking after her? Then calling the vet?"

"You do it. That's what you're here for. Look at me, I'm all dirty!"

That little... Some people didn't deserve to have animals. Luke, to give him credit, looked suitably horrified by the whole exchange.

"Tia, get in the car," he ordered.

"I need to get my bag. And change my boots. And I want a drink."

"Get in the fucking car."

Ooh, I liked angry Luke. About time somebody put Portia in her place, although I was surprised when she actually did as she'd been told with only one small mutter of protest.

After she'd stomped off, Luke walked over to me. "How bad is it?"

"I'm not sure. There's a bit of heat in the ligament just below the knee. I'll cold hose her leg to keep the swelling down, but she needs the vet."

Luke's sigh said it all.

"I'll call him."

Ten minutes later, the vet arrived. Pretty quick, but everything in England was so much closer together than in the States.

"Just finished up with a nasty case of colic in Upper Foxford. Good thing I was passing," he said, ambling across from his Land Rover.

A kind old chap with a soft Scottish accent, he chatted away to Samara about rugby as he examined her leg. Mindless chatter was a tactic I'd used myself with Stan. Horses may not understand your words, but they sure understood your tone and responded to it.

Portia stayed in the car while the vet worked. Luke wandered over briefly and they had words, then she sulked in the passenger seat, arms folded, while Luke paced up and down the central aisle of the barn. At least he steered clear of Samara. If he'd come near and upset her, I'd have had words with him too.

Before long, the vet rose to his feet. "Looks like the suspensory ligament, but she'll need a scan to confirm it. Can you bring her in on Monday?"

Luke stopped wearing a hole in the concrete and turned to me. "If I sort the transport, can you travel with her? Tia'll be at school, and I doubt she could handle her, anyway."

"Yeah, I'll do it. Just let me know the time."

I could get up early and work late to fit everything in. Anything to help the poor horse get her leg treated.

"How about half past eleven?" the vet suggested.

"Works for me," I said.

Luke nodded. "I'll be there."

After that depressing Saturday, I ran myself into the ground on Sunday. Quite literally—I set off early and went for a long run up in the hills. If I hadn't been so bloody miserable, I might have enjoyed it because the scenery was picture perfect. Morning mist swirled around the bare trees, and muntjac deer skipped over the path ahead of me.

I'd regained a little more of my fitness, and I jogged along for hours, covering something in the region of a marathon by sheer determination. The heavens opened in the afternoon, and I spent the remainder of the day curled up in my duvet with hot chocolate and a book I'd borrowed from George on the local area. By the time the moon rose, stiffness had set in, and all I wanted to do was sleep. What was I? A special forces operative having a...hiatus? Unwanted holiday? Breakdown? Or an old-aged pensioner? At this rate, I'd be peeing in the middle of the night and missing the morning shuffleboard tournament while I hunted for my false teeth.

I pushed those thoughts to the back of my mind as I crawled into bed. *Forget the shit in Virginia, Ash. Get some sleep*. With a fun-filled Monday morning to look forward to, I needed the rest more than anything.

CHAPTER 11

ON MONDAY MORNING, I got up an hour early to do my chores and get Samara ready to travel to the vet. Luke had promised to arrange transport for eleven, which I assumed meant a driver for Portia's outrageously expensive horsebox. A horsebox that spent its time parked up behind the barn because, according to Susie, Portia had only used it twice in the last year.

At five past eleven, there was still no sign of a driver. I checked my watch again then compared it to the clock in the tack room. Yes, it was spot on.

"Have you got Luke's number?" I asked Hayley.

"I wish."

Should I call the vet? Hotwire the horsebox and drive it myself? *No, Ash, forget that option.* At ten past eleven, just when I was wondering what Bradley would do in a situation like this, Luke's Porsche swung into the car park. He jumped out and jogged over.

"Ready to go?"

"As I have been for the last half hour. But the driver hasn't turned up."

"Yes, he has. I'm driving."

"You?" Not what I'd been expecting. "You've got an HGV licence?"

"Surprised?"

"You don't strike me as a lorry driver type of guy."

"Don't judge a book by its cover. Or a man by his Porsche."

How many times had I heard that sentiment? An ex once told me I looked like a prom queen and fought like a Velociraptor.

"Fair enough. Dare I ask why you learned to drive a truck? I'm betting it wasn't so you could spend your weekends taking your sister to horse shows."

Luke snorted. "You guessed right. No, I used to go motor racing with a group of friends, and I got the licence to drive the car transporter."

"What kind of racing?" I'd always loved cars, ever since I learned to steal them as a teenager. When I could afford to buy them legitimately, I'd started up a collection. Driving was yet another thing I'd missed since I'd been away.

"We started off with Caterhams then ran a Porsche in the British GT championship. A friend and I shared that drive."

"How long were the races?"

"Anything from one to three hours. I loved that car. There's nothing like driving around Brands Hatch, flat out at the head of the pack."

Hmm... Driving a stolen Camaro with six cop cars chasing you could be pretty exhilarating.

"Did you win?"

"Once or twice. I wasn't too bad."

"You said you used to race. Why did you stop?"

"When my father died, I had to run his company and start living in the real world."

I recognised the flat tone in Luke's voice and the blank look on his face. I used both when I wanted to hide my own feelings.

"I'm sorry," I said, and I meant it. "It must have been hard to give up something you loved."

Luke didn't answer, just walked off to the horsebox. Rather than standing there like an idiot, I went to fetch Samara from her stable. After a brief pause at the foot of the ramp, she followed me into the back of the lorry, and we set off.

"Do we have far to go?" I asked.

"About ten minutes."

Neither of us spoke on the journey, but the silence was strangely comfortable.

"Still hopping lame, isn't she?" the vet said when I trotted Samara up.

"Looks that way. A night's rest doesn't seem to have improved things."

I scratched the mare's neck as she hung her head. Poor girl.

"We'll need to sedate her to do scans, X-rays, and nerve blocks. Can you leave her with us for a couple of hours?"

I raised an eyebrow at Luke. I could stay, but could he hang around?

"Sure, no problem. Do whatever you need to."

The veterinary nurse took the horse, leaving Luke and me on our own in the exam area. Now what?

He turned to me and shrugged.

"Looks like we've got some time to kill."

In my old world, the phrase meant something totally different, but I'd left that girl behind in Virginia.

"I should have brought a book."

"There's a TV in the horsebox." He tapped away at his phone for thirty seconds. "Or we could get lunch?"

If Luke was offering food, that gave me a respite from beans on toast. Burned toast, seeing as my toaster was kind of temperamental.

"Sure. Lunch sounds good."

He strode off, but down the driveway rather than towards the horsebox. After a moment's hesitation, I followed.

"Where are we going?"

Not far in this icy wind, I hoped.

"There's a pub along the road. It's small, but the food's good."

"Anything I don't have to cook is fine by me."

Another plus point was that we weren't going to The Coach and Horses, which seemed to be one of the main sources of village rumours. If I walked in there with Luke, the Women's Institute would be celebrating our engagement by evening.

We arrived at our destination a few minutes later, and Luke hadn't been kidding about the size of the pub. You couldn't fit more than two dozen people inside comfortably. The old wooden bar looked like a relic from the Middle Ages, and a tiny room beyond held a handful of tables. Luke led me to an alcove at the rear beside a roaring log fire.

"You looked cold, so I thought this table would be best," he said.

I smiled gratefully and tucked myself into the seat. The leather may have been worn and cracked, but it was still comfortable. I snagged the menu and looked through the dishes. No macaroni and cheese. Oh well, I couldn't expect the day to be perfect.

"What are you having?" Luke asked.

"I'll go with risotto." I narrowly stopped myself from adding "and chips."

Before we could order, Luke's phone rang. He fished it out of his pocket, grimacing when he saw who was calling.

"Work," he mouthed, covering the mouthpiece. "Could you order at the bar? I'll have cottage pie and mineral water. I've got a tab."

He was already talking into his phone as I followed him back out to the bar, and he continued outside while I told a frighteningly cheerful barmaid what we wanted.

"Ice with the orange juice?" she asked.

"No, thanks."

She pushed the glass towards me, but her eyes were fixed on somebody behind. Assuming it would be Luke, I turned around with an almost-genuine smile, but my face soon fell when I recognised Mr. Wandering-Hands from the previous Thursday night. Was he following me?

"Oh, it's you."

"Hello, sweetheart. Where did you disappear off to last week?" he asked.

"I felt sick."

"You should have stayed. I'd have made it all better."

"I doubt that, since it was you who made me nauseous in the first place. And get your fucking hand off my arm." I'd had enough of playing polite and a little of my old self came to the fore.

The barmaid smothered a snort of laughter, but instead of letting go, the guy's fingers tightened.

"You need to learn some manners—" he started.

I felt another presence behind me, and this time it *was* Luke. He wrapped his arm around my waist and pulled me back against him.

"Your hand's still on her arm, Henry. It's not Ash who needs to learn manners."

Henry sneered and gave my arm one last hard squeeze before letting go. "I didn't realise she was with you, Cain. She didn't mention that the other night."

"What other night?"

"When we had dinner."

With that parting comment, Henry made a swift exit. Luke turned to me, his arm leaving my waist.

"You had dinner with him?"

Why did Luke look so hurt? We'd only known each other for five minutes.

"Only in his dreams. I met him at dinner, yes, but I was eating with Susie and Hayley when he and two of his mates decided to join us uninvited. After I got sick of him pawing at me, I climbed out of the window in the ladies' loo and fu...went home."

That at least got a smile out of Luke. "I'm afraid now he's seen you with me, he may well try even harder."

"I take it you two don't like each other much?"

"Not since we were kids. It started off as a feud between our fathers. His old man's a property developer, and my father refused to sell him a piece of land. I own it now, and I still won't part with it. The bad blood fed down to me and Henry."

"I can see that."

"It's become a game. Henry always wants what I have, and he'll try his best to get it."

"So is that what I am now? The latest pawn in your game?"

"No! Don't ever think that. You're anything but a game."

Well, that was nice to know, although I wasn't convinced Henry shared Luke's sentiments.

"Right. Now we've cleared that up, shall we sit down?"

That self-important arsehole had taken up enough of my time today, and I didn't want to dwell on him.

Luke followed me back to the table, and the food arrived soon after. It wasn't much to look at, but Luke was right—it tasted good. As we ate, he apologised for abandoning me to Henry.

"If I'd known he was here, I'd never have gone out. Work's crazy right now. I rarely take time off, and I had to reschedule things this morning to drive the horsebox."

"You were working this morning? That's why you were late?"

He nodded. "Sorry about that. A meeting ran over."

"It's okay. I just got worried nobody was coming, and I didn't know how to get hold of you."

Luke picked my phone up from next to the salt shaker and tapped away at the keys until his own phone rang with "Ride of the Valkyries." Interesting choice.

"Now I've got your number, and you've got mine. Next time I'm late, I'll call."

Next time? What next time?

"Great. Now when one of the girls at the yard wants your number, I can give it to them." I burst into laughter as he choked on his drink. "Oh, lighten up. I was joking."

"Last year, I had to change my number when a group of girls from Upper Foxford got hold of it. I was getting a hundred calls a day."

"Wow, that's dedication."

He grimaced. "It was something. Can I ask a strange question?"

"You can ask. I won't promise to answer."

But I was curious as to what his question would be.

"Most of the time, what goes on inside the female mind is a mystery I can't even begin to solve, but you seem different. Why don't you act like a lovesick teenager around me when almost every other woman does?"

"Refer to Exhibit A: your earlier comment about not judging books by their covers. I judge people by more than looks and money. They have to earn my respect. I've known millionaires with the personality of a dog turd and beggars who are gold." I gave him a wink. "As I've only met you three times, the jury's still out."

Oh, he looked pretty when he smiled.

"I like that approach. If only other women weren't so shallow and judgemental. At first, the attention was flattering, but after a while it begins to grate, you know? The one place I can escape is at work, and that's only because I'm the boss. Even then, they all talk behind my back."

"What do you do for a living, anyway?"

"I run a cyber security company called HC Systems. Our core business is building bespoke security programs for large corporations and government agencies, but we also test for loopholes in existing systems and fix them."

"This was the company you took over from your father?"

"Yeah, not that I had a choice. He died suddenly, and I needed to support my mother and Tia. Mother and the world of work aren't really compatible."

That I could understand, except the woman who'd shoved me out through her money-maker had mostly been found in crack dens. I bet Luke's mother hung out at the country club.

"You've done well with it by the looks of things."

"My father was good at writing software, but he wasn't much of a businessman. He'd take out loans and use them to make bad investments." A roll of the eyes. "Really bad investments, like a vineyard in the Outer Hebrides. When I took over, the company was nearly broke. I wrote new programs, revamped the marketing, and diversified to bring in more cash."

"Good going."

He gave me a small smile. "It is now. I had a lot of sleepless nights in the beginning, though. And now I'm in the process of expanding overseas. We've been getting more American customers, and it's got to the stage we need an office over there. The time difference is killing me right now—too many late-night phone calls."

He stifled a yawn as if for effect, then apologised.

"Whereabouts are you planning to open the office?" I asked.

"I need to decide between California and Virginia. California's better known in the tech industry, but the education system in Virginia's pushing that way too. That means plenty of workforce availability, and there are some good tax breaks for investing there right now."

Virginia. My home. I could certainly vouch for the state being a good place to start a company because I'd done it myself. Not only was the state government supportive of new business, the proximity to Washington, DC and New York meant a lot of key players were within easy travelling distance. But I couldn't have an intelligent conversation with Luke about corporate affairs because as an ex-nobody, I wouldn't be expected to know about those sorts of things.

Instead, I settled for, "I used to live in Virginia. It's got a good track record for employment and, from what I read in the papers, you're right about the government support packages for new companies."

If only I was being me instead of Ashlyn, I could have offered him more help. After all, I had numerous investments in property and businesses in Virginia, and some of those were tech-based.

"I'm still at the planning stage at the moment. I'll need to take a trip out there in the next few months for meetings."

Where would I be in a few months? Would I feel well enough to go home? And what about the man who'd threatened me? Old me wanted to gut him like a fucking fish, but new me figured crawling under my duvet and squashing the pillow over my head would be the best course of action. And today, new me won the toss.

But I didn't want to stay at Hazelwood Farm forever. I was still pondering my options when Luke changed the subject, unfortunately back to me. Bugger.

"So, what brought you to Lower Foxford

specifically?"

"Uh, the bus?"

"No, seriously."

"I am being serious. It was the last stop on the bus route I randomly ended up taking when the train I flipped a coin for broke down."

Now he laughed. "Strange how an arbitrary decision can lead to a new course for your life, isn't it?"

Wasn't that the truth? Fourteen years ago, I'd made an arbitrary decision to steal a wallet and ended up meeting my husband. Funny the hands that life dealt you, wasn't it? I just hoped Lower Foxford wouldn't turn out to be a complete bust when it came to helping me back to normality.

An interruption from the waitress, asking if our food was okay, allowed me to sidestep further questions. Time to find out more about Luke.

"Have you lived around here for long?"

"My whole life. Mother and Tia still live in the house where I grew up."

"Weren't you lonely in such a small place?"

I'd grown up in London, and while I didn't have family, I'd had acquaintances.

"Not really. I was one of those weird kids who actually liked school, and I made plenty of friends there. Sometimes I thought it would be nice to have a brother to hang out with, but the stork never delivered."

"You got Tia instead." The booby prize.

"Yeah. She was a surprise to all of us." He gave a long sigh and his fork clattered onto his plate. "I worry about her."

"In what way?"

"Mother's got no interest in her at all. She thinks money buys love, and Tia doesn't know anything else. Yeah, I know I should spend more time with my sister, but things are...difficult." He took the last bite of his meal. "You don't need to hear all my personal shit."

I took the hint and looked at my watch. "About time we got back to Samara, anyway. Thanks for lunch—it was good to get away from the farm for a while."

"Yeah, it was. Honestly, you're not what I was expecting. I'm surprised someone like you is mucking out horse stables for a living."

"Now who's being judgmental?" I asked, thinking back to his earlier comment on women.

"Touché. It's just I've met other women who've suffered through what you have, and they've all been bitter shrews. I guess it surprises me that you're not."

If only he knew the half of it.

"As Victor Frankl said, it's 'the last of the human freedoms—to choose one's attitude in any given set of circumstances, to choose one's own way.'"

Before, I'd always been a fighter and nobody could bring me down. A madman took me to my knees, but he didn't knock me out. Big mistake, because I was slowly getting back to my feet. Today, a shard of the old me had made an appearance. Not quite Diamond, but perhaps cubic zirconia.

"Now, that's the attitude. And it brings me back to my first point. It's not often you find a stable girl who quotes Frankl."

He held the door open for me, and outside, the wind had stepped up a gear to biting. My donated jacket may have been quilted, but it sure wasn't up to withstanding a vicious British winter. Another item to add to my shopping list when I next went into town.

"Cold?" Luke asked.

"Mmm hmm. I need a better jacket."

"Want to borrow mine?"

"Nah, I'll live. Thanks for the offer, but it's too cold for you to be without."

"In that case, come here."

I took a step closer, stiffening as Luke put his arm around my shoulders and pulled me into him. While my husband hadn't been affectionate, I'd limited contact like that to a few close friends.

But Luke wasn't to know that. I didn't want to create a scene, nor did I want to delve into my life history, so I forced myself to relax. He was just being nice. A gentleman.

And besides, he did make a good windbreak.

As we strode into the car park at the vet's, a young girl ahead tugged a pony towards a trailer. Her father stood idly by, dressed in a totally unsuitable suit.

"Will you just walk!"

When the pony refused to budge, she walloped it with a riding crop then burst into tears.

"Just give me a minute, would you?" I muttered to Luke.

The girl and pony were in a standoff when I gently removed the stick from her hand.

"That won't help anything. Get me a bucket of food, and I'll have a go."

"Really?"

"Get the food."

She practically threw the reins at me, and over the next fifteen minutes, I coaxed the beast up the ramp one step at a time. A final shake of the bucket got the gelding inside, and I tied him up before returning to Luke.

"Sorry for the delay. I can't stand anyone hitting an animal."

He held up his phone, and even as he did so, it vibrated again. "No rest for the wicked. It's good you cared enough to help."

We had to wait a few minutes for the vet to come out, so I got a cup of terrible coffee from the vending machine while Luke made a phone call. When the vet finally did appear, his expression didn't give much away.

"It's her suspensory ligament, as I suspected. She needs a month of box rest."

Samara wasn't going to enjoy being confined to barracks. "What's the long-term prognosis?"

"She should make a full recovery as long as you don't try to rush her back into work."

"I'll make sure she gets as much time off as she needs," Luke said. "Tia hardly rides her, anyway."

I bandaged Samara's legs up, and she walked straight into the horsebox, eager to get away from the vet. I couldn't blame her. Being a pincushion was no fun.

"That's the best news we could have hoped for," I said as we drove back to Hazelwood Farm.

"I know. If you see Tia doing anything she isn't supposed to, will you call me? I'll deal with her."

"Sure."

I didn't tell him I'd stop his darling sister myself if she risked hurting Samara.

The horse was still dopey when I led her back to her stable at the farm, and I made sure she had hay and plenty of water before I went back out to Luke.

"Thanks for today," he said.

"It's my job."

"I guess." He shifted from foot to foot.

"Don't worry about the lorry. I'll clean out the back. I'm sure you've got enough to do at the office."

"Thanks."

Cue slight awkwardness as he stepped forward and pulled me into a hug. What should I do with my hands? I rested them on his back, curled into tense little fists, as he kissed the top of my head.

"See you soon," he muttered.

He didn't look back as he walked to his car, but I could still feel his arms around me. Why so touchy-feely? Was that just his manner?

Normally, my reputation preceded me, and men gave me a wide berth. How odd for Luke to presume I'd be okay with his affections.

Odd, but not unpleasant. I wasn't sure what to make of that.

I bought a packet of decent coffee in case Luke turned up the following Saturday, but there was no sign of him.

Portia came by herself, dropped off by a polished-looking woman driving a Mercedes. Perfectly coiffed blonde hair that didn't move despite the wind, a tight forehead, that air of superiority that only came with years of practice. Mrs. Halston-Cain, I presumed.

Portia seemed subdued, so at least my poor ears got a break as she groomed Samara. I thought maybe she'd finally grown some compassion, but then I overheard her talking to Arabella. Apparently, Luke had told Portia she had to spend time with Samara as well as her other two horses if she wanted him to pay her livery bill.

As I picked up a broom, I couldn't help wishing Luke had come along. I told myself it was because of the sweeping, but the truth was, I'd enjoyed his company. It had been refreshing to talk to someone with no preconceived notions of me, someone whose eyes didn't flicker with fear when they heard my name. Luke treated me like a normal person.

I was just going back to the trailer for my lunch when the postman wandered onto the yard.

"Got a parcel for Ashlyn Hale. Know who she is?"

"That's me."

He got me to scribble my pretend signature on his electronic pad then handed the box over.

What was it? I hadn't ordered anything. It didn't feel heavy, and the return address was a PO box in Cambridge. Cambridge... Cambridge... I'd killed a man in Cambridge once, a Saudi arms dealer who'd come to visit his old alma mater. But I'd made that look like an accident. No, I quickly ruled out a connection.

Back home, an unexpected parcel would go straight to the lab for testing before I contemplated opening it, but here I didn't have that luxury.

Instead, I used the old-fashioned method and shook it. It didn't rattle.

After staring at it in my trailer for ten minutes, curiosity got the better of me and I slit the tape. It didn't explode. Okay, that was a good start.

I opened the cardboard box then peeled back a

layer of tissue paper. What the...? I held the garment up. A jacket. A top-of-the-range windproof jacket, dark purple with a black collar.

Oh, Luke.

CHAPTER 12

"I'VE GOT A headache," Hayley announced for the tenth time today. It was only 9 a.m. on this glorious Monday morning.

"Aspirin?" I suggested.

"Tried it."

She was hung-over, as was Susie. They'd been out on the sauce last night and part of the morning too. I hadn't slept well either, seeing as they'd woken me with a rendition of "Show Me the Way to Amarillo" as they walked up the driveway in the early hours. Neither would win a recording contract.

"I need a fried breakfast," Hayley said. "That always helps."

Susie dropped her broom with a groan. "It's worth a shot. I'll start cooking while you wash the buckets. We can catch up with work after we've eaten. You coming, Ash?"

"I don't fancy fried stuff, but I wouldn't say no to a couple of boiled eggs."

I'd been trying to eat healthily since I started my exercise routine, and I was less sluggish now I'd cut out the donuts and cream buns. Oh, and I could do my jeans up again—always a bonus. I'd just taken a sip of my coffee when Hayley's fork clattered onto her half-eaten plate of fried eggs, bread, tomatoes, hash browns, and sausages.

"We can't eat all this!"

"Why not?" Susie asked, her mouth full.

"It's the Hunt Ball this Saturday. I was four pounds lighter when I bought my dress. What if it doesn't fit?"

Susie paused, fork in mid-air. "Oh, dammit! You're right. How did we not think of this sooner?"

Alcohol, that was how.

She shoved her plate away. "I bet mine won't fit either. I'll have to buy a new one. Does yours have any stretch in it?"

"No," Hayley wailed. "It's made of silk. I got it at TK Maxx, and I'll never find another one as nice, not for that price. As of now, I'm officially on a diet."

Susie carried her plate to the bin and scraped the remains of her breakfast into it. "I'll do salad for dinner."

"Salad? I'll starve." Hayley picked up her fork again. "I'll start my diet at lunch."

"You both look fine as you are," I told them. "Neither of you needs to diet."

Although the salad wasn't a bad idea. I should be eating more of that.

"You haven't seen the dress yet—it shows everything. Are you coming to the ball?" Hayley asked.

"I didn't even know there *was* a ball. So, no."

"You should go," Susie said. "I can get you a ticket. Mother's on the organising committee."

"I'm not sure it's my type of thing."

In fact, I was more than sure it wasn't my type of thing. Based on the only Hunt Ball I'd attended before, I was well aware they were a euphemism for swimming in alcohol.

"You'll love it!" Hayley said. "Everyone from around here goes. It's the biggest event in the village. You never know, you might even meet a nice fella. You know what they say about getting back on the horse and all that."

"She's right," Susie said. "You need to find a man who'll ruin your lipstick this time and not your mascara."

"I'm not looking to meet anybody at the moment."

Or maybe ever. Inside, I was still raw, like someone had taken a cheese grater to my soul. My husband was the only man I wanted, and nobody else would ever measure up to his standards. Nobody. So why did a picture of Luke pop into my head right then?

"You're coming," Susie informed me. "I'll get you a ticket and lend you a dress. I've got hundreds. Something will fit."

Hayley's head bobbed in agreement. "She's not kidding about the dresses. Her closet's bigger than the lounge in the cottage. I just wish we were the same size."

While Hayley was a career groom who'd been at the stables since she left school two years ago, Susie had a different motive for working there. She'd completed two years of a three-year maths degree, she told me over a glass of wine one evening, before concluding that she hated the subject.

"I walked out right before the exams. I'd have failed them anyway, but Daddy was furious. He said if I didn't go back to uni or get a job, he'd cut off my allowance."

So, Susie had applied for the first job she happened to see, the position of groom advertised on a card in the window of the post office. Her father wasn't happy about her career choice, but she'd done what he said, so he had no choice but to keep forking over the cash. That allowed her to satisfy her designer shoe habit and drive a BMW. And it also meant I knew Hayley was telling the truth about her outfits.

But I still didn't want to go to the ball.

"Someone should stay here and do the late check on the horses."

"George'll do it," Hayley said. "He doesn't mind occasionally. Please say you'll come?"

Shit. The problem with having no social life was that I didn't have any excuses either.

"Fine." Perhaps I could fake an illness? "Okay, I'll come."

If I did end up going, at least it would get me out of the trailer for an evening, away from the microwave and, more importantly, away from my thoughts. *Who knows? It might be interesting to meet more folks from around here.* People-watching was always entertaining, especially when everyone else was drunk.

A week of rain was made more miserable by Hayley's mood, and that mood was caused by a fad diet she'd found in a magazine. Eating only chicken, raw broccoli, carrots, and watermelon would be enough to dull anyone's sparkle, as Bradley would say. Hayley swore she'd lost weight, but the only difference I could see was in her level of grumpiness.

On Friday, Susie invited me to her family home, or rather, their mansion to try on dresses. Hayley came too, smiling for the first time that week despite the bag of carrot sticks she'd brought for company.

"Isn't this amazing?" she breathed when Susie flung open the door to her walk-in closet.

I stifled a groan. The rows of dresses might have been a socialite's dream, but I hated trying on clothes. Bradley had been buying mine for so many years he knew instinctively what fitted me, so usually I avoided the horrors of the fitting room.

"How about this?" Susie asked, holding up something pink and frothy. "Or the red one?"

I tried not to grimace as Susie handed me a rainbow of outfits and sent me into the bathroom to change. We might have been the same size, but all that colour and her flouncy style wasn't me at all. I was wondering how to tell her this when Hayley handed me something black and slippery, perfectly matched to my soul.

Please, let this one fit.

The slinky halterneck had a thigh-high split, and I definitely wouldn't be wearing a bra with it. Or knickers either, since it came dangerously low over my arse.

"That's the one," Hayley shrieked as I emerged into the bedroom.

"Are you sure?" Susie asked. "It's a designer sample my cousin gave me, but I've never been keen on it."

"Definitely."

"Yeah, I like it," I said. It was the lesser of the evils lurking on the rails.

Hayley clapped her hands. "Yay! Now you've found a dress, we can relax in the Jacuzzi."

Hurrah. I'd never been a fan of sitting around until I went wrinkly.

"Or there's a pool if you prefer, Ash?" Susie said.

A pool wouldn't be so bad. When I first moved to

the States, my husband and a merry band of former special forces trainers had taught me to swim like a fish. Being in the water was as natural to me as walking now, and I missed it.

"Can I borrow a swimsuit?"

She tossed me a bikini. "Here you go."

While I swam lengths the pool, the other two shared a bottle of champagne in the spa. So much for their diet. By the time we left, I was exhausted and they were pickled.

On Saturday morning, I went for a run while Susie did the horses. We'd swapped so I'd be doing her Sunday shift instead, working on the assumption that she and Hayley would be unconscious after the ball while I planned to stay sober. I made use of the woods, using tree branches to do pull-ups and logs to do tricep dips, and got back in time for a shower before we left for Susie's at three.

I didn't see how we could possibly need four hours to get ready, but when we got there, all became clear. Susie's mother took the Hunt Ball very seriously. The beautician, make-up artist, and hairdresser waiting for us when we arrived demonstrated that fact.

Normally, I couldn't be bothered with all that shit. People poking and prodding made me shudder. Bradley used to pull stunts like this with annoying regularity, but after he got sick of me turning up late and sending the assorted style gurus home, we'd compromised. If it was an important function, he did my hair and make-up, I had a manicure and pedicure once a fortnight so my nails stayed presentable, and some bitch waxed my legs every month when I was home.

I only let him bring in the big guns for special occasions, like meeting the president or another important dignitary. Even for the president, I couldn't always be bothered to dress up. He'd seen me in sweats in the gym; his view of me wasn't going to change if I was wearing eyeliner.

Today, as a sadist plucked my eyebrows, I realised how much I missed Bradley. He might drive me nuts, but at least he didn't try to insist I had a spray tan.

"You could do with some colour," Susie's mother said.

Sure, I'd faded a bit, but Hayley had just been dyed a frightening shade of orange and there was no way I wanted to look like that.

How were the rest of my friends getting on back home? Bradley wasn't the only one I missed. I'd been watching the news for any signs of trouble, but everything seemed quiet in our little corner of Virginia. The most notable item this week had been a shoot-out and a car chase through Richmond, but that was drugs related. Oh, they didn't say that, but I knew. I'd recognised "Suspect A" as he legged it from the police helicopter. What a drama. Last time I'd gone after the little shit, I'd shot him with one of those tranquilliser guns they use at the zoo, but the cops had all these pesky rules and it didn't look good if they broke them on live TV.

No, Virginia was calm. It was just my mind that was in turmoil. Part of me longed to return home, but I knew from the way my chest tightened every time I thought of getting on a plane that I wasn't ready.

The three of us passed inspection just before seven when the stylists declared us ready.

"You look lovely, darlings," Susie's mother gushed.

Her father had arranged for his chauffeur to drive us, and better still, pick us up. At least we wouldn't be fighting for a cab later.

The ball was being held at a country hotel fifteen miles away. Its drab stone façade was at odds with the raucous guests parading up the steps, and as Susie and Hayley beamed and pouted for the official photographer, I ducked to the side. No, I didn't want a mugshot.

In a stuffy anteroom, white-jacketed waiters offered around trays of champagne. Well, prosecco more likely, but the guests seemed to prefer quantity over quality. Susie and Hayley skipped the bubbles entirely and started on the hard stuff while I sipped a glass of orange juice—one of us had to stay upright.

I studied the partygoers out of habit and spotted a few people I recognised, including Portia and Arabella. What were they doing here?

"Aren't those two underage?" I asked Hayley, jerking my head in their direction.

"Sixteen and seventeen-year-olds are allowed in as long as they're accompanied by an adult family member. They've got to wear a pink wristband to show they shouldn't be served alcohol."

The bands of shame would be lucky to last five minutes. If I'd had one, it would have been snipped off the second I got through the door. As if to prove my point, a piece of jailbait wandered past holding a cocktail and tripped over a chair. Yes, this evening promised to be carnage. *Someone save me now.* The icing on the cake came when I spotted Henry-the-turd from the corner of my eye. You know, that disgustingly thick icing you peel off and hide in a napkin?

He swaggered around with his mates, beer in hand. This evening, he'd swapped the cravat for a wonky bowtie and a tuxedo that might have fitted once, but it hadn't kept up with his expanding waistline. Nice.

With nothing better to do, I worked my way around the room, chatting. I'd always treated gatherings like this as a challenge to find out as much information as possible while revealing as little as I could about myself. I'd become pretty skilled at it, but it was always amusing when I went to a work function where everyone else was playing the same game. This evening was good practice, although I had it easy because this crowd loved to talk about themselves.

Then at eight o'clock, we were called into the dining room. The three of us from Hazelwood Farm were at a table with another girl and four guys.

The new girl was obviously with the short, ginger-haired guy—the way she kept searching for his tonsils with her tongue was a giveaway—and two of the others paired off with Susie and Hayley. That left me with one man to talk to, and I quickly realised he was gay. He didn't mention it, but I'd spent enough time with Bradley to know the signs.

Gay dude was nice enough, but we had nothing in common. There was only so much I could talk about with an accountant who spent his weekends fly fishing.

By the end of dessert, boredom had set in. Hopping

into a cab was oh-so-tempting, but Susie and Hayley were past three sheets to the wind and well on their way to double figures. The responsible part of me said I should stick around to make sure they got in the right car at the end of the night.

Once the tables were cleared away, the DJ came out and the dancing started. Not a good idea for me to join in. I always drew attention when I set foot on a dance floor, no matter how much I tried to tone it down, and I wanted to keep a low profile tonight. I'd slunk back into the shadows by the bar when I felt a presence behind me and hot breath on my neck. Breath that reeked of whisky. Delightful. As I turned, Henry ran his hand up my bare back.

"Managed to lose the boyfriend then? How about trying a real man?"

"I assume you mean yourself? It was just that the 'real man' part confused me."

"Yeah." He reached out and stroked my hair. "Girls always get confused."

Fuckwit. Too drunk to pick up on the sarcasm?

I tried again. "Not even if you were the last man on earth, there were no more batteries, and my fingers were paralysed."

"Oh, come on, don't be frigid. I won't disappoint."

He pressed himself up against me and wrapped his arms around my waist. Fuck, my reflexes had slowed. He'd attempted to kiss me before I got my brain in gear and kneed him in the crown jewels. As he doubled over, clutching his balls, I sidestepped neatly as he threw up. A rare smile played across my lips as he collapsed on the floor, and there was a satisfying rip as the back seam of his trousers split to reveal Winnie the Pooh boxer shorts. Classy. I melted into the gathering crowd and watched from a distance as two waiters helped the bastard out of the ballroom. Boom. Henry was done for the night.

An hour later, I'd had enough. The only thing worse than arseholes hitting on me was drunken arseholes hitting on me. That count ran into double figures. Worse, the DJ clearly had an auditory problem because not only did he have crap taste in music, it could be heard in the next hemisphere, meaning the staff should have been handing out earplugs instead of bar snacks.

Our car wasn't due until 2 a.m., three and a half miserable hours away. I'd rather have been caught in the middle of a battle with the Taliban than spend another three and a half hours there. A gunfight would be easier on my ears too.

Another inebriated guy wobbled past, patting me on the arse as he went. He attempted a smile, but the overall effect was of a lunatic who'd just escaped the asylum. I didn't even try to point out that his zipper was undone. I'm sure he'd have taken that entirely the wrong way.

A sigh from the bartender as he handed over another glass of iced water told me he found this as painful as I did. At least now I had something to empty over the head of my next overzealous admirer. I went back to my spot, only to find it occupied by a couple auditioning for their own porn film.

Why had I agreed to this? The old me would have had enough backbone to say I wasn't going. Now I was stuck in the tenth circle of hell.

Through the disco lights, I spotted the doors that

led back to reception. Surely there must be somewhere else I could hang out until it was time to leave? This was a hotel, after all.

Time for plan B.

Chapter 13

I EXITED THROUGH the double doors and followed the plushly carpeted corridor back towards the hotel reception. A night porter manned the desk, slumped down in his chair and looking as bored as I felt.

"Excuse me?"

He glanced up.

"Is there a bar or a lounge somewhere here? Other than the carnage back there, I mean." I gestured back at the way I came.

"Of course, madam. The Thornton Bar is down that corridor, last door on the right." He straightened up and pointed at a door on the other side of the room.

My eardrums rejoiced as the music faded, and it wasn't long before I found myself in an oak-panelled bar. It was straight out of an old oil painting—the sort of room where a bunch of country gents would retire after dinner. They'd smoke cigars and discuss the important things, like how many pigeons they'd shot that afternoon. A series of dusty tapestries on the walls spoke of a slower-paced life, before the days of cars, aeroplanes, and the internet.

If only things could be so simple now.

The bartender looked like a relic from the past too. I sat down with my water, relishing the peace and resigning myself to a few hours of waiting.

Yes, I was still bored, but at least my head had stopped pounding. The room was almost empty—the only patrons were a couple in the corner having a quiet drink and a man at the bar staring into his glass like it held the answer to life's troubles. Then the door crashed into the wall, disturbing the peace. All heads swivelled toward the newcomer.

"Sorry," he muttered.

He lowered the average age of the customers by a decade or two. I guessed he was around thirty, and he'd have been considered handsome if his nose hadn't been broken one too many times. The guy ordered a round of drinks, and the barman poured them so slowly that watching him would have benefitted from time-lapse photography.

"Have you got a tray?"

The barman shook his head and shrugged. Service with a smile in this place.

I wandered over. "Need a hand?"

"Thanks, you're a lifesaver. Do you want to order one for yourself?"

I looked back at the bar, where the old man was wiping a cloth backwards and forwards across the same bit of surface, over and over again.

"Perhaps not, eh? I have to leave at two, and Mr. Cheerful would still be pouring it."

The stranger laughed and rolled his eyes. Between us, we grabbed the six drinks on the bar plus the glass of water I already had, and I followed him towards the lift.

"I'm Mark. I'd shake hands, but..."

"It's fine. You're staying here?"

"Fortunately not. Have you seen the mess through

there?" He jerked his head towards the Hunt Ball.

"It'd be hard to miss."

"Yeah, you'd have to be deaf. Me and some friends got talked into bringing our kid sisters. They've got to be accompanied by responsible adults." He gave a wry laugh. "My mother thought I fitted the bill."

"I'm here with friends. And when I say 'here with friends,' I mean my job is to shovel them into a car at the end of the night."

"Nightmare, isn't it? We learned from last year, so we've rented a room."

"Sounds cosy."

"Not like that. We're playing poker."

The lift arrived and Mark pressed the button for the second floor with his nose. A poker game. That sounded more fun than the debacle in the ballroom. Would they let me stay? I figured I had two minutes to convince them.

As it turned out, that was easier than I thought. I backed through the door, and when I turned around, I found myself face-to-face with Luke Halston-Cain. The room was more of a suite, and he raised an eyebrow as he thumbed the stack of poker chips on the table in front of him.

"I see you managed to pick up Ash," he said to Mark.

"Less of that talk—I'm spoken for. Anyway, she was the one who came over to me. It must have been my magnetic personality."

"Or your inability to carry a round of drinks. I offered to help with the glasses. That hardly translates as wanting to strip you naked and do you over the bar," I said.

That got a laugh from five of the men and a snort from the sixth.

"Makes a change from most of the women down there," the man sitting next to Luke said. I didn't recognise him.

Mark put his armful of glasses on the table, leaving wet rings on the polished surface. "Yeah, walking into that ballroom would be like taking a shortcut through shark-infested waters on your way home from the butcher's shop."

"Although if Luke doesn't stop eating my crisps, I'll march him downstairs and handcuff him to the bar. The women can take turns," another of the men said.

"I'll buy you another packet," Luke said then turned to me. "Are you staying? You don't seem drunk enough to hang out downstairs."

I grinned at him. "Thought you'd never ask."

He introduced the other players. Ben was the guy on his left, the one who'd had a dim view of the female partygoers, and his dimple distracted me while Luke waved at the other three, so I missed their names. Fuck, I never used to lose my focus like that. In my head, I christened the blanks as Huey, Dewey, and Louie. That seemed to work. As Ben divvied the chips up, I gathered that they weren't close friends of the others, anyway, but rather they'd been brought together by a shared desperation to avoid the havoc downstairs.

"Want me to deal the first game?" I asked.

Luke raised that eyebrow again. At least he hadn't had Botox. "You know how to play poker?"

Come on, dude, it's the twenty-first century. Women were allowed into casinos.

"I've played occasionally."

"In that case..." He pushed the deck of cards in my direction. "Deal away."

Game on.

CHAPTER 14

"ARE WE PLAYING Texas Hold'em?" I asked, naming the variant of the game beloved of casinos and frat boys the world over.

"Yeah," Luke said.

I shuffled the cards and dealt two to each player, face down. They peeked, and betting commenced. Mark tried to hide his smile as he threw a handful of chips into the middle. He had something good.

Huey followed suit. "Come on, boys, make me rich."

Louie tossed his cards down in disgust, muttering, "Did you shuffle these properly?"

"Bad luck, mate," Huey said, although he didn't sound sympathetic.

When everyone had bet or folded, I dealt three cards—the flop—face-up on the table. Mark groaned. He was terrible at this game. I could read him like a large-print book.

"I'm out," he said when his turn came.

I dealt the fourth card, and everyone stayed in. Either they all had good hands, or they thought they could bluff their way through. I found myself watching Luke. What was his tell?

I dealt the fifth and final card, and Luke and Huey folded. Dewey leapt up, fist pumping the air when he won with a full house against Ben's pair of eights.

"Yes, I'm the man!"

That was debatable, considering his choice of drink had been a margarita. As he raked the pile of chips towards him, I gathered the cards up and dealt the next game.

While I wasn't playing, I got the chance to study the others. Mark stayed cautious, and Ben tended towards gung-ho. He thought he could bluff his way through, however terrible his cards were. Most of the time, it didn't work.

"Bollocks," he muttered as his pile of chips dwindled further.

Huey was the easiest to suss out. When nerves got the better of him, his right foot tapped. I could see the slight movement carrying through to his torso. There it was again—tap, tap, tap. He was bluffing. Players like him were easy to take money off. The game lasted another hour, until Luke's face lit up in a grin as he won the last of Mark's chips.

"Hand them over. What were you doing in Vegas last month? Not practising your game, that's for sure."

"No, I was hanging with my posse of showgirls," Mark said.

"And your girlfriend was where?"

Mark rolled his eyes. "Fine, I went to a golf tournament. Anyhow, you just got lucky."

Lucky? I wasn't sure. Luke played with confidence, and he'd rarely had to show his cards. Maybe he was just good at bluffing? I wasn't sure.

"Shall we play again?" Luke asked. The hideous wooden clock on the wall showed it was just after eleven.

There were murmurs of assent.

"You joining in this time, Ash?"

"Love to, but I need to check on Susie and Hayley first." I had visions of them collapsed in a corner somewhere.

"Not a bad idea," Dewey said. "We should check the kids too. We can pick up another round on the way back."

"You might want to order the drinks first if you want them to be ready before morning," I suggested.

"Good point," Mark agreed. "Luke, can you check on Arabella, and I'll go to the bar?"

Ah, so Mark was Arabella's brother. Poor bastard. He seemed so normal in comparison.

If anything, the music downstairs had got louder. I found Susie and Hayley on the dance floor, and while Susie was missing her shoes, at least they were both still upright. I counted that as a win. Back in the bar, the old-timer was making a meal out of pulling a pint.

"Is he almost done?" I asked Mark.

"You've got gin and tonic instead of lime and soda. You're not driving, right?"

I shook my head. "I'll live with it."

While we waited upstairs for the others to come back, I used the bathroom and took a look around. The suite undoubtedly cost more per night than I earned at the stables in a week, but the absence of bags suggested nobody planned to sleep in it. Someone had money to burn. I suspected Luke, from what I'd heard about him.

When everyone had returned, Huey dealt the cards, and my shitty luck held. A two and a five, not even in the same suit. I folded. While the others bet, I stacked my chips—the cheap plastic kind you bought for a few quid off the internet rather than the clay ones used in

Vegas—in colour order. Black, blue, red, green.

Ah, Vegas. The city of sin, and believe me, I'd embraced its reputation. I'd also learned to play poker there. On my first trip, my husband had bought me into a game.

"We're in the gambling capital of the world. Put the drink down and play," he told me.

I knocked back the last of my cosmopolitan while he gave me a five-minute crash course in the rules. Full house, straight flush, three of a kind, yadda, yadda, yadda.

"So, what it boils down to," I said, "is if the cards have people on them, bet. If they're the same suit, bet. Otherwise, fold."

"Something like that."

At three in the morning, I stumbled out of the casino with chips overflowing from my handbag.

"I thought you said you didn't know how to play?" my husband asked.

"I don't."

I didn't even know what my last hand was. The cards had been too blurry. But before I could explain that, I fell off the kerb and he carried me back to our hotel.

After that night, I made an effort to learn the rules of poker properly. Now when I won, it was due to strategy rather than blind luck and alcohol. Whenever I was in Vegas, I played, and the guys at work had a weekly Wednesday night game I joined when I was home. Who was topping the league now? My money was on Dan.

While Vegas was always fun, I'd preferred the underground poker games I sometimes played. Men invariably underestimated the pretty girl, which meant I could act like a ditz then wipe the floor with them. That was always fun, especially when they got angry. I loved a good fight.

But there was none of that tonight. As the moon rose higher, I won a couple of big pots, and soon I had a nice collection of chips. A million imaginary dollars, ten stacks of black ten-thousand-dollar chips, all the same height. OCD city, baby, OCD city.

Ben, Huey and Louie lost their chips and quit before twelve. Lightweights.

"Better go get the brats," Ben said.

Dewey left soon after them, dividing his chips among Luke, Mark, and me. "I promised mother I'd have my sister home by half twelve, and we're already late."

What was it with mothers in this part of the world? They kept grown men firmly under their thumbs. Still, it helped me. I knocked Mark out at a quarter to one with an outrageous bluff—his cautiousness came to the fore, and he folded.

One to go.

"I'll round up Portia and Arabella while you guys fight it out," Mark said, and he disappeared off to search for them.

That left me alone with Luke.

"You're not a bad player," he said. "Where did you learn?"

Err, time for another bluff. "My grandma taught me when I was little. We used to play for pistachios. She was a shark."

"She taught you well. I learned at boarding school, playing for tuck-shop credits."

"You went to boarding school? Isn't that a bit old fashioned?"

"They're still around. I started there at eight. My father liked the idea of having a son, but not the reality of it. We got on better when I wasn't at home."

"How about your mother?"

He rolled his eyes. "You've met Tia."

So, it seemed Luke's childhood hadn't been idyllic either, although his had been eased by liberal applications of money. With the cards dealt, we played another hand and Luke managed to take a few chips off me.

"Nice bluff."

"You don't know I was bluffing."

Not for sure, but I did now, because he looked away when he answered. With only the two of us left in the game, it was easier to figure him out. He clenched his teeth when he had a bad hand. Subtle, but it was there.

When my turn came to deal, I ended up with a pair of aces. "Gonna wipe the floor with you, hot stuff."

"Hot stuff?" Luke asked.

"I've met you four times now."

He chuckled. "You're finally starting to realise that there's more to me than an incredibly handsome face?"

"No, I can see you're self-deprecating and modest too."

I was about to lay out the flop when Luke's phone rang.

"Mark," he mouthed, then put the phone to his ear. "Where? ... Shit, how drunk are they? ... Can they still walk? ... Okay, I'll meet you out front in five."

He dropped the phone on the table and let out a long sigh. "I've got to go."

"What's happened?"

"Mark's found the girls. Since we last checked them, they seem to have got hold of some alcohol. Tia promised she wouldn't drink, but apparently she can't stand up and she's lost her shoes and her handbag."

He rose to his feet and shrugged his jacket on.

I got up as well. "I'll pack up the poker stuff. Where's the box?"

"Just leave it. It belongs to the hotel. What cards did you have, anyway?"

"Not telling."

"Oh, come on…"

"Nope. I never give away my secrets." At least the big ones.

"Fine. A rematch, then?"

"When?"

He grabbed his phone and scrolled through it. "Friday. I can get away on time."

Why not? It wasn't like there was much else to do in Lower Foxford. "You're on."

Luke grabbed my hand and led me into the corridor, his palm hot against mine. The contact made me suppress a shiver—few men in my life would dare touch me in that manner—but at the same time, it was nice for someone else to take control for a change. Fending for myself all the time had left me drained.

We found Mark and the girls in a hallway downstairs. He'd corralled them onto a window seat where the pair of them were bouncing up and down, talking non-stop. Portia's cheeks were flushed, and sweat dripped from Arabella's forehead. When we got close, Portia leapt up and enveloped Luke in a hug.

I caught his look of shock before it turned to

concern.

"She doesn't normally do that, does she?" I asked.

I hadn't seen much of her, but she'd never struck me as the huggy, kissy kind.

"No, never," Luke whispered.

Shit. I peered into her eyes. Yup, pupils dilated. I sat next to Arabella, caught her flailing wrist, and checked her pulse while she chattered away about how much fun she was having. Her heart was hammering.

"Come on, dance with me." She got up and tried to pull me with her.

"I'll pass."

She grabbed Portia instead, and they started waltzing.

"How much have they had to drink?" Mark muttered.

"We only saw them an hour or so ago," Luke said. "They can't have had that much, surely?"

"Guys, I hate to break it to you, but I don't think this is just alcohol."

"What are you getting at?" Mark asked.

Luke was quicker on the uptake. He narrowed his eyes at me. "Are you suggesting my little sister's been taking drugs?"

I put my hands up. "Hey, don't shoot the messenger. But yes, that would be my guess."

"Sorry, I didn't mean to snap. I just can't believe she'd do that. She never has before."

"That you know of."

"Yes, that I know of." His shoulders slumped as his usual confidence ebbed away. "Hell, I should be spending more time with her. Our mother's worse than useless."

Portia danced over to him.

"Cheer up, misery guts," she sang.

He gave her hand a squeeze and focused on me.

"Any ideas what they could have taken?"

"Probably ecstasy. Maybe coke. If it's coke, they'll start coming down from it soon, but I think E's more likely."

"How do you know?"

"Reformed wild child."

I figured I might as well tell the truth for once in my life. It had a terrible habit of catching up, and I just hoped I'd be well away from Lower Foxford before my fabricated life unravelled.

Luke's mouth twitched, and I knew he wanted to ask for details, but Portia chose that moment to puke. Luke held her hair back, looking green.

Meanwhile, Mark wasn't feeling so charitable. He slammed his hand against the wall then winced. "I'm gonna find the little scroat who gave them drugs and arrest him. Then I'll put him in a cell with a bunch of guys who don't take kindly to newcomers. I can have a squad car here in two minutes."

Arrest him? Marvellous. I'd just spent the evening playing poker with a cop.

Mark turned to his sister. "Bella, who did this?"

She clapped his cheeks between her hands and grinned. "I love you. Did I ever tell you that?" When he looked less than amused, she stood on tiptoes and kissed him on the nose.

"No, you never did, actually."

I interrupted their family bonding time. "Look, far be it from me to tell you what to do, but it might be best if you took Arabella home and put her to bed. You can deal with the rest tomorrow."

Mark sighed and some of the anger left him. "You're right."

"You don't think we should take them to hospital?" Luke asked. "Won't there be side effects?"

Given the choice, I'd keep them on drugs all the time. They were both more pleasant that way.

"No, just keep an eye on her and make sure she drinks plenty of water."

"That's it?"

"I'd also suggest not taking her home to your mother like that. And when she comes down from the high, she'll be a bitch. Even more than normal."

Okay, perhaps I shouldn't have said that last part.

But Luke didn't seem to pick up on my insult. "In that case, she'll have to come home with me."

He and Mark eventually managed to shovel the two girls into their respective cars, and Portia turned on the radio in Luke's Porsche and started singing along to Taylor Swift. Badly.

"I'll see you later," Luke muttered as he started the engine.

"Good luck," I said to the night as he roared up the drive. "You're gonna need it."

After they'd gone, I set off in search of Susie and Hayley, hoping my two colleagues hadn't chosen to pop pills as well.

But no, they were sprawled out on the dance floor, fast asleep. Susie was still barefoot. The music had stopped, and with the lights on, the mess was clear to see. Those poor hotel staff. I'd rather clean up after the horses than tackle the ballroom.

Spilled drinks and mushed-up streamers made it

look as though a rainbow had thrown up. Stray corsages grew from the debris, their petals wilting, and a sea of shoes, hair accessories, and bow ties strewn across the dance floor provided evidence of just how much had been drunk that evening. The chances of finding Susie's footwear in that lot were slim. Thankfully, she wasn't short of spares.

I stooped and shook the pair of them awake.

Hayley looked up at me. "Suze, look, there's an angel. With a halo and everything."

I glanced above my head. "That's actually a disco ball but, hey, whatever."

Sidestepping a shard of glass, I hauled them to their feet and held them up as they stumbled through the hotel. *Please, say some fresh air will sober them up a bit.* When we got outside, our car was waiting, bang on time, and I said a silent "thank you" to Susie's father. Had she done this before?

As the car purred through the night, I wondered how Luke was getting on with Tia. She could be a handful at the best of times, but tonight? I didn't envy him. I almost called to check that he was okay, but in the end, I decided I didn't know him well enough. Yet.

Back at Hazelwood Farm, the chauffeur and I half carried, half dragged the near-unconscious pair into the cottage.

"Thanks, buddy," I told him.

"You're welcome, ma'am. I'm quite used to it."

Yup, Susie had definitely done this before.

I finally got to bed with time for three hours sleep before I needed to face the horses. Sometimes, life in Lower Foxford made my old days as an assassin seem relaxing.

Chapter 15

THE RAIN RETURNED to torment us the following week, which meant I had the constant joy of eight muddy horses, and worse, I discovered one of my boots leaked.

By the time Friday evening arrived, I was dead on my feet, and I began to see the attraction of Susie's spa. All I wanted was to sink into a hot bath with a glass of wine, but as I didn't have a bath or any wine, that option was out. And if yesterday and the day before's showers were anything to go by, I didn't have any hot water either.

So I did the next best thing. I changed into my newly acquired yoga pants, wrapped the duvet around myself, then settled onto the good end of the sofa to watch a movie about mutant guinea pigs.

The opening credits were barely over when my phone rang on the other side of the room. Why did phones do that? It was as if they instinctively knew when you'd just got comfortable. With a sigh, I levered myself up and went to answer it.

"Are you still on for poker this evening?"

As I hadn't heard from Luke, I'd assumed he'd changed his mind.

"I thought you'd forgotten about that."

"Of course I didn't. I've been looking forward to

seeing you all week. Do you want me to pick you up?"

At least his memory was better than his communication skills. I almost wished it wasn't, because I could do without going outside in the rain again. Then I looked over at the TV where the guinea pigs were doing a hula-hula dance. Oh dear. Perhaps going out was the lesser of two evils.

"A lift would be good if you don't mind?"

"It's no trouble. I'll be there in ten minutes."

"Can you make it half an hour? I need to take a shower, but I've been putting it off due to a lack of hot water."

"It's broken?"

"Yup, for three days now. George promised to look into it, but he has no sense of urgency when it comes to these things."

Although I imagined if it was him who had to take a cold shower, he'd get onto it pretty sharpish.

"Why don't you bring your stuff with you? I can spare some hot water."

Hallelujah. "I'm not going to turn down that offer. Ten minutes, then."

As Luke swung left into his tree-lined drive, I got my first glimpse of his home. An imposing wall hid the house from the road, but as we rounded a curve, it came into view, lit up by spotlights at the front. The style was mock-Tudor—all exposed beams and imitation leaded light windows.

I couldn't make up my mind whether I liked it or not.

The impeccably decorated, chintzy interior wasn't what I'd expected from a bachelor pad. An overstuffed sofa and ornate credenza flanked the front door, although the fake flowers on the latter looked kind of dusty. Either Luke had been exploring his feminine side, or he'd had help.

My inspection didn't escape his notice. "The decor isn't exactly what I'd have chosen."

I raised an eyebrow.

"When I moved out, mother got a little upset. The only way I could calm her down was to ask her to help with the furnishing. It made her feel wanted."

"You live alone, then?"

"Tia's got a room here, but she doesn't use it much."

"How is she? After the ball, I mean?"

Don't mention the drugs. Be tactful, Ash. A foreign concept to me.

"She's okay. Or at least, as okay as Tia gets. You were right about her being in a foul mood the next day. She slept until one, and when I tried to bring up what happened, she stormed off and refused to speak to me for the rest of the afternoon. Mother picked her up in the evening, and I haven't heard from her since. I don't know what to do."

"I'm sure she'll come round. Just give her time."

"You're female, and didn't you say you went through a wild phase? Any idea how I can get her to behave?"

My wild phase had lasted from the age of twelve until just after I turned fourteen. What can I say? I'd always been precocious. I knew about drugs not because I'd been educated in the dangers of substance abuse by a loving family, but because I'd tried most of them. What snapped me out of it was waking up in a dingy squat one morning to find a guy I'd been partying with the night before dead beside me. An overdose combined with malnutrition, or so I heard.

After that wake-up call, I knew things needed to change, and change they did when I met my father. Not my real father—I had no idea who that arsehole was—but the man I'd nominated for the job. He and his wife took me in and smacked some sense into me. That was the start of my journey to the person I'd become.

I didn't think hearing about my early years would be particularly comforting to Luke, though.

"How about finding her a mentor? Someone she can look up to? If you're not around and your mother isn't up to the job, she needs someone else."

"Where on earth do I find one of those?"

"Could her school help? They might have a program?"

"I'll call them on Monday. Anything else?"

"Does she have any hobbies besides the horses?"

"Shopping."

"Not sure there's much we can do with that."

"I tried cutting off her allowance, but she 'borrowed' my credit card and ran up a five-figure bill on the Selfridges website." He sighed. "But enough about my sister. I'll show you where the bathroom is so you can clean up while I finish dinner."

"You're cooking?"

"Don't act so surprised."

Luke gave me a quick tour. The formal lounge was decorated for show, fussy and uncomfortable with stiff-backed couches and tables full of knick-knacks. The dining room easily seated twelve but looked unused.

"Where do you live?"

"What?"

"Where do you spend your time? Not in these rooms, unless you really do read the copies of *Woman & Home* magazine on your coffee table."

"What? No!" He led me to his den, one hand on the small of my back. "In here."

This was more like the man-cave I'd been expecting. A messy desk dominated one end, with a battered leather sofa facing a large-screen TV at the other. The dartboard on the wall had a photo pinned in the middle.

"Who's that?" I asked, stepping closer.

He sighed. "A programmer at work. Usually, I'm a firm believer in talk rather than action, but he made some really vulgar comments about my secretary and frustration got the better of me."

I admired his restraint. I'd have been throwing the darts at the programmer.

While the row of computers on the desk was undoubtedly for work, the surfboard propped up next to the TV and the snowboard hanging on the wall behind it hinted at Luke's adventurous side. Maybe we had something in common?

"We're playing in here?" I asked, spying the poker set on the coffee table.

"Yes, after we eat."

He walked back along the hallway, and I trailed behind, enjoying the view. The house was quite nice too.

"The gym and pool are down there." He pointed at a doorway. "But it's getting late, so I'll show you the shower. Will half an hour be long enough?"

What did he think I planned to do? Get ready for an evening on the red carpet?

"More than enough."

I hadn't taken a decent shower for a month, but I resisted the temptation to stand under the steaming water until I went pruney and got out after ten minutes. Since the house was blissfully warm, I only needed to put on jeans and a T-shirt, and I found a blow dryer in a drawer and gave my hair a quick blast. Twenty-five minutes. Slow for me.

"How's dinner? I'm starving."

Luke jumped at the sound of my voice. "I was expecting you to be ages yet."

I glanced down at my watch. "I said I'd be half an hour."

"Yes, I know, but normally when a woman says that, she takes at least double. I'll try to hurry the food along."

"What are we having?"

"Cheese soufflé to start, salmon asparagus gratin and steamed vegetables for the main course, then crème brûlée for dessert."

"And you're cooking all that?"

Did he moonlight as a Cordon Bleu chef in his spare time, or was he cheating?

"Yes."

"Really?"

"Well, I'm heating it up." He looked a little sheepish. That was more like it.

"Hey, I'm impressed you're doing that much

instead of hiring a chef and a butler."

"I did consider it," he admitted. "But I decided I'd rather have you all to myself."

I let that last comment slide. "Anything I can do to help?"

"Could you put the salad on the small plates?"

Between us, we got the food dished up and carried it through to the dining room to eat. I'd suggested eating in the kitchen, but Luke said the dining room hardly got used and he had to justify having it somehow.

"You surf?" I asked as I forked soufflé into my mouth.

"I used to, but since I took over the company, I've barely had time to use the gym let alone travel abroad."

"Do you miss it?"

"More than anything. Before my father died, sports were my life. Skiing in the winter, surfing in the summer. I was working the ski season in Switzerland when Mother phoned to tell me he'd died. I figured I'd head back there in a month or two, but it never happened."

"Because you had to run the company?"

He put his fork down and sighed. "That and Mother had a nervous breakdown, and there was nobody else to look after Tia. It took a year for Mother to recover and another two for me to turn HC Systems around."

A nervous breakdown? Miracle of miracles—the two of us had something in common.

"It must have been satisfying to build it up from nothing."

"I guess. Sure, I've made money, but now I'm stuck there. I always liked messing around with computers as a teenager, but I never wanted to do it for a living. The corporate side sucks."

"Couldn't you sell it?"

"I've thought about it, but it would be like selling part of myself. Besides, I still enjoy working on the ideas side of things. It's the day-to-day management that gets me down."

"Get good managers in place and delegate."

"That's the crazy thing—I have good managers." He stared at the wall over my head. "It's the leap into the unknown that scares me."

"Sometimes a gamble can pay off. You could free up enough time to do what you enjoy."

"Maybe I'll try it. Hell, I could do with some excitement in my life." He leaned back in his chair. "Dammit, just listen to me. I invite you over to dinner, and we spend the evening talking about business."

"Talking can help."

Fuck, now I sounded all preachy. It was very much a case of do as I say, not as I do.

The oven timer bleeped from the kitchen, and I helped Luke to clear away the plates and bring out the next course. The salmon and asparagus dish was delicious, better than Susie's cooking and infinitely tastier than mine. While we ate, the discussion turned to Lower Foxford.

"There's a rumour going around that Henry got taken to hospital after the Hunt Ball, but nobody knows why," Luke said. "Have you heard anything?"

I choked, and he looked at me strangely.

"I think it may have been something to do with having his testicles rearranged."

"Who by?"

Oops. I forgot I was talking to Mr. Violence-never-solves-anything, and he sounded kind of shocked. I stayed quiet.

"You did that?"

"He should have kept his hands to himself."

Ten seconds passed. Twenty.

"I suppose he had it coming."

Phew.

After the main course, I helped Luke to stack the plates in the dishwasher. He'd gone a bit quiet. Was he more upset than I thought about the kneeing-in-the-nuts episode?

I turned to face him, and under the brighter lights in the kitchen, he didn't look so good.

"Are you okay?" I asked. "You've gone kind of grey."

"I think I'm just tired. I had to work late every evening this week so I could take the weekend off."

Really? I wasn't totally convinced. *Mental note: don't admit to walloping any more arseholes.*

While Luke slouched over the breakfast bar, I made myself useful by caramelising the tops of the crème brûlées. Wow, it sure smelled better than taking a blowtorch to human skin.

"Here you go." I pushed a tiny dish over to Luke then dug into mine.

He picked at the top, staring at the table. *Should I offer to leave?*

"Are you sure you're okay?"

"Yes. No. I don't..."

He shoved his stool back and ran from the room. Okay, kind of drastic considering my question. Or was it...? A door slammed somewhere along the hallway, and I bit back a groan. Had Luke gone to worship the

porcelain god?
I very much suspected he had.
So much for a relaxing evening.

CHAPTER 16

I WAITED A few minutes, and when Luke didn't reappear, I went to find him.

I'd hoped I was wrong about him being ill, but when I heard the gagging noises coming from the downstairs loo, that hope faded. When I pushed the door open, he was kneeling over the toilet, and judging by the mess on the floor, he hadn't made it in time.

He groaned when he looked up and saw me. "Please go out. I'm fine."

No, he wasn't "fine." Embarrassed, yes, but definitely not fine.

"I've seen worse." Although not by much. He'd gone from nought to Norovirus in sixty seconds. "Somebody has to look after you."

"Yes, but not you. I don't want you here while I'm like this."

Under his grey pallor, a red tinge spread across his cheeks.

"Well, do you want me to call someone else? Your mother? Or your sister?"

"No! My mother would totally overreact. I'd end up at the hospital, probably in intensive care. And Tia would just call my mother. She doesn't deal with things like this."

"You're stuck with me, then. Suck it up."

He didn't argue further, which showed how rough he must have been feeling. That and the fact he puked again. I dampened a wad of tissue and handed it to him, then averted my gaze while he wiped his mouth.

"Think you can stand?" I asked.

Did that groan mean yes? I had to assume so.

With my arm around his waist, I guided him past the mess and towards the stairs that wound up both sides of the entrance hall.

"Just lean on me. We can go as slow as you like." He'd have given a tortoise a run for its money, but we made it to the top. "Now where?"

"To the right, last door on the left." His voice was barely audible.

I hadn't planned on ending up in Luke's bedroom tonight, but that was where I found myself. The elegant decor spoke of his mother's touch again.

He sank onto the bed and leaned forward, head in his hands. His face was paler than the cream quilt, and I couldn't help wrinkling my nose at the splashes of vomit on his clothes. The smell turned my stomach.

"Lean back," I said, then unbuttoned his shirt.

Hmm... Not bad at all. He had a gym, and he knew how to use it. There was no time to stop and admire, though. I needed to find him something clean to wear.

Opposite the bed, two doors hung ajar. I tried the left one first. Unlucky—that was the bathroom, complete with whirlpool bath. Did every house around here have one?

The right door hid what I was looking for—Luke's dressing room. I rummaged around until I found a clean T-shirt, old but soft with a faded slogan:

Binary

It's as easy as

01.10.11

Okay, geek alert. That was one for Mack, not me. She was probably sitting at her computer in Virginia right now. She rarely left it.

Luke made no attempt to help as I tried to shove his spaghetti arms through the holes. Good grief. Dressing Nate's four-year-old was easier. Luke's jeans were dirty too, and I reached for his belt.

"Tell me you don't go commando?"

He managed a weak shake of his head, so I stripped him down to his underwear and shoved him under the duvet.

Drugs. I needed drugs. Oh, don't look at me like that—I meant painkillers. His bathroom cabinet yielded a box of condoms, vitamins, and four kinds of moisturiser. Surely he had paracetamol? Ah, there it was, a half-empty packet of Anadin shoved behind his spare razor blades.

By the time I got back to the bed, Luke had fallen asleep, and I didn't want to wake him. Instead, I filled a glass of water and left the pills next to it on his nightstand. He could take them when he woke up.

Wonderful. What promised to be a pleasant evening had turned to shit, just like everything else in my life. Was I cursed? I stuffed Luke's dirty clothes into the washing machine and found a pair of rubber gloves and disinfectant in the cupboard under the sink so I could sort out the downstairs toilet. Even after it was spotless, the smell of vomit lingered in my nose.

Back in the bedroom I'd borrowed earlier, I stripped down to my T-shirt and knickers. The door had a lock, but just to be on the safe side, I hid the key and dragged a chest of drawers across in front of it too. Not to keep Luke out, but to keep me in.

I checked on him once during the night, and although the covers lay twisted, he was still sleeping soundly. That was more than could be said for me. I'd barely dropped off when the sun rose over the balcony outside, waking me. Once, I'd thought of each sunrise as a new beginning, something to be thankful for, but now it signalled another day of sadness.

How much more of this could I take?

I was sipping a cup of coffee as I read the doom and gloom in the morning paper when Luke stumbled into the kitchen in his underwear.

"What the...?" He stopped short when he caught sight of me at the breakfast bar. "You didn't leave."

I looked down at myself. "Nope, still here."

"But I threw up in front of you."

"I wasn't kidding when I said I'd seen worse." He shuffled closer, and I laid a hand on his forehead. "You've got a fever."

"I was freezing five minutes ago."

"You should have stayed in bed. Did you take the painkillers?"

"Yeah, but they're not working yet."

"Go and lie down. I'll bring up some Lucozade."

And for fuck's sake, put a shirt on. Trousers would be good too. I was having a hard time keeping my eyes on his face.

Luke did as he was told and went back to bed, and when I took his drink up five minutes later, he was dead to the world again. No, the universe. He didn't stir for the rest of the day. As he hadn't kicked me out, I took advantage of his pool table and dartboard, not to mention the giant TV and the well-stocked fridge. I was tempted to skinny dip in the pool, but sod's law would have ensured he woke up and caught me.

Swimming or no swimming, it was a far more pleasant Saturday than I'd have had at Hazelwood Farm. Susie had drawn today's shift, and she was no doubt enjoying the company of the whining brats.

As the hours ticked by, I used my phone to find a recipe for macaroni and cheese and attempted that for dinner. Since it was my comfort food, I figured it would be good for a sick person as well.

"You didn't have to cook," Luke said when he appeared in the early evening, thankfully dressed this time.

"Don't get too excited. I might end up poisoning you."

And for once, it wouldn't be intentional. At least I'd fished out the fingernail I'd accidentally grated into the cheese.

"Didn't you cook when you lived in America?"

"Not much. We just ate a lot of takeaways."

He must have been hungry, because he shovelled his plateful down, despite the pasta not being entirely cooked. Not bad for a first attempt, but was I brave enough to try a second? At least Luke had some colour back.

"I'll clear up the dishes before I head off. I'm glad you're getting better."

"Stay. Please. I like having you here."

Stay? What did he have in mind? "Why?"

"It's nice to have company."

I wasn't sure whether to be pleased or disappointed by such a bland response, but in the end, hot water won the day. That and the central heating were too good to turn down.

I shrugged, careful not to appear too enthusiastic. "Okay, I'll stay."

"Fancy a movie?"

"Sure."

I vetoed the rom-com that Luke half-heartedly suggested and let him pick out a spy thriller instead. The storyline was vaguely interesting, but I couldn't help picking out all the factual inaccuracies in my head as it played. Although I had a movie theatre at home, watching a film from start to finish was a novelty for me. Usually if I fancied seeing some action, I only had to pop into the control room at work. Assuming I wasn't in the middle of it, of course.

After a family-sized bowl of popcorn and an unrealistic ending where the bad guy's chest exploded after being shot with a .22, my eyelids grew heavy.

"You look like you're ready for bed," Luke said. "After all the chores you've done today, you'll sleep well."

"I doubt it. I rarely do."

"You suffer from insomnia?"

"Not insomnia, exactly. I have a few problems at night."

Problems. What an understatement. Murderous tendencies more like, but I didn't want to explain that one.

"Doesn't everybody, sometimes?"

"With me, it's more than that. Promise that if you ever hear me cry out, or see me sleepwalking, you won't come near."

"Why not?"

"I once hurt someone in my sleep, and I can't let it happen again. It's why I always sleep alone."

"Hurt someone? How?"

"I'd rather not talk about it."

He rolled his eyes, clearly convinced I was exaggerating. "If it makes you feel better, I promise."

It was Luke's turn to make breakfast the next morning, and mine to wake up sweating. I kicked the sheets away from my feet and stumbled out onto the balcony, gripping the railing as I gulped in air. The peaceful view turned black as I screwed my eyes shut. *No, no, no.* I'd seen my husband's death again, played out in all its fiery horror. Why couldn't I forget? The noise, the flash of heat, the smoke. Would it ever fade?

The delicious aroma of bacon filled the air as I shuffled into the kitchen, and Luke greeted me with a smile more genuine than my own.

"My specialty," he said, pointing at the frying pan with a spatula. "Something I can actually cook from scratch."

"I'm impressed." I headed for the coffee machine, drawn like a magnet. "Let me show you my specialty."

I'd made us both cappuccinos by the time Luke set two bacon rolls on the counter. I could work a coffee machine as well as I could fire a gun. My survival depended on both.

"Ketchup?" he asked.

"Lots of it."

He slid a plate over, and I bit into my roll and groaned. "You know if you ever wanted to quit your job, you could become a bacon chef."

"Keep that up, and I'll make you breakfast every morning."

Two weeks ago, I couldn't have contemplated that, but now... The idea didn't seem so bad. I could wake up to worse than Luke's easy grin.

"Anything you want to do today?" he asked when we'd both finished eating.

"I've been eyeing up your gym."

"Knock yourself out."

"I'll try not to take that literally." I'd always preferred to knock out other people instead. "I'll have to pass for the moment, though—I don't have any shorts with me."

"Have a look in my wardrobe—there's probably something with a drawstring you can make do with."

I used to "borrow" my husband's shirts all the time. Would it feel weird wearing another man's clothes?

"They're clean, I promise," Luke added.

Ash, stop being sentimental. "Thanks. I'd like that."

The air-conditioned gym would make a pleasant change to running through mud. I found a new pair of navy blue boxer shorts in Luke's closet, relieved to note the lack of novelty underwear. Nothing killed a girl's libido faster than Bugs Bunny hopping over a man's package. Not that my libido needed killing, of course. Nope. No way.

The boxers sat low on my hips, but I was only wearing them in private, so they'd do. I snagged one of his T-shirts too. Comfy. What were the chances of me taking it home without him noticing?

"I'm tired just watching you," Luke said a couple of hours later. He'd spent the last thirty minutes sitting on the floor with his tablet while I ran on the treadmill.

"Perhaps you should try joining in?"

"Not today. I'm still groggy. I will next weekend."

Next weekend? He'd made a big assumption there. I opened my mouth and closed it again. What was stopping me from setting him straight? Maybe how sweet he was. When I staggered off the treadmill, he had a towel and a smoothie waiting for me.

"I put protein powder in it. You need it after that run." Then, despite me being all sweaty, he put an arm around my shoulders and pulled me close. "Thanks for looking after me yesterday. Nobody's ever done that before."

In the gloom beyond the floor-to-ceiling windows, movement caught my eye. What was it? A fox? An owl? I tried to focus, but Luke blocked my view with his chest, and I gave up.

"Everybody needs a hand when they're down," I muttered.

Or lips. Lips would do. He leaned down and softly kissed the top of my head.

A shiver ran through me, and my heart pounded faster than it had on the treadmill. Not just because Luke was hot, but because that was the first moment since I'd left home that I started to feel human.

Maybe the first moment ever.

Chapter 17

"DO YOU WANT to stay over again tonight?" Luke asked once I'd rinsed the sweat from the gym off in the shower.

"Tempting, but I've got to start work at seven tomorrow. I'm better off going back to the farm."

"Don't remind me about work. I've got a conference call with a Japanese supplier at eight. Last time, the translator didn't turn up, and it was a nightmare."

I nearly offered my services, but I bit my tongue.

"Sounds like it," I said. So damn lame.

"At least stay for dinner?"

Another day off cooking? "Deal."

Our pizzas arrived an hour later, delivered lukewarm by a dude on a moped. We skipped the formality of the dining room and opened the boxes at the breakfast bar.

"Ugh, Hawaiian?" I crinkled my nose in disgust when Luke flipped his lid back.

"What's wrong with it?"

"It has pineapple. Fruit doesn't belong on pizza."

"Tomatoes are a fruit, and yours is covered in them."

"Okay, technically they *are* a fruit, but they're also not."

"You're using women's logic."

I grinned. "It's the best kind."

After we'd eaten, Luke offered to drive me home, and as I climbed into his car, I almost changed my mind and stayed for the night. My trailer didn't have Netflix or a shower with three nozzles.

It didn't have Luke, either.

"Better stop at the end of the drive," I told him as we got close to Hazelwood Farm.

If Susie or Hayley noticed me getting out of his car, I'd never hear the end of it.

"Can we do this again next weekend?" he asked as we sat in darkness. "It's... It was... I had a good time."

"Me too. I'd like that."

It may have been difficult to admit, but I sort of liked him. Luke was totally different to any of the men in my past, but he was kind. Sweet. Gentle. And right then, that was exactly what I needed.

Despite the miserable weather and the amount of mess the owners had left over the weekend for me to clear up, I was smiling on Monday morning.

"What's made you so cheerful?" Hayley asked.

"I won fifty quid on the lottery on Saturday." I held up Coco's rug in front of me. "Honestly, how does somebody get lipstick all over a horse blanket?"

"Practice."

I wouldn't have been so cheerful if I'd known a steaming pile of horse shit was about to hit the fan. The day passed uneventfully, and even when Tia and Arabella showed up after school, dropped off by Arabella's mum, it didn't dampen my spirits. Had Luke spoken to Tia about paying more attention to her horses? She was still there at five when I went in to catch up on the TV news. *Please, don't let her leave the place a tip.* I shook my head as I settled onto the couch. She was sixteen and hated getting her hands dirty—surely she couldn't wreak too much havoc?

I'd underestimated her.

When I heard a knock on the door at seven, I expected Susie or Hayley, but I got George.

Had he come to fix the shower? A glance at his expression told me the answer was no. He shifted from foot to foot, hands stuffed in his pockets.

"Is there a problem?" I asked.

"Um, I don't really know how to say this." He refused to look me in the eye—never a good sign. "It's not something I've had to deal with before, and I don't take it lightly."

Oh, spit it out, man. "Say what?"

"I've had a complaint."

"About what?"

Me? Was this about the Henry episode?

"One of the owners said she saw you hitting her horse."

Of all the things someone could accuse me of, that hurt the most. I'd never hit an animal. A person, sure, if they deserved it, but never an innocent animal.

"That's ridiculous."

"I guess it surprised me too, and Susie and Hayley when I spoke to them just now. They said you were always kind to the horses. But the girl had a witness."

The purpose behind Tia's earlier visit suddenly became clear. I knew she wasn't my biggest fan, but how had I pissed her off enough to want me fired?

Because surely that was where we were heading...

"So, you want me to leave?"

"I think that might be best."

I could try to clear my name, but two witnesses against me made that difficult. Plus George would be left in an awkward position—Tia and Arabella's horses were worth several thousand pounds to him each month, so he had to keep them happy. Not only that, I needed to maintain a low profile. Singing the injustice from the rooftops would hardly help my cause.

No, the easiest option was to leave. To walk away from Lower Foxford and everyone in it and start over. I'd done it once; I could do it again. Sure, I'd miss Susie and Hayley, but they weren't close friends. Luke flitted through my mind, the only cause for hesitation before I answered George.

"I'll go tonight."

"You don't have to leave straight away. You're welcome to stay in the mobile home until you get something else sorted." The relief that I'd agreed to go quietly was all too evident in his voice.

"I haven't got much to pack, and I'd prefer to leave as soon as possible."

Why hang around where I wasn't wanted? I closed the door, leaving George on the lopsided step. It only took me ten minutes to stuff my belongings into a bag. Where should I go? Far from this village, that was for sure. Thanks to the rumour mill, most people already thought my piano was a few octaves short, and this latest episode wouldn't help matters.

I glanced at my watch. If I got a bus to the train station, I might be able to catch a sleeper service up north. At least that way, I wouldn't have to find a hotel room.

But I'd have to hurry. I scribbled a note out for Susie and Hayley, thanking them for everything, and left it propped up on the table. They'd be thrilled when they realised they had to do all the horses between them tomorrow. I needed to let Luke know he'd have to make his own coffee next Saturday too, but I'd call him in the morning. No point in disturbing him when he was probably still at work.

The thought of never seeing him again stung more than it should. Perhaps we could have become friends if we'd met under different circumstances. Like at a point in my life where every other thing that came out of my mouth wasn't a lie and my head wasn't fucked. Those kind of circumstances.

I took one last look around the trailer that I'd called home, however briefly. The end of another chapter in my story, albeit a short and not particularly sweet one. My phone was running low on battery, so I turned it off. Who would I call, anyway? My bag was heavier than when I arrived, thanks to my efforts at shopping, but I slung it over my shoulder and tramped off. The bus stop wasn't far.

The driver who took my money for the next leg of my journey was the same one who'd dumped me off in Lower Foxford a month ago. I might have considered that poetic if I'd had any light left in my soul.

But only darkness remained.

CHAPTER 18

LUKE'S DAY STARTED at six with a call about a server issue. He'd barely sorted that out before it was time for his conference call, which overran, and no sooner had he hung up from that, a young blonde admin assistant knocked on his office door.

"Luke, have you seen the Spires contract?"

Shouldn't that be his question?

"Try the filing tray."

Before Luke could pick up his coffee, a developer poked his head in. "Do you know when Mike's back from his holiday?"

"It'll be on his calendar."

And so it continued—a succession of simple queries that could easily be solved by the people asking them if they'd only *think*.

Why did Luke have to do everything around here?

Because he let his staff walk all over him, that was why. He reflected on his conversation with Ash about delegation. Would it really be that difficult? Maybe it was time to find out.

He picked up the phone to his PA. "Blanche, I need you to arrange a meeting."

As Luke made himself a coffee at lunchtime, whispers followed him across the open-plan office.

"The control freak's finally loosening his grip."

"Some people will need to start pulling their weight in this place."

"Is Luke ill? He looks a bit...different."

Was that really what they thought of him? A control freak? The looks of shock on the managers' faces when he'd started delegating tasks in the meeting earlier had been priceless. Yes, things would be changing in the office. But what did that woman mean, he looked different?

When he got back to his office, he peered at himself in the mirror he kept in his desk drawer. No, nothing out of the ordinary. Except, maybe.... He peered closer. ... Shit! Was that a wrinkle? Dammit. Yes, adjustments to his lifestyle were definitely required.

At the end of the day, when he left on time for the first time in well, ever, it was with a tentative smile and no small amount of guilt. And when he arrived home in time for the opening credits of *EastEnders*, he didn't know what to do with himself. Should he start watching soap operas? Did Ash like that kind of program?

The time he'd spent with her over the weekend had made him see things differently. She'd had so many knocks over the past few months, but still she'd stayed positive. And here he was with a seemingly perfect life —more money than he could ever spend, a huge house, his own successful company, girls falling at his feet— and let's face it, he was miserable.

The steps taken today may have been small, but at least they were headed in the right direction. Closer to Hazelwood Farm and a certain new stable girl.

How long until the weekend? Four long, long days. Should he invite Ash over sooner? Maybe they could go out for dinner? Yesterday, his finance director had been raving about a London restaurant where every dish was colour-coded. Hideously expensive, no doubt, but Ash was worth it. Although for someone with so little money, she'd so far seemed strangely unaffected by his. Should he be pleased by that or worried?

She didn't obsess over looks either—not his or hers. Hell, he'd never met a woman who could take a shower in thirty minutes. One ex-girlfriend had refused to stay at his house at all until he had a bigger hot water tank installed—that was just one of many reasons she'd become an ex. But Ash? Even with no make-up, unfashionable glasses, and a shabby haircut, Luke had still needed a cold shower when she came downstairs in his T-shirt and boxers. Would the curves that outfit hinted at live up to their promise?

Luke fetched a beer from the fridge and went through to the den. With time on his hands, he picked up a pool cue. Did Ash play? If not, he'd teach her. Anything to see her cute ass bent over the pool table. His trousers tightened uncomfortably thinking about it. Should he call her? He wanted to call her?

He'd just potted a red when the front door slammed, and he flung the pool cue across the table then groaned. Only three people had a key—his housekeeper, his mother, and his sister. Nora had gone home for the day, and either of the other two was bad news.

For a moment, he considered escaping out the back door, but he'd left it too late. Tia walked in wearing a self-satisfied smirk.

"Why do you look so pleased?" he asked.

"The gold-digging bitch from the stables is finally gone."

"What are you talking about?"

"That crazy woman. I got her sacked." Tia's grin got wider, and she clapped her hands in glee.

"What crazy woman?"

"Ash, of course. How many other crazy women are there?

"Hold on. You got Ash sacked?"

"It was easier than I ever dreamed. I just told George I saw her walloping Samara, and the gullible old fool believed me."

Luke recalled his recent visit to the vet. The way Ash had stepped in to stop that teenager from hitting her horse, he couldn't imagine Ash hurting an animal herself.

"So you lied, and Ash lost her job?"

"Well, yeah. But something like that was bound to happen sooner or later. Everyone knows she's psycho. Arabella heard from Bethany at school that she got done for assault on her ex-husband. She might even have escaped from prison. Nobody's quite sure."

"You've got no idea what you're saying," Luke said, his chest tight.

"Yes, I do. You should be thanking me. I saw her here at the weekend, standing in the kitchen like she owned the place. She'd soon have stuck her claws into you and taken all your money."

"You saw her? I didn't even know you were here."

"Well, I didn't come in, obviously, not after I looked through the window. I didn't want to walk in on the two of you fucking."

"Tia! Mind your language. And that's not why she was here."

"Oh, please. I'm sixteen, not stupid." Tia's voice rose an octave. "She was wearing your underwear for goodness' sake."

Ouch.

"You don't know her. She's not interested in my money," Luke said, teeth gritted.

More than ever before, he felt the urge to throttle his sister.

"Of course she is. She works on a farm. She earns less in a week than I spend on manicures."

"So? That doesn't make her a bad person. Wait a second—how much do you spend on manicures?"

"I'm not going to a cheap place. The polish chips too easily, and it's a false economy. Anyway, Ash is a nasty cow. She even told you I'd been taking drugs. Then you told school, and I got called in to see the counsellor. Do you realise how embarrassing that was?"

Luke resisted the urge to cover his ears. Tia's voice was so high, he half expected the neighbourhood's dogs to come running.

"Well you *had* been taking drugs, hadn't you?"

"That's not the point." Tia came back with impeccable women's logic.

Luke knew he'd never win that argument, and he wasn't going to waste time trying. No, he had something more important to do: find Ash.

He turned his back on his sister and tried calling. Voicemail. Bloody voicemail. He cursed under his breath before the beep.

"It's Luke. Can you call me? Urgently?" He rattled off his number again, just in case, then grabbed his car keys. He'd deal with his sister later.

The Porsche slewed to a halt in front of Ash's place, leaving a line of black rubber. Luke leapt out and hammered on the door. Nothing. The trailer was in darkness, and nothing stirred inside Dammit! She'd left already.

Next door, the curtain twitched. By the time Susie answered his hasty knock, she'd had time to cover herself in perfume and put on some lipstick. The cloud of scent that wafted out made Luke cough.

"Luke, what a nice surprise! Would you like a cappuccino?" She twirled her hair around one finger and stuck out her chest.

Couldn't a girl have a normal conversation with him, just for once?

"Save it, Susie. I need to find Ash. Do you know where she went?"

Susie's face fell, and now he felt guilty. He'd get Blanche to send a box of chocolates or something.

"I've got no idea. George sacked her over some ridiculous story about hitting a horse, but I don't know what happened after that."

"Does she have any friends around here?"

"No, I don't think so. She stayed with Carol in *Melrose* for a while, but she seemed glad to get out of there. She reckoned Carol bugged her room." Susie paused, still twirling. "She can't drive, so she must have walked or gone by public transport. Cabs are pricey, and George pays a pittance. Maybe the bus? Or a train? That would be faster."

"Thanks."

Luke turned on his tail and headed back to his car, ignoring Susie's cry behind him.

"Luke? Why do you care, anyway?"

He broke most of the speed limits on his way to the train station, praying Susie had guessed right. With the car park packed, he abandoned his Porsche in a no-parking zone right outside the entrance and ran inside.

The two platforms offered Ash two chances to leave. He paused to scan them, trying to pick out a pretty brunette among the groups of Christmas shoppers lugging their bags.

Movement at the far end of the northern platform caught his eye. He could spot Ash's arse anywhere, and there it was, climbing onto a train. He sprinted down the platform and ran into the same carriage. A woman tutted as he jostled her, but Luke didn't care because he'd spotted Ash at the far end, sliding into a seat.

When he skidded to a stop in front of her, her eyes widened.

"You're leaving? Without telling me?" he spluttered, trying to catch his breath. *Way to go, Luke.* He'd wanted to impress her with his suaveness, but what came out was more desperation.

"What good would that have done?" She didn't smile. "Would you have tried to talk me out of it?"

"Of course I would."

"Why? Everyone in the village reckons I'm only one step down from being an axe murderer. It would hardly do your reputation any good to be seen with me."

"You think I give a fuck about my reputation? Look, I like you. I mean, I really like you. I want to get to know you, and I can't do that if you run off, can I?"

Luke had wanted to tell her that on Saturday. Being honest, he'd wanted to do more than tell her, but Norovirus had thrown up on that plan.

Ash didn't speak. Not in words, and not with her eyes. Her face was a blank mask as the guard on the platform whistled the one-minute signal.

Luke tried again. "Please stay, if only for tonight. Just to talk. Otherwise I'll have to go with you to..." Luke looked around. "Wherever the hell this train is going."

A lady sitting opposite spoke up with the husky voice of a forty-a-day smoker. "Better stay here, love. He's obviously sweet on you. What have you got to lose?" Turning to Luke, she added, "This train's going to Manchester, cutie."

Silence descended on the carriage. Luke wasn't the only one waiting for Ash's answer, and she withered under the gaze of thirty travellers.

"Please, Ash?"

"Okay," she whispered.

A round of applause echoed as Luke slung Ash's bag over his shoulder and grabbed her hand. They made it onto the platform a second before the doors closed. As the red lights on the final carriage faded into the distance, he put his arm around her waist and guided her out to his Porsche.

"Come on, let's give the village something to gossip about."

CHAPTER 19

THE ROAR OF the Porsche's engine drowned out anything I might have wanted to say as we rode back to Luke's place, making the silence more bearable. Was I doing the right thing? Head battled heart, but neither had much to lose at that point. If nothing else, I could rest for a few days then head north as I'd originally planned.

Luke took my hand again as he led me from the car. Sweaty palms. Caused by his dash through the station, or nerves? I was getting used to his touch, and while old me would have stepped back and glared, new me took a deep breath and swallowed. *Relax, Ash.* Grasshoppers invaded my stomach as he fitted his key in the front door. When I left on Sunday, I'd expected to come back but not under these circumstances.

"Have you eaten?" Luke asked.

I shook my head. My appetite had deserted me again.

"What the...?" Luke started as the door swung open.

"Fuck," I muttered, leaping in front of him. The house had been trashed. "Stay here; I'll check the place."

Shit! I forgot I was supposed to be playing the helpless female.

Luckily, Luke didn't notice. "Don't bother. It was

Tia."

The vase from the hall table lay shattered on the floor, a puddle of water spreading from the remains. The table itself rested on its side, the polished surface chipped and scratched. I picked up a screwdriver from the floor and looked up at an abstract painting now more fucked than the artist originally intended.

"Your sister did...this?"

"We had an argument."

The carnage continued from the dining room to the den. A tornado would have done less damage.

"Must have been some fight."

Luke's sigh settled in the still air. "It was."

"What was—?" Never mind. "You fought about me, didn't you?"

"She told me what she'd done, about getting you sacked, and I blew up at her." He nudged his broken surfboard with his foot. "She didn't take it too well."

"I'm sorry," I whispered.

"No reason for you to be sorry. It's Tia who's the problem."

I bent to pick up a stray pool ball from the den floor. "I'm contributing to it."

How did one teenager make so much mess in so little time?

"Hey, leave that." Luke crouched beside me and turned my chin to face him. "Nora can clear that up tomorrow."

"Nora?"

"My housekeeper. She works Monday to Friday. Now, will you leave it?"

"I'll help her in the morning."

"Fine. But tonight we're going to bed."

He stood, lifting me with him, then wrapped me up in his arms. His motives were a mystery, but he'd cared enough to come after me.

"Were you planning on doing that together?"

"Do you want to?"

Did I? Good question. I totted up the months I'd been without in my head and found it reached double figures. That last time hadn't even been in a bed. A rather rushed effort on a kitchen island, if I recalled correctly. A certain blond CIA agent had lured me into his apartment with a promise of donuts, and we'd been tearing at each other's clothes before the door swung closed. I'd got a bruise on my elbow from bumping into his fridge, and my backside nearly froze on the marble counter. Worse, I never did get my donut. Asshole.

And no, he wasn't my husband. Surprised? Well, I'll explain that part later. Right now, I had more important things on my mind. Like the bulge in Luke's trousers.

Oh, fuck it. A girl had needs.

"Make me forget," I whispered, then kissed him.

On tiptoes, my mouth was level with his, and as I nibbled on his bottom lip, he pressed into me and let his tongue explore. No complaints about his technique.

Before I knew it, we'd fallen back on the sofa, and I'd lost my top in the process. That was hardly fair, so I sat up and dragged Luke's shirt over his head. Now I was free to explore those abs I'd glimpsed last weekend.

He ran his tongue along my collarbone and I shivered, but not from the cold—the atmosphere had turned steamy, and the mercury was still rising. My breasts were treated to equal attention before he slowly, slowly continued his journey south. Heat pooled between my legs as he paused at my belly button. *Oh, for fuck's sake, hurry up!*

Before he unzipped my jeans, he met my eyes. "Are you okay with this?"

"If you don't get a fucking move on, I'm gonna spontaneously combust."

"Can't have that."

He peeled my jeans off, and my knickers swiftly followed. Before he got to the good bit, he propped himself up on one elbow and inspected me.

"So, that's what you've been hiding."

I wriggled as he ran a fingertip down my side, cursing myself for being ticklish. "Which part of hurry up didn't you understand?"

The vibrations of his laughter rippled through me, followed by a surge of warmth as he slid a finger into my pussy. His mouth muffled my gasp as he added a second, hitting exactly the right spot. Wars had been won and lost since I last had an orgasm, even a DIY one, so it didn't take long for the fireworks to go off. When the explosion came, my back arched up off the sofa, and when I fell back to planet Luke, my grin matched his.

"I love being able to make you smile like that," he said.

Cheesy, yeah. But cute.

I gave myself a minute to recover, but fair was fair. Luke deserved payback. I unbuttoned his jeans and found a gift as impressive as the rest of him. Happy birthday to me. Okay, so I'd actually turned thirty a few days ago, and my fake birthday wasn't until May, but I didn't care about the small things today. Just the big things. Luke breathed harder as I trailed my lips across his smooth chest, matching my kisses to my strokes.

I'd got halfway down his stomach when he stopped me. "Wait."

"What's wrong?"

"Nothing, but if you keep that up, I won't last long. And I don't have any protection downstairs."

"Not the kind of guy to carry a condom in your wallet then?"

"Despite rumours to the contrary, no, I'm not."

"Perhaps you should start?"

Luke levered himself off the sofa then pulled me up. We tried to run for the stairs, but my gait was more of a stagger. Thanks, buddy.

The serenity of Luke's bedroom décor contrasted with our desperation. Somewhere between the stairs and the door, Luke lost his trousers, and we landed on the bed in a tangle of limbs. Having spent a bit of time at the stables lately, I'd become well educated on the origins of the phrase "hung like a horse." And he was.

"I need you to fuck me." I never minced my words. Often that got me into trouble, but tonight it got me into Luke's bed.

He grabbed a condom from his nightstand, and I ripped it open with my teeth and rolled it on. Look, no hands.

"Ash, that's the hottest thing I've ever seen."

"Practice makes perfect."

"Shut up. I don't even want to think about you doing that with another man."

I'd actually perfected the technique with Dan, a courgette, and a bottle of Patrón. We got kicked out of the bar after that.

Luke didn't hang around. He rolled me over and

thrust himself inside so quickly, I banged my head on his fancy wood-and-leather headboard.

"Sorry." He winced more than I did.

"Don't apologise. Just bloody get on with it."

And he did. Oh boy, did he. It was only afterwards I thought to ask, "How close are your neighbours?" I'd never bothered to look past the tree line—slacking during my time away.

"Far enough, thank goodness. Otherwise the police would be on their way with the amount you were screaming."

I bit my lip. "Sorry. Just got a bit carried away."

"Don't apologise. It made me feel like a man."

"You'll be going to hunt dinner next." Probably at Waitrose.

"Oh come on, admit it. I was fantastic."

"You were...okay." I couldn't help grinning.

We stared at each other then burst out laughing.

All right, so I'd understated things. Fantastic didn't do Luke justice, and lying there in bed beside him, the corners of the jigsaw puzzle that made up my soul slotted into place. I was far from whole again, but I felt...something. Something other than the empty numbness that had ruled me for the last few months.

Despite the nickname given to me by one of the men in my life, I was no angel. I didn't make a habit of hopping into bed with virtual strangers, but every so often, I met a guy who wormed his way past my defences. They'd varied from friends with benefits, to kind and gentle, to adventurous, to a brief foray over to the dark side during a phase when I didn't like myself much. It was a long while since I'd had sweet.

Instead of leaving straight away, my usual modus

operandi, I snuggled into Luke's arms. His strength seeped into me and held my demons at bay. I could have curled up there for hours, but inevitably, my eyes started to close.

"Luke, I can't stay here." Even if for the first time in years, I wanted to.

"If it's about the sleepwalking thing, I don't mind." He brushed it off as a triviality, but he'd never met the monster I became on my worst nights.

"But *I* mind. I don't want to hurt you."

"I'm a big guy. I can look after myself."

And the guy I'd hospitalised had been a Navy SEAL. Guilt gnawed at me, both for what I'd done to Nick all those years ago and what I was about to do to Luke.

"I can't. Please, don't do this."

"It can't be that bad."

Oh, it could. A ride in an ambulance if he was lucky, the morgue if he wasn't.

"Not tonight, okay?"

He nodded, still far from happy. I leaned in and kissed him again, an apology for being unable to give him what we both wanted.

"Are you up for round two before you go?" he asked.

"Sounds like a plan." I giggled as he rolled me over. What the hell? Giggled? I sounded like a vapid idiot. Had I lost my mind?

No, but I did when Luke kissed me again.

The sun hovered above the trees when I woke the next morning, and the clock on the guest-room wall showed

I'd slept for eight hours.

Holy crap, I was late for work!

I had a foot out of bed when I remembered I didn't have a job anymore, at least, not at the stables. The jury was still out on my previous occupation.

Ah well, at least I had a bed and a duvet. At the moment, they seemed the better option, but I couldn't succumb to the temptation. Had Luke overslept too?

I dashed through to his bedroom—empty. The smell of bacon wafted past me, making my mouth water. I threw on a robe I found on the back of the bathroom door then found Luke downstairs at the breakfast bar, drinking coffee while he scrolled through emails on his phone.

"Aren't you late?"

"I'm taking the day off."

"Seriously? I thought you never took time off."

"A couple of weeks ago, I wouldn't have dreamed of it. But you made me realise there's more to life than making money." He gave me a lopsided grin. "Especially when I don't enjoy it."

"Bravo. So you're up for another go?" I eyed up his sandwich. "Well, after breakfast?"

"You want one?"

I nodded.

"I'm always up for you." He paused to kiss me on his way to the stove. "Apart from an hour this morning —I've got a conference call at ten."

The backdoor opened and a pleasantly plump woman in her fifties bustled in. She did a double take when she saw me.

"Nora, this is Ash. She'll be staying here for...well, I'm not sure."

Nora pushed a few stray strands of grey hair back into her bun, fighting a losing battle. "Pleased to meet you, ma'am."

For crying out loud, don't call me that. I wasn't a bloody relic. "Ash is fine. It's good to meet you too."

Her eyes widened as she took in the destruction behind me. Tia had thrown eggs at the wall and swept a pile of plates off the counter.

"Didn't the burglar alarm work?"

"It was Tia," Luke said.

Nora's lack of surprise said a lot about his sister's character.

"That girl'll be the death of everyone," she muttered. "I'll get the bin bags."

Despite Nora's protests, I lent a hand with the clean-up. By the time Luke finished his call, the house looked presentable other than the black scribbles on the dining room wall. That needed to be repainted.

"I'll make soup for lunch," Nora said. "We could do with a filling meal after all that work."

"I'm sorry." Luke apologised on behalf of his sister with the resignation of a man who did that regularly.

"These things can't be helped. I'll put up the Christmas tree after we've eaten—the delivery man left it by the front door."

Living in a bubble at Hazelwood Farm, the run-up to the festive season had all but passed me by. Just as well, because I'd had nothing to celebrate.

But did I now?

The three of us hauled the tree inside and set it upright in the hallway. Nora produced boxes of ornaments, and soon the tree sparkled in red, green, and gold. As I wound tinsel over the boughs, I wondered what Bradley was getting up to. I never wanted to make a fuss over the festive season, but he went all out.

Every year, he did something bigger and better, and usually, I let him. It made him happy. Everyone needed a little happiness in their lives, even if my darling assistant shoved it down their throats.

Would he make such an effort this year without me there?

Yes, most likely.

I said a silent prayer that one of my friends would apply the brakes if he tried anything too wild. Last year, I'd had to veto his plan to install a life-size nativity scene on my front lawn. No way were the sheep and cows going to stand peacefully and nibble hay. They'd shit everywhere. We'd compromised, and he'd arranged for the gifts to be delivered in a sleigh pulled by reindeer. The year before, he'd insisted on using my helicopter to install a giant star on the roof. A decade of special-ops training, and I used my skills to dangle at the end of a rope while he kept changing his mind about the angle.

Luke's tree seemed tame by comparison, but once we'd hung all the crap on it, we stood back and admired our work.

"I'm looking forward to unwrapping my present," Luke said, snaking an arm around my waist.

"You've only got a few days to wait."

"I wasn't talking about the one under the tree." He kissed his way up my jaw. "It's been purgatory keeping my hands off you. Get upstairs."

"Nora's still here."

"Then you'd better be quieter than you were last

night."

"What are you going to do? Gag me?"

Without warning, he picked me up and slung me over his shoulder, caveman style. I shrieked, cursed myself for being such a girl, then enjoyed the ride. When he dumped me on the bed and peeled me out of my clothes, I managed to keep the noise down until Nora slammed the front door on her way out.

Then I got loud, and I wasn't the only one.

CHAPTER 20

I LAY WITH my head on Luke's chest, threading my fingers through the smattering of blond hair that led to the good bits. We'd had our workout for the afternoon —Luke had certainly put in an effort holding me up against the wall. I was debating whether I could muster up the energy to go down on him when "Nightmare" by Avenged Sevenfold blared out from his phone.

He raised his head and groaned. "Shit."

"Just leave it."

"I can't. It's my mother."

Ah, yes. Mothers. In Lower Foxford, ignoring a call from one was probably punishable with a lifetime ban from the country club. He grabbed the phone from the nightstand and jabbed his finger at it.

"Yes, Mother?"

The woman's cut-glass accent and lack of a volume control meant I heard every word.

"I'm just going to drop Tia off with you. We'll be there in ten minutes."

Luke stiffened. "You can't. I've got company."

"I'm sure she'll be no trouble, darling."

"She's sixteen. Why can't she stay home on her own?"

"The gardener caught her smoking cigarettes behind the pool house again, so she's grounded. I don't trust her to stay put, so she'll have to spend the evening with you."

"She can't come here."

"Don't be silly. She's your sister. Ooh, got to go; Mabel's calling me. It'll be about bridge night."

She hung up, and Luke threw his phone down on the bed.

"I take it you heard all that?"

"I could hardly avoid it. Shall I go out for a while? It would be the easiest thing for everyone."

"No." Luke's tone left no room for argument. "I'm hoping you'll stick around, so Tia will have to get used to you."

Hmm, so he wanted to spend more than a few nights with me? A part of me was happy to hear that. For the first time in weeks, a chink of light shone through the fog in my mind. Today, the simple act of decorating a tree had been fun because he did it with me.

That—dare I say it—happiness competed with worry. My increasing strength meant the journey home loomed on the horizon. I was starting to care for Luke, and if he felt the same way, he'd end up getting hurt when I left. There was also the small matter of having lied to him about my entire existence, but with Tia on the way, I pushed that out of my mind.

"I'd better put some clothes on." I rolled out of bed. "And find my riot shield."

Tia did indeed arrive in the promised ten minutes. By that time, I was in the kitchen, pulling out a casserole

Nora had left in the oven.

The demon child stomped into the kitchen and stopped short when she saw me there. Even with my back turned, I knew that, because her footsteps came to an abrupt halt and it felt like all the air had been sucked out of the room.

"What's *she* doing here?" Tia's voice ended on a shriek.

"She's staying with me," Luke said. "Thanks to you, she doesn't have anywhere else to live."

Oh, the horror on her face as she realised the result of her actions was a joy to behold.

"You're dating her now?"

We hadn't exactly talked about that. We hadn't exactly talked much full stop. Sure, we'd slept together, but fucking and dating were two completely different kettles of fish. Luke looked at me, eyebrows raised. I shrugged.

"Yes," he said.

Well, that cleared that up, then.

"B-but...you can't!" spluttered Tia.

"Under whose rules?"

"She's just a stable girl. Mother will go mad."

"But she's not a stable girl anymore, is she? At the moment, she's a lady of leisure. Which is exactly what mother is, so she can hardly complain."

Tia had no reply for that. She stood open-mouthed, hands on her hips.

"Well, are you eating with us or not?" Luke asked, getting the cutlery out.

"I'm not sharing a table with *her*. Hell would have to freeze over first."

She looked so indignant at having to breathe the

same air as me, I stifled a laugh. That earned me a glare.

"Well," I said, looking at my watch. "The temperature's dropping, and the devil's wearing thermals."

"Fine. But I'm not speaking to you."

I set out an extra place, and she moved the utensils to the furthest end of the table. That suited me fine.

While Tia gave herself an aneurysm, I spooned the casserole onto plates. Luke even had a plate-warming drawer in his over-specced kitchen. For a moment I was impressed, but the chances were, I had one too. It wasn't as if I'd spent enough time in my own kitchen to check.

Tia ate in silence, staring daggers at me from across the table. It could have been worse—at least she'd stopped shrieking. I ignored her attitude and chatted to Luke about the ridiculousness of Christmas traditions. When we started discussing who on earth came up with the idea of stuffing bread up a turkey's backside, even Tia giggled. Then she remembered she hated me and went back to glowering instead.

After dinner, I left Luke to spend some brother-sister time with Tia. Judging by the shouting, it didn't go too well. Tension levels in the house rose, so I did the adult thing and hid upstairs with a glass of wine and Netflix. After their mother turned up to ferry Tia home again, Luke trudged into the bedroom, frowning. I reached out and smoothed the wrinkles on his forehead.

"You didn't deserve that."

He sighed. "I don't know what to do about her. I tried to discuss the smoking, and she went crazy again."

"Look on the bright side; at least it was only a cigarette."

His glare suggested I wasn't helping, so I tried again.

"I'm not sure what to say, other than she'll probably grow out of it."

"Did you ever smoke?"

"A long time ago."

"How old were you when you stopped?"

"Fifteen."

"Fifteen when you stopped?" His eyes bugged out. "How old were you when you started?"

"Twelve, I think." I shrugged. "Maybe eleven. I forget."

"You're kidding?"

"Told you I was a wild child."

"What did your parents say?"

"Not a lot." Nothing, in fact.

"What made you stop?"

"I met someone who showed me I was worth more."

"Who?"

"That's not important. Now, why don't I take your mind off things?"

Luke lay back on the bed, happy with the change of subject. Tia was quickly forgotten as we continued what we didn't get to finish earlier.

The next week passed peacefully enough. Luke had to go back into the office, of course, but he made an effort to come home on time each day.

"I should've started this delegation lark years ago,"

he told me on Tuesday evening after we'd done something on the pool table that may have involved balls but definitely wasn't pool. "Although my staff seem slightly disgruntled."

"They'll get used to it. Don't back down."

Don't back down. I used to live by that mantra, right until the moment I'd run to England. I needed to abide by my own rules.

"Not planning to. Not if it means I have more time for this." He flicked his tongue along my lips and I surrendered.

Maybe rules were meant to be broken.

While Luke worked, I took advantage of his gym. With that and the running I'd been doing, most of my strength had returned. The little potbelly I'd developed had shrunk away, and the outline of my muscles became clear again. At least my body had returned to its previous state—now only my head needed work.

Having no responsibilities and nothing pressing to do all day was a novelty at first, but I soon found mid-morning television didn't deliver.

"What's this?" Luke asked as I plonked his dinner on the table in front of him.

"It's supposed to be coq au vin."

Except I'd burned the chicken and drunk most of the wine. Despite Nora's efforts to teach me, I was a terrible cook.

"You don't have to do this, you know. Nora can make us dinner."

"I was bored, so I thought I'd experiment."

"I hate to tell you this, sweetheart, but it looks like a science project gone wrong."

Wasn't that the truth? How come I could make a bomb out of store-cupboard staples but not a meal?

"Sorry. I'll find something else to occupy my time. I suppose another job would be the sensible thing."

He reached over and squeezed my hand. "You don't need to work. I've got plenty of money."

That may have been the case, but it didn't mean I enjoyed spending it. I'd always prided myself on being self-sufficient. Sponging off a man didn't sit well with me.

On Thursday, Luke dropped me off in town, and I spent a day rounding up Christmas presents from the list he'd hastily scribbled over breakfast. Wrapping was a bitch, and I got tape stuck to everything. Who did this for fun? Knots were a specialty of mine, though, so I went to town with the curly ribbon, and by the time I'd finished, the parcels looked passable.

But I still had one gift left to buy. What should I get Luke?

According to Wikipedia, The Times Rich List reckoned he was worth sixty million pounds. *Glamour* magazine had him at a more conservative fifty million in their "UK's 50 most eligible bachelors" feature last year. I could hardly get him a packet of socks and a paperback, could I?

Inspiration hit when I was standing in the den. The skis hanging on the wall reminded me of Luke's past love of winter sports, and didn't he say he hadn't seen snow for ages? I found an indoor ski centre nearby and booked us a session.

Despite time ticking by slowly, I had little to complain about. Luke was good company, and we spent our evenings watching TV, talking, and fucking. Okay, mostly the latter if I was honest. By the end of the week, the lines on Luke's forehead were less pronounced, and my numbness had receded a little more. The only sore point was my continued refusal to sleep in Luke's bed at night.

"Stay?" he'd asked yesterday evening.

"I can't."

He turned his back on me and pulled the duvet up to his chin. "Fine."

I thumped the wall on my way back to the guest room. Why couldn't my subconscious behave? I longed to return to Luke's side, but I'd be risking his life if I did.

The incident with Nick happened almost a decade ago, but when I closed my eyes, I still saw his bruised and bloodied face as if it were yesterday. One touch, that's all it had taken. He'd tried to comfort me as I writhed in the throes of a nightmare, and I'd attacked him. It took two people to pull me off, but not before I'd broken his nose and three of his ribs. One of the people who'd dragged me away was my husband.

Embarrassing much? I'd never even contemplated sleeping in the same bed as a man since.

Other, more disturbing, episodes had followed, and it was more by luck than judgement that I hadn't damaged anyone else. My house had borne the brunt of my night-time rampages, and I didn't want Luke to be next.

Breakfast on Saturday started off frosty, but Luke thawed out over coffee.

"Are you taking Tia to the stables today?" I asked.

"I'm due to pick her up in half an hour, but I can make an excuse if you want?"

"She hates me quite enough already without me monopolising your time."

"I could drop her off and come back. It's not as if she talks to me while we're there."

"She won't see it like that, trust me."

Trust me? I almost choked on those words. I barely trusted myself anymore.

Luke called me mid-morning from his hiding place in the feed room. "George's hired a replacement girl already."

"At least he hasn't shafted Susie and Hayley. What's she called?"

"No idea. I said hello, and she flipped out. Just kept staring at me. I thought she might be having one of those petit-mal seizures, and I nearly called an ambulance, but then Susie walked past and told her to snap out of it."

"Try looking less hot. That would solve the problem."

"You think I'm hot?"

"I wouldn't have sucked your cock last night if I didn't."

It was his turn to lose his train of thought. When he located his vocabulary again, he asked if I fancied going to the cinema when he got back.

"Why not? We can make out in the back row like teenagers."

Not that I'd ever done that—I'd be making up for lost time.

"It's a date."

Except that plan got scuppered when the first fat flakes of snow fell after lunch. When it snowed in the US, people hauled their big-ass trucks out of the garage, stuck snow chains on, and kept driving. In the UK, panic set in and the whole country ground to a halt.

Not wanting to break that great British tradition, we stayed at home. I started to make lunch, but Luke's appetite was for something else, and he led me upstairs.

"You can finish lunch after," he said.

"If I can still walk to the kitchen after, you don't deserve lunch."

"Challenge accepted."

Luke aced it, and it was him who ended up making the sandwiches. We ate cuddled in bed, watching the snow fall over his garden through the floor-to-ceiling windows. By mid-afternoon, a thick blanket of white covered the ground. On a hill in the distance, kids dragged their sleds up to the top before riding down, arms and legs flying.

I envied their freedom. I'd been trapped my whole life—first by circumstances, then finances, and finally by work. Living with Luke, my responsibilities got shoved on the back burner, and I had no commitments, just the company of a wonderful man who cared about me. Or at least, cared about the person he thought I was. But I was still shackled to my mind.

What direction would my life have taken if I'd been born into a family with loving parents, a brother or sister, and maybe a dog, instead of having a mother who treated me like the spawn of Satan and spent her days pretending I didn't exist? I'd never have met my husband, the man who taught me life was about living rather than merely existing, but I might have avoided a world of heartache.

What would have happened if I hadn't made the snap decision fourteen years ago to follow him to the other side of the world so he could turn me into what I was today? Would I be with a man like Luke, truly happy and content? Or lying in the gutter somewhere? I'd never know. I could only make the best of what I had now.

And as the snowstorm eased, I had a sudden urge to live my failed childhood. I got up and tugged my clothes on.

"Where are you going?" Luke asked.

"Come on, get dressed. Wear something warm!" I yelled over my shoulder as I ran towards the stairs.

Luke caught up with me as I got outside.

"What are you doing?"

"I want to build a snowman."

"A snowman? How old are you?"

Shit—for a minute, I couldn't remember. There was only one person in the world apart from me who knew my real birthday, so I just went off whatever passport I happened to be using.

"Uh, thirty-two. But I've never built a snowman before, so I think I'm entitled to have a go."

"Never? What sort of childhood did you have?"

"Not a great one," I admitted.

Luke sensed my change in mood and turned serious. "Do you want to talk about it?"

"No. I don't even want to think about it. If I could erase it from my memory, I would. Can we just build the damn snowman?"

Luke wrapped me up in his arms and kissed my hair. "Sure."

Like I said, he was sweet.

By the time daylight dimmed, we had a rather lopsided snowman sitting in the middle of Luke's lawn, with a carrot for a nose and eyes made from dates. A cashmere scarf from Luke's wardrobe completed the ensemble.

"His head's wonky," Luke said.

He was right. The snowman was looking down at his feet. At least, he would have been if he had any.

"Maybe he's texting?" I suggested.

We gave him a pair of twiggy arms and stuck Luke's phone to them. Yeah, that worked. I took a few photos of the snowman then aimed the lens at Luke. This was one of those rare days I wanted to remember. I hated cameras, but I put up with it when Luke reclaimed his phone and made me pose—today I was determined to have fun.

Snow crunched underfoot as we walked back to the house. I couldn't resist—I bent and scooped up a handful, packed it into a ball, and launched it at Luke. He swiftly retaliated, and any pretence at being grown-ups stopped as we slung snowballs at each other across the garden.

"Where the hell did you learn to throw? Did you play baseball or something?" Luke yelled at me, ducking.

"No, just beginner's luck."

Beginner's luck my arse. It was incredibly useful to know I could throw an object and have it land bang on target, so I'd practised. A lot. I had a party trick with knives and fruit, but it wasn't appropriate to show that one to Luke.

Eventually, he gave up trying to hit me and braved the barrage to stuff snow down my jacket.

"Hey, that's freezing!"

I didn't want to fight back, so I tripped him instead. We both ended up lying in the snow, breathing hard. I rolled over and made a snow angel, flapping my arms and legs to form the wings and dress. Being a child was fun. When we started to get cold, we retired to the den and Luke lit a wood fire. The flames were soon leaping into the chimney.

"You have any marshmallows?" I asked.

Turned out he had a sweet tooth too, so I taught him how to make s'mores.

"Why haven't these caught on in England yet?" he asked with his mouth full.

I shrugged. "Who knows? I'll take these over pie and mash any day."

He squashed closer. "And I'll take you. What do you say we try out this rug?"

Making snacks in front of the fire turned into something rather more interesting as Luke discovered a new use for melted chocolate. The perfect end to a perfect afternoon.

But as with most things in my life, the perfection wasn't to last.

CHAPTER 21

AT 7 A.M. on Sunday, Luke's phone rang with the theme song from *The Office*. At least it wasn't his mother again.

"Some bastard's attacking our biggest client's servers," he said when he hung up. "I can't leave this to anyone else."

"You want me to make you a coffee before you go?"

He already had his trousers on. "No time." He leaned over and gave me a quick kiss. "I'll be back as soon as I can."

Noon arrived, and I cobbled together a sandwich. Luke rang while I was eating.

"Can you do me a favour?"

"Sure."

"I need a file off the memory stick in my desk drawer. Could you email it?"

"No problem."

He explained what he wanted, and my breath hitched when he told me his laptop password. My name, and the date we'd met. Fuck. I was going to end up hurting him, wasn't I? Every time the sun set, my return to Virginia came closer. I wasn't strong enough to leave yet, but that day would soon arrive.

Back in the kitchen, I opened the internet browser on my phone and googled my company. How were things back home? Ticking along, it seemed. Unlike Luke, I'd been perfecting the art of delegation for years. We'd won several large contracts, and the Japanese office, a pet project of mine, had finally opened. A few more searches revealed no drama in the Richmond area. My husband's killer had held up his end of the bargain, at least for the moment. My friends were safe.

And what about me? I typed my real name into the search box. I didn't expect much—my tech guys and legal team were good at shutting down any mention of me—but it never hurt to check.

Coverage was limited to three small stories in Virginia newspapers. One speculated I'd fled to Panama. Yeah, I wished. The weather would certainly be better. Another informed me the police had no other leads in my husband's murder—good to see my tax dollars hard at work. The third article advertised an upcoming ball being held in Richmond to support a homeless charity. It listed all the projects they'd run with the $100,000 donation I'd made last year. That cause was close to my heart, and I smiled as I read.

My final search was for Luke again. Rumours abounded that he was dating Mitzi, a reality TV star famed for having her breast implant surgery live on television. Really? I happened to know he preferred the real thing. I'd got halfway through reading how Mitzi was considering an increase in her cup size when my phone rang.

This time, Luke sounded frantic. "George just called. Tia went out riding, and Gameela's turned up back at the farm on her own."

"Has anyone heard from Tia?"

"No, and she left her phone on the locker outside

Gameela's stable. They've got people out searching, but there's no sign of her yet."

A teenage girl who wasn't surgically attached to her phone? Great.

"I'll go down to the farm and help look—I'll call as soon as I arrive."

"I'm getting in the car right now—should take me forty-five minutes to get there."

The snow was still thick, so I yanked on a pair of sturdy boots. Where was the first aid kit? Ah yes, in the cupboard by the back door. I shoved that in a rucksack along with a bottle of water.

Out in the garage, I eyed Luke's Porsche SUV with regret before hopping on his mountain bike. I'd told him I didn't drive, so I could hardly borrow his car. Luckily, the lanes had been gritted, and I made it to the stables in ten minutes on two wheels.

Chaos reigned.

George stood in the middle of the car park, flapping his arms. His tomato-coloured face made me fear for his health. Arabella perched on the mounting block crying, and several girls were riding down the drive. Marianne helped a woman in an expensively cut coat to breathe into a paper bag. Luke's mother? I'd seen her drop Tia off once, and up close, I saw the similarities in their features.

I waved to get George's attention. "What's happening with Tia?"

"What are you doing here?"

"Answer the question, would you?"

He did a double take at my tone, but answered nonetheless. "She rode off and the horse came back on its own so she must have fallen off and we can't find her," he said, all in one breath.

Luke had told me that much already. "When did she leave?"

"I don't know. Arabella—when did Tia leave?"

"About eleven? Susie said it was when she went in for a tea break." She sobbed harder. "What if she's dead?"

Nothing like looking on the bright side, was there?

So, Tia had been out for two hours, but how far she'd got would depend on her speed and Gameela's sense of direction. How long had the horse taken to find her way home? I did a quick calculation and estimated we were looking at a six-mile search radius. A snowflake landed on my arm, and I glanced up. Clouds were gathering overhead. Great. Even if Tia wasn't injured, we had exposure to contend with.

"Where have people looked?" I asked.

George did the deer-in-headlights thing. "Some of the girls rode up the lane, and Mr. and Mrs. Jackson from next door went out on foot. At least, I think they've left—Mrs. Jackson said she had to find her hiking boots first."

My eyes started to roll all of their own accord, and I blinked to stop them. "Which way up the lane?"

He scratched his chin. "I'm almost sure they went left."

Well, wasn't this organisation at its best? A well-oiled machine. Tia would be a popsicle at this rate.

"Who's still here?"

"Arabella, Marianne, and Mrs. Halston-Cain."

And me.

"Right, you stay here in case Tia comes back. Her mother can stay with you—get her a cup of tea and try to keep her calm." I turned to Arabella and Marianne. "It won't be dark for a couple of hours—saddle up and head right up the lane. Look for any single sets of hoof prints, medium sized. Has anyone called the police?"

George shook his head.

I took a deep breath and gritted my teeth. "Well, could you please phone them?"

The sweetness in my voice was at odds with the acid building up in my stomach. George's colour had lightened by that point, which was a relief. I didn't have time to deal with him stroking out as well.

He bobbed his head up and down. "I'll do it right away."

Moving at a steady amble, he headed for his house —he must have been the only person left in the country who didn't own a cell phone.

Next, I called Luke and gave him an update, brief because he was driving. Fast. I could hear the roar of the engine. After quickly reminding him it wouldn't help if he ended up in a ditch, I went to join the hunt myself.

Gameela was back in her stable, head hanging low. A quick examination revealed cuts on her legs, and although none of them looked serious, she still needed a visit from the vet. Apart from the crusts of blood, she was clean—hardly surprising given the frozen ground. It was in her mane that I spotted the clue I was searching for. Twigs with tiny, spidery yellow flowers attached.

Witch hazel. A shrub with many medicinal uses and one of the few that flowered in winter. The plants weren't common in the wild, but I'd spotted a clump at the entrance to a thicket when I'd been out running. It lay about five miles away, if I remembered rightly.

But how could I get there?

The quickest way would be by horse, but only Tia's were in the barn. I hurried past the two invalids and eyed up Majesty. I'd never seen him ridden, but his reputation preceded him. Still, he couldn't be worse than Stan. Nothing could be worse than Stan. I painted the bottoms of his feet with hoof grease the way Dustin had taught me, an old trick to stop the snow balling up in them, then tacked him up and hopped on.

Luke drove into the yard as Majesty, thrilled to be out of his stable, had a bucking fit then stood up on his hind legs.

"Come on, you pig-headed bastard—that the best you can do?"

The look on Luke's face was priceless.

"I meant the horse, not you."

"I got that. Are you sure he's safe?"

His face suggested he thought Majesty should be shot at the first opportunity.

"I'll be fine."

With those words, Majesty decided that trying to unseat me wasted too much energy and did what he was told instead. We trotted up the lane, and as soon as I hit open fields, I urged him into a gallop. The world lay silent apart from the rhythmic beat of his hooves. While we flew over the white-blanketed landscape, snow crunching underfoot, all I could do was hope my hunch was correct. I didn't fancy Tia's chances out here after the sun dropped. That posh school she went to undoubtedly taught Latin and Shakespeare rather than survival training.

A couple of miles from the thicket, we crossed a

small ridge. On the other side, in an otherwise pristine layer of snow, I spotted a single set of hoof prints heading towards the thicket at a trot. Another set came back, much faster. Unless there was another nutter out galloping their horse in the snow, I was heading in the right direction. Thank fuck for that.

I went to call Luke, but the bloody signal had disappeared. Welcome to the world of mobile communications. The woods loomed closer as I carried on at a fast trot, only slowing as I ducked under the first boughs. The branches hung low, heavy with ice that twinkled in the last of the afternoon sun.

Hoof prints wound through the trees, deeper and deeper into the frosty wonderland. Majesty danced on the spot as a rabbit shot out of the bushes in front of him. At least somebody was having fun.

For some reason, an old children's song popped into my head. "The Teddy Bears' Picnic."

If you go down to the woods today, you're sure of a big surprise...

I never had been keen on surprises. What was I going to find?

Chapter 22

"SHH, MAJESTY. IT'S okay."

The horse spooked at a rabbit as I peered into the undergrowth beside the path. Light was fading, and the woods were gloomy as hell. Should I get a torch out? No, I'd ruin my vision. We'd been in the woods for ten minutes when I heard crying and knew we were in the right place. Up ahead, Tia hobbled along the path, tears streaming down both cheeks.

Was she okay? Not quite—she was dragging her left foot and holding her right arm crossed over her chest. Thank goodness I'd brought the first aid kit.

"Tia?"

She looked up, her face a juxtaposition of relief and peevishness. Should she be grateful someone had come to help or pissed off because it was me?

Eventually, she settled for whining.

"Why did you take so long? I've been out here for ages, and I can hardly move. And I'm freezing."

I hopped off Majesty, who'd behaved impeccably after his initial high jinks, and tied his reins to a nearby tree. He snuffled for grass, then gave up and pawed the ground.

Taking Tia's good arm, I steered her over to a nearby log and sat her down.

"What hurts? Your arm and leg, obviously, but

anywhere else?"

"N-n-no, just my arm and my ankle."

"What happened?"

"Gameela spooked, and I came off and landed on my side. I wrenched my ankle in the stirrup as I fell."

I knelt and studied her. No, I didn't like her colour, or rather, the lack of it.

"Did you hit your head?"

"I don't think so."

"Okay, I'm going to have a look. Tell me if the pain gets worse."

"Can't you just call an ambulance?" she demanded, some of her attitude coming back. "One of those helicopter ones."

"We're half a mile into dense woodland. Where exactly do you think it would land?"

"Fine. A normal ambulance, then."

"Which would have to drive a couple of miles up a rutted track in the snow. Not gonna happen, sweetheart. Plus, I lost phone signal at the start of that track, so I can't call anyone from here, anyway."

"You're not being very sympathetic."

"Nope. Sympathy isn't one of my strong points. Getting things done is."

"So what are you going to do? It'll be dark soon, and there are wild animals out here."

"The worst thing in these woods is a fox, and I can guarantee it'll be more scared of you than you are of it. Now, let me look at your arm and ankle."

Tia finally shut up and let me examine her. She shrieked when I touched her ankle, making Majesty leap in alarm, but at least she didn't get too hysterical.

"Your arm's broken. It'll need to be pinned. I think

your ankle's just badly sprained."

"So now what?"

"I'm going to strap up your arm then you can sit on Majesty while I lead you back to civilisation."

"I'm not riding that evil horse! He bucks and rears."

"Yes, I found that out first-hand, but he's tired now. He'll be fine if I lead him." I gave her a saccharine smile. "Or you can wait here while I go for help."

"Wait here? On my own?"

"There's a few spiders around. Maybe some rats. They'll keep you company."

"You'll have to help me get on."

I found a straight branch to act as a splint, then bandaged Tia's arm and ankle so they were supported. I gave her my jacket, and with the buttons done halfway up, it formed a makeshift sling. A handy log provided a step for her to get on board, I handed her the phone to watch for a signal, and we set off down the hill. Majesty pricked his ears forward, eager to be heading home. I knew that feeling. It was colder than a witch's tit out here.

We'd got halfway along the track when Tia broke the silence. Good things never lasted.

"Why did you come?"

"What do you mean?"

"To find me. Why did you come to find me? I mean, you hate me, so why are you helping?"

"I don't hate you." It took a lot for me to hate someone, and usually resulted in the loss of body parts. "I care about your brother, and he's worried sick about you."

"But you *must* hate me." Her voice dropped to a whisper. "I've been really nasty to you."

"Yes, you have, and I'll confess you didn't exactly endear yourself when you got me sacked, but I can understand why you did it. You were looking out for your brother, in your own way, and you're scared of losing him."

My words must have hit close to home because a tear rolled from her eye.

"He's all I've got. Apart from Mother, who ignores me, and Arabella, who only likes me when I'm wearing the right clothes and the latest accessories."

"How about other friends at school?"

"Mother made me go to private school. It's two towns away, and nobody except Arabella lives near here. They all hang out together after school, but I have to come home."

"Can't you go out with them in the evenings sometimes?"

"Mother won't let me. She won't even let me get the bus to school. She sends me and Arabella in a car every day."

"I'm sure she cares about you."

Except I wasn't. Not after Luke's comments on the subject.

"But she's never there! She's always at bridge or a supper party or the theatre or the tennis club. I tried sneaking out, but Mrs. Squires told on me, and I got grounded again."

"Who's Mrs. Squires?"

"Part housekeeper, part dragon."

"Have you told all this to Luke?"

"I tried, but he's always busy with work. He said I should find a hobby, that he'd pay for me to take classes in something, but Mother vetoed everything I suggested. Painting's too messy, apparently."

Despite our earlier run-ins, I kind of felt sorry for Tia. Somewhere under her spoilt, bitchy exterior was an insecure kid who just wanted attention. I'd been there myself.

"Do you want me to speak to Luke? See if he can have a word with your mother?"

"Would you?" She sniffled and wiped her nose on her sleeve. "He'll listen if you say it."

Tia went quiet, giving me space to think. It was hard to believe she was the same person as the brat who destroyed Luke's house. If I'd realised breaking an arm could have such a dramatic effect on somebody's personality, I'd have done it more often.

Calm down, I was only joking.

"A signal! There's a signal!" Tia shouted.

Oh, happy days. I took the phone back and called Luke.

"I've got her."

"You're serious?"

"Unfortunately."

"Thank fuck for that. Is she okay?"

"No damage that can't be fixed. We'll need an ambulance to come and meet us, though."

"How bad is it?" His voice cracked. Yeah, he really did care.

"A broken arm and an injured ankle. I don't think the ankle's broken, but she'll need an X-ray to make sure. The arm's likely to need pinning."

"I'll arrange it. The police have just turned up, so they can help. Where are you?"

"Good question." I turned to Tia. "Do you know the name of that rise over there?" I pointed ahead.

"Christmas Hill."

Well, at least we were in keeping with the festive season. "We're heading for Christmas Hill. Tia's on horseback, so we can make it to the road. I remember crossing a lane next to a cottage with a caved-in roof—ring any bells?"

"Yes, I know where that is. I used to mess around in it when I was a kid. I'll meet you there with an ambulance. The roads should be passable up to that point."

Tia had turned ashen by the time we made it to the cottage. Shock was setting in now the adrenaline had worn off, but thankfully, the ambulance was waiting next to Luke's car. He leapt out when he saw us coming.

"You're going straight to hospital," he told Tia. "The doctors are waiting. Where does it hurt? Just your arm and your ankle?"

Two medics helped her from the horse as I flexed my frozen fingers to get some feeling back into them.

"Everything hurts," she mumbled.

He leaned over and squeezed her good hand. "You'll be okay."

While Luke went to the hospital with Tia, I rode Majesty back to Hazelwood Farm by the light of the moon. Stars twinkled overhead in the clear sky, and with the light reflecting off the snow, it never truly got dark. So peaceful, so serene. As Majesty strode forward, ears pricked, I was reminded that despite the evil in the world, it could still be a beautiful place.

The vet waved from his Land Rover as we walked up the drive, and back in the barn, I was relieved to see Gameela happily munching her hay with her legs bandaged.

Majesty nosed at my pockets as I put him to bed, and I pinched a handful of Marianne's carrots.

"Good boy. You mostly redeemed yourself today."

His biggest crimes were being smart and being bored. Somebody needed to take him for the long rides he enjoyed and tire him out, then he'd behave better.

Now, where was Luke? He didn't answer when I called, so I cycled home, dodging cars in the dark. Made a change from bullets. Luke wasn't there, so despite my hatred of hospitals, I hopped in a cab to go and lend some moral support.

As the car got closer, the knot in my stomach grew tighter. Over the years, I'd spent too many hours in the emergency room, most of them because someone was hurt or dying, and I couldn't stand the feeling of helplessness that came with waiting. Sitting around made me feel useless. I much preferred to be out doing something constructive. Or destructive, depending on which was more appropriate.

I found Luke slumped in a chair, staring into space, and I perched on the edge of an adjacent seat. The black circles under his eyes showed how much the day had taken out of him.

"How's Tia?"

"In surgery. She's got a displaced fracture, and the doctor wanted to repair it straight away."

"At least then she can start recovering."

He rubbed his temples and sighed. "Mother lost the plot, and they had to sedate her."

"Do you want to go and sit with her? I can stay here and wait for news on Tia."

"Sitting with my mother is the last thing I want to do. Besides, she's still sleeping."

"That's probably for the best."

He nodded. "The world always has to revolve around her, and I'm tired of it. She behaves like this all the time."

"It feels wrong, doesn't it? That you have to be the adult while she acts like a child?"

"Between her and Tia... Everyone thinks I've got this perfect life, and yes, I've got money. But the old saying's true. It doesn't buy happiness."

Yeah. It bought big houses and cars and yachts and diamonds and even a bloody jet, but without my husband by my side, I might as well live in a shack.

"Ain't that the truth."

Luke slumped down in his chair, while I stared at the wall opposite and got lost in my thoughts.

The last time I sat in a hospital like this was on *that* day. My husband had died at the scene, but the medical staff were trying to save one of the men who'd killed him.

Why was I there? Why did I want that fucker to live?

Firstly, because he was hired help—I'd worked that much out—and I wanted to ask him nicely who'd paid for the hit. Secondly, because I wanted the pleasure of peeling his skin off, piece by tiny piece.

This isn't happening. This isn't happening. I'd repeated the mantra over and over, wedged between Nick and Dan, until the doctor came out in bloodstained scrubs to tell us the murdering scum hadn't made it.

But it was better news for Tia. Three hours later, a smiling nurse told us we could go in and sit with her. Hooray.

"You want to go in alone?" I asked Luke.

An appropriate answer would have been "yes," but he pulled me into the room alongside him. At least Tia was still unconscious. I much preferred her that way.

But the anaesthetic soon wore off, and I mustered up a smile.

"Welcome back," Luke said, stroking her hair back from her forehead.

"My tongue feels too big for my mouth," she mumbled.

"Do you need more painkillers?"

She shook her head. I suspected they'd put something good in her drip.

A commotion in the corridor made us all turn our heads, and Tia's mother swept in to join the party, followed by a pissed-looking doctor.

"Tia, you're awake! I was so worried, darling, but the doctor says you're going to be just fine."

Tia mumbled something that sounded suspiciously like, "No thanks to you," but Mrs. Halston-Cain had already turned to the doctor.

"When can she come home?"

The doctor scanned Tia's chart, still looking far from happy about her mother's presence.

"Assuming there are no setbacks overnight, she can be discharged tomorrow. I'll check on her in the morning."

"That's wonderful, isn't it darling? I have tennis first thing and the spa in the afternoon, but I'll make sure Mrs. Squires is at home to look after you."

Tia took on the same air of resignation as Luke had earlier when talking about his mother. "Okay. Whatever."

Now Mrs. H knew Tia wasn't at death's door, she lost interest and looked at her watch.

"I'm late for the rotary club meeting, darling." She air-kissed Tia on both cheeks, continental-style. "I'll see you at supper tomorrow."

While the members of the Lower Foxford Rotary Club were no doubt wonderful people, I found it somewhat tragic that she considered them more important than her own child. The bitch was so wrapped up in herself, she'd barely acknowledged Luke either. Had she even noticed I was in the room? I doubted it.

No wonder Tia was lonely.

And that loneliness was something I understood. The donor of my own chromosomes had been no better.

"How are you feeling?" Luke asked his sister, and I knew he was asking about their mother's visit rather than Tia's arm.

"Fine."

"That's good." Didn't he understand that when a woman said she was fine, she meant the complete opposite? "Shall I bring you a magazine or something?"

Oh, for goodness' sake... I rolled my eyes at him.

"How are you really feeling?" I asked Tia.

She burst into tears. Shit.

Between sobs, her true feelings came pouring out. "I hate everything. I hate being at home, and now I'm stuck there. I'd rather be at school, and now I can't go.

Mother won't be around; it'll just be me and the nosey old cow, and I'm not allowed to do anything. I can't even make myself a snack without her moaning about the mess, and if I try to watch a movie, she says it's unsuitable or too loud. And I've got no privacy. She pokes through all my stuff." Tia let out a loud sniffle. "I want to go to boarding school, but Mother won't let me. I wish I was dead."

"Uh…" Luke looked to me for help as Tia rolled over and carried on crying. "What the hell do I do? Normally if a woman cries, I buy her stuff, but I'm not sure that'll work?"

Good grief. "Could you go and find some tissues?"

Luke shot from the room, no doubt relieved to have a task that didn't involve comforting an upset teenager. After he'd left, I sat on the edge of the bed.

"Are you still speaking to me, Portia, or am I back to being the devil incarnate?"

"I don't hate you anymore. And call me Tia. All my friends do."

Well, that was progress. "Let's try and fix this. In an ideal world, what would make you happy?"

A minute passed. Then another. I stayed quiet and gave her space to think.

"I want a family that cares about me and some friends other than Arabella. I want to live in my own house without feeling I'm always in the way, and I want to be allowed out. I'm sick of being treated like a kid. Like, I'm sixteen now."

Despite the differences in our upbringings, we'd both had shitty childhoods. Perhaps that's why I felt compelled to make the offer I did.

"If Luke agrees, how would you like to stay with us

for a while? I'm around all day, so I could help with the things you can't manage with your arm."

"Do you really mean that?"

"I wouldn't have suggested it otherwise."

A pause. "I think I'd like that."

When I broached the subject with Luke in the corridor a few minutes later, he glanced up at the sign for the psych unit.

"Did you take a wrong turn?"

"No."

"But why would you want to help her after the way she's treated you?"

"Because somebody has to, and your mother isn't up to the job."

I hoped Luke wouldn't take offence, but I couldn't bite my tongue.

No worries there. "It's hard to imagine how she could be worse."

Oh, I could offer a couple of suggestions.

"I didn't realise things had got so bad for Tia," he continued. "I've spent too much time working. I'm a pretty second-rate brother, aren't I?"

"You've done your best. It's not like you asked to run the company at such a young age. You supported your family financially, but now Tia needs a different kind of help."

"I'll agree to her staying, but it's you who'll be with her all day. How do you feel about it?"

"I think we have to try."

He wrapped his arms around me, pulled me close, and kissed me chastely on the lips.

"In that case, you'll need to learn to fuck quietly. Or else I'll have to gag you."

"Ooh, kinky. Deal."

The following morning, Luke hammered on my door while it was still dark. Not that I was asleep. I'd been standing at the window for an hour, staring at the stars. Somewhere on the other side of the world, my friends were lying under those same stars, and that thought made me feel a little less lonely.

What did Luke want? He never normally got up this early.

"Is something wrong?"

"Two things, actually." He slid an arm around my waist and pulled me towards him. "Firstly, my sister's moving in and that's going to put a dent in my plans to christen every room in this house."

"And the second thing?"

"You're wearing too many clothes."

Okay, I liked this kind of emergency.

"What are you planning to do about it?"

He leaned into me, running his tongue along the outside edge of my ear, then murmured, "I'm going to peel off this T-shirt you stole from my wardrobe, then I'm going to sit you on the dining table so I can eat you for breakfast."

Funny how a few simple words could make my pulse race faster than a wild sprint from a gun-wielding terrorist, wasn't it? Even so, I couldn't help teasing.

"But I haven't had my coffee yet."

"You can drink the coffee while I fuck you over the kitchen counter."

"Fair enough. And then?"

"The lounge. The gym. Maybe we can screw in my car like a couple of horny teenagers?"

Heat crackled in the air as he brushed his lips against mine, and as his kisses became more intense, he gave up on the idea of peeling and tore his T-shirt clean in two. Luckily, he'd turned up in his boxer shorts so I didn't have to ruin any more clothing, just push them down his legs until his cock sprang free, hot and hard and heavy.

Did I stroke? Lick? Suck? As heat coursed through my veins, it felt like Christmas had come early. Or was that me? Because as I dropped to my knees and tasted Luke, an exquisite tension wound tighter and tighter in my core. I slid one hand between my legs to relieve the ache, but he tsk-tsk-tsked at me.

"That's my job, sweetheart."

I ignored him, but he stepped back, pulling me to my feet as he did so.

"You don't like doing what you're told, do you?"

So he'd noticed? "Not really."

That earned me a slap on the arse, and I bit his shoulder to keep from laughing because he was still so damn polite. That wouldn't even leave a handprint, let alone a bruise.

"Is that the best you can do, Mr. Cain?"

He squeezed one breast then lifted me up against the wall. His cock notched at my entrance, and he grinned as he lowered me down on top of it, deeper, deeper, then thrust hard as he sucked my lip.

"With you, I'm always on the verge of losing control. But you're this...this delicate flower and I don't want to break you."

Delicate? Fucking delicate? Wow. I was even better

at pretending than I thought.

"You won't break me. I'm tougher than I look."

He feathered kisses along my jaw then hoisted me up further, one hand under each knee. I wrapped my legs around his waist, holding myself in place as a delicious burn started in my pussy.

"Are you sure?" he asked.

"I'm more of a diamond than a flower."

Multi-faceted and difficult to scratch through the surface. But Luke didn't understand that. Only one man ever would.

Instead, Luke tangled his hands in my hair as he surged into me, bringing us closer to what we both needed at that moment in time.

For me, a distraction.

For him? Something more.

CHAPTER 23

"SLOWLY, TIA."

LUKE helped her into the back seat of the SUV he rarely drove while I stuffed her bag of medication into the footwell on the other side. The doctor had prescribed so many pills Tia would rattle if she jumped up and down, and she'd been discharged with a long list of dos and don'ts. No horse riding for at least six months.

On the way home, we stopped off at Woodley Hall, the house Luke grew up in and where Tia still lived with their mother. The country pile screamed old money.

"Nice," I said as we turned into the drive.

"It is now. It was in an awful state when our father died," Luke said. "We almost lost it after he ran out of money. I'm sure that's what caused his heart attack."

Tia gasped from the behind me. "We nearly lost our home?"

Luke nodded.

"I didn't know that."

"Well, you do now."

Luke had tried to shield her as she grew up, convinced he was doing the right thing. I wasn't so sure —the world might be full of shit, but living in a bubble was no better.

"I always knew he was an arsehole," Tia muttered.

"Tia, don't call him that. He was still our father."

"Some father. Did you know he cheated on Mum with the girl from the florist?"

Luke slammed the brakes on. "He what? What makes you think that?"

"Because I saw them when I was little. I was supposed to be asleep, but I woke up and saw them in one of the spare bedrooms, doing..." She closed her eyes and shuddered. "It."

"Fucking arsehole." Luke walloped his palm against the dashboard. "Shit."

Wow. This family was almost as dysfunctional as my own.

Luke's mother was reading a novel in the lounge when we arrived. When he'd called earlier to tell her Tia would be staying with us for a while, the news was met with a vague comment of, "I hope you both have a good time, darling," and that was that, almost as if Tia was popping over for a brief visit rather than moving out for weeks.

Even now, Mrs. Halston-Cain made the effort of raising her eyes from the book seem like a chore. When she saw me standing behind Luke, a slight look of puzzlement came over her face. I say slight because most of her facial features had been frozen in place by Botox.

"Who are you? Do I know you?"

"I'm Ashlyn. You saw me yesterday at the hospital." And ignored me completely.

"Ash is my girlfriend," Luke said.

"Oh. What happened to Caroline?"

"I broke up with Caroline three months ago."

"Such a shame. Caroline was a lovely girl. It would have been a wonderful family for you to marry into, what with her father being a banker and her mother being such an active member of the hospital fundraising committee. Girls like Caroline don't grow on trees, you know. Are you sure there's no chance of you getting back together?"

Hey, don't mind me, lady. I'm only standing right next to your son.

"Mother! Show some tact and don't be so rude to Ash."

"Sorry, darling," she said, when in reality she was anything but. "So, Ashlyn, what do your parents do?"

"My dad's an accountant, and my mum's a teacher."

Nice, normal professions, I thought, but still her face fell. I was tempted to tell her the truth, that my mother was a drugged-out hooker and my father was a sperm donor, just to see her reaction. But I couldn't do that to Luke.

"Never mind, dear, I'm sure you'll find a nice man to marry one day, in spite of that." The words, "Just not my son," remained unspoken at the end of her sentence.

Her attitude didn't go unnoticed by Luke. "That's it. We're getting Tia's things, and we're leaving," he snapped.

Tia rolled her eyes at me and mouthed, "See."

Yes, I did indeed see.

When we arrived back home, Luke supported Tia while she hobbled up the steps into the house. Her ankle may not have been broken, but it was still the size of a grapefruit, and her newly pinned arm prevented her from using crutches. The hospital had given her a cane instead.

"It makes me feel a hundred years old," she said as she shuffled through the hallway.

"Better than hopping. Want me to get you a top hat and a pair of tap-dancing shoes to go with it?"

She glared at me, but this time she was smiling.

Luke got Tia settled on the sofa in the den while I carried her stuff upstairs. Six suitcases, three trips. How long did she plan on staying?

The following morning found me in the kitchen, eating breakfast with the newest addition to the household. I'd got pretty good at making egg white omelettes without too many burnt bits, but I couldn't help wishing I had the bowl of Lucky Charms Tia was snarfing down with her good arm. In the background, the TV played one advert after another for all things festive. The Christmas season now started in September and ran until Easter took over on the first of January.

"What are you and my brother doing at Christmas?" Tia asked.

"Luke's made dinner reservations for the pair of us at a restaurant in town. Have you got plans with your mother, or do you want me to see if they've got space for one more?"

"Mother has plans, but I'm not part of them. I never am. She said Mrs. Squires would make me something nice for dinner, but she won't. She hates me."

"I doubt she hates you."

"For Christmas dinner last year, she gave me chicken nuggets and microwave chips."

"Okay, I'll admit it doesn't sound like she went all out."

Tia dropped her spoon into the bowl. "She's rubbish at cooking, she doesn't clean properly, and she gets in everyone's business. She's been our housekeeper since Dad was alive, and I'm sure she's only around because she has too much dirt on Mother to be fired."

"So you want to come with us to the restaurant, then?"

"Yes, please."

I sent Luke a text asking him to change the booking, and a few minutes later, he called me back.

"The restaurant's full. The manager said there's no way they can accommodate an extra person."

"Did you tell them we wouldn't need a bigger table? We can all squash onto ours."

"I tried that, but no go."

"Shit. Tia's dreading Christmas Day with Mrs. Squires."

"I can understand that—Mrs. Squires makes Ilse Koch look like she was just a bit misunderstood."

"If she's that bad, we can't leave Tia on her own. Is there another restaurant we could try?"

"I doubt we'd get a table at this short notice. How about we stay home?"

How about we dish up cardboard with a side of charcoal? Because that was how bad my version of a roast dinner would be.

"Nora's off, and you realise my culinary skills are limited?"

"Doesn't matter. I'm not fussy. Could you pick up some pre-prepared meals and bung them in the oven? And maybe something for dessert?"

Okay, that sounded doable. "I can probably manage that."

Oh, what I would have given to be able to call Bradley at that moment. He'd have rustled up a four-course dinner and a couple of waiters to serve it without batting an eyelid. And knowing Bradley, probably a band and some dancing girls as well.

My mind wandered back to the year he'd attempted to recreate the "Twelve days of Christmas" out of the well-known carol. The five gold rings were all right, but let me tell you, swans are not as peaceful and serene as they look.

"Bradley, what were you thinking?" I'd asked.

"I was thinking they'd stay in the swimming pool where I put them."

Mack wandered past, looking at her phone. "According to Wikipedia, swans pair for life. That's so romantic."

Deep breaths. "And we've got seven? What's the spare one gonna do? Have a three-way?"

"They can fight to the death in territorial disputes."

Marvellous. A bloodbath for Christmas. "Will you put the phone down and help us look? Does anybody know where they went?"

Bradley held up his thumb, complete with a nasty red welt. "One of them pecked me."

My husband gave Bradley a death stare. "Somebody get me a gun. We can have them for lunch."

Bradley's face turned the colour of the swan feathers stuck all over his sweater. "No bullet holes in the walls! I've just redecorated."

Half an hour later, I'd rugby tackled the last bird in an upstairs hallway and gone to take a well-deserved shower. Five of the birds got relocated, and the last pair still lived on the lake out back.

Perhaps Christmas at Luke's wouldn't be so bad after all. I broke the news about us cooking to Tia, and she cheered up a bit.

"I'd better go to the supermarket, then," I said.

While I lived at Hazelwood Farm, I'd got by with provisions from the local shop, but they didn't have much of a selection.

"Can I come? I never get out much, and my ankle feels much better today."

"Sure, why not?" That way, she could pick out her own ready-meal. "I'll call a cab."

"No need. Mother's driver can take us. She's hosting some boozy lunch at home today, so it's not as if she'll need him."

"Sounds like a plan."

I'd never had to do my own shopping—Toby decided what I should eat, and my housekeeper went out and bought it—so the whole experience was a novelty. And then somehow, on the drive into town, "we'll just pick up a lasagne or something and maybe a trifle," turned into "we might as well get a turkey and all the stuff that goes with it. I mean how hard can it be?"

The car park was packed, but the driver dropped us off right at the entrance to the store. Being rich did have some advantages.

"Call when you want to be picked up," he said. "I'll wait somewhere safer."

Safer? *Safer?* What did he mean, safer?

All became clear when we found a trolley and headed inside.

Over the previous decade, I'd probably visited every war zone in the world. I'd swum with the Navy SEALs and slogged through survival training in the jungles of Belize. I'd trekked across the Antarctic, and I'd completed the Marathon de Sables. But none of that compared with the horrors of Sainsbury's the day before Christmas.

To say it was chaos was like saying World War II was a minor disagreement. We could barely move for people, and not two minutes after we got inside a catfight broke out over a packet of Brussels sprouts. Seriously. I mean, who even liked those? At home, we had our own tradition. Toby bought the nasty little suckers, and after lunch, my friends and I lined them up out back and used them for target practice. First person to shoot three from a hundred yards won an Easter egg.

But today, I had no gun and no bullets and also no clue what I was doing.

"We could start with the turkey?" Tia suggested. "We'll need one of those for sure."

"Okay, poultry. Aisle three."

Except when we got there, we were greeted with a bewildering array of choice. Big turkeys, small turkeys, organic turkeys, RSPCA certified turkeys, turkey bits in packages.

I stared at the shelves. "Why the fuck are there so many different kinds? Oh shit, Luke'll kill me if he hears me swearing around you."

"I have no idea. And I won't tell him about the

swearing if you don't."

"Deal. How about this one? The turkeys on the label look happy."

And that seemed as good a reason as any to buy it.

"That'll do. Who wants to eat an unhappy turkey?"

Next up, we hit the produce section. Recalling Toby's insistence that I should eat variety, I tossed a vegetable of every colour into the trolley. I had no idea how to cook most of them, but I could work that out later. What was a Romanesco cauliflower? Was it supposed to be green like that?

"What do you th— Hey!" I hauled Tia out of the path of a speeding trolley pushed by a woman who could barely see over the handle. "Watch it."

She gave me a barely apologetic shrug. "It's every woman for herself."

Tia clutched at a shelf for support. "I think I twisted my ankle."

"Do you want to sit down? I'll find somewhere."

"I'm not abandoning you in this mayhem."

Hmm... "Why don't you sit in the trolley? It's big enough."

"Is that allowed?"

"Do I look like I give a shit?"

Her giggles bubbled over. "Okay."

With me lifting, Tia scrambling, and a bit of assistance from a handily placed vegetable rack, she ended up in the trolley with her leg stuck awkwardly over the top as I steered towards the dairy aisle. Now we were making faster progress. This was a good thing.

I added cream, milk, and ready-made custard to the trolley then leaned back against a shelf to take stock of the situation.

"What else do we need?" I asked.

Tia had made herself useful by googling the ingredients for a traditional Christmas dinner on her smartphone.

"I think we've got everything for the starter and main course, but we haven't got anything for dessert. Head for the bakery aisle."

I wheeled the trolley in that direction, dodging sprinting toddlers and lost husbands. A Christmas pudding whizzed past my ear, thrown by a red-faced man shouting at a harried-looking mother in an argument over the last carton of eggnog. I should have worn body armour. Honestly, this was worse than being on the frontline. At least the rules of engagement were easy to understand out there.

We finally made it to the checkout, and Tia passed the groceries up to me as I stacked them on the conveyor belt. The shop assistant gave her a dirty look for sitting in the trolley.

I pointed at her puffy ankle and cast. "She got wounded in a battle over cranberry sauce in aisle twelve."

The shop assistant looked confused, but a couple of people behind us sniggered. After a nasty moment with an unreadable barcode, we got everything bagged up and paid for, and I called for an evacuation.

The car sped towards us, the chauffeur wearing the grim look of a man under siege. I hauled Tia into the back seat, threw the bags in the boot, and leapt in after her.

"Drive! Drive!" Tia shouted, then collapsed into a fit of laughter as the man stepped on it.

At times in my life, I'd wondered whether it was

really necessary to employ someone to do my shopping for me. Never again. The first thing I'd do when I got back home was give my housekeeper a raise.

Luke arrived home that evening to find the kitchen looking like a crime scene. Tia and I had arranged stools in front of the oven so we could watch our cake cook through the glass window.

"I've just had mother on the phone," he said. "Apparently Mrs. Wilkinson from the bridge club saw someone looking remarkably like Tia riding around Sainsbury's in a trolley this afternoon, holding a turkey in her lap and wearing a Santa hat."

"Really?"

"Mother was horrified. Said it was most unladylike. You guys wouldn't happen to know anything about that, would you?"

"Nuh-uh," Tia said. "Of course not."

"Had Mrs. Wilkinson been drinking?" I asked, not daring to make eye contact with my partner in crime.

"Hmmph." Luke didn't look entirely convinced but chose to head upstairs.

"The Santa hat was a nice touch," I said. "What did you do with it, anyway?"

"I stuffed it in the cupboard above the blender."

The kitchen timer dinged. *Well, here we go. My first cake.* It was a team effort, really. Tia had read the instructions off the internet while I measured and mixed. I just hoped it turned out edible.

"Ready?"

I grabbed a tea towel, fetched the cake from the

oven, and put it on the counter.

"It looks cooked," Tia said, peering at it. "But why is one side lower than the other?"

"Buggered if I know." I gave it a prod. "Maybe that side got hotter or something."

"We could hide it with icing."

"Or cut a slice off. We'll manage something; don't worry."

With the hard part done, we'd be having a good Christmas, of that I was determined.

CHAPTER 24

THE NEXT MORNING—Christmas Day—I rolled out of bed at six and stretched. I needed to get up before Tia to give Luke the first part of his Christmas present, which was, well, me.

I checked my hair in the bathroom mirror and brushed my teeth, then wrapped myself up in a red satin ribbon, centring the bow over my breasts. A pair of stilettos and the Santa hat I'd retrieved from the kitchen cupboard completed the ensemble. Just in case Tia rose early, I slipped into the short silk robe Luke had bought me last week. Running into his sister almost naked wouldn't be a great start to the day.

I tiptoed along the hallway to Luke's room, and the look on his face when I shed the robe and woke him with a kiss said my efforts had been worth it. He grinned from ear to ear as he pulled the bow undone.

"Best Christmas present ever."

"Lie back, hot stuff. I'm doing all the work this morning."

He settled his head back onto the pillow, and I feathered kisses over his chest, feeling a hitch in my own as my heart skipped a beat. Getting sick of this man's body would be impossible. I moved slowly downwards, rewarded by Luke's sharp intake of breath as my mouth closed over its prize.

When he neared the edge, I rose to my knees then lowered myself onto him until he filled me completely. Time for my morning workout, and I didn't mean the gym.

"Hurry up, baby," Luke urged. "I'm not gonna last long."

I stopped moving. "Patience is a virtue."

"And lust is a sin. I prefer that one."

Seeing as I was no saint, I gave in and obliged him. And myself, obviously.

Afterwards, I lay there, boneless, draped over Luke, lazily kissing along his jawline. I confess, this Christmas present was for me as well as him. Gradually his breathing slowed, and he dropped into a slumber.

I stayed with him, his arms wrapped around me, careful not to fall asleep myself. A bittersweet moment. Luke was a beautiful man, inside and out, and in sleep he looked younger, without the worries that usually haunted his features. Kind and gentle, generous and thoughtful—one day, he'd make somebody a wonderful husband. But it couldn't be me.

I sensed Luke's feelings were becoming deeper, and sooner or later, he'd want more commitment. Commitment I couldn't offer. Right now, being in Lower Foxford made me happy, and it was so, so tempting to stay. Luke was easy to live with, and I saw potential in Tia. Life was good. So, why did I have a problem?

Well, because it wasn't *my* life.

Work was more than just a job to me. For years, I'd believed it was what I'd been born to do, no matter how challenging or unpleasant it could be. Conflict raged within me—should I stick with straightforward or return to my destiny?

If I stayed, would I be able to keep my past a secret? Easy in the short term, but what if Luke fancied a holiday? Or wanted me to accompany him to functions? Staying within the boundaries of the village forever wasn't an option.

Hammering at the door interrupted my thoughts.

"Come on, get up!" Tia yelled. "It's Christmas and there are presents to open! Hurry and put your clothes on."

Luke stirred awake. "Tell me again, why did we let her move in?"

"Because she's your sister and you love her dearly."

"Not at this moment, I don't."

Tia decided to open half of her presents before lunch and save the rest for later. Either her mother was shit at buying gifts, or she'd delegated the task to Mrs. Squires. Tia's delights included a Barry Manilow CD, fluffy dice for a car she wasn't old enough to drive, and a pair of comedy socks meant for a three- to five-year-old.

"Lame," she said, and I couldn't blame her. Someone had clearly put seconds of thought into that little lot.

She brightened up when I suggested we start cooking Christmas dinner, but I didn't share her enthusiasm.

"This is gonna be a disaster."

"Don't be so pessimistic. I've found a YouTube video on how to prepare a turkey. All we need to do is follow the instructions."

"Yeah. *All* we need to do."

Tia may have said *we*, but she didn't help in the slightest, mainly because she couldn't stop laughing.

"See, I told you we could do it."

Right. "If you ever tell anyone I was standing here with my hand stuck up a turkey's arse, I'll kill you."

"I'm not planning to tell anyone. I'm just going to put a photo on Facebook."

"No, you're not!"

Fortunately, she couldn't run away with her ankle strapped up, so it was easy enough to grab her phone and delete the offending picture.

"Spoilsport."

Luke came in. "Are you two going to stop messing around and cook? Or are we having Christmas dinner for breakfast?"

Tia stuck her tongue out. "Slave driver."

Dinner made it to the table by early evening. It was, without doubt, the worst meal I'd ever eaten, but Tia's happiness was infectious.

"That was so much fun," she squealed. "This is the best Christmas ever!"

"The cake tasted all right," said Luke. "I liked the skiing snowmen. How did you get it to slope downhill like that?"

I tapped my nose. "Trade secret."

TV repeats were the order of the evening, and we all sat around the fire wearing dodgy jumpers Tia had dredged up.

"You have to wear them," she insisted. "It's not Christmas otherwise."

Hers had a tree with sparkly tinsel, mine had a

snowman, and the red nose on Luke's reindeer lit up. The true meaning of Christmas, twenty-first-century style. We opened the rest of the presents while drinking a nice bottle of red.

"Tia shouldn't have wine," Luke said.

"Oh, let her have a glass. If she's going to become an adult, she needs to be treated like one."

I mean, at sixteen I'd been drinking a lot more than wine, and look how I'd turned out. Okay, so maybe that was a bad example.

Tia got a top from Arabella, and Luke had bought her a stack of gift cards from both of us. She'd got him a model racing car and me a spa voucher. I'd never been a "spa day" sort of girl, but I appreciated the sentiment, especially considering she hadn't been speaking to me a few days before.

Perhaps I should try to relax more? After all, the last time I went to a spa was on a stakeout. Surely I'd enjoy it more if I didn't have to eavesdrop on a senator's ex-wife?

I unwrapped my next gift, an iPod from Luke, and he gave me a shy smile.

"You said you wanted one for running."

"That was ages ago. I'm impressed you remembered."

"I can't lie—I saved a note on my phone."

The card I gave Luke contained a message telling him to take the twenty-seventh off.

"What for?" he asked.

"It's a surprise."

"Is it anything like this morning's surprise? I'd take the whole week off for that."

"La la la," Tia sang, stuffing her fingers in her ears.

"Guys, I don't want to know."

We spent Boxing Day pigging out on chocolate and lazing around the house—a pleasant contrast to last year, when I'd parachuted into a territory where the inhabitants didn't celebrate Christmas.

The day after, I enlisted Tia's help to distract Luke while I snuck his snowboard and warm clothes into the boot of his SUV.

"He still doesn't know where you're going," she whispered.

"Good. Are you coming to watch?"

"Ooh, can I?"

"Why not?"

I gave directions, and when we arrived at the Snozone in Milton Keynes, Luke's eyes lit up.

"It's been ages since I've seen a ski slope. I never even thought of going indoor snowboarding."

It had been a while since I'd seen proper snow too. Over a year, in fact. My husband had a chalet in Chamonix, where the snow was perfect in winter and we could go climbing in summer, but we'd been too busy to visit recently. I'd been sixteen on my first trip there, and I got hooked, first on skiing then later on snowboarding.

With Chamonix came memories of friends and fun. And maybe a teeny tiny bit of alcohol. I recalled the drunken bet that resulted in my husband and I skiing off a mountain, James Bond style, my parachute with the Union Jack, and his with the Stars and Stripes. The Snozone would be tame in comparison.

I tried to block those thoughts from my mind, not wanting the man I missed so terribly to cast a shadow over the day. But he was always there, lurking. I pasted on a smile and rented myself a snowboard while Luke went to change.

By the time we reached the top of the slope, I felt more upbeat. Something about the crunch of snow underfoot.

"Ready?" Luke asked.

"Three."

"Two."

"One."

We took off, racing to the bottom, and it turned out we were pretty evenly matched. Before long, we headed over to the rails and jumps of the freestyle course.

"Nice," said Luke, as I flew through the air.

"Not bad yourself."

Of course, our competitive streaks emerged, and we tried to outdo each other. Tia declared herself the judge and pronounced it a draw.

"Thank goodness for that," Luke said, stretching out his legs. "I'm not sure I'll be able to walk tomorrow."

"I'm glad you had a good time."

"Not as good as your last surprise, but a close second." He drew me in for a kiss. "Maybe we could come here again?"

"Sounds good to me."

"By the way, where the hell did you learn to snowboard? I worked as an instructor, yet you were matching me at every turn."

"My parents started me young, and I used to go each winter with my ex." I shrugged. "I picked it up over the years."

Every time I lied to Luke, the pit I was digging myself into got a little deeper. It would be a tough climb out.

Luke went back to work the next day while I stayed at home with Tia, who still had a week of school holidays left.

"Do you want to go out?" I asked, recalling her comments about being stuck at home.

"I'd love to. Can we go shopping? I could spend my gift cards."

Her mother proved to have one use when she lent us her chauffeur again, and after a brief detour to the charity shop to drop off Tia's unwanted gifts, we headed into London. I kept my head down as Tia bought half of Selfridges, then hid in the shadows at a West End show.

"I bought you a necklace," she said in the car on the way home, presenting me with a silver letter A on a chain. "It's no fun if I'm the only one getting new things."

"That's sweet of you. Thanks."

As she fastened it around my neck, the guilt weighing me down grew heavier. It wasn't only Luke I was going to end up hurting.

When Tia returned to school the following week, I worried she might revert to her old ways, but it seemed her new attitude was there to stay.

"Do you think Luke would let me go out with friends from school?" she asked one evening. "They're going to the cinema."

Friends? Well, at least she was making some. "I'll deal with Luke. But you've got to promise you won't drink and you'll come back at a sensible time."

I'll admit I paced a little while I was waiting for her to return, but she didn't let me down. Someone's mother dropped her off at ten, and she could still walk in a straight line.

That was the same week I discovered Luke wasn't quite as squeaky clean as he made out. Embracing his new-found delegation skills, he'd been working from home more, and his desk in the den was a sea of empty crisp packets and post-it notes.

"You want a coffee?" I asked him one evening.

His eyes shot up. "Huh? What did you say?"

Why the surprise? I looked at the image of his screen reflected in the window behind him. Wasn't that the police national database? I recognised the logo.

He flipped over to a spreadsheet as I walked behind the desk, but I knew what I'd seen. And I very much suspected he wasn't supposed to be in there.

"I said, would you like a coffee?"

"Oh, er...yes, please."

I bent and kissed him. So, he wasn't quite the angel I thought he was? Good. I liked my men with a streak of bad in them.

And I loved the time spent with Luke and Tia, but when they were out, I got restless. A seed of boredom germinated inside me, twining with guilt that was growing ever stronger. As soon as Luke left in the mornings, I'd hit the gym to take my mind off things, but there was only so much exercise I could do.

"Why don't you join the country club?" Luke asked.

I stifled a laugh. "I'm not a lady who lunches."

In fact, nobody who knew the real me would even describe me as a lady.

"You might like it if you tried it."

How could I tell him I felt more at home navigating my way through the underbelly of society than I did making small talk with a bunch of women whose main concern was that their hair looked good? The answer? I couldn't

"Thanks for the offer, but I'll pass."

Right now, I was leading the life many women dreamed of. I had free time, a hot boyfriend, and a luxury home. But the more time passed, the more sure I became that it wasn't for me.

I missed the little things—Stan's scowls in the morning, Bradley's incessant chatter, Nick's crap dumped on every surface, Dan stumbling in at three in the morning. Hell, I even longed for Toby's disgusting smoothies on occasion. I hadn't quite managed to replicate the vile taste myself. And all those feelings that had been locked up inside? Luke had somehow found the key, and now that the door was cracked open, my stupid emotions threatened to leak out around the edges.

I craved my old life, or at least the remnants of it.

But how would my friends react if I turned up in Virginia saying, "Hey, did you miss me?"

And it wasn't only *their* reaction. I hadn't forgotten the threat from my husband's killer. Was I ready to expose my people to that? Would I ever be?

Every time I was on the verge of leaving, Luke and Tia changed my mind. I'd never been one to show emotion in the past—my training had knocked that out of me—but I found myself smiling and laughing. Two things that had once been foreign concepts.

And Luke was so damn *nice*. The other guys I'd dated had mostly been in the same line of work as me, and yeah, we'd had a lot of fun, but they'd all had a toughness about them. An edge. With Luke, I could curl up on the sofa and he'd help me escape from reality. Well, not the guilt. I'd never escape that.

Tia became the sister I'd never had, once the shit on the outside of her was stripped off. We'd been shopping for art supplies, and now she channelled any angst she had left into painting and drawing. Her talent floored me. She'd started sketching my portrait, and every evening it got more detailed.

"I can't believe the change in her," Luke said. "Normally by this point in term, the headmistress has called me into school at least twice to discuss Tia's behaviour, but she hasn't had a single detention. Her grades are up too."

"Did she tell you one of her paintings got selected for an exhibition?"

Luke snuggled me closer on the couch and nuzzled my ear.

"Yes, she mentioned it."

"She's happy."

"That's because of you." He kissed me deeply and laid his forehead against mine. "Meeting you was the best thing ever to happen to me. To us. I think I've fallen in love with you, Ash."

Fuck.

Leaving would be one of the hardest things I'd ever done.

Chapter 25

MONDAY MORNING ARRIVED, and it was a relief when Luke went back to work. Breakfast had been an awkward affair, a mix of politeness and avoidance. Hardly surprising after his confession the night before —he'd told me he loved me, and I didn't say it back. Normally, lies came easily, but the words stuck in my throat. I'd never told anyone I loved them. How could I start now, in a relationship built on a foundation of half-truths and hope?

I'd kissed him instead, but it was no consolation. When I'd pulled back, his eyes filled with hurt and disappointment, and as he walked away, the pit of dread in my stomach grew ever deeper. How could I repair things? I'd never had this problem in my deep and meaningful relationship with my Walther P88.

We'd reached mid-February now, and each day got a little lighter. I'd taken to running in the early mornings as soon as Luke left then heading to the gym until lunchtime. For the last few days, I'd borrowed Majesty in the afternoons and gone out riding. Apart from a small difference of opinion over a pheasant, we were getting along famously.

When we'd been chatting, Tia had told me more of his history.

"I saw a video on the internet and fell in love with

him, back when he lived in Qatar and his name was Majnoon. Luke bought him for my birthday."

"You know *majnoon* is Arabic for crazy, right?"

A blank look. "Is it?"

I tried to stop laughing, unsuccessfully. "The guy who sold him to you must have been laughing his head off."

"He seemed so nice in the emails."

I gave her shoulders a squeeze. "A lot of pricks do. Majesty's not a bad horse, though. We'll sort him out."

Yes, it had started as another routine week in the life of Luke, Ash, and Tia. Quiet, easy, kind of dull.

Things changed on Wednesday evening when a feeling absent for months made a reappearance. A prickle. A tingle in the base of my spine and a tension that spread across my shoulders. I'd relied heavily on my instincts over the last couple of decades, and they were usually bang on the money. Something wasn't right.

My mind cycled through the possibilities before settling on the problem. Where was Tia?

She'd gone to Arabella's house after school, but when she called me at lunchtime, she said she'd be home for dinner. My version of macaroni and cheese might have been crude, but she still claimed to like it.

And right now, it was going crispy around the edges. I glanced at my watch—she'd been due at half past six, and the clock said five to seven.

I tried calling her. Voicemail.

"It's Ash. Just checking you've remembered dinner. Can you call me?" I kept my tone light, not wanting to scare her if everything was fine. I sent a text message saying the same thing. No reply.

Had her battery run out?

I dug Arabella's number out of Luke's computer, and she answered almost instantly.

"It's Ash. Could you give Tia a shove out the front door? Dinner's nearly ready."

"She left ages ago." A pause. "Maybe an hour?" Another pause. "Is everything okay?"

"I'm sure it's fine. Honestly, don't worry. I had the music on loud so I bet she's snuck up to her room."

I didn't want to panic Arabella, but I knew damn well Tia wasn't in the house. I may have been rusty, but I wasn't dead. And that meant I wanted to check the route myself before calling Luke. A bit of the real me stirred deep in my soul, and I ran upstairs to change. Dark colours were the order of the day—a navy blue jacket, dark red jeans, and brown boots.

Why didn't I wear black? Because I wasn't a fucking ninja, that's why. Sure, it went with everything, but if you're skulking around in the dark dressed in black from head to foot, you might as well tattoo "burglar" across your forehead.

Before I left, I slipped a knife into my pocket. When Luke wasn't around, I'd got back into the habit of carrying a little something, and thanks to a dude in the pub, I had my weapon of choice. Over the years, I'd become so familiar with carrying an Emerson CQC-7, it was like an extension of my hand. I'd worked the mechanism on this one until it was smooth as Sean Connery.

Right, time to go. I set the alarm on my way out the door, although it wouldn't stop someone like me. Hell, it'd barely even slow me down.

The streetlight between Luke's home and Arabella's

was out, the lane pitch black. Coincidence? I checked underneath—no broken glass. Keeping to the shadows, I traced Tia's usual route. On the plus side, I didn't find her lying in a ditch. The not so good news? I didn't find any sign of her at all. On the way back, I slowed down and used my torch.

I'd almost got back to Luke's when I saw something that made my chest seize. A few scuffs, barely visible at the edge of the kerb. A fresh tyre track marked the dirt in the gutter, its tread distinct. I flipped a coin next to it for scale and took a photo with my phone.

It might be nothing, but my intuition wasn't convinced.

Luke turned into the driveway as I got back. He'd taken his SUV today, grumbling about the salty roads. A Porsche Cayenne the same as my husband used to drive, except Luke's was red instead of black and it didn't have the souped-up engine. Right now, the sight of it felt like an omen.

As Luke pulled into the garage, I let myself in through the front door. By the time he came through the internal door, I was waiting.

"Have you heard from Tia?"

"Why would I? She always calls you."

"She hasn't come home, and she left Arabella's over an hour ago."

He shrugged. "Maybe she went to see Mother? She mentioned picking up some art stuff. Or she could be visiting another friend. She always used to sneak out in the evenings."

Once, possibly, but not now. "Could you give your mother a call and check?"

Luke's sigh told me I was overreacting, but he

humoured me and pulled out his phone. He wandered upstairs to change while he made the call.

A few minutes later, he came back, looking marginally more concerned. "Mother hasn't seen her for over a week. She can't remember exactly when."

Figured.

I called Arabella back. "Turns out Luke and Tia had a bust up. She's run off, and I need to track her down. Can you give me the numbers of her friends? I don't know if she's got money on her for a taxi back."

Luke looked peeved when I ended the call. "We didn't have a bust up."

"I know that, but I don't want to worry more people than necessary."

"Are you worried?"

I was when I got off the phone to her friends. Nobody had seen Tia since school that afternoon.

"I'm calling the police," Luke said.

I could hardly tell him not to, but inwardly I groaned. My cover was on thin ice. He paced the lounge as he muttered into the phone then hung up with a frown.

"Graham says nobody's reported any accidents, and if she hasn't turned up by morning, he'll stop by and take a report."

"Graham? Is that the prick we met in the pub the other day?"

Luke nodded. Marvellous. Graham, the local constable, had struggled to detect his own vehicle in the car park at the end of the evening. Finding a missing person was well beyond his abilities. Now what? If harm had come to Tia, I wasn't averse to getting the chief constable out of bed, but I wanted to rule out other possibilities first.

"I'm calling the hospitals. I don't trust Graham," I said.

"I'll go out in the car. She might have gone to the stables. Or the shop." A note of desperation crept into Luke's voice. "Or the pub."

I drew a blank on the phone and set out on foot again. A more thorough check wouldn't hurt, although I had a sinking feeling I knew what had happened. I'd been involved in plenty of child abduction cases, although never from such an early stage. And never somebody I was close to.

I tramped down the road and checked each footpath leading off it. As I rooted around in the undergrowth, I thought over the scenarios.

If Tia had been taken, why? Was it because of Luke, me, or Tia herself?

Luke was the obvious answer. Because of his money, Tia would make a great target for a hefty ransom. Then there was the business angle—had Luke pissed off any competitors lately? Revenge was so often a motivator.

Then there was the possibility Tia had been abducted by a wack job who simply wanted a pretty young girl. Perhaps they had a long-running infatuation or saw an easy opportunity? I was inclined to discount the first option because if she'd been receiving unwanted attention, surely she'd have told me? The latter was a very real possibility, though.

The plus point of those scenarios was that Tia would still be alive, most likely, and she'd remain that way until the kidnapper achieved their goal.

What worried me most was the slim chance she'd

been taken because of me. What if one of my associates had started looking into my husband's murder and trodden on someone's toes? Had I been traced here? I thought I'd taken enough precautions to stay hidden, but what if I'd screwed up? The people who took out my husband had access to heavy weapons and didn't hesitate to kill. If they had Tia and she was still alive, she wouldn't have long.

That thought was at the forefront of my mind as I walked back to the house. Luke was pacing the hallway as I came through the door.

"Anything?" he asked.

"No. You?"

"Nothing."

I hadn't truly been expecting any other answer.

"Luke, I need to talk to you," I started, but the ping of an incoming text message interrupted me.

Luke snatched his phone out of his pocket. "Thank goodness, it's from Tia. She probably wants me to pick her up from somewhere."

"Where is she?"

Time slowed as the colour drained out of his face.

"Luke, what does it say?"

His hand shook as he passed the phone over. Tia filled the screen, bound and gagged, lying on a grubby floor. Her eyes were closed, and the words underneath left no room for interpretation.

Unknown: You and the bitch girlfriend keep your mouths shut. No police or she dies. We're watching. Further instructions will follow.

The strong man I knew disintegrated in front of me, tearing at his hair.

"Someone's taken her. Fuck! What the hell do we

do?"

I didn't share Luke's surprise. For the last hour, I'd kind of been expecting the news. And in fact, there were plus points to the message—it confirmed she'd been abducted, and it wasn't a random sex crime. They also said she was alive, although I couldn't be certain from the photo.

The bit that bothered me was the reference to Luke's girlfriend. Whoever took Tia knew of my existence, so there was still a possibility I was connected.

And now I was about to make Luke's evening worse with the most uncomfortable conversation of my life.

"We wait," I said.

"That's it? That's your answer?"

He paced up and down the hallway, and I itched to join him. Pacing was a bad habit of mine.

"The other options are going to the police or looking for her ourselves."

"We're not going to the police. Oh, hell, do you think they know I called Graham? What if he stirs something up?"

"He won't. If you don't call him back, he'll forget all about it."

"I hope you're right."

I agreed with avoiding the police, at least for the moment. They couldn't do much with a scuff and a tyre print in any case. Little traffic went down the lane, and none of the neighbours had CCTV. It was one reason I liked the place so much.

"How about calling a private investigation firm?" I suggested.

"That's as bad as the police."

"They're more discreet."

He paused, eyes narrowed. "Don't you dare."

We'll see.

"Uh, I need to speak to you about something."

"Is it about Tia?"

"Not totally."

"Then can't it wait?"

"No."

"You sure know how to pick your damn moments. Fine, say it so we can get back to the things that matter. Like my little sister."

I took a deep breath. "I know you're going to hate me, and I accept that. Please just understand that right now all I want to do is get Tia back, the same as you do."

"Why do I get the feeling I won't like this?"

Because if Tia disappearing broke your world, now I'm going to shatter it.

"I'm not who you think I am. I told you I came here to get away from my cheating fiancé, but that's not exactly true."

"Go on."

Fantastic, he sounded pissed already. *Good start, Ash.* Or whatever the hell my name was.

"I had a run-in with a guy, and I was struggling to deal with it. So much happened three months ago." I closed my eyes for a second. "He threatened my friends if I didn't keep out of his way, so I ran. I ran here. A few lies at the beginning spiraled out of control, and I couldn't find a way to tell you the truth. I'm not proud of what I did, and I'm so, so sorry."

"So what *is* the truth?"

I turned away, because it hurt to look at him. At the

fury on his face.

"I can't tell you everything. I don't want to put you in danger as well."

It only took seconds for Luke to put two and two together and come up with my greatest fear. "You think Tia's been kidnapped because of something you've done?"

He looked like he was about to punch me, and I deserved it.

"I don't know. I don't think so. There are more plausible reasons for her being abducted."

"But it's possible?"

"Yes, it's possible."

He stood toe-to-toe with me, his voice hard, his eyes unforgiving. I'd never seen this side of him, but he'd only seen a tiny piece of me so I had no right to complain.

"Get out."

"I can help you if I stay. I know what I'm doing in situations like this."

"Just get out!"

He shoved me towards the front door. Yes, I could have stopped him, but there was no point in making him angrier. I covered my ears as he carried on shouting.

"You came into my life and made me and my sister care about you, and all the time we were in danger. You selfish bitch! Tia could die because of you."

How could I argue with the truth?

I let him push me outside, and the door slammed shut behind me. My last glimpse of Luke was as a broken man, fear and anger and hurt etched on his usually handsome face.

The lock clicked.

So, that went well.

CHAPTER 26

LUKE MAY HAVE kicked me out, but no way was I giving up.

Old me never gave up, and tonight, I felt more alive than I had in months. I also felt kind of guilty about that.

What did I have in my pockets? A wad of cash, a set of lock picks I'd got at the same time as the knife, and the phone I'd bought after I got to England. Not enough. If I was going to help Luke, I needed more equipment, especially as he wasn't keen on my assistance.

Based on past experience, the kidnappers wouldn't be in touch straight away. Now the first contact had been made, my money was on them leaving Luke to stew for a while. They wanted him tired and unable to think straight.

Not too long, though, because that had other risks. The longer Tia was missing, the more likely others would notice and involve the police. My educated guess was that the next contact would be in the early hours. That gave me a bit of time. I just hoped it would be long enough to do everything I needed to do before the circus started.

I set off on foot into the village, keeping in the shadows. The kidnapper's message had said "they" were watching, but I was fairly sure there was nobody out the front of the house. I hadn't seen anyone in the lane earlier, and more importantly, I hadn't *felt* anyone.

The woods out the back would provide a better hiding place, but I'd check those later, and the gardens next door. The kidnapper had referred to "we" rather than "I," but a gang was unlikely. A pair, maybe, but more than that tended to lead to infighting. I'd worked one case where three idiots argued so much, one ended up in hospital while the abductee snuck out the back. Made my job a heck of a lot easier. I had a feeling this case wasn't going to be so simple, though.

As I neared the village, I called a taxi to meet me outside The Coach and Horses. Nobody would bat an eyelid at a cab picking somebody up from a pub. Within ten minutes, an ancient Vauxhall Vectra with a taxi plate on the back rolled into the car park.

"Where to, love?" the driver asked.

"London, please. Belgravia. I'll give you directions when we get closer."

It took just under an hour to reach my destination, a part of the world I hadn't visited since last year. I had the cab pull over to the side of the main road and hopped out.

"Keep the change." Money wouldn't be so much of a problem now.

"Thanks, love. Do you want me to wait?"

"No, I'm fine from here."

I walked along a couple of side streets until an eight-foot wall loomed ahead. Cameras watched me—I could see their red eyes in the gloom. I crossed the road and hopped up on a rubbish bin, one installed by the council last year in an effort to keep the borough tidy. The extra height allowed me to see the house beyond the wall. No lights. No movement.

Good.

As the occasional car trundled past, I walked around the block and went through the same routine at the front. A single window glowed next to the front door. Ruth, the housekeeper, had always been a creature of habit, and she turned the hall light on when she left each day, a welcome for anyone coming home late.

I smiled in the darkness. Albany House looked the same as the last time I visited, and better still, it appeared nobody was home.

Ten minutes. I had ten minutes to get in and out, and I set the timer on my watch. The instant I breached the perimeter, a unit would be dispatched from the London base of my company, but even if the driver broke the speed limit, they'd take fifteen minutes to get there.

How about the police? Well, they didn't worry me. Nobody would make that call. After all, it wasn't against the law for me to break into my own home, was it?

I put my head down, vaulted over the gate, and jogged along the driveway. High up on the wall, the camera swivelled around as it tracked me. I didn't have my key, but it only took me thirty seconds with my lock picks. Then I looked into the retina scanner. What, you didn't think I'd entrust my security to a single lock, did you?

The deadbolts shot back with a muffled thunk, and I pushed my way inside.

One minute gone. I flicked the lights on and ran straight to the study on the ground floor, pulling back the mirror on the wall to reveal a hidden door. A sixteen-digit code punched into the recessed keypad got me through it and into the basement. Two minutes gone.

The basement contained a carefully amassed arsenal of everything one could possibly desire to either start a small war or prevent one, all neatly arranged in racks and lockers. The really good stuff was hidden in an armoured room at the back, but I didn't need any of that today.

I grabbed a couple of bags and filled them with equipment. Bugs, tracking devices, a spare phone, night vision goggles, infrared goggles, a parabolic microphone, and a handy little scanner that would detect the transmissions of any wireless cameras or listening devices. I was a kid in a candy store, one who'd been living on muesli for months.

Should I take a gun? Decisions, decisions... I opted against it. They were illegal to carry in the UK, and the drawbacks of getting caught with one would outweigh the benefits. I picked up an extra knife, though.

Thankfully, I insisted on everything being kept in its proper place, and it only took me three minutes to find the equipment I wanted. I removed more cash from one of the safes, gave my perfectly ordered playroom one last wistful glance, re-locked the basement, secured the mirror back over the door, and ran through to the kitchen. Five minutes gone.

Food. I needed food. Luckily, Toby had left a pile of shit-flavoured protein bars in the cupboard, and I grabbed a handful. They tasted like sawdust, but I wouldn't starve. Those and some bottled water went into my bag.

Six and a half minutes gone.

The phone on the kitchen wall rang. The moment my eye was scanned, alarms would have blared in the control room. That call was someone wanting to find out what the hell I was playing at, and I bet I knew who. I could just picture the scowl on his face as I ignored him.

The noise was driving me nuts, and I stared into the hidden camera.

"Pack it in!" I shouted at Nate. The house was wired for sound as well.

The phone stopped, but five seconds later, it started up again.

I didn't have time to deal with this. I'd been thrown into this situation, and despite having three months to think of what to say to my friends about my breakdown, I hadn't got around to it. Now wasn't the right time, not with my head all over the place.

The phone didn't stop. Nate would be pacing the control room in Richmond now, an earpiece wedged into each ear.

"Nate, you'll wear a hole in the floor."

He didn't answer. He couldn't—the house only contained microphones, not speakers. Although I bet myself $100 that the next time I set foot in there, he'd have wired one in.

I dashed up the stairs, trying to block out the ringing, and grabbed some warm clothes and a blanket. A quick glance at my watch told me my time was almost up. I ran to the other side of the house and took the stairs to the underground garage.

Eight minutes.

What was in there? A BMW X5, an Audi A4, a sporty Yamaha motorcycle, and my latest toy, a shiny black Aston Martin V12 Vantage tucked up under a cover in the corner. I'd been hoping for the Land Rover Discovery I'd driven on my last visit to the UK in case I needed to go off-road, but no such luck. The X5 would have to do.

I liberated the keys from the lockbox in the corner and bleeped open the car. The bags got slung in the back, then I popped the bonnet. Twenty seconds later, I'd disabled the tracker hidden in the engine bay.

As I hopped into the front seat, I hoped I remembered how to drive. I had no idea who the BMW belonged to—my friends had a tendency to abandon their cars in my garage—so I kept my fingers crossed I wouldn't break it. Breaking cars was Dan's job.

I aimed the key fob at the garage door and tapped my fingernails on the steering wheel as it slowly rolled up. At the end of the driveway, the gates creaked open.

Nine minutes and fifty-seven seconds. Nice.

Back behind the wheel at last, I took the odd liberty at traffic lights but drove sensibly enough that I didn't attract attention. The response unit would be coming from the opposite direction, although the chances were they'd called off the dogs when they saw me leave. They weren't about to chase me through the streets of London, not when they knew they didn't have a hope in hell of catching me.

Once I was sure I hadn't picked up a tail, I pulled into a lay-by, savouring the adrenaline rush. Fuck, I'd missed this. I'd missed the challenges and the danger and the risk.

But I was back now.

I smiled to myself.

I was back. And I had a kidnapper to catch.

Seeing as I'd missed dinner, I gulped down a protein bar and took a slug of water. Midnight was fast approaching when I punched Luke's postcode into the satnav and headed back to Lower Foxford.

As I drove, guilt chewed away at me. I owed my friends and colleagues an explanation for what I'd just done, but I didn't know how to put it into words. The calm, rational part of my brain was still suffering from a serious malfunction. Every time I tried to *think*, my head filled with fuzz, like static from an old television.

Yes, I had to talk to them, and sooner rather than later. But first I needed to help Luke.

When I reached the village, I parked on the far side of the woods behind Luke's house and assembled my kit. I wanted to check for prying eyes.

An hour later, I'd been through the woods and neighbouring properties with infrared goggles and the transmission scanner. Nothing. Apart from several hundred rabbits and a couple of deer, I was alone. For completeness' sake, I checked the front of the house too, but nobody was watching. They just wanted Luke to think they were.

My next job was to get into the house. I swapped out the goggles for a handful of Nate's custom bugs. Each incorporated a tiny camera and microphone and worked on motion sensors. I'd selected the battery-operated version as they didn't need to last long. If Tia was missing for more than their natural life, we had bigger problems.

I did a quick circuit around the outside of the

house. Luke was sitting in the den, staring into space as he tore pages of a notepad into pieces. Did he even realise he was doing it? I squinted through the window at the computer in front of him. He'd been trying to track Tia's cell phone, but by the looks of things, he hadn't had any luck. Hardly surprising—the kidnapper would have to be stupider than a rock to leave the phone on. Any teenager with an internet connection could track them nowadays.

My chest seized as I watched Luke. Guilt. Fear. Guilt that I'd hurt him. Fear that we wouldn't get Tia back. Before my husband's death, I'd locked all those pesky emotions firmly away, but I'd gone soft in my little sabbatical. I wished I could offer Luke some comfort, but my presence would only make things worse.

A few minutes later, I swung myself up onto the balcony outside my old bedroom and picked the lock on the sliding door. Before venturing into the rest of the house, I packed everything I wanted to keep into the rucksack I'd brought and left it outside. There wasn't much—my old phone, a bit of cash, and Ashlyn's passport. While I was at it, I put my wedding ring back in its rightful place. I'd missed the feel of it on my finger.

I inched open the door to the upstairs hallway and tiptoed to Luke's bedroom. It only took seconds to install a bug in the light fitting. No, I didn't expect Luke to get much sleep until Tia was found, but I had the opportunity, so I took it.

Next, I crept downstairs and hid another device in the kitchen, peeping out from behind a stack of plates in the dresser. Ideally, I'd have put a camera in the den, but even though Luke was now dozing over his desk, I didn't want to risk venturing in there. I settled for putting a third bug in the flower arrangement opposite the den door instead.

With that done, I fitted tracking devices to both of his vehicles then went back to the BMW to watch and listen. An alarm would alert me to any sound or movement, so I lay back under the blanket to wait.

At 8 a.m. one of the sensors woke me with its insistent beeping. Luke was moving through the house. On the screen in the receiving unit, I watched him open the safe hidden behind a Picasso print in the bedroom and count the cash inside. Why? Had a ransom demand come in? If it had, it must have been by text message, because I hadn't heard the phone ring.

At eight thirty, he did get a call. Arabella wanted to know where Tia was. Tia normally walked to her house in the morning so they could ride to school together.

"She's not feeling well," Luke said. "She ate something that disagreed with her."

A pause.

"Yes, I'll tell her. I'm sure she'll be very grateful if you take notes."

Another beat.

"No, I don't think she'll be in for a few days. She's sleeping at the moment, but she's been really sick. I'll get her to call you when she's feeling better."

His voice shook as he spoke. He was a terrible liar.

Not like some people.

At nine, Luke left the house carrying a briefcase—empty from the way he threw it into the back of the car. I followed him to the bank, staying well back and letting the tracker do its work.

He'd obviously gone to pick up more money for the ransom, but how much? What story had he come up with? Banks tended to get a bit funny about handing over large bundles of cash in this day and age of electronic transfers. I knew Luke kept £150,000 in the safe because I'd watched over his shoulder and memorised the combination then looked while he was out, but clearly that wasn't enough.

No detours on the way back—Luke went straight home. Back in the bedroom, he piled up the cash from the briefcase and the safe, counting as he went, and I tallied up the bundles on my phone. £250,000, if I'd estimated correctly, and he packed the lot into a duffel bag he dug out of the closet.

That was it? £250,000? That was all Tia was worth? Luke could and would pay a lot more. Why such a low amount? Was the kidnapper being sensible, knowing the tricky logistics of obtaining cash under the radar? Or was I missing a bigger picture?

Luke piqued my curiosity when he disappeared into the den. He was only in there for twenty minutes, but when he came back, he added a memory stick to the bag. What was on there?

As he stood up, he looked directly at the camera. Haggard and scared, he was a shadow of his former self. When he started pacing, I wanted to tell him to rest, or at least eat something. He'd need his strength later. My frustration had no outlet, and I made myself unclench my teeth.

Heeding my own advice, I had a snack then relieved myself in the bushes. Oh, the joys of being on a stakeout. Not for the first time in my life, I questioned my sanity. Why hadn't I bought myself a tropical island

and marooned myself on it? Somewhere idyllic like the Bahamas or the French West Indies? I could have been getting a tan instead of frostbite.

I sighed. Who was I kidding? No matter how uncomfortable I might be, I'd stop at nothing to get Tia back. I slouched down in the front seat, ready to play the waiting game.

CHAPTER 27

THE SUN SET. Luke was still inside the house, but he'd paced so much the bottom of his shoes must have worn thin. I covered my mouth as I yawned, out of both tiredness and boredom. There was a good reason I delegated surveillance work whenever possible. I'd much rather be out shooting people.

Relax, I was just kidding.

Maybe.

At six, Luke lay back on the bed and dozed, which meant I got some sleep myself without bloody movement alarms going off. That relief was short-lived, however, because at nine he got up and resumed his now familiar route. Through the hall to the kitchen. Turn. Back to the front door. Turn. In every step, his fear and frustration was evident, and it hurt to watch.

I got out of the car for a stretch and another pee then huddled under the blanket again. The car thermometer said six degrees, and I swore under my breath—the bloody kidnapper could at least have picked the summer to make his move. Throughout his torturous routine, Luke kept glancing at his watch. What was he waiting for?

I found out at midnight when he climbed into his SUV, carrying the holdall. A ransom drop?

I sure hoped so. All that waiting had given me too

much time to think, and there were only so many times I could go through things in my head without second guessing myself. I was always happier getting on with things.

With the tracker still on Luke's car, I didn't need to follow too closely. I hung back and watched the other vehicles instead, but I didn't spot anyone else tailing him. The M40 motorway was quiet at that time of night, and it didn't take long for Luke to drive north a couple of junctions before winding his way through the countryside again.

I dropped back further on the narrow lanes. It was either that or turn my lights off, and I didn't fancy crashing. I didn't even know who this car was registered to—sorting out the aftermath of an accident would be a bureaucratic nightmare. Luke was two miles ahead when his car stopped moving. I sped up to catch him, flicking my headlights off when I got close. A three-quarter moon bathed the countryside in a dim glow, and ghosts danced as trees and bushes swayed in the wind.

The only thing pitch black was my mind.

The tracker put Luke's vehicle in a woodland car park, and I pulled up at the entrance. What was waiting in there? I needed to find out, so I reversed the BMW up an overgrown track further along the lane before returning on foot.

That sodding nursery rhyme came into my head again. *If you go down to the woods tonight...* The last time I had a surprise in the woods, I'd discovered Tia wasn't actually Satan's daughter. I was certain tonight's wouldn't be quite so pleasant.

The pale moonlight threw long, soft shadows over

the waiting forest. My eyes slowly adjusted to the darkness, but it was still difficult to spot anything in the foreboding tangle of tree limbs rising up in front of me, the night-time playground of rabbits, foxes, deer, and of course, little old me.

Luke was nowhere to be seen, and I cursed in my head. I'd have given my Aston Martin to have a tracker in the duffel bag. Ahead of me, paths branched off into the woods, left and right. Which one did he take?

I listened out for a clue. The crack of a twig, maybe, or the soft thunk of footsteps on the humus-strewn ground. Nothing. Just the low hoot of an owl as it whispered through the bare branches overhead.

Messy footprints littered the damp ground— evidently, the place was popular with walkers. Which were Luke's? He wore a size nine, but that didn't narrow it down. Okay, time for infrared goggles. I slipped the slim rucksack off my back, but I'd barely opened it when a shout came from my left. *Luke*. The words might have been muffled, but I recognised the voice, and the argumentative tone meant I had no time to waste.

I dropped the bag and ran towards the noise. There was enough moonlight for me to leave my torch in my pocket, and I preferred the element of surprise over the assistance of its beam. Throughout the years, I'd become proficient at moving quickly and quietly through difficult terrain, and I doubted they'd hear my approach over the yelling in any case.

I'd almost reached the voices when...nothing. They stopped. I crept forward, and the path opened up into a clearing, beams of moonlight slanting through the trees. A body lay on the ground, sprawled motionless among the rotting leaves. A second figure loomed over it, pointing a gun towards its head. I could tell from the build the standing figure wasn't Luke, which meant it must be him on the ground.

I didn't hesitate.

I flicked on my torch, hitting the stranger full in the face with the beam, careful to hold it at arm's length. That way, if the dude got trigger happy, he'd aim at the light rather than my head. A bullet through the arm I could recover from. Through the brain? Not so much.

My CQC-7 had found its way into my right hand—an automatic reflex. As soon as I'd double checked it was Luke on the ground, I let the knife fly towards the man trying to kill him.

Good to see I hadn't lost my touch. The knife buried itself in the stranger's biceps just as he fired at Luke. His arm jerked, and dirt kicked up a foot from Luke's head.

"Aaaaaah!"

The man's startled yowl cut through the night, and he took off, keeping the hold of his bloody gun. I wanted to go after him, but since Luke hadn't moved, I stopped to check on him first.

Blood seeped from a gash across his temple, and although he was unconscious, his breathing was steady and his pulse beat strongly. He'd be fine for five minutes, but would Tia? The best chance of finding her was crashing through the woods ahead of me, and I sprinted off in pursuit.

Muffled curses came from the darkness ahead of me as the arsehole crashed into branches. Either he hadn't brought a torch or he wanted to poke his eye out on a branch. Both good news for me.

I was gaining, but he had a good head start, and a moment of silence was interrupted by the slam of a door and the growl of an engine.

Shit! I reached a second car park just in time to see a transit van spin its wheels out of the entrance. Before it disappeared from view, I burned the registration number into my mind. There was no chance of catching up—my car was half a mile away, and I didn't know the area. With a heavy heart, I returned to Luke.

On my jog back, I almost tripped over the holdall, still heavy and unopened. Now the kidnapper would be doubly pissed—no ransom as well as a damaged arm. What if he took his anger out on Tia? Bile rose in my throat at the thought of it.

Pack it in, Diamond. Emotion only clouded my judgement in situations like this.

When I reached the clearing, Luke was regaining consciousness, flopping from side to side. He tried to get up, but I held him down while I checked for damage.

"He's going to spill the tea," he mumbled.

"Tea? What tea?"

"Kill the tea."

"Tia? Do you mean Tia?"

"Kill Tia."

Great. Tell me something I didn't know.

Before I could help Luke to his feet, he doubled over and puked, reminding me of my first night at his house. Seemed like somebody had a touch of concussion. I gave him a few more minutes on the ground then pulled him to a sitting position. He couldn't stay in the woods all night. Blood was running from his head, and he needed it stitched. I took my jumper off and pressed it against the wound to try and stem the flow.

"Can you try getting up again?"

"I think so."

Between us, we got him to his feet, where he swayed and clutched at a nearby sapling.

"We need to get to the car."

He gritted his teeth. "Okay."

With me half carrying him as well as the bag and pausing on the way to pick up my rucksack, we made our way to the BMW. Slowly. Painfully slowly. The woods closed up behind us, hiding their secrets in the inky blackness. Those trees had seen more than most humans ever would.

When we reached the car, I propped Luke up in the passenger seat and retrieved the first aid kit from the boot—company rules, everybody carried one. Luke's gash was nasty, most likely inflicted by the sight on his assailant's pistol, and I wound a temporary bandage around the cut until I could clean it up properly. He'd be sporting a scar in years to come if he didn't get professional help. And that wasn't his only injury—the back of his head had a cracking lump on it. No wonder he'd ended up unconscious.

Ready to go, I did up his seatbelt. Safety first, right? He was still groggy, his head lolling to one side, but his faculties were returning.

"What are you doing here?" he slurred.

"Currently? Making sure you still have a head on your shoulders."

Although whether he had a fully functioning brain in it was debatable. What the hell had he been thinking, skipping through the woods at night carrying quarter of a mil?

"Where's Tia?"

"Still missing. I'll find her, but I need help to do it. We're doing this my way now."

"No! He said he'd kill her. You can't call the police."

"I'm not intending to, but you're not doing this alone. I'm going to call some friends."

He groaned and slumped back into the seat but didn't argue any further.

Good. It would have been a waste of his breath.

As he was talking and making a certain amount of sense, I decided to steer clear of the hospital and the inevitable questions that would come from a visit there. We both wanted to avoid the police, which would likely be the end result. I'd had enough medical training to believe he wasn't in serious danger. I'd had worse damage myself and still run a half marathon the next day.

The guy who tried to kill Luke was a different story, though. For him, the danger was very real. Boy, I itched to get my hands on him.

I hopped in the driver's seat and started the engine. Before setting off, I shoved the battery back in my red phone and turned it on for the first time in three months. One bar of power. I plugged it into the charger and connected it to the car's Bluetooth system. Seconds later, I was on my way back to Belgravia for the second time that week.

The night was deathly quiet as I sped down country lanes towards the motorway. With the adrenaline of the chase no longer flowing through my bloodstream, the journey back seemed to take twice as long. Or perhaps it was the sense of dread building in my veins that made time slow? What was I going to tell my friends? And Luke? How would I explain my life to him?

I had no words.

At one point, he turned to me and mumbled, "I thought you couldn't drive?"

"Technically, I said I didn't drive, not that I couldn't."

"Do you always go this fast?"

I noticed he was gripping the sides of the seat, and his knuckles had gone a bit white.

"Yes."

He closed his eyes and whispered a prayer.

Old life, meet Luke. Luke, meet my old life. I hope you enjoy the ride.

CHAPTER 28

ONCE WE HIT the motorway, I scrolled through the phone's memory to the number I wanted, took a deep breath, and hit dial. The line crackled as someone on the other side of the world answered.

"Nate?"

"Emmy?" Surprise was evident in his voice, but also a tinge of something else. Anger? Relief?

"Yeah."

"Thank fuck. Why the hell didn't you answer the phone the other day?"

Yes, anger and relief, both present and correct. In truth, I hadn't expected him to be anything but pissed off. It was his normal demeanour, even when I hadn't done something really, really stupid.

"I was busy. Are you at home?"

Virginia was five hours behind, and any normal person would be in front of the TV at nine in the evening. But, like me, Nate wasn't normal and often slept in the office.

"Busy? Busy? I could see you were busy. What in the devil's name did you need all that equipment for? And no, I'm in the control room. Someone's got to run this company, and it sure as shit hasn't been you."

"Uh, there was a small situation. Actually, there still is. I could use some help."

"What kind of situation? Are *you* okay?"

"I'm fine. Someone else is in trouble, and I'm trying to fix things."

"If you're 'fine,' where the fuck have you been for the last three months? You vanished without a trace and left some cryptic fucking note. I've been monitoring hospitals and morgues the world over."

Yep, he definitely had a scowl plastered across his not-so-pretty face.

"I'm sorry. I was messed up."

"That's it? You were messed up? You've put us all through hell, and now you phone one night out of the blue asking for help?"

I stared at the road, barely seeing the way ahead. I deserved his anger, but that didn't make it any easier to take.

"Please, Nate, I'll explain later. I promise. Right now, a girl's been kidnapped, and her life's at stake. Could you put the animosity aside and lend a hand?" I thought of Tia, bound and gagged on the floor. "Please?"

"You know we'll do whatever you need. But, Emmy, we *will* talk about this later."

Hurrah. That gave me something to look forward to, but I'd deal with it once we'd resolved the Tia situation.

"I need manpower. The girl's been gone thirty-two hours now, and the ransom drop just got botched."

"Got it. Now you've turned your phone on again, I can see where you are. You going to Albany House?"

"That's the plan. I need you to get a team together at the office, and I'll go and brief them. Can you pull in everyone not working on a priority level one case?"

"Everyone? Do you have any damn clue what that'll do to the running of everything else?"

Yes, I was perfectly aware of the havoc it would create with the scheduling of all the other jobs for weeks afterwards.

"Everyone," I confirmed.

Nate gave an exasperated sigh but didn't try to argue. He knew I wouldn't pull a stunt like this lightly.

"Fine." He sounded more like me than he'd ever admit. "I'll make the calls and speak to you when you get back to London. By the way, Nick and Dan flew over to the UK when we spotted you in the house. They'll be waiting for you to arrive."

"That's the best news I've had all day. I'll let you know when I get there."

"You'd better. If you do another runner, I'll hunt you to the ends of the fucking earth."

Aw, at least he still cared.

"I'm back now, and I'm staying back. And Nate, I'm so, so sorry."

"You can grace me with an explanation later. I'll be waiting with bated breath. Now, get off the phone so I can make some calls."

Well, that went about as well as expected. I was definitely on Nate's shit list, but I deserved it. And at least he stayed professional rather than letting his feelings towards me impede the hunt for Tia.

When we arrived at the house, I drove straight into the garage. Luke was still unsteady on his feet as I bundled him into the lift. Usually, I hated the thing and took the stairs, but it did have its uses.

I helped him into the kitchen and found Dan seated at the breakfast bar, a mug of coffee cupped in her hands. Nick was speaking on the phone, staring out of the window, but he hung up when he saw me.

I'd known Nick Goldman since I was eighteen. My husband introduced us. They'd worked together on various black-ops projects until my husband quit his not-so-cushy government job to strike out with Nate instead.

When I'd come onto the scene, Nick had helped to train me, and not just on the job. He'd educated me in the bedroom as well. Things didn't work out between us, but we remained close, and when I was twenty-two, he'd become the fourth shareholder in our security company.

Daniela di Grassi's background was similar to mine. We'd met by accident in not-so-pleasant circumstances and just clicked. She'd moved in with us for a while, and over bottles of wine and cold case files, we discovered she had hidden talents.

Dan could ferret, wheedle, and cajole information out of people better than anyone. Her mind could assemble a jigsaw puzzle of clues into a work of art. Aside from my husband, she was the best investigator we'd ever had.

Along with Nate and his wife, Carmen, and Mack, the office geek, Nick and Dan made up my inner circle. I trusted them with my life.

And neither of them looked happy.

I balanced Luke on a leather and chrome stool then walked over to where Nick and Dan now stood in silence. What should I say? They just stared, seemingly lost for words too. Finally, Dan stepped forward and hugged me tightly.

"Ease up. Can't...breathe."

When she let go, Nick still hadn't moved. He'd turned into a statue, arms folded, brows furrowed.

Dan's eyes were damp as she mumbled, "Where have you been, you stupid bitch? We thought you were dead."

"You think I'm that easy to kill?"

"I s'pose not. Where the fuck have you been, then?"

I jerked my head towards Luke. "Living with him."

She shot him a sideways glance. "Hot. But who is he?"

"Luke. It's a long story, but his sister's missing, and I need your help to find her. They know me as Ash, and neither has a clue what I do for a living. I'd like to keep it that way." Luke groaned from the other side of the kitchen. "Before we do anything else, he needs his head stitched up."

"Want me to do the honours?"

"Please. Your hands are probably steadier than mine right now, plus he can't stand the sight of me."

She gave me a puzzled look. My hands never shook, at least, not before.

"Okay."

"I need to call Nate, see where we are with a team."

Nick followed me into...well, I called it my home office, but it was more than that—it served as a backup control room should anything happen to our primary location in Kings Cross. He still hadn't said a word, which stung, and now he slammed the door behind us.

"What the fuck, Emmy?"

Great. In the last two days, I'd managed to upset

almost everyone I cared about.

"I'm sorry."

I was doing a lot of apologising tonight. If this kept up, I might just record a message.

"Sorry? *Sorry?* Sorry doesn't cut it, babe. You ran off without a word to any of us."

"I left a note."

I tried to defend myself, but half-heartedly because I knew he was right.

"A half-assed note that didn't explain anything, just asked us to stop a fucking murder investigation."

"Did you stop it?" I asked, holding my breath.

"Yes."

I inhaled again. "Then it did its job."

"That's it? That's all you're gonna say?"

"Nicky, can we do this later?" Say, sometime next century? "Finding Tia's the most important thing here."

"Fine."

He echoed Nate's comment from earlier, and as a woman, I understood what that meant. I had two grumpy, monosyllabic men to deal with.

I settled myself into a seat and Nick grudgingly took the one beside me. Nate soon appeared on the wall of screens in front of us.

At forty-one, Nate was a couple of years older than my husband, and his dark brown hair had grown too long again. Carmen would be nagging him to cut it, no doubt. His tan skin spoke of his Cuban heritage, and on a normal day, women the world over would kill for his complexion. Not today, though. Today, worry lines marred his forehead. The last few months had taken their toll on him too.

He could see me as well, and his first words weren't

exactly sympathetic.

"What the hell, Emmy? Have you seen yourself in a mirror recently? You look like a librarian on crack, and your hair's full of twigs."

"Nice to see you too, Nate."

I ditched the glasses I'd put back on out of habit.

"Your team's being assembled." He was all business. "I've assigned Nye as team leader, and he's in the office already. You've got nine more people on their way in and another thirty-seven on standby for the morning."

The monitor chimed and Nye, one of the supervisors in the London-based investigations team, popped up beside Nate.

"Evening, Emmy. Glad to have you back. Bloody hell, what happened to your hair?"

At least one person was happy to see me, but was my hair really that bad? I toggled a few buttons so I could see what they did. Eek! I looked like I'd been in a fight with a hedge trimmer and come out the loser.

I explained the situation with Tia, going over the chain of events since the evening before last. "I'll send over the photos of the tyre print. Get someone on tracing the van right away, would you?"

"Tom's looking up the registration as we speak." Tom was the control room supervisor, drafted in to help.

I'd liberated Luke's phone from his pocket without him noticing, and now I forwarded the text messages he'd received. There were three in total: the initial one with the photo of Tia, the ransom demand, and directions to the drop site. The first was sent from Tia's phone, and each of the others came from a different number. Burner phones, most likely, but we'd try to trace them anyway.

As I'd suspected, the ransom was for £250,000, but it also requested a copy of the source code for Luke's latest piece of business security software. That explained the low cash demand. The software was in final testing right now, and worth a fortune in the right hands. A competitor or someone wanting to maliciously exploit the vulnerabilities it prevented would kill for it.

I discussed strategy with Nye, and we assigned teams to the phones, the van, and the tyre track. Another team would go out to canvas for witnesses first thing in the morning, and the remaining staff were to comb through Luke's life for possible links. The demand for the source code meant I'd all but discounted Tia being taken by an infatuated admirer or someone connected with me.

"Check a guy called Henry Forster. He lives in Lower Foxford or somewhere near it. I'm fairly certain he's too stupid to have done this, but he and Luke don't see eye to eye," I told Nye.

"I'm planning to look at everyone in the village, but I'll start with him."

"How can I help?" I asked. Nye raised an eyebrow, because I didn't normally get involved at that level. "Tia's important to me. I'll do whatever's needed to get her back."

"Could you ask around your network? If we get any leads that need chasing down, I'll call you."

After Nye signed off, Nate folded his arms. "Are you going to grace us with an explanation yet?"

I sighed. "When Dan's here, and Mack too. I'm not

going through it three times."

It would be painful enough once.

"In that case, I'll go and track down Mack."

While he did that, I trudged back to the kitchen to see how Dan was doing. She had Luke laid out on the white marble breakfast bar where the lighting was good, his feet hanging off over the end. His cut looked better now she'd cleaned it up, and she'd almost finished stitching the edges together.

"Nearly done," she said. "I don't think the scar will be too noticeable."

"Does she know what she's doing?" Luke mumbled.

It was a bit late now if she didn't. "She took a sewing class in college."

He groaned and tried to get up. I shoved him down again.

"I was kidding, okay? Dan's a trained medic. She's stitched up more people than most doctors. I'd trust her far more than some junior in the ER who's only awake because his veins are circulating more caffeine than blood."

When Dan had finished her neat row of sutures, I led Luke upstairs to one of the spare bedrooms and helped him out of his bloodstained clothes.

"What happened in the woods?" I asked him as he sat on the edge of the bed.

He rubbed his temples, remembering too late about the stitches. "Ouch, fuck. I can't remember."

"Nothing?"

"It's all fuzz. There was a guy, I think. Then you came."

"You said earlier that he spoke to you?"

"I don't know. He might have."

"Get some rest. You might recall more in the morning."

"What about Tia? I need to look for her."

"You're in no state to do that right now. Leave it to the professionals."

"But..."

"Lie down. Sleep. I'll talk to you when you wake up."

His blue eyes were already closing and his arguments ceased, soon followed by soft breathing as he drifted off. Once I was satisfied he wouldn't do anything stupid, like try to get out of bed, I headed back to the others.

Nick had made coffee for everyone. Mack appeared on screen next to Nate, and she didn't look any cheerier than he did. Marvellous.

Mack was Mackenzie Fox, a flame-haired former CIA agent who'd been with us for almost a decade. She was a year older than me and certainly saner. I took a seat and leaned back, trying to separate the story I was about to tell from the emotions underlying it. My voice flat, I rehashed the chain of events from the funeral onwards.

When I'd finished, Dan rolled her chair next to mine and hugged me.

"You stupid bint, you didn't have to run away. We'd have been all right."

I looked up at the others.

Nick's face was blank, and Mack rose to her feet. "I've got work to do."

I watched her back as she walked off.

Then Nate took his turn to make me feel worse. "I thought we'd taught you better than to run away from your problems. *Our* problems. We're supposed to be a team. What happened to the real Emmy? The stubborn bitch who faced up to her enemies and never flinched?"

"I don't know what happened, okay? My head was fucked, and I couldn't think straight. I still can't think straight. Nothing makes sense. I didn't want to risk you guys getting hurt, not when I'd already lost my husband. I'm sorrier than I can put into words. Now I've come to my senses, I realise how stupid I was."

"Promise you won't do anything that dumb again, yeah?"

He seemed to have come round, just a little. The band circling my chest loosened infinitesimally.

"I promise. No more running."

"So, what are you planning to do with the murder investigation now?"

"Nothing."

"Nothing? You're going to let them get away with it?"

Uh oh. He was back to angry again.

"For the moment. My head's not completely back in the game yet. Going all out to find who was behind it won't bring the dead back to life, but it may make us lose more. We can't let a need for revenge blind us so we fail to factor in the possible cost."

"Well, at least that sounds more like the old Emmy. The one who looked at everything objectively."

The old me. Who was that girl, and would I ever find her again? The one who never lost her head. The one who weighed up all the options before selecting the one that would give the most advantageous result, no matter how difficult it may be, or how strange the choice might seem to others. The one who was a dispassionate, cold-hearted bitch.

Tonight, I channelled her. "That's my decision."

Nate leaned back in his chair, face dark as a storm cloud on a winter's day. "We'll respect it." Without a doubt, those words were hard for him to say. "But you should know everyone hopes you'll change your mind."

With that parting shot, Nate signed off for the night, saying he'd find Mack and get her to contact the UK team directly to assist. He didn't need to tell me how upset she was—I'd seen that for myself.

Time to get some sleep, or at least, to lie down and stare at the ceiling. Dan gripped my hand as we walked upstairs while Nick stomped off in front. Hopefully, he'd feel more charitable towards me in the morning.

I yawned as I headed towards my bedroom, which was far from everyone else's. Part of me wanted to stay up and do something, but Nye had it under control. I was back in a team now. Enough people were working overnight already, and I'd be more use after a few hours' rest.

I'd get up first thing to sharpen my claws.

Chapter 29

LUKE TURNED HIS head slowly from side to side, his neck stiff. The pillow was soft, the mattress firm. It smelled different to normal—something floral. He cracked an eyelid open. Since when did he have a pale pink duvet? Nope, definitely not his bed. Where was he?

Sunlight spilled between the half-closed curtains, and he squinted at the brightness. Was it morning or afternoon? Luke didn't know the day of the week, let alone how he got there or even what country he'd landed up in. His mind blurred around the edges.

Through the window, buildings clad in cream stonework with grey slate roofs stood out against the blue sky. The occasional purr of a car rolling past told him he was within reach of civilisation, at least.

He tried to get up, but his head had other ideas. A wrecking ball pounded inside, doing its worst. Giddiness overcame him, the room spinning as he sank back onto the mattress, but when he closed his eyes, the events of yesterday slowly, slowly trickled into his brain. That awful walk through the woods with the bagful of money. The brief conversation with the sick bastard who took Tia. Then his memory went fuzzy again.

And no wonder. He thumped his head against the

pillow in frustration then bit his tongue to save from crying out. What the...? Probing gently, he winced as he found a golf ball-sized knot on the back of his head, and when he ran a hand over his forehead, he discovered a line of stitches on his temple. What happened? Who stitched him up? This place sure didn't look like a hospital.

A vague picture of Ash floated into his head, her face in shadow, lit only by the moon flickering through leafless trees. Had she been there? In the woods? Why would she when he'd sent her away?

Thinking of Ash made his chest tighten. Partly with sadness, but mostly with anger.

He'd told her he loved her, for pity's sake—but she clearly hadn't felt the same way. What had gone so wrong? She was the first woman he'd lived with, the first woman he'd wanted in his bed night after night, and although she'd seemed reluctant to commit, he'd hoped she'd stay indefinitely. Hadn't he offered her everything? His home, his heart, even his damn credit card. What was with her attitude towards money, anyway? Even though she had none, she'd never wanted his. She'd even suggested getting a job, for crying out loud. As if he'd let her work for minimum wage when he earned a hundred times that.

Ash had genuinely cared about Tia, of that he was sure. Past girlfriends had treated his sister as an irritation to be avoided at all costs, but Ash connected with her. Tia had become a different person, a much nicer one, since they met.

But Ash had betrayed him.

Who was she, really? She admitted she'd lied, but what was the truth? Maybe, with hindsight, he'd been a little hasty in kicking her out, because now questions were eating away at him.

What did she want?

Why had she come to Lower Foxford?

Could she be working with the kidnapper? Was that why she'd been in the woods?

So many unknowns. Half-formed thoughts swam around Luke's head, but each time he tried to grab one, it disappeared into the mire.

Think. Think. Think.

Okay, got one. A question. Why was he in this room? Had he been kidnapped too?

Muscles screaming in protest, he forced himself out of bed. Hmm. Who had undressed him? He'd certainly been wearing more than boxer shorts when he left home. A pile of clothes on a chair by the window caught his attention, and he shuffled over. Mud and reddish-brown stains covered his jeans and shirt. Blood? He sniffed, and a metallic tang wafted into his nostrils. His blood? The kidnapper's? Tia's? *Hell, please don't let it be Tia's.*

Outside the window, a small flock of birds landed in the park opposite. No, not a park. Tall iron railings surrounded the greenery, and a pair of sturdy gates kept the riffraff out. One of those private squares that made the expensive parts of London so desirable? A car hooted its horn, and a black cab pulled up below.

Yes, this was definitely London.

Luke cringed at the thought of putting on his filthy clothes, but what other option was there? He opened the nearest door and found himself in a large bathroom. A stranger stared back from the mirror above the basin—sunken eyes, a couple of days' worth of stubble, smudges of dirt on his cheeks. He turned to get a better look at the line of stitches. Fuck, that was a nasty-looking cut, and it stung like hell.

How had he got it? Why couldn't he remember?

A washcloth sat on the marble vanity, and he used it to clean up his face. Next to the basin, a row of pale pink toiletry bottles reminded him of an upmarket hotel. Who did they belong to? *Was* this a hotel? If he had indeed been kidnapped, there were certainly worse places to be held.

The cold water helped him to think straight, and he returned to the luxuriously appointed bedroom. Despite the opulent curtains and fifty throw-pillows, there were no personal touches, and whoever chose the paintings was either schizophrenic or seriously indecisive. A rose in a vase. A pair of dice. A green tiger drinking from a rippling pool. Luke squinted at the signatures, but he didn't recognise any of the artists.

A selection of clothes hung in the wardrobe, both male and female, some cheap, some expensive. Probably not a hotel, then. The nightstand held a torch, tissues, and an economy-sized box of condoms. Had the previous occupant hunted pussy for a hobby?

Finding the other door unlocked, he overcame his nerves and walked out into a long hallway. More doors, more paintings. He peered at the closest, a vibrant abstract in acrylics, a mixture of purples and pinks. Looked original. *What was this place?*

He counted the doors—five in total, all closed. Both ends of the hallway disappeared around corners, and apart from the faint sounds of the street outside, silence reigned.

Should he go left or right? Even that decision

seemed too difficult today. *Just pick one.* Left, he'd go left. Around the corner, sweeping staircases framed a landing and led down two floors to a grand atrium dominated by a magnificent chandelier. In between, a lift door stood closed. He looked up, momentarily dizzy again, and saw the stairs continued up, seemingly for eternity. How big was this place? It reminded him of the mazes he used to program on his first computer.

Do you want to open the door? Yes or no? Yes? Haha. You're dead.

Unsteady on his feet, he descended to the next floor, paused, and listened. Nothing. Another flight of stairs, and he stood below the chandelier he'd glimpsed from above—a work of art at least four feet high, made from multi-coloured blown glass. It belonged in a museum, not a private home.

But he had no time to stop and marvel. He continued past a cream leather couch and matching sideboard complete with fresh flowers, searching for signs of life.

Three archways led off the atrium, and he caught a snippet of sound coming from the left. Voices? Did they have something to do with Tia's disappearance?

Luke continued in that direction, stomach fluttering. Past a dining room, past a cavernous lounge, past a music room with a grand piano sitting silent in one corner. Who played it? This place made his home look like a shack.

Finally, he made it to the kitchen. A kitchen bigger than his first apartment, the one he'd rented in Switzerland. Two strangers looked up as he entered, and a curvy, dark-haired girl put down her mug of coffee.

"Welcome back. You want coffee? Something to eat?"

The accent said New York, and the clothes said hooker.

"Should I know you?"

"Probably not. We met last night, but you were pretty much out of it. I'm Dan, and this is Nick."

Luke sized Nick up and found himself wanting. Nick looked as if he'd just stepped off the cover of GQ magazine whereas Luke had only graced the inside pages.

"Why am I here?" he asked. "Thanks for the offer of coffee, but I need to get home."

Every time Luke thought about Tia, a ripple of fear went through him. If his heart hammered any harder, he'd have a coronary.

"Ash brought you. She asked us to help with your problem."

"My problem?" Luke played dumb. The kidnapper had said to keep his mouth shut. "What problem?"

"With your sister? How bad *was* that bang on the head?"

Luke's knees buckled, and he collapsed onto a stool.

"You okay? Don't worry—we've investigated kidnappings before." She took a bite out of a pastry, calm as anything.

A groan escaped Luke's lips. "Are you the police? The man who took Tia said he'd kill her if the police got involved."

"Relax, we work for a private security firm."

Before Dan could elaborate, Nick broke in. "Nice though this chat is, we have to get to work. We need all the information we can get to find your sister."

"I'm not sure about this."

"The way I see it, you don't have a lot of choice. I don't know how much you remember about last night, but you nearly got shot in the head. Trust me when I say you can't do this alone."

Ever swim out of your depth as a kid and panic when your feet couldn't touch the bottom? Luke was just surprised he hadn't drowned yet. He needed help, and he needed it badly.

Anyone who could afford this place had to be good at their job, right?

"What do we do now?"

A look passed between the pair. Relief? Suspicion?

"First, we need to work out why Tia was taken," Dan said. "That's the key to finding her."

"But I don't know why. Honestly, I don't."

Dan got up and poured another mug of coffee from a filter jug then slid it in Luke's direction.

"Has anyone threatened you?" Nick asked. "Or Tia? Any problems at work?

"Nothing. This came out of the blue." Luke sipped, hoping the caffeine would give him some much-needed energy.

"Have you noticed anybody following you? Seen any cars parked up in strange places?"

"No and no. Believe me, I've been thinking this through myself."

"I thought as much. Ash would have noticed even if you didn't."

Ash again. "How is she involved in this?"

Nick ignored the question. "What are your thoughts on the ransom?"

"They wanted £250,000 plus the source code for

my company's new product."

"I know."

"How?"

Nick shrugged. "Not important. How much is that source code worth?"

"Millions, in the right hands."

"What does it do?"

"Incorporates the usual firewall and anti-virus software, but the key feature is when it detects a threat, instead of just blocking it, the code I wrote starts tracking it back to its source. Simply put, it turns the tables on malicious hackers. There are a lot of people who don't want it to see the light of day."

"So who would steal it? Hackers?"

"Possibly. Or our competitors. It's light years ahead of anything else on the market at the moment. Some individuals in the industry have dubious morals, and they'd be quite happy to use it as a base for their own software."

"So hackers, competitors. Who else?"

Luke sighed. "Anyone looking to make a quick buck. They wouldn't have to use the product themselves—buyers would be lining up for it. If the program gets out, my reputation will be trashed. What kind of cyber security expert lets his code get stolen? Plus my company will end up in the toilet. We've sunk a lot of resources into that program."

"Who knows about its existence?"

"Everyone who reads the industry press. I've been doing interviews about it for months."

"So the person who took it wouldn't necessarily need to be a techie then? Not if they could simply sell it on?" Dan asked.

"No, although I spent a few hours modifying the code so it didn't quite work. Nothing too obvious, though, in case they noticed and took it out on Tia. A good programmer could probably fix the changes in a couple of months."

Dan stood to pour herself another coffee.

"Top up?" she asked Nick.

He nodded and handed his cup over. Luke felt too sick to drink his. How could they stay so relaxed? When Dan sat down again, Luke averted his eyes as her skirt rode up so high it was almost indecent.

She didn't seem to notice. "This guy you gave the ransom to, what do you remember about him?"

Luke fought through the sludge in his head. "Not much. Things are coming back in bits and pieces, but I'm still not sure what happened."

"Talk us through what you do recall."

"The message gave me coordinates for a clearing in the woods. I was supposed to leave the bag there." Insane, now he thought about it. But desperate men did stupid things. "Except when I arrived, I saw a man on the far side, watching me."

"You're sure it was a male?" Nick asked.

"I didn't get a good look at his face, but when he punched me, it bloody hurt. I doubt a woman would have such a vicious right hook."

Nick laughed at that. "You'd be surprised."

"It wasn't fucking funny." Luke's jaw still ached from the hit.

Nick grew serious again. "Sorry. Wind back a bit. What happened when you saw the guy?"

"I walked towards him, but he held a hand up, so I stopped. He came to me instead."

"Then what?"

"He pointed a gun at me and asked for the money."

"And you gave it to him?" Dan asked, and it was impossible to miss the incredulity in her voice.

"What would you have done? Taken his gun off him?"

"Probably. You remember much about the gun?"

"Only that he pointed it in my damn face. And when I asked where Tia was, he told me I'd find out when I handed the bag over. But when I gave it to him, he just laughed."

"That was it? He laughed?"

"No, he spoke as well."

"And...?" Dan prompted.

Luke rubbed his temples as if the motion could clear the fog in his head. What had the man said? He caught the edge of his stitches with one finger, and the pain helped to focus his mind.

"He said I disappointed him. That he never expected me to be such a pushover. I told him I just wanted my sister back, and that we had a deal." Luke closed his eyes as the man's voice echoed in his ears. "And he said, 'Deal? I never said we had a deal. You took my life, and I'm getting it back.' At least I think that's right."

"Any idea what he meant by that?"

"Not a clue. It doesn't make much sense, does it?"

"Did he seem familiar?"

"Not at all. He wore a hat, and he'd covered the bottom half of his face with a scarf. His voice... His voice was kind of high-pitched for a man, but I didn't recognise that either."

"And were those his exact words?"

"I'm not a hundred percent sure. Everything's fuzzy."

"A little haziness is to be expected. Can you remember what happened next?" Dan asked.

"I saw his finger move on the trigger. No way could I outrun a bullet, so I leapt at him. What other option did I have? That was when he punched me." Luke gingerly touched his cut again. "Then I ended up on the ground, but everything's black after that."

It was more than he'd remembered this morning, and he half wished he could forget again.

Dan tapped her nails on the counter. She'd painted them turquoise with black dots, too playful for such a serious situation.

"That's okay. We've got more to work with now. His comment about you taking his life suggests your paths have crossed before, so we'll concentrate our efforts on your past. Can we get access to your employee files? Have you fired anybody who might have borne a grudge?"

She thought he hadn't considered that?

"I can't think of anyone, but I'll arrange access to the files. Whoever this guy is, he's well on his way to taking my life now, isn't he? I mean, he's got my sister, a chunk of my money, and the software I've spent years developing. What else is there?"

Luke groaned as Ash popped into his head. A week ago, she'd have been on that list, but where did they stand now?

"Oh, he didn't get the ransom," Dan said chirpily. "Ash did. It's in the strong room."

"What?"

"I guess you forgot that part. The guy was about to

shoot you when Ash got there. She stopped him, but when she paused to check on you, she lost ground in the chase. The asshole jumped in a van and escaped, but he'd already dropped the bag. Probably the knife lodged in his biceps made it tricky to carry."

"Have I missed something? How did he get a knife in his biceps?"

"Ash."

Ash?

"Let me get this straight—Ash got close enough to a man carrying a gun to stab him in the arm? He could have shot her! Does she have a death wish?"

"Oh, she wasn't that close. About twenty metres away by all accounts. She threw the knife."

Dan made Ash's actions sound like the most natural thing in the world.

"You're shitting me. Is she crazy?"

Nick and Dan just looked at each other.

"Yes," they replied in unison.

CHAPTER 30

THE DAY AFTER the attempted ransom drop, I got up at five, but not out of choice. A mistaken assumption that I'd sleep better in my own bed led to me running through the house in the early hours, only waking when I fell over a coffee table in the lounge.

I sat on the floor breathing hard, and the pain across my shins told me I'd have a lovely bruise later. Why did this have to happen? I hadn't suffered from such an awful sleepwalking episode for months. Since before I met Luke, in fact. I swore under my breath then froze as I heard a noise behind me. Strong hands reached under my armpits and pulled me to my feet. Nick. I recognised the aftershave and his own earthy smell under it.

He spun me around to face him. "Fucking hell. Are the nightmares getting worse?"

"They were bad after the funeral, but then they got better. I went two weeks without one before Tia disappeared."

"What did you dream of this time? I could hardly keep up. You've done a couple of laps of each floor and been up and down all four staircases."

"The kidnapper. I was chasing the kidnapper, but no matter how fast I ran, I couldn't catch him. Then I fell and woke up."

"It'll be a nightmare for everyone if those demons are back."

"I know that, Nick. Believe me, I know it."

Even in my sleep, I couldn't do right.

His face softened. "Come on, let's go back to bed."

"What's the point? I won't sleep. I might as well head into the office and do something useful."

"Are you sure you're ready for that?" His voice held more than a hint of concern. That was Nick all over. He rarely bore a grudge for long.

"I've got to go sometime, haven't I? Why not today? Everyone'll be whispering behind my back, anyway, so they might as well do it to my face."

The weather forecast predicted a crisp, clear day, so I whipped the cover off the Aston Martin. I'd barely driven the thing since I bought it, and I needed to lift my spirits. Metallic black with a black leather interior, it had a paddle shift gearbox and a top speed of 205 mph. Not that I'd ever drive so fast. At least, not in London. Too many traffic lights.

The journey left me smiling—I had to take pleasure in the small things nowadays—and when I walked into the large, modern building hidden away on a backstreet in Kings Cross, I found one of the conference rooms had already been commandeered as a base for the investigation. Nye and a few others had spent the night there, and what little information we'd gathered was projected onto the wall in an electronic index card system. That didn't stop Nye from having a pile of paper on his desk, though. He loved to print *everything*.

Despite the team's efforts, the only concrete lead was the van, and that didn't look hopeful. Mack *might* have snuck into the police database overnight and found the plates were stolen. They'd been taken almost four months ago from a silver Mercedes Sprinter van parked in South London.

Despite the multitude of automatic number plate recognition cameras dotted around the city, the registration number hadn't been spotted since. Either the kidnapper only put the plates on his van recently, or he'd been driving it outside London. Or maybe the bastard had just been plain lucky.

If it was the latter, I intended to make that luck run out.

"I've sent a pair of guys to the owner's address in case the theft report wasn't genuine," Nye said.

"I saw a Ford in the woods, not a Mercedes."

Nye leaned back in his seat. "I wanted to cover all bases, and we haven't found any other leads."

"You were right to send them. I'll get the cops to keep an eye out as well, off the record."

For that, I called an acquaintance in the Metropolitan Police. Jason Bridges was a good guy, one of the few cops I trusted. He saw the bigger picture rather than striving to keep his paperwork shipshape and his statistics up.

His methods meant he wasn't always popular with his superiors, and more than once he'd shared his frustrations over a drink. I'd offered him a job several times, but for the moment his loyalty lay with the Met. He genuinely believed he could help to make the city a better place, and I had to respect his tenacity.

Months had passed since I'd spoken to him. Did he know about my break?

"It's Emmy. Long time, no speak."

"You're not kidding, mate. I heard you'd gone AWOL."

"I needed some time off. You know, with everything that happened."

"Fair enough. Look, I'm sorry about your husband. Nobody deserves that."

"Thanks. It was a shock to lose him." I didn't want Jason's sympathy, and I didn't want to discuss the past either, so I moved the conversation back to the problem at hand. "I need a favour."

"I had a feeling this wasn't a social call. What do you want?"

He was right. I didn't do social calls. Although perhaps I should start? Spending so much time away from my old life had made me realise just how much my friends meant to me. But now wasn't the time to think about that.

"Can you keep an eye out for a white Ford Transit?" I read out the registration number.

"Sure thing. If anything gets picked up, what do you want done?"

"Nothing, just call me with the details. Quickly, yeah?"

"Right-oh. Don't suppose you want to tell me what this is about?"

I laughed. "You know me better than that, Jase."

"Always did play your cards close to your chest. Talk to you soon."

"You can count on it. And thanks."

I hung up, shoving the amber phone I'd recently

been reunited with into my pocket alongside the red phone and Ash's phone. At this rate, I was going to need more pockets.

Living with Luke, I hadn't needed to cart so much crap around with me. Today, I'd stuffed my jacket with the bare essentials—the phones, my wallet, a couple of knives, lip balm, flex-cuffs, tissues, a tactical pen, pepper spray, a torch bright enough to blind a man, my favourite Zippo lighter, and a tube of mascara—I felt like a pack pony.

Bradley's voice played in my head. "Emmy, you're ruining the line of your jacket. It's by Ishmael, and it wasn't designed to be used as luggage."

Sigh.

At a quarter to ten, my pocket started playing "Put Your Arms Around Me" by Texas, the ringtone I'd set for Nick back in happier days. I fumbled to get the red phone out, dropped it, then cursed as the screen cracked. Ah well, another one bites the dust. The amber phone rang ten seconds later, and this time I managed to answer successfully.

"Yeah?"

"Did you know Luke had a conversation with the kidnapper before you got there?"

"No, I didn't. Luke wasn't exactly coherent last night when I tried to speak to him. What did the bastard say?"

"Something about Luke ruining his life. I'll send over the recording of the interview. You'll want to hear it for yourself."

That would have been my next request. He knew me too well. "Thanks, Nicky."

Upstairs in my office, I wiped the dust off my laptop and turned it on. Thirty seconds later, my breath hitched as my husband smouldered back at me from the screen, one arm around me and the other held up to ward off Bradley, who'd been intent on replacing his white silk pocket square with a linen one that matched my purple dress. Bradley liked to be absolutely correct when it came to black tie.

Funny how the little things became so unimportant, wasn't it? Right now, the idea of tarting myself up and going out to a party made me want to crawl under the duvet and hide.

So, I stuck with my favourite distraction: work. Sloane had been busy—my inbox only contained eleven emails, all dated today.

Did she know I was back yet? Things had happened so quickly last night, I wasn't sure anyone had mentioned my return to her. I bashed out a quick message to let her know.

When I took a closer look at the screen, I spotted a new folder she'd set up titled *IMPORTANT—For Emmy to read when she comes back*. Uh-oh. Ninety-seven messages. At least she hadn't assumed I was dead. On the downside, it looked as if I had some bedtime reading to do.

But it could wait. I ignored the emails for the moment and put my headphones on. The file from Nick had arrived already, and I listened to it twice all the way through before pausing and rewinding the end, replaying the kidnapper's comments several times over.

The man's actions bugged me. When I saw him

standing over Luke, I could have sworn he was about to pull the trigger. He'd had his finger on it for sure. But Luke was unconscious by that point. What would the bastard have achieved by killing him? Any "professional" kidnapper, and by that I mean one after an easy payoff, would have been long gone. Committing murder would complicate affairs to no end.

My gut said the kidnapper had a personal vendetta against Luke, and that was borne out by Luke's memories. He wanted Luke's life? What were the main things in it? His work, his sister, a stack of money, and at one time, me. My chest tightened when I thought of what we'd once had.

Emmy, stop it. Concentrate.

The kidnapper almost took three of those pillars, and indeed Luke himself, out of the picture. Oh, how I wished he'd tried for the fourth. I'd relish the day that arsehole came for me.

But he'd escaped, and now we needed to comb through Luke's life for anyone with a grudge. Nick's idea of starting with employees was a good one. For the time I'd been with Luke, he'd done nothing but work and hang out with me. Hardly contentious, and he'd always seemed too damn nice to make enemies. But did he have any dark secrets lurking in his past?

I sat at the back of the room as Nye briefed the team, preferring to delegate the lead role for the time being. Nye certainly had the experience, and although I might have had seniority on paper, my head still wasn't in the game. But I did add my thoughts at the end.

"We need to look for someone with a personal grudge against Luke. Try work, ex-girlfriends, their boyfriends, previous domestic staff. Everyone." Everyone but Henry. He'd panned out as a lead—on the night of the ransom drop, he'd passed out in The Coach and Horses after being slapped by the barmaid.

"Family?" Nye asked.

"There's only his mother and Tia. His mother's a bitch, but she'd be shooting herself in the foot if she killed the golden goose."

"What about neighbours?"

"In the time I spent in Lower Foxford, we barely saw them, but check anyway."

The team drifted off to their stations, ready to start work, and Nye slumped down behind his laptop. Had he slept at all in the last twenty-four hours? Judging by his yawn, I suspected not.

"Nye, you look shit," I told him. "Get some sleep."

"Someone needs to supervise the team."

Yes, but not him. "I'll do it."

"You?"

"I think I'm qualified."

The rest of the guys looked as surprised as Nye when I settled into the top seat in the control room. Hardly surprising—at least three years had passed since I'd spent a whole day in there. So why now? I told myself it would help in the hunt for Tia, but the truth was, I didn't want to speak to Luke.

Was I being a coward? Hell, yeah. I'd rather face the business end of a machine gun than my inner self, any day, and the curious glances of the staff as I called my contacts in the city were easier to deal with than a single moment with Luke. I didn't enjoy the scrutiny, but after a while, I tuned out the discomfort. They'd get bored with me after a day or two.

Don't think, don't feel, just do. *Be a robot, Emmy*. I missed the simplicity of my life with Luke. Why hadn't I told him the truth in the first place? What if he'd known my true identity all along? Maybe, just maybe, there was a chance he'd have liked Emmy as well as Ash. Instead, I'd fucked up my first serious relationship in years, probably since Nick, in fact, with no chance of salvaging it. I mean, who would choose to continue a relationship based almost entirely on lies?

All I could do now was concentrate my efforts on finding Tia then getting her safely back.

Tia. I missed her too.

She'd been the sunshine in my life lately, making me smile in the evenings while I waited for Luke to get home. Was she keeping herself together? Had the kidnapper hurt her? The thought of her being held prisoner saw me planning ways to make him pay. And believe me, when it came to making lives a misery, my résumé was second to none. Which reminded me... I needed to fit in some target practice.

Mid-morning, the team who'd gone to check on the stolen number plates returned. The registered owner was one Gabir Hassani, an Iraqi refugee now settled in South London, according to Mack.

"He wasn't there. His sister said he went home to visit their parents," the operative told me.

"In Iraq?"

"He left over a week ago."

"Any chance she was lying?"

My guy shrugged. "If she was, she did a good job of it. Showed us a family photo. Gabir Hassani's missing his right arm and his left leg."

Fuck. It may have been dark, but there was no way the man I chased through the woods was missing two limbs.

Which meant that avenue was a bust.

I spent the afternoon calling up old acquaintances and even went out to visit a couple, but nobody had heard a whisper about a kidnapping. All the other leads evaporated too. We were chasing shadows in an Arctic winter.

No hospital in the south of England had treated a stab wound to an upper arm last night. Disappointing, but at the same time, I hoped the kidnapper was in a lot of pain. The tyre prints belonged to a common set of Goodyears, the perfect size for a transit van. You could buy them from almost any tyre fitter, and it would be an impossible task trying to trace them all.

Six people had canvassed Lower Foxford, and while four villagers thought they might have seen transit vans in the vicinity, none could give a description of the driver. A further two operatives were in Luke's house and reported all was quiet there. They'd opened the mail, but only found a credit card bill and a circular from the local Porsche dealership inviting Luke to a canapé party.

"The credit card bill's interesting, though," our man told me.

"How so?"

"The man goes to a tanning salon every week."

Yes, thanks, I had noticed.

"And he spent a fortune on that holiday to the Bahamas. Even rented a private plane for the transfers. Are you still going?"

Luke had been planning to surprise me with a holiday? Fuck. Just when I'd thought I couldn't feel any shittier, I did.

"Is there anything relevant to the case?" I growled, then felt guilty because this was my problem, not anybody else's.

"What? Oh, no. Nothing at all."

My fists balled automatically, a subconscious reminder that I needed to speak to Jimmy.

Deep breaths, Emmy. Act professionally.

"Send the canvassers on to Middleton Foxford, would you? Keep one person with you at Luke's, just in case. Make yourselves at home, but do me a favour and don't drink the expensive wine."

"Right-o, boss."

Next up, I bit the bullet and called Mack. I couldn't put it off any longer.

"Hey, it's me." I forced a smile, knowing it would transfer to my voice.

"What can I do?"

Not her usual, "Hey, honey," or even a "How are ya?"

I'd never been great at handling these situations. With strangers, I could slip into a role, but when one of my best friends in the world treated me with such indifference, it hurt worse than a bullet.

"Uh, could you take a look through Luke's bank accounts?"

"Yes. Anything else?"

"You know the drill. See what else you can get into.

Home computers, work network, anything interesting on the web."

"Sure."

"Thanks."

Click.

Talk about strained. Usually, Mack was the bubbliest out of all of us, but she'd barely given me the time of day. Boy, did I have a lot of bridges to mend.

With that in mind, I fired off an email to Bradley to let him know I was back. If he found out last, he'd never forgive me, but if I phoned him, that would be the entire day gone. Okay, one final call left to make. Would it be as painful as talking to Mack? Time to find out. I'd lived with Jimmy and his wife, Jackie, for almost two years, until just before my sixteenth birthday. He was the closest thing I had to a father.

"Jimmy?" my voice cracked, and I took a sip from the glass of water on my desk.

"Amanda, that you?"

Few people knew me as Amanda. My birth certificate agreed with them, but I hated the name. Why? Because my mother chose it. And by chose it, I mean she opened a book of baby names and got bored before she'd got to the end of the A's. But Jimmy had always called me Amanda, and so I let it be.

"Yeah, it's me."

"Blimey, girl, you had us worried the way you dropped off the face of the earth."

"I needed to be on my own for a while. I'm sorry."

"I get you, sweet thing, but next time you gotta promise to call Jimmy, you got it?"

"Hoping there won't be a next time."

"You won't be replacing that husband of yours in a

hurry, then?"

"Doubt I'll ever replace him. He was one of a kind."

"That he was, girl. That he was. Now, you know I wasn't keen on him at first, but he grew on me over the years. He did you proud."

I choked back a laugh. Wasn't keen on him? A bit of an understatement from Jimmy. When my husband announced he wanted me to move to the States with him, Jimmy had threatened to fold him in half, hang him from the ceiling, and use him as a punchbag. They were about the same size. It would have been an interesting match.

"I know he did me proud," I sniffed.

"No tears, girl. Gotta keep your chin up. You in town at the moment?"

"Yeah, working."

"Well, try and fit in a few minutes to come and see us."

"I'll try, Jimmy. I'll visit as soon as I can. I promise."

Something else for my to-do list. At least Jimmy didn't sound as unhappy with me as everyone else. Meanwhile, I had to sort out this mess with Tia so she and Luke could get on with their lives while I got on with mine.

Whatever was left of it.

CHAPTER 31

THUNK. THUNK. THUNK.

One last roundhouse kick to the punchbag, and I stripped off my boxing gloves. A good session in the gym always made me feel better. Took some of the edge off. An edge so sharp right now that it could slice through titanium. A quick shower to get rid of the sheen of sweat, and I was ready to face the world again.

But first, food.

We always kept the staff kitchens fully stocked, but when I opened the fridge on the fifth floor, all I found was turkey on rye, falafel with carrot, chicken salad sans mayo, apples, grapes, celery.

"Has Toby been here?" I asked Tina, one of our London assistants.

"He sent a directive. The catering staff took all the junk food out an hour ago."

"But I *need* cookies."

"I think that's why he did it."

Gah. I also craved a meatball marinara sub, but I didn't have time to go out and buy one. Instead, I grabbed a bowl of fruit salad and headed for the conference room. Judging by the glum faces looking back at me from around the table, frustratingly little had happened.

"Can you give me an update?"

"We've been through the employee files, but there's little in there in the way of disputes," a woman told me.

What was she called? She'd joined just before I left. Helena? Melanie? Usually, I remembered names, but I couldn't think straight.

"That doesn't surprise me. Luke isn't the type to go around upsetting his employees. So there's nothing?"

"We found one complaint that looked kind of juicy. Luke sacked a programmer for lying that a project had passed beta testing when it hadn't, and the guy wasn't happy about it."

"I take it you followed up?"

"Oh, yes, straight away. He was surprisingly cooperative. Said he'd been going through a nasty divorce and things just got on top of him."

"Did he seem the type to bear a grudge?"

"He admitted he hadn't been happy at the time, but he didn't blame Luke anymore. Even said he'd have done the same. He reckons he's got a new perspective on life now he's moved to Sydney with his boyfriend."

"As in Sydney, Australia?"

Helena/Melanie nodded.

"Did you corroborate?"

"We sent an operative from the Sydney office to check on the happy couple. They offered him a beer and invited him back for a barbecue."

A complete bust, then.

Mack called back at five past eight, just as I was rooting through my desk drawers for a stray chocolate bar. No luck.

"I've got good news and bad news."

"Hit me with it."

"I've got into Luke's bank accounts, and his mother's. And through the firewall on his home computer and his work servers."

"And what's the bad news?"

"I haven't found anything concrete. But from the log files on the server, I'd say someone else has been trying to do the same as me; they just haven't been so successful."

"Any idea who?"

"No, but I'll keep trying to find out."

"Thanks. We could use a break. Was that the only thing of interest?"

"Oh, there's plenty that's interesting. Do you know how much money Luke gives to his mother each month? It's thousands, Ems. And she spends it all on hairdressers and clothes and golf and manicures."

"I've met the woman, and that comes as no surprise. But I meant anything of interest to the case?"

"No. I don't think so."

Mack hesitated a little too long before answering for my liking. What was she holding back? I was tempted to push, but my name already graced her shit list. No, I trusted she'd tell me if it was important.

"All right, we'll speak later."

At least she hadn't frozen me out today. This was progress.

At nine in the evening, I headed home. I needed to recharge, and although I had a fold-out bed in my office, after last night, I didn't want to risk sleeping in it. Bad enough to have Nick catch me sleepwalking without my entire staff finding out about my nocturnal adventures.

When I got back to Albany House, I snuck up the rear stairs from the garage, keeping my fingers crossed Luke had gone to bed so I could avoid talking to him. Stupid for someone who'd once thrived on confrontation.

"How was the office?" Dan asked.

Shit. Should have used the front door. Because Luke was sitting next to Dan, typing away on his laptop with Nick the other side of him.

Smile, Emmy. It intimidates those who want to destroy you, so said my husband.

"Yeah. Good. Great. I had spinach salad for lunch."

Dan laughed then grew serious again. "Luke might have found something."

Really? "Like what?"

Luke looked me in the eye for the first time since our argument. "I got an email alert a couple of hours ago to say someone was in my mainframe at work. They tripped an alarm while they were looking at the code for my new program, the same one the kidnapper wanted. I'm trying to track them."

I had a bad feeling about this. "Have you got very far?"

"Yes and no. Might sound crazy but, I think I know who it is."

"Go on."

"Well... You see... The thing is... I'm involved on the fringes of the online hacking community."

I recalled the time I'd caught him in the police

database. Fringes my arse. "I already knew that. And?"

"You did?"

"Sure, and it makes perfect sense. You build cyber security products. The best way to defend something is to know every possible way to attack it."

I worked that way as well, except in the physical world rather than virtual.

"And you're not judging me for being a hacker?"

"That's not the sort of person I am. You'd know that if you thought about it. I didn't lie to you about everything."

Plus, I'd be a complete hypocrite if I got upset at Luke for skirting the bounds of legality.

"I guess." He paused to type in another command. "Anyway, there's this hacker called Diablo. He's one of the best, and we've always had a rivalry. Until now, I thought it was friendly, but I'm ninety percent sure that's who broke into my system. I recognise his footprint. So, if we can find Diablo, we might also find the kidnapper."

"I hate to rain on your parade, but I doubt that."

Dan looked at Nick, Nick looked at Dan, and Nick raised an eyebrow.

"Bloody Mack," I muttered to him.

Did Mack use the name Diablo? I'd lost count of her aliases over the years, but she was a hacker, and she'd just been in Luke's system.

Nick rolled his eyes. "You really think so?"

"Let's find out, shall we?"

Luke narrowed his eyes as I slid his laptop over to my side of the table, but he didn't try to stop me. A minute later, I'd navigated through our company website to the internal messenger program Mack herself had written. She'd clear out his browser history afterwards.

Diamond: Diablo???

A second later, her reply came.

Mack: Shit.

I spun the laptop back to Luke. "Now, you two play nice."

"Huh?"

"Diablo isn't our kidnapper. Diablo's on our side. Meet Mack."

"Who's Mack?"

"One of my closest friends. Happy hacking."

As I left the kitchen to go to bed, Dan and Nick trailing behind me, I heard the keys clicking as Luke typed out a reply to Mack. Hopefully, this would be the start of a beautiful friendship.

I woke at six the next morning in my own bed—a definite improvement. Barely coherent, I stumbled downstairs, zombie-like, my arms outstretched for the coffee machine. Two minutes later, I took my first sip of espresso, savouring the burn from the rich Colombian. An old friend was branching out into the coffee business, and he'd sent me the beans to try. Not bad.

"How are you feeling today?" Ruth asked. She'd been my housekeeper for years now, and knew not to ask questions before I'd had my first hit of caffeine.

"I need to call the control room."

"Young Nick already did that. Nothing new came in overnight."

I reached over for my phone, but Mack was offline and therefore asleep. She didn't keep office hours like a normal person. Most of the time, she worked unsociable hours as the sunshine battled with her inner vampire.

"An impasse," I muttered. "I hate playing the waiting game."

"You need to take your mind off things, love. You know you don't do well when you overthink. Why don't you spend half an hour in the pool?"

"I should help with the case instead."

"From the chatter in here earlier, they've got enough people working on that already. I don't know about you, but I do my best thinking in the peace and quiet. Maybe you'll come up with a few ideas?"

Okay, so she was right on that part. More than once, I'd had a brainwave out running or cycling or, yes, stroking lazily up and down the pool.

But today, I swam a couple of miles without any light bulbs pinging on, and my fingers turned into little prunes. My stress levels dropped in the water, but they soon rose again as I got dressed in jeans; an old, worn T-shirt; and a fresh pair of contacts. I was still wearing the lenses for Luke's sake. I wasn't sure where I stood with him, and if I was going to make a clean break at the end of this, it seemed easier to give him as little of the real me as possible.

"Breakfast?" Ruth asked when I got back to the kitchen.

My stomach answered with a loud rumble.

"Toast?"

"Sounds good to me."

Except before I could get the Nutella out of the

cupboard, a commotion in the hallway caught my attention. I raised an eyebrow at Ruth, and she shrugged.

Okay, better investigate. As I got closer, a high-pitched voice made me groan.

"Where's Emmy? Is she up yet?"

And Luke replied. Shit.

"I don't think there's anyone called Emmy here."

"Nonsense, it's her... Oh! There you are! Sweet mother of Gaultier, who did that to your hair? It's just not nice. In fact, it's nasty! You look like a librarian who just escaped from the 1980s."

Luke's brow furrowed as a short but exuberant man marched over to me. His pink skinny jeans were studded with diamantes and matched his off-the-shoulder Pringle sweater—tame in comparison to some of his outfits. He held up the ends of my hair for closer examination.

"I cut it a bit," I confessed without thinking.

"What did you use? An axe?"

Deep breaths, Emmy. "Bradley, what the hell are you doing here?"

"You said you were back, so I flew over on the red eye and, well, SURPRISE!" He gave me jazz hands. "It was awful. There were no business class seats left, and I had to fly economy. Economy! Thank goodness I had my travel pillow and a cashmere throw with me. And a really cute member of the cabin crew gave me an eye mask and a pair of earplugs. And his phone number too, but I'd better not tell Miles that."

Miles, Bradley's boyfriend, spent his waking hours writing papers on ancient Egyptian burial sites, when he wasn't overseas digging them up himself, anyway.

I'd never quite fathomed out how they worked as a couple. Bradley loved bright colours and changed his hairstyle the way most men changed their socks, which is to say about once a fortnight. Today's effort was platinum blond and gelled up in a faux-hawk. Miles, on the other hand, was as drab as the beige jumpers he favoured. But they'd been together for a decade now, so they had to be doing something right.

Before I could throttle Bradley, the front door opened and one person after another walked in, dumping packages on the floor and couch before going back out for more.

"Hey!" Bradley screeched as a guy lifted up a tall, thin cardboard box. "Watch out for the chandelier—it's a Dale Chihuly."

"Bradley, I'm sure I'll regret asking, but what is all this stuff?"

"I didn't know when you were coming back, so I had clothes from the spring collections on hold all over the place. And now you're here, so I'm having them delivered," he said, speaking slowly as if explaining the obvious to a small child. "I had to call in a lot of favours to get everything brought over this morning." He must have caught my look of horror because he patted me on the arm reassuringly. "Don't worry; you'll barely notice I'm here."

I glanced at the pile of shit that had taken over one side of the entrance hall. "Somehow I doubt that."

"Besides, I need to clear out your closet," Bradley continued, oblivious. "I mean, what are you wearing?"

I looked down at myself. "Jeans?"

"Not just jeans, Emmy. Those are last season's jeans."

"So? They're comfy."

"But now you have new jeans, which are both comfy and *fashionable*."

Oh, Bradley. I loved him dearly, but sometimes he exasperated me. On the plus side, he was fearsomely efficient at organising my clothes, houses, schedule, and life in general, so I couldn't get too upset with him.

"Fine, Bradley, do what you need to do."

Attempting to argue with him was pointless—I'd learned that the hard way over the years. Instead, I made a mental note to hide my favourite old clothes before he recycled them.

"I intend to." He tilted his head to one side. "Starting with your hair. The colour's so drab. Does it have to stay brown?"

"I meant with my clothes. The hair will have to wait. We're in the middle of a kidnap investigation, and I need to go into the office."

"Do we just have time for an argan oil conditioning pack?"

"No!"

I started for the stairs, but Luke caught my arm. "Emmy?"

Thanks, Bradley.

"Most people call me by a shortened version of my middle name." That was sort of mostly true. And Luke thought my middle name was Emily, which fitted. "Call me Ash or Emmy, it doesn't matter. I'll answer to either."

I had to get out of the house, mainly to avoid Luke but also to keep out the way of Bradley's wardrobe shenanigans, so I drove into the office, hoping there was something I could do. Rain was falling heavily, so I left the Aston snugly under its cover and took the X5 instead. Turned out it belonged to me, part of Bradley's car rotation program. The Land Rover was apparently being fixed after Dan used it for a bit of impromptu off-roading while trying to avoid a deer. Dan assured me the deer came out of it just fine, which was better than the Land Rover's suspension did.

In the incident room, phones rang, keyboards clicked, and the information board gradually filled up. The problem was, we had nothing significant.

While I waited on hold for one of my contacts to dig out some information, I flicked idly through the emails Sloane had flagged for me. I needed to start pulling my weight in the company again. My husband's death had left me as majority shareholder, with my fifteen percent and his forty combined. Nate owned thirty-five percent and Nick the remaining ten.

There had always been four of us splitting the administrative burden, but Nate and Nick had been carrying the can by themselves for over three months now, which I didn't think was helping our relationship. If I'd had that lot dumped in my lap, I wouldn't have been happy about it either.

I skimmed financial and operational reports first— we needed more staff in the Japanese office, and we'd won a big new contract in LA. Okay, that was good news. Then I found a message that had me itching to pick up my gun. My husband's Aunt Miriam was taking legal action over his estate because, basically, she wanted it. A letter from her solicitor gave me thirty days to file his will for probate, a deadline I'd missed, oh, twenty-seven days ago. Marvellous. I added a note on my to-do list to call my own lawyer.

"Emmy," Nye called from across the room.

Oh, thank goodness. A distraction.

"What?"

"A gardener working three doors up from Luke's house reckons he saw a transit van a few days before Tia got taken. I'm going to send someone to speak to him."

"Forget that—I'll go."

I was sick of sitting on my ass, waiting for something to happen. Plus if I was driving, I could avoid reading my emails.

Despite its size, the BMW was surprisingly speedy, and it wasn't long before I arrived in Lower Foxford. Could this be the break we needed?

No, was the short answer. The gardener only saw a white van drive past a couple of times a week previously. It could have been the kidnapper, or it could have been a lost courier. He was almost sure the driver was a man, but the only description he managed was, "I think he had brown hair."

Along with half the male population. Back to square one.

As I stomped into Luke's house, I needed coffee, preferably by intravenous drip. Lack of sleep was getting to me.

"Oi, love, could you sign for this?" a voice called from behind. The postman ambled up the drive, whistling tunelessly.

"Sure."

Anyone else want to keep me from the caffeine I so

desperately needed?

He handed me a padded envelope—small, brown, nondescript. Alarm bells rang as I flipped it over. There was no sender's address.

I scribbled something unintelligible on the postman's pad and backed into the house, clutching the mystery package.

"What you got, boss?" one of the men stationed there asked.

"No idea, but at least it's not ticking."

CHAPTER 32

I RAN MY gloved fingers across the package. What was inside? A small bump in the bottom left-hand corner told me it wasn't simply a letter.

I pulled out my phone. "Nick, can you find out whether Luke's expecting a package? Something small in a padded envelope?"

"Have you got something?"

"Maybe. Can you ask him?"

"Gimme a second."

Muttering followed then Nick came back. "The only thing he's expecting is a portable hard drive, and that's being sent to his office."

Unless this was Barbie's portable hard drive, it looked like we had a problem. "Can you get the lab on standby?"

"I'm on it. How long will you be?"

"Leaving now."

We had our own forensics lab in the basement at the office. It didn't do the flashy stuff—we contracted that out—but the small team could cover most of what we needed. As I pulled into the car park, Nick was waiting.

"Where is it?"

I held up the envelope between a thumb and finger. "Let's go."

In the lab, the head technician, Test-tube, pushed back his chair and sauntered over. Of course, his mother didn't actually name him Test-tube, but I'd never known him as anything else.

"All right, boss?" he asked.

"Just peachy. Let's see what we've got, shall we?"

He ran the package through a scanner, much like the ones at airports. An indistinct blob showed up in the corner. What was it?

Test-tube donned a pair of latex gloves, gingerly sliced through the flap, and peered inside.

"Well?"

He looked up at me. "Have some patience."

He'd known me too long to take my shit. Dammit. I nearly snatched the bloody thing off him, but I forced my hands to my sides as he tilted it over a tray. Something tumbled out, and I took a step closer.

"Oh, fuck."

It was a fingernail. As in a whole fingernail, yanked out at the root. The gaudy paint job, shocking pink with silver and black stars, spoke of happier times for its owner.

"Tia's?" Nick asked.

I swallowed down the lump in my throat and nodded. No doubt about it. My toes sported the same design, painted by her last week as we'd watched a movie. I borrowed a pair of tweezers and angled the nail under the light. Yep, I even recognised the wonky star where the brush and her language had both slipped. Luckily, Luke hadn't been around to hear her turn the air blue.

While I planned which parts of the kidnapper's anatomy I was going to remove, Test-tube fished around in the envelope and extracted a note. One line, typed on plain white paper:

Further instructions will follow.

Relief jostled with my anger. We had another chance.

Meanwhile, Test-tube dug out evidence bags and gathered everything up.

"I'll take this lot for analysis."

He'd cover all bases, but I doubted we'd find anything. Everyone and their dog watched *CSI* nowadays and knew not to lick the envelope, and I couldn't believe we'd be that lucky.

"Where was it posted?" I asked.

Test-tube turned it over. "Penge, South London."

Two minutes later, I was in the Aston.

Traffic wasn't kind, and it took me almost an hour to reach the post office, a tiny kiosk at the back of a convenience store.

"Hi." I smiled at the blond kid sitting behind the counter, and he looked at his hands. "Were you working yesterday?"

He shifted nervously on his stool, struggling to make eye contact. Was he even old enough to have a job?

"Hang on, I'll check the rota." He made a show of flipping through a wedge of papers. "Uh, yeah."

If he couldn't remember being there yesterday himself, how would he remember if the kidnapper came in? I should have brought a shovel to dig for his IQ. His answer to my question about the package was an echo of the gardener's.

"It might have been a man that posted it."

I dropped a tenner onto the counter. His eyes lit up then rolled back in his head as he tried to remember.

"His hair might have been brown."

Arrrgh!

"I don't suppose you've got CCTV?"

He shook his head. "Do you want to post a letter?"

I refrained from suggesting he return his brain to sender and left before I kicked something. A quick walk along the residential road didn't reveal a single camera. This was a game of snakes and ladders, and I'd just slid all the way down a boa constrictor.

We were back to square one again. I ground my teeth, something I hadn't done since my teenage years because it gave me a headache. The kidnapper had promised further instructions, so all we could do was wait.

I ate dinner alone in the office, picking at the pizza I'd had delivered with the enthusiasm of a sloth. I'd told myself I needed to stay in case we got a break in the investigation, but I was lying. In a quiet corner of the canteen, there were no reminders of the husband I'd lost. At home, the reminders lay everywhere.

The rest of Sloane's saved emails held nothing of interest, and my calendar stretched ahead, empty. My mind had nothing to distract it from memories of my husband and Tia, fighting it out for prime position. And as I'd told Sloane I wouldn't return to the States until Tia was found, I'd have to live with that.

Back in the control room, I found Nye had gone to

get some sleep, and Tom, who was running things in his absence, took one look at me and told me to do the same.

"I should stay. What if something comes up?"

He gave me a gentle push towards the door. "Then we'll deal with it. If this becomes a rescue situation, we need you ready to do what you do best."

At that moment, the only things I felt capable of were drinking coffee and staring into space.

"Fine. Promise you'll call if you need me?"

"You know I will. Now, get out of here."

I drove home, sticking to the speed limit for once as I didn't want the journey to end. Luke was pacing around the kitchen when I arrived, and my heart seized when I saw him. Not because he was upset, but because his hands held my husband's mug. To the casual eye, it was nothing special—oversized china with *black is the new black* written on it—but it had been his favourite, and I wasn't ready to see another man drinking from it.

As Luke turned, tea sloshed out and hit the tiles. "Why the hell aren't you doing more? This'll be the fourth night she's been gone. What's that maniac doing to her? He ripped her nail out for fuck's sake. She must be in agony."

Dan and Nick looked on, silent, and it was me who spoke. "I know it's not easy, but believe me, we're doing everything we can. There's so little to go on, we don't have much choice but to wait."

"Believe you? Yeah, right. How would you like it if your nail had been ripped out?"

Been there, done that. "It hurts, but it'll grow back. He could have done a lot worse."

I'd seen everything from fingers to ears being sent

to parents. One poor bastard got sent their kid's foot, still stuffed into the tiny Nike trainer he'd got for his birthday the previous weekend. A fingernail was nothing compared to that.

But I had a feeling Luke wouldn't appreciate me pointing that out, so I stayed quiet.

And he didn't like that either.

"How can you act so calm? I suppose it's because it's not your sister that's been abducted. You've got me stuck here in this bloody palace with this pair..." he jerked his thumb at Nick and Dan, "who could be doing something far more useful than babysitting me. I should have called the damn police."

"I'm calm because getting worked up won't solve the problem," I answered, although at that moment I felt anything but calm inside. "We've got over fifty people working on this, most of whom were cherry picked from the police or military for being the best in their field. We've chased down every lead as it's come in, but there's been precious little to go on."

Luke paused in his steps to glare at me, but this time I didn't back down.

"Nobody's got a good look at the kidnapper, and if I hadn't followed you to the woods that night, you'd be lying dead, and I'd be the only one who even knew Tia was missing."

His eyes softened slightly, but still he didn't speak. Well, fuck him. He wasn't the only one hurting right now. I walked from the room with a parting shot of, "If you don't want to be here, Dan will call you a car and you can go home."

Yes, the bitch was back.

I wandered the house aimlessly, ruing an awful day

that only got worse with each passing minute. Even though people surrounded me, I felt horribly alone. Part of me wanted to grab a bag, climb into the Aston, and run again, but I couldn't break my promise to Nate. While it might have helped my sanity, I'd done quite enough damage when I left the first time, and I needed to search for Tia.

On the first floor, my feet carried me to the study I'd shared with my husband. Small and cosy, we'd used it as an alternative to the control room downstairs when we needed peace.

I hadn't been in there since he died, and it looked like nobody else had either. His favourite pen still sat in the middle of his desk. A book he'd been reading sat on the coffee table, the bookmark showing he'd never get to finish a quarter of the pages. One of his jumpers hung over the back of the couch under his favourite painting.

It was on the couch that Nick found me, squashed into one corner, knees drawn up, arms wrapped around my legs, and my head resting on the jumper. I could have sworn it still smelled of my husband, but it had been three months, so perhaps that was just my imagination.

"Why are you sitting here in the dark?"

"I don't really know. I thought it might help."

"Has it?"

"No."

Nick sat down beside me. "Want to talk?"

I wasn't sure what to say, but I couldn't keep everything bottled up inside any longer. The pressure had built, and it was either let it out or end up exploding, and that wouldn't be pretty. I smacked my head back on the couch.

"I'm so fucked up, Nicky. Inside. I'm not capable of having a normal relationship without making a mess of it. Everything I do ends up hurting someone."

"That's not true, Emmy."

"Yes, it is. Look at my track record. My mother disliked me so much she didn't bother to see me after the age of ten. When I moved to the States, I upset Jimmy, and after that, there was my succession of sleep disasters and..." I counted on my fingers. "Six relationships I managed to screw up. Seven if you count my marriage. Then with Luke, I lived a normal life for the first time and managed to make a mess of that too, and to top it all I've made you, Nate, and Mack hate me. The only person who can stand to be near me is Dan, and that's only because she's made of bloody Teflon."

I turned away from Nick, gulping in air as I tried to control my runaway tongue, but he shuffled closer and laid a hand on my thigh. "I don't hate you, and neither do Nate or Mack. We were just hurt you didn't talk to us. We only wanted to help."

"Logically, I know that, but three months ago all I wanted to do was get as far away as possible. I had visions of that maniac picking you off one by one."

Running had seemed like the best option at the time, and besides, avoidance was a tactic that had worked well for me in the past.

Nick sighed and shook his head, showing me his opinion of my thought process. "And I don't blame you for the whole sleep episode; I've made that clear," he said. "Nobody, least of all you, knew that you'd react like that."

A decade had passed since I'd tried to kill Nick, but

it seemed like yesterday. "It wasn't just you, Nick. What kind of woman tries to stab her own husband?"

For me, that was perhaps worse than what I did to Nick. CCTV had shown me wandering through the house, my movements smooth, my face blank. Moonlight glinted off the four-inch Sabatier paring knife I'd selected from the block on the kitchen worktop—perfect for getting in between a person's ribs.

I moved with purpose, looking for something. *Someone.* I found him in the study. My husband had been sitting at his desk, concentrating on paperwork until I'd darkened the doorway, and he only had time for half a smile before I launched myself at him, knife in my outstretched hand. Luck was on my side, and he managed to fight me off long enough to Taser me. If it had been anyone else, I'd have woken up with a body in the house.

And to this day, I have no idea why I did it.

"He never blamed you for that either. He loved you more than anything," Nick said.

"Loved me? Did he really? Because he never once told me that. I was more of a project to him, and perhaps that's just as well. It's not like I could ever have been a real wife."

"You were far more than a project. Maybe that's how it was at first, but he'd moved on a long way since the beginning. Don't underestimate the strength of his feelings for you."

"He kissed me once," I blurted. "Then told me it was a mistake."

"I know."

Huh? He'd told Nick that?

Nick chuckled. "Don't act so surprised. Men talk occasionally too."

That kiss happened four long years ago. At first, our marriage had been purely one of convenience. The training my husband put me through was hardly compatible with a romantic relationship. He pushed me. Hard. So hard I almost broke. He had more confidence in me than I had in myself, and he understood my limits better than I did.

Some days, I hated him.

No, most days. Back then, it never occurred to me to sleep with a man whose death I plotted over breakfast each morning.

The change happened gradually. As I became stronger, my animosity turned to gratitude because it was him who'd made me that way. He was always there for me, for richer, for poorer, in sickness and in health. And finally until death do us part. My husband became more than just my mentor and trainer—he was my confidante, my rock, and my best friend.

I fell in love with him, but until that night, he'd never shown the slightest inclination he might have felt the same way.

Hungry and tired, we'd stopped for a break halfway through a journey upstate. Heavy rain soaked us as we ran from his Porsche to some little honky-tonk bar, the only sign of life in the middle of nowhere. Dinner was nothing special, but sick of the cramped car, I dragged him onto the dance floor afterwards to delay our journey a little more.

An upbeat country song on the scratchy jukebox turned to "Desperado" by the Eagles. I went to sit down, but he grabbed my hand and pulled me into him.

Never before had I felt his heart beat so hard against mine. I recalled resting my cheek on his shoulder while we danced as if it had happened last night.

Then his eyes darkened, and he kissed me.

Lost in the music and lost in him, I kissed him back. The magic lasted as long as the song, and then my brain short-circuited. What had I done? I'd fucked up every other important relationship in my life—I didn't want to lose what I had with my husband by trying to change it into something never meant to be. So I flipped out and took off. See? Avoidance—it was my speciality.

That night, I walked for miles, until the rain soaked me to my knickers and blisters blossomed on my feet. By morning, my mind had twisted my thoughts. What if we *were* meant to be together? I couldn't shake the feel of his lips on mine, and my soul craved his touch.

At breakfast the next morning, the words got stuck in my throat. How could I tell him I wanted more of what he'd given me?

It turned out I didn't have to. As I picked at my plate of eggs, he spoke first.

"Diamond, I'm sorry. What happened last night... I shouldn't have done it." He shook his head. "I need to lay off the beer before I make any more mistakes."

A mistake? I was a mistake? Shattering my already damaged heart was a fucking mistake? I swallowed down tears and pain and lust and longing, and the whole mess settled in my stomach like a bad ulcer.

But he wasn't done. "Can we turn the clock back? Forget it ever happened?"

What could I do but nod?

That night still played on my mind, years later. Why

had he told Nick about it?

"So, what did he say?" I asked.

"Just that the moment felt right, and he'd kissed you."

"That's it?"

"Not quite. He said you broke away, looked at him like he'd gone crazy, and sprinted out the bar. He didn't know where you'd disappeared to, and he spent the rest of the night terrified you wouldn't want anything to do with him again."

"He was terrified of nothing."

"Except losing you."

"But he said the next day it was a mistake."

"He only thought it was a mistake because of the way you reacted."

"I was scared," I admitted. "Scared that if I fucked things up the way I do any time I get close to someone, I'd lose him. And I couldn't lose him."

"You never would have."

"You think? He always was way out of my league. Anyhow, I decided I'd rather keep what we had than put all my chips on black with a chance of losing the lot. Except now I've lost him anyway." I smacked my palm on my forehead. "I'm so *fucking* stupid."

"Not stupid, Em. Nobody could ever describe you as stupid."

"Well, I am. I wish I'd told him how I really felt, because I'll never feel that way about anyone again. He was it for me."

My heart ached once more, a yawning chasm that would never be filled. What if Nick was right? What if my husband *had* felt the same things for me as I did for him? I'd never know. But I did know I'd always blame myself for not having the courage to find out.

"You need to stop being so hard on yourself. You can't change what happened, so you need to get closure and move on. Learn from the past, but don't live in it."

"How the hell do I get closure? There are reminders of him everywhere in this house. *Everywhere.* He's all I've been able to think about since I've been back." I motioned at the jumper draped over my lap, the photos of us on the wall that I couldn't look directly at.

"When Jana died, it helped to talk."

Except six years on, Nick's voice still cracked when he mentioned her name.

"I'm not one for talking."

He squeezed my hand. "I've noticed. I guess it doesn't work for everyone."

"If someone got a look in my head, they'd lock me up and chuck the key down a mineshaft."

"How about writing a letter? There were so many things I wished I'd said to Jana, and that's what hurt more than anything—knowing I never would. The therapist I saw made me put them down on paper."

"How does that help?"

"It lets the grief escape. She told me to leave the letter somewhere I associated with Jana—I left it under the tree where the eagles live at the back of my house. Maybe doing that would help to get the grief out of your system?"

"Maybe."

And then I made the mistake of thinking about what I would write. When I felt the words "I love you" on my tongue, I lost it. Big time. I guess not crying for over twenty years meant I had a lot of tears stored up because I dissolved in a puddle of them in Nick's lap.

The old Nick came back, and he held me until I had nothing left inside. My eyes were as empty as my soul, and my dead hopes dampened his shirt. When I stopped shaking, he kissed my hair and hugged me tighter, then lifted me into his arms and carried me upstairs to bed.

CHAPTER 33

TURNED OUT MY meltdown chased the nightmares away. Perhaps I should try it more often? When I woke, dark storm clouds still raged in my mind, but this time there was something else. A chink of sunlight. While it hadn't vanquished the shadows, it had lightened the gloom in places, and with that glow came a newfound positivity. I'd spent the last three months running away from things. Now, the time had come to fight.

But before that, I had to speak to Nick. Embarrassed couldn't begin to describe how I felt. That girl last night, the one overflowing with tears, dramas, emotions—that wasn't me. How was I supposed to face him?

I lay in bed pondering this as the door clicked open. With all the mess last night, I'd forgotten to lock it.

Nick peered around the edge. "Is it safe?"

I inhaled deeply as the rich aroma of coffee floated over to me.

"Don't worry, I'm awake."

He stepped into the room and perched on the edge of my bed, his battered jeans a contrast to Bradley's choice of plum velvet throw. My eyes alighted on the cup in his hands. Please, say that was for me?

"I brought you coffee," he said.

Hallelujah. "Did I ever tell you how fucking

fantastic you are?"

"Many times, each of them when I was carrying something hot and steamy."

I took a sip—black and strong, just the way I liked it. My ecstasy, however, was short lived when I realised Nick wasn't leaving.

"Look, about last night, I'm so sorr—" I began, but he interrupted me.

"Nothing to be sorry for. It was about time you let go of all that crap stored up inside. You need an outlet before it poisons you."

He was right; of course he was right. I did need an outlet. Or, I should say, a new outlet. I'd always unloaded on my husband, and he'd known what to say or do to make the pain go away. Talking to Nick was different, but his stepping in had been a blessing.

"I know I do."

"I'm always here, baby. Talk to me, don't bottle it up. Please."

If Nick was offering to be my sounding board, I had to accept. Nobody left could do the job better. Did he understand what he was letting himself in for? The black parts of my mind scared even me.

I reached over and squeezed his hand. "Thanks, Nicky."

"No need for thanks. I'll do anything for you; you know that. And remember, it's always darkest before dawn."

"I hope that's true."

Surely something had to give? If not my sanity, then something on the case. The longer the kidnapper held onto Tia, the greater the chance of something going wrong.

"Another ransom demand's gonna come in soon," I said. "I'm sure of it."

"Agreed. Are you planning to lead the team at the drop?"

"I was hoping you would. Luke may well have to go too, and it's not good for me to be around him. This situation's stressful enough without adding the atmosphere between the pair of us into the mix."

Nick shrugged. "Guess I'm with you there. I'll get a team together this morning. What are you planning to do?"

"Get my head back in the game, firstly." I'd been wandering around in a daze, but at last, the fog was lifting. "I'll start with a visit to JJ's."

JJ's gym belonged to James James. Yes, his parents really did that to him, but everyone called him Jimmy. Over a beer I wasn't supposed to be drinking, he'd once confessed the endless taunts he'd received as a child were what drove him to become so good with his fists.

I'd stayed fit while I was living with Luke, but nothing compared to a good fight, and I hadn't been in one for months. If I wanted to get back in top form, I had to pay Jimmy a visit.

"It'll be good to have you back at a hundred percent," Nick said, leaning over to give me a hug. "We've all missed you, even Nate, no matter how much he pretends otherwise. You go do your thing."

Once he'd left, I got dressed in running tights and a sports bra then zipped a hoodie over the top. It was still only six thirty. JJ's was in East London, just off the Mile End Road, and I'd use the six-mile run as a warm up.

When I arrived forty minutes later, I found Jimmy

next to one of the boxing rings, watching a pair of welterweight fighters go at each other. He always had been an early riser.

I crept up behind him. "Boo."

He spun around, and when he saw it was me, he crushed me to his massive chest. "Amanda! You should have said you were gonna stop by."

Jimmy had once been a super heavyweight fighter, and to say he was big was like saying the Empire State Building was a little on the tall side. He topped out at six foot six and had the width to match. Beside him, I felt all dainty, like a Barbie doll. Luckily, he let go before he cracked any of my ribs.

"Didn't really plan this trip, Jimmy. I just woke up and decided I could do with a session. Are you busy?"

"I've got a guy in for training at eight thirty, but I'm all yours till then. Come to think of it, you can go in the cage with him. Keep him on his toes."

Over the past few years, Jimmy had branched out from boxing into the world of MMA. The gym now sported a pair of cages as well as the more traditional boxing rings. He spent the next hour drilling me through kicks, punches, blocks, and grapples. I needed to borrow a towel when we'd finished.

"Not bad, girl, but I can tell you've taken a few months off. You need to find a new partner and keep up with the training. Don't want you going soft again."

I paused to get my breath back. "Easier said than done."

My husband had been the only person who'd put up with me apart from Alex, my ex-Spetsnaz trainer back in Virginia, and I didn't feel up to facing him right now. I may have been depressed, but I wasn't suicidal.

Jimmy chuckled and looked at his watch. "Too early for beer. Want a protein shake?"

"Why not?"

Jimmy's shakes always tasted better than Toby's, and I'd got my breath back by the time eight-thirty guy arrived.

Jimmy introduced us. "Amanda, this is Lee Belmont. Lee, meet Amanda."

Lee looked me up and down, his eyes pausing a fraction too long on my chest. I put him in the lightweight class, which meant he had about ten kilos on me.

"She the new ring girl?"

Jimmy grinned wide. "Nope. She's your new sparring partner."

"You're kidding?"

"Get on with it."

For a second, I thought Lee was going to refuse, but then he shrugged and climbed into the ring. I hopped up behind him.

I'd never seen him at the gym before, and his strong northern accent suggested he was new to the area. I'd got a bit out of touch with who was who in the world of MMA, but I trusted Jimmy wouldn't ask me to fight someone without a few decent matches under his belt.

I stuck my mouth guard in and waited for Lee to strip off his tracksuit. A small crowd gathered to watch, and cash began to change hands. One guy I recognised gave me a wink, and I suppressed a smile. How much money had he bet?

Jimmy rang the bell.

Quick off the mark, I almost got Lee with my first punch. He fell to his knees, but when I stepped back, he scrambled up, a new determination in his eyes. Guess I wasn't going to be as easy to beat as he'd assumed.

And once he put in some effort, he wasn't a bad fighter. We were halfway through the third round when he got me against the side of the cage with a couple of jabs. The small crowd gasped as he came at me again. In for the kill, or so he thought. I feinted with a high right hook. As my fist swung, his eyes cut to it, and I got him under the jaw with a left-handed uppercut. My ears relished the satisfying thump of leather on flesh.

That dropped them every time, and he'd left himself wide open.

"He'll have a hell of a headache when he wakes up," I said, stripping my gloves off.

"All part of the game, sweet pea," Jimmy said.

He and another of the trainers tended to Lee, and once he started to come round, I headed off for a quick shower.

"Won fifty quid on that one, darlin'," the guy who'd winked at me called as I headed upstairs to Jimmy's flat.

I returned his thumbs-up. "Drinks are on you, then."

I still kept a few clothes in a drawer there, and Jackie made me an egg-white omelette while I got dressed.

"You staying all day?" she asked.

"Can't. Got things to do."

"That missing girl?"

I nodded. "There's no sign of her yet."

"Poor child. Let us know if there's anything we can do."

I promised to stop by when I had more time then

headed back downstairs to say goodbye to Jimmy. Lee had woken up by that point, and he was slumped on a bench, holding an ice pack to his face.

"Who the hell *are* you?" he asked.

"This is my almost daughter," Jimmy told him, and the pride in his voice made my breath hitch. I didn't deserve his admiration right now.

"Wish I'd known that beforehand," Lee said, holding out his hand for me to shake. "No hard feelings, eh?"

"She's taken down far bigger men than you," Jimmy said. "Just shows you have to train harder and lose some of that cockiness."

I left Lee and Jimmy to it and began the jog home. My legs felt heavy after their workout, and I took it slow. Yes, I still had a way to go fitness-wise. I chose a different route back, backstreets rather than the main roads—it was always good to keep up with how the city was changing. I'd learned that the hard way on the night I met my husband, although it turned out to be a blessing in disguise.

Having settled into a steady rhythm, I took a right onto Laburnum Avenue. Why did that name sound familiar? I'd heard it somewhere recently. Half a minute later, it came back to me—Mack had mentioned this was where the owner of the stolen number plates lived. Was he back from his trip abroad yet? It wouldn't hurt to check while I was in the vicinity, and it only took a second to call Nye and get the house number.

Number forty-three turned out to be the bottom half of a Victorian, once a modest family home and now converted into two flats. The door looked freshly painted, a contrast with that of forty-three-A's, which was peeling at the edges.

A small, dark-skinned man opened the door with a frown. "Are you selling something?"

"No, I'm not." I stuck to the same story as the original team and explained the number plates had been used in a burglary.

He broke into a smile. "Oh, come in, come in. My sister said somebody had called, but she was not sure who. Her English is not so good. I wondered if you would return."

"Thanks. Are you Gabir Hassani, then?" I asked, although the fact he shook with his left hand rather than his right and walked with a slight limp was a bit of a giveaway.

"Yes, I am. Would you like some tea?" His English was careful, precise.

"I'd love a cup."

Lesson number one, build rapport.

If he was surprised by a slightly sweaty woman showing up on his doorstep, he didn't show it as he bustled around the kitchen with teabags and sugar.

"Could you tell me more about the missing plates?" I asked as he handed me a mug. "When you noticed they were gone, whether you saw anyone suspicious hanging around, anything like that?"

"I noticed straight away they had been taken. They were there in the morning, and in the evening when I went to get in my van, they were gone. And just to be certain I was not wrong, I checked on my CCTV. The man stole them at precisely seventeen minutes past six."

CCTV? He had CCTV? How the hell had we missed that?

"You mean you actually have the person who stole them on video?"

"Oh, yes. My brother owns a company that sells security cameras, and he says I cannot be too careful on my own in the shop at night. He installed me an excellent system. I told the police this, but they did not seem interested. They said they would send somebody to look at the film, but nobody came."

"Do you have a copy of the footage I can watch?"

"Certainly, but it is in my shop in Clapham. That is where the van is kept. My delivery driver uses it. We will have to go there."

Sod the cup of tea. I hailed a passing cab while Gabir locked up. As he hunted for his jacket, I called Dan and asked her to meet me in Clapham.

"Put the incident room on standby as well, would you?"

"You think this might be a break?"

"Keep everything crossed. Fingers, toes, the lot."

"Eyes?"

"If you think it'll help."

We were halfway there when my phone pinged again. Nye was calling.

"We've just had the new ransom demand."

About bloody time. "How much?"

"A million plus the software."

"Where's the drop?" If the guy had picked the woods again, I was going and so was my gun. Sod the legality.

"A shopping centre in East London at six this evening. I've sent a team to check the place over."

A shopping centre? If anything, that was worse than the previous location. We'd have to be careful with the public around. I dialled Nick to get an update on Luke.

"How is he?"

"Just about holding it together. But if this goes on much longer, he'll give himself an aneurysm."

I gave Nick a brief outline of where I was heading.

"Shall I fill Luke in?" he asked.

"No. I want him to concentrate on what he has to do this evening, and besides, I don't want to get his hopes up."

I couldn't say much more with Gabir sitting beside me, but I promised to call Nick back once I got out of the range of unwanted ears.

The cab pulled up outside a small supermarket called, imaginatively enough, Gabir's Supermarket, and we both hopped out. As I followed Gabir into the store, he proudly pointed out the ridiculous number of cameras in the completely over-the-top security system his brother had installed. I fell a little bit in love with the second Mr. Hassani at that point.

In the cupboard-like office at the back of the store, Gabir cued up the footage. The picture was crystal clear. I held my breath as a man walked into shot, head down, and unscrewed the plate from the front of the van. He crossed to a different camera and did the same at the rear. The guy was the same size and build as the arsehole I'd chased through the woods, but due to the hood pulled low over his eyes, I couldn't see his face.

I said as much to Gabir, who stared off into space for a second, pondering.

"This man, I could not be sure, but I think I saw him before. His jacket is very unusual."

The black hoodie had *YOLO* graffitied in white across the back and the front—quite distinctive. *You*

Only Live Once. I hoped to change his philosophy to *YODO.* Can you guess what the *D* stood for?

"I think he came into the store," Gabir continued. "Earlier in the day."

"I don't suppose you've got that on film as well, have you?"

"Of course. I saved it all. I do watch *CSI*, you know."

Thank goodness for that. What would we do without American crime drama?

Once again, Gabir clicked onto a file, and I watched the man walk around the store from sixteen different camera angles, picking up a roll of duct tape, two kinds of Pop-Tarts, and a couple of bottles of water. Was he making Tia eat Pop-Tarts? That was inhumane. When he reached the register, he added a pack of cigarettes, and thank heavens for nicotine. Because as he selected his brand, he stared straight into a camera he clearly didn't realise was there, giving us a perfect head-on shot.

The second I saw his face, synapses fired in my brain, and I swear I almost squealed. I was about to call up Gabir's brother and offer to have his babies.

Holy shit.

Five seconds later, my phone rang, and it was Dan.

"I'm ten minutes out."

"Drive faster."

I never thought I'd hear myself ask her to do that.

While I waited, Gabir copied both videos onto a USB stick. I clutched it as if it was the Rosetta stone.

"I hope I have been helpful?" he asked.

"More than you could ever know."

His ever-present smile grew wider. "The USB stick is nine pounds ninety-nine. Is there anything else you need before you go?"

"A bottle of water and some gum would be good. Oh, and give me twenty quid's worth of lottery scratch cards."

The way my luck was changing today, I figured it couldn't hurt.

Dan pulled up outside, and I thanked Gabir again before I left. On my way to the car, I passed a homeless man huddled under a blanket and dropped the scratch cards into his lap.

"Good luck, mate."

He raised his hand in a silent thank you.

"How was JJ's?" Dan asked as I climbed into the Aston.

She hadn't been able to resist its lure, and I made a mental note to check the other side for scratches later.

"I knocked out my sparring partner again."

"Who'd Jimmy put you up against this time?"

"Some dude called Lee Belmont."

"As in Lee Belmont who just won the UK MMA title in the lightweight division?"

"Dunno, I didn't ask. Probably. Jimmy seemed to think he needed taking down a peg or two."

"Well, you sure did that if he ended up on the mat. Now, tell me, why have you got me over here? Not that I'm complaining or anything, because this car is freaking awesome."

I pulled out my phone. Gabir had also emailed me some stills from the videos, and I got the clearest photo up on the screen.

"I want you to quickly look at a photo then tell me your first impressions."

Dan gave me a quizzical glance. "Okay."

I held the screen up for a few seconds, and her brows pinched together.

"Luke? What does a picture of Luke have to do with the kidnapper?"

"Look again."

Dan chewed her lip as she took in the subtle differences between the two men—a slightly broader nose, a squarer jaw, a steeper slope to his forehead, and longer hair being the main ones.

"A brother? Cousin?"

"He told me he doesn't have either. I don't think he'd have tried to hide it—in the same conversation, he said he always wished he'd had a brother growing up."

"Well, that guy looks so much like Luke, it's hard to imagine he's anything but."

"And it would fit with his comment about Luke having taken his life. Maybe it's not something Luke's knowingly done at all. This bastard wants what he sees as his birthright: Luke's money, Luke's job, Luke's sister."

"Luke's girlfriend?" Dan suggested.

"If only. You have no idea how many times I've wished he took me instead of Tia."

"I'd love to be a fly on the wall if he tried that."

I winced as Dan started the engine. It had been ages since she drove me anywhere, and I hadn't missed the experience.

"So, the possible brother—mother or father?" she continued as she pulled out into traffic, narrowly missing a cyclist.

"Luke looks nothing like his mother. It's Tia who has her features. So, I'm gonna go with daddy dearest."

Plus didn't Tia tell us her father played around?

"Where do we find him?"

"Six feet under, unfortunately."

"Recent?"

"Nope. He died years ago, and Luke's been picking up the pieces ever since."

"Maybe the mother knows something? The guy in the photo looks pretty close in age to Luke. Perhaps she suspected an affair?"

"Head to Lower Foxford," I settled back in my seat. "Let's see what the mother of the year's take on all of this is."

Had she even noticed Tia was missing yet?

CHAPTER 34

DAN DIDN'T DRIVE as fast as I would have, but on the plus side, she didn't total my car and traffic was mercifully light, so we still made good time. On the way, I gave Nick a call to see what was happening at his end.

"Have you sorted out the logistics?"

"More or less. We found someone in the investigations division who looks enough like Luke that we could use him as a decoy, but Luke's determined he's doing the drop himself. He says he's not taking any chances with Tia's life."

"So he'd rather risk his own as well?"

After his idiotic trip to the woods, why did that surprise me?

"I can't change his mind, and believe me, I've tried."

More than once, I'd seen Luke's stubborn side. He'd be doing the drop whether we liked it or not.

"Right, we're on damage limitation, now."

"Understood. We also need to come up with £1 million in cash. Again, Luke's insisting. He doesn't want to risk pissing this guy off if anything goes wrong and he gets away with the ransom. He says he'll cover it."

"He's good for the money, but I wasn't planning on letting this arsehole get away for a second time. That cash will be coming back, one way or another."

"Any ideas where we can get £750,000 in used bills without having to bribe a bank manager?"

I gave Nick the code for a safe in the basement that contained enough to make up the million. It was the least I could do after the shit I'd pulled with Luke. My husband had always liked to keep a quantity of cash on hand for emergencies, and I'd say this qualified.

Once Nick had repeated the code back to me, I updated him on our progress, and we both felt it was best not to get Luke involved in my end of things. He had enough on his plate already without having to deal with the havoc I was undoubtedly about to wreak at his old home.

"Oh, and Nick, whatever you do, don't let him answer the phone to his mother if she calls. He doesn't need her hysterics on top of everything else."

"Got it. I'll make sure his phone stays with me."

I received one more call on the way. Jason called to say a speed camera caught the kidnapper's van doing thirty-seven in a thirty limit on the outskirts of Bromley two days ago. South London again, and not too far from where the ransom note was posted. Together with the initial theft of the plates, that made three connections with the area.

We had to be on the right track, didn't we?

As Dan and I neared Lower Foxford, I kept half an eye on the cars she was slicing past and focused the rest of my thoughts on what to say to Luke's mother. How did I get the information I needed without alerting her to the fact Tia had disappeared? I foresaw hysterics if she found out, swiftly followed by a call to the police, and if I gagged her and tossed her in the closet, that might be taking things a step too far. Once again, I decided to lie through my teeth. I already knew I was going to hell—at this point, it was go big or go home.

Dan slewed to a halt in front of the Halston-Cain family residence, covering the front porch in a hail of gravel. I hopped out and rang the bell.

Mrs. Squires answered the door, looking as if she was sucking a lemon. If someone gave her the gin to go with it, she might loosen up a bit. Her expression didn't change as she showed me into the formal sitting room with all the enthusiasm of a stripper in the Arctic.

"Madam will be with you shortly."

Fantastic. I could hardly wait.

Luke's mother swanned in a few minutes later. As usual, she was perfectly attired, and her face screwed up in disgust as she registered me sitting on her Laura Ashley sofa. Guess she didn't appreciate my jogging outfit.

"You're Luke's little friend, aren't you? I'm sorry; I don't remember your name?"

"It's Ash."

"Oh, yes, like the leftovers from a bonfire. How appropriate. What can I do for you?"

Bitch.

"Luke asked me to come. A man claiming to be his brother turned up on the doorstep this morning, and as you can imagine, that was a bit of a shock. Right now, he doesn't know what to believe."

How would she react?

"Well, that's just ridiculous. Luke doesn't have a brother. I hope he sent the man away with a flea in his ear."

I could almost swear she was telling the truth. She

didn't hesitate as she answered, and her eyes remained fixed on mine, narrowed slightly because she was pissed off rather than shifty.

"That's what I said at first, but this guy looks so much like Luke he reckons he's telling the truth. He's quite upset."

Quite upset. Got to love the British penchant for understatement.

"For goodness' sake, tell him he's mistaken."

On the way over, I'd had a graphics wizard on the marketing team put together a mock-up of the suspect standing in Luke's living room, and he'd done a remarkably good job. Suspect number one glowered back from among the chintz as I pulled the photo up on my phone screen and handed it over.

Mrs. H-C leaned forward, squinting, then huffed.

"Well, I'll admit there's a similarity, but that's all it is. A similarity. I think I'd remember having a third child, don't you?" She focused back on me, her eyes tiny slits. "Why are *you* here, anyway? Did you get lost on the way back to your street corner?"

So far, I'd done my best to be semi-polite, what with it being Luke's mother and all. But now the gloves were off.

"Why am I here? Isn't it obvious? Luke reckons you've been hiding things from him, and he's so furious he can't even bring himself to speak to you."

"Nonsense. Luke would never stop speaking to me. I'm his mother."

She fetched her own phone from her handbag, and I suppressed a smile as she dialled Luke. I just about managed to keep a straight face as she got cut off once, twice, three times. Thanks, Nicky.

"I don't understand," she said, glaring at the screen.

Time for some fun.

"So if the kid isn't yours, who else was your husband screwing? Some sweet little piece who gave him what you couldn't? Because having breathed the same air as you for a few minutes, I can see why he'd look elsewhere."

Come on lady, get angry. Let something slip.

"You nasty little trollop! I gave my husband everything he needed. He knew I was the best he'd ever get, and he'd never have swapped someone with my breeding for a slut. Now, get out of my house!"

"Even heifers have a pedigree. That doesn't mean men want to fuck them."

My cheek stung where she slapped me, and I resisted the urge to pound her face into the coffee table.

"Get out! Just get out!" she screeched. "My husband only had eyes for me."

She shoved me towards the hallway, heels clacking on the wooden floor. Dammit! She genuinely seemed to believe what she was saying, which meant we needed to come at this problem from a different angle.

As I neared the door, it opened before me. Mrs. Squires held the handle, a self-satisfied smirk spread across her ferrety face. A smirk mixed with smugness—she'd clearly heard every word.

But something was missing. Surprise.

What had Tia told me about Mrs. Squires a while back? Her voice played over in my head: *I'm sure she's only around because she has too much dirt on Mother to fire.*

She knew! The old dragon fucking knew.

Instead of walking out the front door, I turned right

into another sitting room, this one decorated in muted shades of green and peach. Kind of like the vomit one saw outside a nightclub offering 2-for-1 shots on a Friday evening.

"Where are you going?" dragon-lady asked. "Mrs. Halston-Cain told you to leave."

"I thought we'd have a chat first."

"I have nothing to talk to you about."

Her tone was haughty, but she refused to meet my eyes. Worried about something?

"Yes, you do. All I want are the names, and then I'll leave."

"I'm not telling you anything."

"Fair enough. But if you don't spill, I'll unleash so much shit on you that it'll make your nightmares seem like a happy place. I'll have a team of investigators rake through your entire life, and when they find out who you've been blackmailing, and why, and how much for, I'll tear you apart for it. With tweezers." I said it with a smile, but my tone stayed icy. "And I'll take pleasure in every moment."

Please let my guess be right. From what Tia had said, there must be some blackmail involved somewhere.

But the dragon only laughed. "What makes you think you can do any of that? Mrs. Halston-Cain told me you were just a stable girl."

"Mrs. Halston-Cain has no clue who I am. See the Aston Martin out there?"

I pointed through the window. Dan was sitting on the bonnet, looking bored, her skirt short enough to cause a scandal in Lower Foxford. Mrs. Squires followed my gaze.

"Does that look like the kind of car a stable girl would drive?" I asked. "No? You'd better believe I can make good on that promise."

Ah, a flicker of fear. Now we were getting somewhere.

"Did you know that under the Theft Act 1968, section 21, the maximum sentence for blackmail is fourteen years? Wonder what the food's like in prison?"

She swallowed hard and took a step back.

"If I tell you what I know, you promise you'll leave me alone?"

Wow. That was easier than I thought. Guess it was true that bullies were just cowards in disguise.

"Sure. Brownie's honour." Just in case, I kept my fingers crossed behind my back. I felt no loyalty to the snivelling woman in front of me. "Talk."

"I don't know much. Mr. Halston-Cain had several affairs over the years, but the woman who gave birth to his child was named Fiona. I remember her coming to the house one day while she was pregnant. Mr. H wanted her to have an abortion."

"Nice."

"They had a huge argument, and Mr. Halston-Cain said he wanted nothing more to do with her. He accused her of trying to trap him, and judging by the look of her, he was right. Common as muck, that girl was. He said he'd give her money each month, but if she ever tried to contact him again, the payments would stop. That was more than generous if you ask me."

"What was her last name?"

"I don't know."

I took a step closer, feeling satisfaction as she

cowered. "Fucking tell me."

"I don't know, I swear."

"How long ago did it happen?"

She shrunk before my eyes. "Right before Luke's birth. Odd how Mr. H managed to get two women pregnant at the same time."

What a prick. Mrs. Squires glanced towards the door, looking for a way out. Tough shit. She could leave when I'd finished with her.

"Where did Fiona live?"

"Not around here. London, I think."

South London, by any chance? All roads led to the city. I didn't bother bidding the dragon goodbye as I strode out to the car, already planning our next move. Dan had the engine started by the time I pulled the door open.

"Where to, kemosabe?"

"London. We're going back to London."

Four and a half hours until the ransom drop. I'd filled Dan in, and now my stomach grumbled because I'd missed lunch. But I had no time to think about food. I needed Mack instead.

Except Mack didn't answer, and my call got transferred to her assistant.

"Can you put me through to Mack? Where is she?"

"Emmy? I can't believe you're back. We've all missed you."

Guilt. Trip. "I've missed you too. Where's Mack?"

"On a plane. We've got a data issue at the LA office, and she had to fly there pronto. Something about a drive failure."

Bloody marvellous. "How about Nate? Is he there?"

Nate—Mr. Gadget himself—came a close second in the hacking stakes. A few seconds later, he picked up, and I didn't waste time with small talk.

"I've got a lead. I need to find a woman called Fiona with a son born around the same time as Luke."

"Do you have any idea how many women called Fiona there are in England?"

"Narrow it down to South London."

"That doesn't help much, Em. Why couldn't you have a suspect called Esmeralda or Persephone?"

"I'll bear that in mind next time I go after a kidnapper. Could you just start looking?"

Keys clicked in the background. "Already am."

"Thanks, Nate. I'll get back to you when we have something more."

Next, I called the incident room and asked Nye to cross-reference the name Fiona and the approximate age of her son with the records in our database. Could the name have popped up somewhere previously?

As Dan crunched through the gears, I was so deep in thought I barely cringed. How could we find one Fiona in thousands? I began to fear Nate was right and this was a lost cause. Should I change the plan and go to the drop site instead?

Traffic ground to a halt, and I cursed under my breath. Bloody road works. Six men in hi-vis standing around drinking tea, and not a shovel in sight.

The car lurched forward and Dan stomped on the brake, stopping mere inches from the car in front. Why had I let her behind the wheel again?

"Don't kill my car. I love this car."

She jerked her head sideways. "At least we're in the right place for a funeral."

I stared past her at the old church, complete with grimacing gargoyles glowering down from its grey stone walls. Such a contrast in London beside the glass-fronted office buildings and blocks of flats. The graveyard formed a tiny green oasis in the sea of concrete, and for a brief moment, I envied the dead their tranquillity.

Then it hit me.

The dead.

I called Nate again, drumming my fingers on the dash as the phone rang on speaker. *Pick up.*

"Missing me already?"

"Nate, try dead Fionas."

"What? Start from the beginning."

"I reckon Fiona might be dead."

"What? How'd you work that one out?"

Beside me, Dan let out a whoop. "Of course! The son's got to be Luke's age, and why start this campaign when he's in his thirties? Why not five years ago? Ten, even. Something triggered it."

I gave Dan a high-five. "And that something might have been the death of his mother. They had to have been close for her to tell him who his real father was."

Nate gave a low whistle. "You know, you could be right. I'm on it."

The second I got back into the office, I began putting a team of my own together. If we found an address, the best time to pay a visit would be this evening when we knew the kidnapper would be out leading Nick, Luke, and the rest of their gang on a merry dance.

I chose Dan, of course, plus another four men from the UK office to assist. Six would be enough to search a building. Now all we needed to do was locate the damn property.

Nick called at five. "We're leaving for the drop point."

Luke had three tracking devices sewn into his clothes and another two in the bag with the ransom. We'd given him an earpiece to keep in contact with the team, and he took his phone as backup. The kidnapper's message had told him to go to a shopping centre in Sydenham, South London and await further instructions.

Half an hour later, my phone rang as I paced the control room.

"Nate, tell me you've got good news."

"Three possibilities for the woman. I'm looking for pictures of the sons."

It wasn't long before he started firing emails at me. The first photo was a bust—the guy was too chubby, grinning into the camera with a big dimple in his chin. Nothing like Luke, and another fifteen minutes wasted.

But we struck gold with son number two.

"That's him," I told Nate. "Simon Howard."

I scanned through the background information as Nate plucked it out of cyberspace. Simon had been born to Fiona Howard just eight days before Luke came into the world.

Which made a certain amount of sense.

"First born son," Nate muttered.

"No wonder he's got a chip on his shoulder the size

of Texas."

Simon's life had not been one of privilege. He'd grown up in a ground-floor maisonette not too far from JJ's, an area I knew all too well and not one conducive to an idyllic childhood. In his teens, he'd attended the local state school, where he'd passed his exams despite a poor attendance record, excelling in computer studies and electronics before going on to study computer science at university. Had he been aware of his father's identity at that point? Was he trying to emulate him? Or seek his approval? If that had been his plan, it hadn't worked, because Luke still ended up as the golden boy. That must have stung.

"Address, Nate?"

"Flat 403, Shelton House, which looks like a block of flats in Bromley. On a side road just off the high street."

Nate pulled up the satellite photo onto the screen. Simon lived in the middle of a heavily built-up estate, his block one of four that surrounded a patch of scrubby grass. What were there plenty of in that area? Pedestrians. And what was missing? Car parking spaces. Flat 403 would be on the fourth floor—how would Howard have got Tia up there? Wheeled her through the streets in a shopping trolley then shoved her into the lift?

"No good. Try the mother?"

It was six thirty by the time Nate came back with the news that Fiona Howard had lived in a small, detached house in a quiet cul-de-sac in Lewisham.

"I can't find a record of it being sold since her death."

I couldn't help smiling. "Fifty bucks says that's

where Tia is."

"No way I'm taking that bet."

My team was already packed and ready to go, so within two minutes, we were in the back of a specially modified van, ready for our eight-mile trip from the office to Lewisham.

As we sped through darkened streets, a surge of adrenaline rushed through me. I'd tried to convince myself I could live a normal life, but the truth was, I'd felt dead inside. Now I was ready to face the darkness again.

Once more unto the breach, dear friends. Once more.

Because this was who I was.

CHAPTER 35

LUKE SAT BESIDE Nick in a nondescript black SUV as they drove to the specified location. He rarely visited this part of London, and right now, he never wanted to set foot in the city again. If—when—he got Tia back, they could move somewhere far away from this life and its hellish complications. Their mother, Ash, a criminal who'd turned their lives upside down. Luke should have been on holiday in the Bahamas right now, sipping a beer with Ash lying next to him in a bikini, and the injustice of it all brought a pulse of anger that overrode his fear for a second.

But only for a second.

The bag containing the ransom jiggled up and down on his lap as he bounced his feet, trying to dissipate some of his nervous energy. A million pounds was a lifetime's work for most people, yet it all fitted in one small holdall.

Where had the cash even come from? Luke still didn't know, but Nick assured him it was genuine. At least Luke hadn't had to try and withdraw it from the bank. The manager had been as suspicious as hell about his tale of buying a second-hand Ferrari last time, and Luke doubted the man would have fallen for it if he showed up at the branch claiming he wanted to buy a Bugatti Veyron as well.

But the bundle of cash was of little comfort as the driver pulled up a short distance from the shopping centre with five minutes to spare. Luke would walk the last part alone with Nick as his shadow.

As he exited the car, he felt giddy, dazed almost, and he couldn't help thinking of the disaster in the woods. What would happen if he messed up this time? Would he receive Tia's hand? Her foot?

"Careful, buddy," Nick said, pressing down on Luke's head in time to stop him hitting it on top of the doorframe.

"Thanks," Luke muttered, preoccupied with thoughts of his sister. What if they couldn't get her back?

Outside the car, Nick patted Luke on the back. "Good luck."

He melted into the darkness before Luke had a chance to reply.

Luke walked slowly along the pavement, his eyes darting from side to side. Where was the kidnapper? A door slammed, and he jumped sideways, splashing dirty water up his legs as he landed in a puddle. Shit. Why had he agreed to this? Why did he turn down the offer of a decoy? Shabby homes gave way to derelict buildings, and his hand trembled as he gripped the handle of the bag tighter. Nick and his people may have been in the surrounding shadows, but Luke had never felt more alone in his life.

He'd always thought he could look after himself, but recent events had shaken him. First, his misjudgement of Ash, then his injury in the woods, and finally, his inability to get Tia back all left him racked with self-doubt.

What if he failed?

No, don't think like that.

At the appointed time, Luke stood beside the entrance to the shopping centre, desperately trying to look more in control than he felt. Nick had returned his phone to him in the car, fully charged, and at one minute past six, it vibrated with a message.

Unknown: Follow road to left of shopping centre two hundred metres. Self-storage unit on left. Key at desk in name of Johnson.

Luke relayed the instructions to Nick over the radio, keeping his voice to a whisper in case the kidnapper was nearby.

Nick's voice came back through his earpiece. "Copy. I'm right behind you, and I'll send a couple of teams ahead to the storage place."

Luke increased his pace as he walked, anxious to get the drop over with. A hundred yards to go, then fifty. Could Nick hear his heart hammering over the airwaves?

Ah, there was the storage place, a neon sign out front proclaiming " elf S ore." Like the surrounding area, it had seen better days, but possibly not this century.

In the faded lobby, an old lady sat at a desk with the remains of a cheese sandwich on a cracked plate in front of her, cackling at an episode of *The Jeremy Kyle Show*. She squinted up at Luke through rheumy eyes and attempted a toothless smile.

"Do you have a key for Johnson?" he asked.

"Oh, yes, your brother said you'd be by. Look just like him, you do."

Really? He looked like the guy? That thought gave

Luke the creeps, but he made a mental note to mention it to Nick in case it provided a clue. And what about the name Johnson? Did that mean anything?

Following the old lady's directions, Luke took the stairs to the first floor, where he found himself outside a shabby wooden door secured by a hasp and a shiny padlock. Was anybody watching? He looked both ways along the corridor, squinting into the gloom at the far end. Nothing, at least, nothing that he could see. The key felt cool in his palm. Should he open the door? What if it was a trap?

His voice shook so much, it took three attempts to speak.

"What do you think?" Luke asked after he'd finally explained the situation. "Should I go in?"

"Not sure you've got a choice. Just go slowly and carefully, and stop if you feel any resistance."

"All right." Luke slid the key into the lock. "I'm not sure if it means anything, but the old lady on the desk reckoned I look like the man who rented this storage unit. Does that help? Maybe we have the same colour hair?"

"We'll bear that in mind. Now, try the door."

The padlock was well oiled, and the door swung open smoothly. A single, bare bulb lit the small space, swinging in a hint of a draught. Ahead of him, Luke saw a bag, a pile of clothes, a cheap mobile phone, and a note.

He picked up the note first.

Swap the money and the software into the bag on the floor. Strip off all your clothes and shoes and put on the ones next to the bag. Don't even think of keeping any electronics on you other than the phone supplied, or your sister dies. And smile, you're on camera.

In the far corner above Luke's head, the red light of a CCTV camera blinked among the cobwebs. Shit. He didn't dare speak to Nick—he wasn't a ventriloquist, after all. And what if the camera also had a microphone?

Instead, he followed the instructions and began transferring the ransom into the new bag. His hands shook so much he dropped a handful of bundles on the floor, and one burst open. He didn't bother to hold back his curses as he wasted precious time retrieving the notes. When he got his hands on this arsehole, he'd...he'd... Okay, so he didn't exactly know, but it wouldn't be pretty. Worse even than making him sit through the *Fifty Shades of Grey* movie without the ability to mute or fast-forward.

Next, Luke needed to change. The kidnapper had left a pair of jogging bottoms, a T-shirt, and a red sweatshirt, plus cheap trainers. Should he take off his underwear and socks? He glanced at the camera again, its beady eye steady, then stripped to his skin. The scratchy sweatshirt was too small, and the shoes slopped around on his feet. How far would he have to walk in them?

As he tied the second lace, the phone on the floor vibrated, signalling the arrival of a message.

Unknown: Go back to the shopping centre and take the 180 bus. Use the travel card in the trouser pocket. Run - you have 2 minutes.

Luke took off down the stairs, reaching the bus just as the doors were closing. Nobody boarded after him. Had the following team kept up? He looked out the window, but all he could see was the glare of headlights and the occasional glow from homes on the tired street.

Was Nick in one of the vehicles nearby? Or the kidnapper?

The bus wound its way through South East London for forty minutes. Luke tried to memorise the route, but he wasn't familiar with the area and soon lost track of where he was. Ten stops, twenty, and after the twenty-third, he received another message.

Unknown: Get off at next stop. Take the ferry.

Ferry? What ferry? Was he near the Thames?

He hopped off the bus at the twenty-fourth stop, clutching the bag as if his life depended on it. Or rather, Tia's life. At the end of a nearby pier, a boat floated gently on the river, and he dashed in that direction. *Please, don't go without me.* A sign told him the ferry was free to use, and he leapt on among the multitude of cars, lorries, and foot passengers.

Exhausted both by the wild run and a lack of sleep for the last few days, Luke sank into a seat beside a businessman in a rumpled suit.

"Can you tell me where this boat goes?"

The businessman raised an eyebrow but answered anyway, his voice weary. "It's the Woolwich ferry. It'll dock on the other side of the river in five minutes."

"Thanks."

Did Luke dare to call Nick? Was the kidnapper watching? He studied his fellow passengers, but none seemed to be paying the slightest attention, and this could be his only chance. He punched the number Nick had made him memorise into the cheap phone the kidnapper gave him.

Dammit! No credit.

Feeling desperate, he turned to the businessman

again. "Any chance I could borrow your phone?"

The guy just stared. Understandable, since even making eye contact with a stranger in London was frowned upon.

"Please. I've got a family emergency."

"You're not calling overseas, right?"

"No, just local."

The man sighed and handed his phone over. "Make it quick, okay?"

The last of Luke's hope leached away when Nick's number went straight to voicemail. What was he playing at? How could he call himself a professional if he didn't even answer his damn phone?

Luke left a garbled message telling Nick his whereabouts then got swept up in the exodus of passengers as the ferry reached the opposite bank. Thirty seconds after he stepped onto dry land, another message arrived. He was to travel on foot this time.

Unknown: Two miles, twenty minutes. Go down the road next to the hair salon then take the first left, second right, third left, fifth right, second right, fourth left. Don't be late.

Luke set off at a sprint. He may have been fit, but the heavy bag banged against his legs and slowed him down. Running the ten-minute miles specified would be uncomfortable, especially in a pair of shoes that didn't fit. Worse, he had no idea where he was or where he should be going, and he didn't even have street names to confirm whether he was heading in the right direction. Was he alone now? He hadn't seen a familiar face since he left the storage place.

Could things have gone any more wrong?

Luke had been running for eighteen minutes when

a police car overtook him, blue lights flashing and siren wailing, closely followed by a second and then a third, all rushing in the same direction as him. What was going on up there?

A few seconds later, the phone rang.

Luke skidded to a halt, hands on his knees as he tried to catch his breath and answer at the same time.

"Yes?"

The voice on the other end was harsh. "I said no police. Such a simple instruction, and you fucked it up. I'll tell your sister you said goodbye."

"Wait! I didn't call the police. I don't know why..." Luke started, then realised he was talking to dead air.

Shit, shit, shit. His heart hammered against his ribcage, and not just from the exertion. He'd screwed up, and his sister was about to die.

What were his options? He had no phone to call for help, even if he knew where he was. Sure, he had cash, but if he waved a fistful of twenties around in this place, he'd probably get mugged. He tore at his hair in despair.

Think, Luke, think.

Okay. He'd been two minutes from his destination when the kidnapper called, and the bastard assumed the police were there for him. Which meant the police must be two minutes away. If he... Hold on. What was that? Something the size of a grain of rice clung to his finger. He tried to flick it off, but it was stuck fast. What was it? He moved under a streetlight to get a better look at the tiny black object.

"I see you found the extra tracker, then."

Nick's voice coming from behind made Luke jump out of his skin, and he dropped the bag on his foot.

Curses turned the air blue as Nick's words sank in.

"Tracker? You put another tracker on me?"

"Call it an insurance policy. So, what's happening? Why have you stopped?"

"The kidnapper got spooked by the police ahead, and he's going to kill Tia. Did you call them? Did you call the cops?"

Nick scoffed at that idea. "Hell, no. We got unlucky. They're doing a drug bust. A bunch of potheads have turned a family home into a cannabis factory, and it looks like they've called half the force in to pull the place apart. Must have been a slow day at the station."

Images flashed through Luke's mind—his sister as a baby, a toddler, her first day at school, her twelfth birthday party. He couldn't give up. Not now.

"The guy must be nearby, and so are the police. Can't they set up a roadblock or something?"

"That'd take too long. I need to make a call."

"Who to?"

"Just give me a minute."

Luke paced the dirty pavement as Nick spoke. Who was on the other end? Luke had no idea.

"Things have gone to pot here. Quite literally. If you're gonna act, you need to do it now because the asshole told Luke he's on his way to Tia."

Luke strained his ears but couldn't catch the reply.

"Right, I'll let you get on with it," Nick said, then hung up.

"Who were you speaking to?" Luke asked again. "What are they doing?"

"The other team. The one out looking for Tia."

"What do you mean? What other team? I thought there weren't any leads?"

Before Dan left that morning, he'd asked her if there was anything new. Her apologetic shake of the head had left him close to despair.

"Well, you'd better hope our esteemed leader's back on form and her hunch of a couple of hours ago turns out to be right," Nick said. The words, "Because that's the last chance Tia has," were left unspoken, but the implication was clear.

"What can we do to help?"

Luke wanted to keep busy, anything to take his mind off what could be happening to Tia at that moment.

"Nothing. We can only wait."

How many times had Luke been told to do that? He hated being kept out of the loop like this. It was *his* sister in trouble, for fuck's sake.

A car pulled up, and they both climbed in, Luke on his own in the back while Nick sat up front with the driver. Luke hadn't felt so alone since his father died, or so scared.

Nick put in an earpiece and spoke to someone, presumably a colleague. "Patch me into the feed from the control room, would you?"

A giant's fist squeezed Luke's chest, and he struggled to breathe. Outside the window, dark streets passed by, and his head filled with "what ifs?" What if he'd spent more time with Tia? What if he'd insisted she didn't go out alone? What if they'd lived in an area that wasn't so isolated?

Luke had never advocated violence, but sitting alone, impotent when it came to saving his sister, he dreamed of throttling the kidnapper with his bare hands. His fingers tightened around his thigh, imagining it was the man's neck. No, that wouldn't bring Tia back, but it would stop the bastard doing the same to another girl. What if she didn't come home? What was he supposed to tell their mother? She'd have another breakdown, wouldn't she?

"We've got her," Nick said.

"What?"

"Tia. The other team's got her."

"Is she alive?"

"She was tied up and dehydrated, but the only damage seems to be to her fingernail."

Tension seeped out of Luke like water from a sponge.

"Can I see her?" He wanted to confirm the news with his own eyes.

"Give it a few minutes. They're not fully extracted from the scene, and I don't know where they're taking her yet."

Nick put the audio from the control room onto the car speakers so Luke could listen too. The first voice he heard was Dan's, her harsh New York accent crystal clear.

"Are you staying behind?"

"No point." This voice was female too, but English and softer. "There were fucking cameras everywhere, transmitting wirelessly. A hundred bucks says he knows we've found her and he won't be coming back. I'd also bet money on him being royally pissed."

"I'd tend to agree with you," came a man's voice, American this time. "Leave one team, and we'll start planning the next phase."

"Next phase?" Luke whispered.

"We still need to find the man," Nick said.

The soft voice spoke again. "In that case, I'm gonna take Tia home—it's where she said she wants to go. Nye, can you arrange for an ambulance to meet us there? She could do with a check over."

"Will do. Do you want the police involved now?"

"I'll call Jason. Might as well utilise our tax dollars and get them to look for Mr. Howard too, even if all they've managed to do so far is prove they can't fill in the details on a witness statement properly."

What witness statement? And who was Mr. Howard? Luke had a lot of questions, but right now, his first concern was getting to Tia.

"Any chance of a lift home?" he asked Nick.

"No problem, buddy."

They weren't sharing in the rest of the team's luck, and ten minutes after they got on the M25, the motorway came to a standstill.

"There's a lorry crash up ahead," their driver said.

"Can we go around it?" Nick asked.

"They've closed the motorway. We'll have to wait it out."

An hour passed before they reached an exit, but Tia was safely back in Lower Foxford, complete with a team of bodyguards, and that was all that mattered. They were crawling along in a never-ending line of cars when Nick's phone rang. A few muttered words, and he held it out to Luke.

"It's your sister."

Luke grabbed the phone and held it to his ear. "Are you okay? I'll be there as soon as I can."

"I'm all right," Tia said, although she sounded exhausted. "I just want something to eat, and then I want to go to bed."

"Where were you? What happened?" Luke heard the muffled sound of a yawn and felt guilty for asking questions. "Or we can talk later."

"Yes, later, when you get back."

"Okay. Are you being looked after?"

"There're loads of people here. Did you tell Mother I was gone?"

"Why? Do you want me to call her?"

"No way! I can't deal with her tonight."

"You don't have to, and no, I didn't tell her you were missing."

"Thank goodness."

"Just stay safe, okay?"

It was after nine o'clock when Luke arrived in Lower Foxford, tired now that the earlier adrenaline rush had worn off. He looked forward to seeing Tia, having dinner, and getting some sleep, in that order. Everything else could be dealt with tomorrow. Luke didn't even want to think about the rest of the mess.

As the car pulled into the drive, he pictured the glass of wine he was going to pour after he'd seen his sister. After such a shitty day, he deserved at least one drink. Then Tia's idea of going to bed was a good one.

Luke's thoughts turned to the future, a future with his sister, no hassle, no drama. Perhaps she could take Ash's place on that holiday he'd booked? The danger was over now, right?

Wrong.

CHAPTER 36

THE FAR END of Luke's driveway looked like the forecourt of a car dealership. Matching black SUVs formed a row, presumably belonging to Nick's crew, and just for variety, a couple of police cars and an ambulance were lined up opposite. All very neat and tidy. But between them, a white van blocked the driveway, more abandoned than parked.

"Looks like Mr. Howard found us instead," Nick said.

Howard? That was the second time Luke had heard the name.

"Who the hell is Mr. Howard?"

"Our kidnapper."

Luke reached for the door handle as anger flared in his belly. The man who'd taken his sister had dared to come here? To his house? He itched to get his hands on the bastard, but Nick held him back.

"Stay put, would you? We'll deal with it."

"It wasn't *your* sister he took."

Luke tried to open the door, but the handle didn't work. What was wrong with the bloody thing?

Nick grinned at him. "I put the kiddie lock on."

Suddenly, the kidnapper wasn't the only man Luke wanted to hurt.

But then Nick motioned out of the window, and

Luke took a closer look at the scene outside. In the shadow of an old oak tree, a man dressed all in black held a policewoman at gunpoint. He shouted something, but the glass muffled his words.

"Would you wind the window down?" he asked Nick, fresh fear blossoming in his chest.

Nick shrugged and opened it a few inches, and Luke caught the tail end of what the man was yelling.

"...the girl back, or I'll shoot the cop."

His jerky movements, his high-pitched voice, they both suggested the man's self-control hung by a hair. Where was Tia? Did she know what was going on? That she was being used as a bargaining chip by a madman?

"Don't worry," Nick said. "Not going to happen. No way is she gonna give up Tia."

"Do you think he'll really shoot that policewoman?"

The woman's face shimmered white in the glare from the van's headlights, and she stumbled as the man dragged her backwards.

"Who knows? He looks like he's lost his mind. If he ever had it in the first place."

"Somebody's got to do something! We can't sit here and wait for her head to get blown off."

"Don't panic. Somebody will."

Nick gestured to the front door, and Luke watched, heart thumping, as Ash walked calmly towards the kidnapper. She stopped ten metres away and her lips moved as she spoke. What was she saying? Luke strained to hear, but he couldn't make the words out.

The kidnapper nodded in agreement then jerked his head towards his van, where the sliding side door gaped open like the entrance to the underworld.

What was going on?

Ash took her phone out of her pocket and placed it on the ground, then walked in the direction indicated. When she got to the van, she reached inside and emerged with a pair of handcuffs and a length of rope.

"What's she doing?" Luke asked. "What's Ash doing?"

"Going with him."

"Stop her! We've got to stop her." Luke tried the handle again, but it rattled uselessly. The window wouldn't open any further either.

"Nobody can stop her. Sit still, would you?"

"No, I won't sit still! That's my girlfriend facing a man with a gun."

Nick swivelled in his seat to face him. "I thought you split up?"

"We did, but..." Luke trailed off as Ash sat on the sill of the van and tied her feet together before holding up the handcuffs.

"Put them on," Howard yelled.

Ash shook her head, talking to the kidnapper again. A few seconds later, he huffed and pushed the policewoman away before turning back to Ash, the gun trained on her instead.

Luke pounded on the window, trying to break the glass.

"Good luck with that—it's bulletproof," Nick said.

"Let me out of the damn car."

"No chance."

Luke had no choice but to watch as Ash fastened one cuff around her wrist then attached the other to a cargo ring set into the floor of the van. The kidnapper strode over and looked in at her, his face hidden under a black hoodie. Then he slammed the side door of the van shut before turning back to the frozen crowd of onlookers, waving the gun wildly.

"If anyone follows me, she dies. I mean it," he screeched.

Nick was right; he'd lost the plot.

Howard jumped into the van and peeled out of the driveway, onlookers scattering and tyres squealing. Luke gripped the edges of the window, his heart threatening to claw its way out of his chest. Yes, he and Ash had had their problems, but now he understood that she'd only been trying to help him. What if the kidnapper planned to kill her the way he'd threatened with Tia?

The locks clicked as Nick released them, and Luke sprang out of the car.

Nick followed, muttering, "Poor bastard."

Luke paused to stare at him. "What? What are you talking about?"

Dan strolled over, smiling, her hands relaxed by her sides.

"This is handy. At least it saves us the trouble of looking for him. Might get a lie in tomorrow," she said.

Nick nodded his agreement. "Yeah, although I'm getting kind of hungry."

Hungry? The man was hungry? Luke felt like he was about to throw up.

Dan looked at her watch. "Are you joining in the pool?"

"Count me in," Nick said. "What are we doing? Ten-minute slots?"

"Five. The US offices are joining in too. Nate's gone off to make popcorn."

Luke couldn't hold back any longer. "What the fuck

are you two talking about? In case you hadn't noticed, your friend has just been abducted at gunpoint."

How could they be joking right now? Someone needed to tell him what the hell was going on.

One of the policemen wandered over, greeting Nick with a complicated handshake.

"Jason, it's been a while."

"All right, Nick? How do you want us to play this?"

"Hold back for a bit, would you? Dan and I will head off in a minute. Can you follow behind us?"

"Sure. Give me a shout when you're leaving."

"No worries. Will do. Your woman okay?" Nick asked.

"Shaken up, but someone's taken her into the house for a sit down and a cuppa. She'll be fine."

Everyone had clearly gone mad.

"A woman's been kidnapped," Luke told the policeman, as that seemed to have escaped his notice.

"Yeah, I know. Don't worry about it."

Luke's jaw dropped as the cop strolled back to his group of colleagues in front of the house. The ones in uniform shifted from foot to foot, unsure of what to do with themselves, but a couple in plain-clothes were laughing.

"What about Ash? Nobody seems to be taking this seriously."

"She'll be fine," Nick said.

"You don't know that. The last time we saw her, she was decidedly un-fine."

Was Luke the only one who cared?

"I *do* know. She just messaged me."

"What? But she left her phone here." Luke pointed to where it still sat on the ground.

"Correction. She left *one* of her phones here. She still has another two with her."

"But she was handcuffed."

"*Was* being the operative word. She won't still be handcuffed. Trust me," Nick added, seeing the disbelieving look on Luke's face.

"I'd better get going," Dan said, fishing a set of car keys out of her pocket. "She left her coat in the car, and it's chilly out. She won't be happy if we keep her waiting for ages in the cold."

"I'm coming with you," Luke insisted.

"I don't think that's a good idea," Nick said. "Besides, you should go in and see Tia."

Luke hesitated. He'd desperately wanted to check on his sister, but that was before his girlfriend got abducted.

"I'm worried about Ash," he mumbled.

Nick gave an exasperated sigh and relented. "Dan, take Nye with you and go on ahead. I'll stop with Luke and Tia for a few minutes then follow."

Dan looked as if she was about to protest, but Nick held up a hand.

"Look, he was living with her for two or three months. She'll have got under his skin like she does with everyone else."

He was right. Ash had wormed her way under Luke's skin and into his heart.

Nick turned back to him. "But Luke, you will *not* get involved. Just see that Ash's okay, and I'll bring you back. Agreed?"

"Agreed." Luke understood he didn't have much choice.

Not wanting to waste any more time, he hurried

into the house and found Tia curled up on the couch in the den, arms wrapped around her knees. When she saw Luke, she leapt up and hugged him.

"I missed you," she sniffed.

"I missed you too."

"Ash told me you tried to deliver the ransom?"

"Yeah, I did, but it went a bit wrong."

"You were so brave."

He didn't want to let on he'd been terrified the entire time. "I'd have done anything to get you back."

Nick came into view, tapping his watch, and Luke steered Tia towards the door. "Let's get you to bed. We can talk more in the morning."

"Okay. I'm really tired, but I didn't want to go to sleep until I saw you."

The instant his sister was tucked under her duvet, Luke sprinted for Nick's car. As they left the drive, a screen on the dashboard displayed several pulsating blobs. Nick pointed at a white blob a mile or two behind the others. "That's us, and the other white dot is Dan."

"Is the red one Ash?"

"Yeah."

The red dot was ahead of Dan, moving steadily.

Their strange convoy continued for half an hour, first along the main roads then out into the countryside again. When the red blob suddenly stopped, Luke's heart stuttered too. From the map, it looked as if the van had pulled up in an area of woodland.

"Oh, fuck, he's planning to shoot her like he tried with me." Panic rose in his chest, icy fingers clawing at his insides.

Nick glanced at his watch. "Ten twenty. Shit. My

pool time isn't until eleven. I've lost this one unless a miracle happens."

Luke stared at him. "You're insane."

They rode on in a tense silence until Nick's phone buzzed, and the woman's voice Luke heard earlier filled the cabin.

"Time's ten twenty-six, Nicky. So, tell me, who got the pool?"

"Pool?"

"I'm crazy, not fucking stupid."

"Fine, it was Luther."

"Didn't he win the last one, too?"

"Yeah, the lucky son of a bitch."

"Gotta go. Jason's just turned up. See you in a minute."

Nick turned to Luke. "Told you she'd be fine."

"That was Ash?"

The woman on the radio had sounded so different from the Ash Luke knew, confident and self-assured in contrast to his Ash's sweet hesitancy.

"Yeah, it was. She changes her accent more times than she changes her mind."

Why would she need to do that? Luke was about to ask when Nick pointed out their destination just ahead.

"We're heading for a clearing just around that bend."

When they arrived, Nick held Luke to his promise and made him stay in the vehicle. Luke watched Jason and another policeman ask Ash questions as she perched on the bonnet of their car, eyes downcast. Was she okay? Had the kidnapper hurt her? He looked over at the van, slewed at an angle with its doors wide open. Was that the kidnapper on the ground next to it? Luke pressed his face against the glass to get a better look. Yes, it was him in the black hoodie. Howard.

"Is he dead?" Luke asked, pointing.

"Don't think so," Nick said. "He's got cuffs on. Those cops next to him are waiting for him to come round."

Luke's hands curled into fists as he thought of what he'd like to do to the man. How dare the bastard hurt his family? If the police hadn't been present, he'd have marched right over and punched him, but instead, he had to settle for watching as the guy slowly stirred and got hauled to his feet by two officers.

Shoulders slumped, head down, he didn't look quite so scary now. At least, until he got close to Ash. The bastard tried to lunge at her, cuffed arms outstretched, but she stood her ground and the police hauled him back. Why was she laughing? And more to the point, why did the man hate Luke's family so much?

The kidnapper got closer, and as he passed by Dan's SUV, the headlights lit up his features. Of all the shocks Luke had received in the last few days, this one was perhaps the most unexpected. He froze, unable to tear his eyes away from the man's face. It was almost, but not quite, like looking into a mirror.

"What the...?" Luke started. He stepped out of the car, and Nick didn't try to stop him this time. "Who are you?"

The prisoner glowered back, unspeaking.

Ash stepped in to do the honours. "Luke, meet Simon Howard, your half-brother. Simon, I'd introduce Luke, but I'm sure you already know who he is."

"You're a bitch," was Simon's only reply.

"Oh, you're wrong there. I'm not a bitch. I'm *the*

bitch. The queen bitch, in fact. I lost my crown for a while, but I need to thank you for helping me to get it back. It was almost a pleasure doing business with you."

Ash took a mock bow and laughed again. Was there something in the water? That wasn't the Ash Luke knew. Simon still looked like he wanted to punch her as the police marched him towards their car.

"See, fucking crazy," Nick said.

Who was he talking about? Ash or Simon? Luke felt like he'd fallen down a rabbit hole and ended up in the eighth circle of hell.

He faced his...girlfriend? Ex-girlfriend? "You okay?"

She shrugged, looking at her feet. "Yeah."

"Did he hurt you?"

She shook her head and followed up with a bark of laughter.

"No."

Fuck, he'd never been in this situation before. What was he supposed to say? He barely knew Ash anymore, and right now, he wasn't sure whether to love her for saving Tia or hate her for lying to him. *Okay, think logically*. They should talk. He should ask her to come home so they could discuss this. That would do for starters.

"Will you—"

A cop interrupted. "Good to see you!" He clapped Ash on the back like she was one of the guys. "Can I borrow you for a few minutes?"

"Sure."

She practically ran off, leaving Luke with his mouth hanging open, the rest of the sentence stuck in his throat. Great. That went well. Still, it gave Luke breathing space to work out exactly what he needed to say.

On the far side of the clearing, Simon Howard got unceremoniously loaded into the back of a police van, and before Luke could stop her, Ash climbed into the SUV with Dan and took off after them. He was left with little choice but to ride with Nick.

"Do you really think that man's my half-brother?" Luke asked.

The revelation made him feel sick, not just because his father had kept him in the dark all these years, but because Howard was evil personified. How could they be related?

"Yes, we do."

"How did you find him?"

"I don't have all the details. We'll have to get Dan to fill us both in when we get back to the house."

The background chatter on the radio provided a soundtrack to Luke's thoughts. He got so engrossed in trying to unravel the mess in his mind, he barely noticed Dan's car parked in a lay-by a few miles down the road.

"Why have they stopped?" Nick muttered, pulling in behind.

They both got out and walked to the driver's side, where Dan sat with both hands on the steering wheel, staring pointedly out of the windscreen. In the passenger seat, Ash had her hands in her lap and her eyes fixed forwards.

"Are you two okay?" Nick asked.

No answer. Then Dan glanced over at Ash, catching her eye, and the first hint of giggles escaped from her lips. That did it. Ash and Dan both collapsed in hysterics, with Dan laughing until tears fell from her eyes.

"Oh, for fuck's sake. What?" Nick asked.

Dan waved her hand in front of her face, signalling she couldn't speak.

"Maybe it's some kind of delayed shock?" Luke suggested.

"No," Ash spat. "It's just he was the worst kidnapper ever." Another burst of laughter. "He was waving the gun around, and he had the safety on. The safety! It was my lucky day when he agreed to take me instead of that poor policewoman."

"Saved us a bunch of trouble tomorrow," Dan said.

"Yeah, and I got to spend a little alone time with him."

"But you were handcuffed," Luke said. "And tied up."

Ash rolled her eyes. "I had a handcuff key, and when I tied my feet together, I used a quick-release knot. The idiot didn't even check it."

"What about when he opened the door? He had a gun."

"I wasn't even in the van at that point. When he stopped, I climbed out the back door and onto the roof. My only regret was missing his face when he realised I wasn't there."

"I'd like to have seen that, too," Nick said.

"When I dropped down behind him, he tried to swing the gun around, but I twisted it out of his hand. And it still had the fucking safety on."

There was another pause as Ash and Dan dissolved into laughter again, with Nick joining in this time. But Luke still didn't see the funny side. What did Ash know about guns? He didn't even know where the safety was, so how did she?

"The *safety*," Ash continued. "Can you believe that? When I got him with an uppercut, he dropped faster than a second-rate hooker on a deadline. He'd even given me the cuffs and rope to tie him up with."

"Not bad, baby," Nick said.

Baby?

"Three minutes, Nicky. Shame it was over so fast—I was having fun." Then she smiled brightly. "I wonder what the prison doctor will make of his mysterious groin pain?"

She turned to Dan, and they high-fived.

Another vehicle pulled up behind Nick's, and the girls climbed out of their car as Jason unfolded himself from the passenger seat of his.

"What's this? A convention?" Jason asked.

"Oh, just feeling a little car sick," Ash told him, voice sweet as pie.

"Strange, that. The prisoner's complaining he feels sick too, except my officer reports he's clutching his balls. You wouldn't happen to know anything about that, would you?"

Ash glanced at Dan then quickly looked away. "Can't help you there, I'm afraid. Maybe he caught himself on the door sill as he fell?"

Jason didn't look convinced, but he let it go. Everyone climbed back into their respective cars, Ash driving the SUV this time. Her car shot off into the distance, leaving the smell of burnt rubber in its wake and Luke more confused than ever.

Who was Ash, really?

CHAPTER 37

I PULLED AWAY from the lay-by with Dan beside me, leaving Nick and Luke behind to get into their car. Jason watched me in the rear-view mirror as I sped off, hands on hips. No doubt he'd be pissed when he found out I wasn't going back to the house, but he knew how to get hold of me if he needed to. He'd get over it. He always did. I made a mental note to give him a call later to smooth things over.

Dan reached over and keyed our destination into satnav. Forty minutes. At least Howard chose to hold his final showdown close to the airbase so we didn't have far to travel. Today had turned out to be a good day, and I felt more upbeat than I had in ages. Not only was Tia back home in one piece, but I'd also proven this morning with Jimmy that I still had a good fight in me. And best of all, Luke's crackpot half-brother was making friends with his new cell mate, who I hoped was six-foot-seven with a penchant for tall, blonde, and grouchy.

Nope, not a bad day at the office.

Of course, the day wasn't without its low points. My life wouldn't be complete at the moment without a dash of darkness to even out the light.

The first low occurred as I rode in the van, but not for the reasons you'd think. No, the sadness came when

I freed myself, because my handcuff key was built into my wedding ring. Unlocking the cuffs brought back memories of my husband and the heartache that came with losing him.

When we first got married in Vegas, we'd had crappy off-the-shelf rings, engraved on the inside with "CB & MB 4EVA"—Crazy Bastard and Mental Bitch Forever. Nate's idea of a joke. We didn't manage forever, though, did we? Although the rest of my life would feel like forever without my husband in it.

We'd put up with the shitty rings for a week before my husband flicked his across the breakfast table.

"Diamond, if I've got to wear a permanent reminder of my supposed undying love, I'd prefer something that doesn't look as if it came from an arcade machine."

"Agreed. What are you thinking?"

"Surprise me."

My husband's new ring had been titanium with two bands, one made from dinosaur bone and the other from a meteorite. The designer told me it would symbolise our love lasting for all time. Back then, I thought he was talking shit, but it turned out he'd been right. When I gave it to my husband, I told him I wanted to get something as ancient as he was—he may have only been nine-and-a-half years older than me, but that didn't stop me from reminding him about it at every opportunity.

My platinum ring with its hidden handcuff key was beautiful as well as practical. And, of course, we'd had the engraving transferred over as a reminder of our drunken wedding.

When I'd unlocked my handcuffs in the van, I sent him a silent thank you. Was he up there somewhere, watching me? If so, I hoped I'd redeemed myself just a little with today's performance.

The next low point had been leaving Luke and Tia. Guilt gnawed away at me, and I felt kind of sad too. It wouldn't be easy for Luke at first, dealing with the revelation that his brother was a head case, but he had the strength to deal with it. That much I knew. He'd lent me some of that steel over the past few months and helped me through the worst time of my life. I'd always be grateful to him, but the kindest thing I could do now would be to let him go. He didn't need me and my troubles weighing him down further. My problems were my own, and I needed to face up to them.

At least Luke and Tia had each other for support. I'd watched them grow closer over the last two months, and now they had the relationship a brother and sister should have. Yes, they'd get through this together.

And me? Well, Luke had dug the pit in my chest a little bit deeper. My life would be worse for not having him in it, but the time had come for me to return to Virginia. Luke belonged in England, and I couldn't ask him to change everything for me.

Nor could I change for him. I'd been away from home too long, and while I'd salvaged my relationship with Nick and Dan, I still had a way to go with Mack and Nate. That was something best done face to face.

Dan interrupted my thoughts. "What happened to the ransom?"

"It's in the back of Nick's car. Can you put my share back in the safe?"

"Sure."

"And Jason's gonna want to speak to you. There'll be paperwork."

She groaned. "Yeah, I know. Thanks for leaving me all that."

"I'm sorry. I'll call him—I need to have a word about Simon. He's whacked."

"I got that."

"You don't have the whole picture yet. In the van, he told me he couldn't wait to feel my tight pussy around his dick. Jason needs to look into his history."

"The sick fuck. Did you check Tia?"

"He didn't touch her. If he had, he wouldn't be breathing now."

"That kick in the nuts you gave him let him off easy."

"I broke his trigger finger too. I heard it crack when I wrenched the gun out of his hand."

"That was a nice trade off for Tia's fingernail."

"Exactly what I thought." I gripped the steering wheel tighter. "He's not getting out of prison. I'll fix it. He's never going to interfere in Luke or Tia's life again."

Dan reached over and squeezed my hand. "You obviously care about them. Are you sure you're doing the right thing by leaving?"

"I don't see another way. I've fucked up Luke's life for quite long enough."

"You should speak to him."

Did she think I didn't know that? "I can't."

Her answering shrug left me under no illusion that she thought I was doing the wrong thing. I glanced at the satnav. Ten minutes to the airbase.

"Will you say goodbye to Luke and Tia for me?" I asked. "Tell them I'll miss them."

"I will, but you should do it yourself."

My turn to shrug. Dealing with more emotion was beyond my current capabilities. "Let me know if they need anything."

We lapsed into silence and soon pulled up at the gates of RAF Northolt, where my Learjet waited next to the taxiway. The stairs were already lowered, and as I approached, Bradley bounced down to meet me. Didn't the guy ever run out of energy?

"I've loaded your bag with your laptop, clothes, a cashmere throw, and three kinds of moisturiser. And I've picked up a fresh bulgur wheat and rocket salad for you to eat on the flight."

"Have you been talking to Toby again?"

"Yes, and he's thrilled you're on your way back. He's so worried you've been neglecting your diet. Most of your groceries have arrived—it's just the Wagyu beef that's stuck on the tarmac in Japan, and the caviar's on back order. He mentioned a detox."

Great, that would mean living on spinach smoothies and lemon tea for a week, and I didn't even like caviar. Was it too late to change my mind about going home? A little break in the Caribbean seemed like an excellent idea right now.

Dan read my thoughts and mouthed, "Don't even think about it."

I rolled my eyes.

"Stop being like that. You know how much you love nettle juice," she said.

"Bitch," I whispered in her ear as I hugged her tightly. "I'll see you in a few days."

"Yeah," she said quietly. "I'm glad you're back. I mean really back."

"Me too."

Leaving Dan on the tarmac, I turned and walked up the stairs onto the plane. It was just as I remembered, cream leather seats with walnut trim. At least Bradley hadn't refitted the interior while I was away. I wouldn't have put it past him, not after the time I spent a week in Atlanta and got home to find my gym painted a pale purple. Calming, apparently. I didn't want to be calm in my damn gym. I wanted to punch things.

Deep breaths, Emmy. Think happy, purple thoughts. I pushed the memory away and took a left into the cockpit to greet Brett, my pilot.

"It's good to see you back, Emmy," he said. "Will you be flying her today?"

"I might as well." Seeing as I was still wide-awake, and I never slept on planes, anyway. I could do far too much damage at forty-five thousand feet. "I'll take a break in the middle. I understand Bradley has salad for me."

"He mentioned it earlier while I was tucking into my cheeseburger and fries."

"Sometimes, I don't like you very much."

Brett chuckled as we buckled ourselves into our seats, and I shouted back to Bradley to fasten his seatbelt for take-off. With eight seats, it was the smaller of our two planes. We had a larger Global 8000 as well, but that was apparently in Seattle. First world problems. Today's flight plan called for us to fly to Teterboro, New Jersey, a seven-hour journey that took the plane to the limit of its range. From Teterboro, we'd refuel and make the short hop over to Richmond International where my husband's helicopter, a shiny black Eurocopter he'd purchased two months before his death, was waiting to take me home. Maybe a fourteen-seat helicopter was overkill for Bradley and me, but we'd sold the smaller one just before I left, and I hadn't got around to replacing it. Something else on my to-do list, which grew longer by the minute.

I started the plane's engines, and once they'd warmed up, I taxied over to the runway. *Was* I doing the right thing by leaving? Part of me wanted to go back to Lower Foxford, my sanctuary of sorts. But I couldn't, not now. No more running.

"Ready?" Brett asked.

"As I'll ever be."

As I powered up for take-off, I felt the first rush of adrenaline, but there was something else too.

What was it?

Was I...? No, I couldn't be. Was I nervous?

CHAPTER 38

LUKE AND NICK made the drive back to the house without further incident. The place was still lit up like a nightclub by emergency service vehicles, blue and red lights flashing everywhere, so Nick parked at the far end of the driveway.

"You okay, buddy?" Nick asked when Luke didn't move.

"Yeah. Just thinking."

Which was always dangerous. Luke got out of the car and shuffled towards the house, thankful that Tia had gone to bed. He wanted to tell her they'd caught the kidnapper, but at the same time, he didn't know how to explain that Simon Howard appeared to be a relative. They'd gone through their whole lives believing it was just the two of them and their mother. The news he had a half-brother was still sinking in, not to mention the shock of Howard being a criminal. How would Tia take it?

Perhaps Ash could help him break the news? Luke was still cross at her for lying, but that anger had been tempered when she came through on the kidnapping problem. Without her, he'd most likely be lying in a shallow grave, and even if he'd survived, he wouldn't have known where to go for help. He'd always be grateful to her for getting her friends involved, doubly so for the way she'd selflessly exchanged herself for the police officer at gunpoint.

Her hysterical reaction afterwards still baffled him, though.

And where was Ash, anyway? She and Dan weren't among those gathered outside. Come to think of it, their car wasn't even in the driveway. Nick had stopped to talk to the police who'd stayed to ensure Tia's safety while the whole mess unravelled, and Luke wandered in that direction.

"Has anybody seen Ash? I'm surprised she's not back by now."

Especially with the way she'd smoked the tyres when she left ahead of them. Could she have crashed?

Nick excused himself from the group and led Luke out of earshot. "The thing is, she's not coming back."

"What do you mean? Tonight? She's not coming back tonight? Have you got her number? I could meet her somewhere tomorrow."

"Sorry, buddy." Nick shook his head. "She's not coming back at all. She's on her way home."

"To America?"

"Yeah. She thought it would be better that way, what with not being your favourite person right now."

Shit. Luke tore a hand through his hair as Nick's words sank in. "I need to talk to her. Surely if she left at the same time as us, she'll still be on her way to the airport? I'll go after her. Is she flying out of Heathrow?"

Nick looked at his watch. "No, out of Northolt, and she's already taken off."

Since when did commercial airlines fly out of Northolt? It had been over a year since Luke last chartered a jet from there, so maybe things had changed?

Movement by the front door caught his eye, and an awful evening became even worse. Why wasn't Tia in bed? Her eyes settled on him, and she veered in his direction.

Now he'd have to break the news about Simon, Ash, and everything else himself. Tia would be devastated Ash had left. They'd grown so close in the time she'd been with them, and of course, she didn't yet know about Ash's deception.

He walked over to her, slowly, as if by dragging his feet he could somehow put off that talk forever. Tia looked so young and vulnerable at that moment, lit up by the security lights on the outside of the house, her face pale and her frame gaunt. The ordeal of the past few days showed in the way she carried herself.

Luke put his arm around her, but she shook it off. Seemed that having a big brother who cared was still totally uncool. Instead, he put his hand on her back and gently steered her inside. People milled around all over the place downstairs, talking into phones and writing notes, and he didn't want to have this conversation with an audience.

A policewoman started towards them and he waved her off, bypassing the rest of the crowd. They could wait. He led Tia back up to her room where she sat at the top of the bed, hugging a pillow to her chest. Luke perched on the edge, facing her. For a few minutes, they just stared at each other. Luke didn't know what to say, and it seemed Tia was in the same boat.

Finally, Luke broke the silence. "Are you okay?"

"I don't know."

"What happened? Can you talk about it?"

He wasn't sure whether Tia would tell him all the details, or even if he wanted her to, but the masochist in him couldn't stand being kept in the dark.

"I want to tell you, but I'm not sure I remember everything right. It's hazy."

He reached over and squeezed her hand. "It doesn't matter if you forget things." *It might be better that way.* "Just tell me what you can."

"I was walking home from Arabella's. I remember seeing a van up ahead, and I was going to cross the road to avoid it. But then you got out the driver's door. What were you doing in a van?"

"It wasn't me. The man who took you, we look alike."

Tia shuddered. "Creepy."

"What did he do?"

"I don't remember anything else until I woke up in a bathroom. I was on my own, but my wrist was chained to the radiator. The taps didn't work, and I had to drink funny tasting water out of a bottle. I think he put something in it. I didn't want to drink it, but there was nothing else."

Tia paused, and a tear rolled down her cheek. Luke reached out and wiped it away with his sleeve as thoughts of murder ran through his mind.

"I needed to use the toilet, but it didn't flush." She screwed up her face at the memory. "The smell was disgusting. I thought I'd been abandoned. One night, I dreamed you came through the door, but then you left. You didn't leave, did you?"

Tia dissolved in tears, and Luke struggled to keep his own eyes dry.

"It wasn't me. I swear, it wasn't me."

Should he hug her? Or leave her to calm down? This was why he needed Ash—she'd know what to do. In the end, he opted for the middle ground and stayed on the bed while Tia continued.

"The room didn't have any windows, so I didn't know if it was day or night. My thoughts were all jumbled. Maybe that's what they mean when they say someone's lost their mind?"

"You hadn't lost your mind. That situation would make anybody think odd thoughts."

"Nothing made sense. But then I remembered Ash reading me a poem once. She made me a copy. It started 'If you can keep your head when all around you are losing theirs...' And that was funny, because it wasn't those all around me who'd lost their heads; it was me. I'd lost *my* head. But I kept repeating the poem over and over, to have something in my head that wasn't fog. But I couldn't remember one part, and that annoyed me more than anything."

"What part couldn't you remember?" Luke asked. He'd look it up.

"'If you can make a heap of all your winnings; and risk it on one turn of pitch-and-toss; and lose, and start again at your beginnings...' I just can't remember the line that comes next."

"'And never breathe a word about your loss,'" Dan completed softly from the doorway.

"You know it, too?"

"It's 'If' by Rudyard Kipling. Ash has a copy of the poem hanging on her office wall back in Virginia. I've read those lines many times when I've been sitting in there."

"She said it was special to her, that when she was

my age and struggling with how she should live her life, someone read it to her like she did to me."

"She told me that tale too."

Dan might have smiled on the surface, but her eyes told a different story as they fixed on the far wall. Haunted. She looked haunted.

"It helped so much," Tia said. "I'd have gone mad in that room otherwise."

"She'll be very glad to hear it offered some comfort."

"She saved me again. That's three times now. Once when I fell off my horse, once with the poem, and then when she got me out of that room. It was her, wasn't it? Or did I imagine her like I imagined Luke?"

"It was her," Dan confirmed. "She put all the pieces together and realised who'd taken you."

Really? Luke knew Ash had been there at the end, but he hadn't realised she'd been so hands-on in the search. What exactly had her role in all this been?

"I thought I was dreaming when she opened the bathroom door," Tia said. "She wrinkled her nose and said, 'He's been making you eat Pop-Tarts? What kind of sick animal would do that?' I'd been stuck in that filthy room for days, and she still managed to make me laugh. Then she got the chain off my wrist and carried me out of the house."

Luke wasn't sure laughter was appropriate. Ash sure found humour in strange places. Although when Tia asked her next question, he almost let out a nervous giggle himself.

"Where is Ash, anyway?"

So, this was how a deer in headlights felt. Ready to get flattened and unable to do anything about it.

"She needed to leave, honey," Dan said.

"Leave? Why would she leave? She lives here. Where else would she go?"

"Ash wasn't totally truthful with us about who she was and why she came here," Luke said. "It was for the best that she went back to her real home."

Wherever that was. Luke realised he didn't have a clue. Virginia was a big place.

"But this is her real home now. She was happy. We were all happy. You have to make her come back!"

Now what? Luke didn't know what to do, other than somehow get Ash to return. And that was impossible, because according to Nick, she was over the Atlantic right now.

"Ash had a few problems in her life, sweetie." Dan stepped in once again. "Just before she came to England some awful things happened, and she needed to get away for a while. But the time's come when she needs to face up to those things rather than keep running from them, and that's what she's gone to do."

"Will she ever come back?" Tia asked, tears flooding down her cheeks.

"I don't know. I honestly don't. She told me to tell you that she'd miss you, though." Dan looked at Luke. "Both of you."

Luke couldn't meet her gaze, and at that moment, he understood just what he'd lost. He'd never truly known Ash—the quiet woman with what in hindsight was an underlying sadness about her despite her efforts to put on a mask for the world. Yes, she'd lied, but she'd never set out to hurt him, and she'd come through for them both when it really mattered.

"Are you going to see her?" Tia asked Dan.

"Yes, in a day or two. I can give her a message if you like?"

"What am I supposed to say to her?" Tia rolled over and faced the wall. "I can't believe she left."

Dan's phone trilled, and she looked at the screen. "I have to take this. I'll be downstairs if you need me."

Luke slid to the floor and leaned back against the bed. In less than a week, his life had fallen apart. His sister wasn't the only one broken inside. Hurt battled with confusion, a rivalry that left him drained. As well as being cut up about Ash, his view of the world had changed.

He'd once been convinced that violence never fixed anything, that right and wrong were black and white. But when Tia had been rescued, Luke suspected the methods used slipped into shades of grey. Once, he'd have had a problem with that, but now? His only regret was that Ash had inflicted the damage on Howard instead of Luke doing it himself.

He thought of his own online exploits. He'd never minded skirting the boundaries of legality with hacking by telling himself the only people he hurt were up to no good. Was what Ash did to Simon Howard any different? He couldn't deny the satisfaction he'd felt when he saw the man holding his nuts.

No, Luke wanted to throw the man under a train for what he'd done to his family. What would have happened if Howard hadn't come on the scene? Would Ash have stayed? He'd never know.

"I miss her," Tia sobbed from behind him.

Luke reached up and squeezed her hand. "I miss her too."

The question was what, if anything, could he do

about it?

CHAPTER 39

AS THE LIGHTS of London faded beneath me, the flutters didn't leave, no matter how much I willed them away. I'd tried to kid myself the feeling was due to my lack of flying practice, but now we were airborne, I had to admit to the possibility of another cause.

"Do you want your salad?" Bradley asked.

I shook my head. My appetite had deserted me, left behind somewhere in the vicinity of Lower Foxford.

Along with a small piece of heart and a lightness I hadn't felt in years. Maybe ever. Had I made the right decision to leave? Had I really? When I thought of Luke and Tia, I almost turned the plane around once, twice, three times, but head overruled heart, and I continued on my course. They were better off without me. What did I have to offer apart from hassle and heartache?

Not a lot on current form.

I let out a thin breath. No, I needed to go home. That chapter of my life was closed, my one attempt at normality, and it was time for a new book to begin. The tatters of my life awaited me, scattered in the wind. I could spend a lifetime gathering the pieces together, but the biggest one would always be missing.

My husband. What would my future hold without my husband?

I gripped the control yoke as another mile zipped

past, England dark below us apart from the glowing lines of streetlights. It wouldn't be long before I found out...

WHAT'S NEXT?

If you'd like to find out what became of Simon Howard, you can get FREE Pitch Black bonus chapters by following this link:

www.elise-noble.com/pitch-black-bonus

The Blackwood Security series continues with Into the Black...

Diamond may be used to saving the world, but can she save her own relationship?

With her husband's killer still on the loose and her life in England a disaster, Diamond returns to the only thing she knows: work. As the star of special ops takes on enemies from the States to Syria, she finds the toughest battle is the one going on in her own head.

While she faces her demons, the man she left behind is involved in his own struggle when a beautiful stranger crosses his path. Will Luke give in to the ultimate temptation?

You can buy Into the Black via this link:

www.elise-noble.com/into-the-black

If you enjoyed Pitch Black, please consider leaving a review.

For an author, every review is incredibly important. Not only do they make us feel warm and fuzzy inside, readers consider them when making their decision whether or not to buy a book. Even a line saying you enjoyed the book or what your favourite part was helps a lot.

WANT TO STALK ME?

For updates on my new releases, giveaways, and other random stuff, you can sign up for my newsletter on my website:
www.elise-noble.com

Facebook:
www.facebook.com/EliseNobleAuthor

Twitter: @EliseANoble

Instagram: @elise_noble

I also have a group on Facebook for my fans to hang out. They love the characters from my Blackwood and Trouble books almost as much as I do, and they're the first to find out about my new stories as well as throwing in their own ideas that sometimes make it into print!

And if you'd like to read my books for FREE, you can also find details of how to join my review team.

Would you like to join Team Blackwood?
www.elise-noble.com/team-blackwood

END OF BOOK STUFF

Ash started off as a niggle in my brain many years ago and stuttered into life in a truly terrible attempt at a novel that I'm relieved nobody else ever set eyes on. After much feedback from early readers and a whole lot of cursing from me, she finally made it into the light of day. Or, in her case, the darkness.

Fast-forward three years, and more people have read Emmy's story than I ever dreamed of. I've also done a bunch more writing and a hell of a lot more learning. So I thought it was about time these first three Blackwood books had an overhaul because I always want to give readers the best experience I can :)

For those of you who don't know me, I live in England and combine my love of writing with my adventures(!) as an accountant. My horse, Trev, eats most of my money (can you guess who Stan is based on?) but at least he looks pretty while he does it.

Apart from horse riding, my hobbies include eating chocolate, listening to true crime podcasts, scuba diving, and thinking up excuses not to go to the gym. I also spend too much time on Facebook, so if you want to chat, you can find me hanging out in the Team Blackwood group most days.

While I'm good at spending hours making up stories in my head, I couldn't publish my books properly without the help of my awesome team. I'm awful at spotting my own typos, for one thing. A recent gem saw a kindly old lady with grey hair asking another character if he would like someone to eat, which turned my romantic suspense into some dodgy version of Hansel and Gretel.

So, in no particular order, huge thanks to Abigail Sins, cosplayer and artist extraordinaire, who designs most of my covers. Thanks also to Amanda, my editor for this series, for helping me to fix up all the plot gremlins and educating me on the names of American breakfast products. And thank you to my three proof readers for these books—Lisbeth, John, and Noel—for spotting all those pesky typos.

Finally, a huge thank-you to you, the reader, for taking a chance on me and reading this book. I hope you've enjoyed it!

OTHER BOOKS BY ELISE NOBLE

Platinum
Lead
Copper
Bronze
Nickel (2020)

The Blackwood UK Series
Joker in the Pack
Cherry on Top (novella)
Roses are Dead
Shallow Graves
Indigo Rain
Pass the Parcel (TBA)

Blackwood Casefiles
Stolen Hearts

Blackstone House
Hard Lines (TBA)
Hard Tide (TBA)

The Electi Series
Cursed
Spooked
Possessed
Demented

The Trouble Series
Trouble in Paradise
Nothing but Trouble
24 Hours of Trouble

Standalone

Life
Coco du Ciel (TBA)
Twisted (short stories)
A Very Happy Christmas (novella)